LITHIUM TIDES

A
LITHIUM SPRINGS
NOVEL

CARMEL RHODES

Copyright © 2018 by Carmel Rhodes

ISBN-13: 978-1987705829
ISBN-10: 1987705823

All rights reserved. No part of this publication may be reproduced, distributed, or transmitted in any form or by any means, including photocopying, recording, or other electronic or mechanical methods, without the prior written permission of the publisher, except in the case of brief quotations embodied in critical reviews and certain other noncommercial uses permitted by copyright law.

This is a work of fiction. Names, characters, businesses, places, events and incidents are either the products of the author's imagination or used in a fictitious manner. Any resemblance to actual persons, living or dead, or actual events is purely coincidental.

Editing: Kristen—Your Editing Lounge
Proofreading: Judy's Proofreading
Cover Design: Designs by Kirsty-Anne Still
Interior Formatting: Champagne Book Design

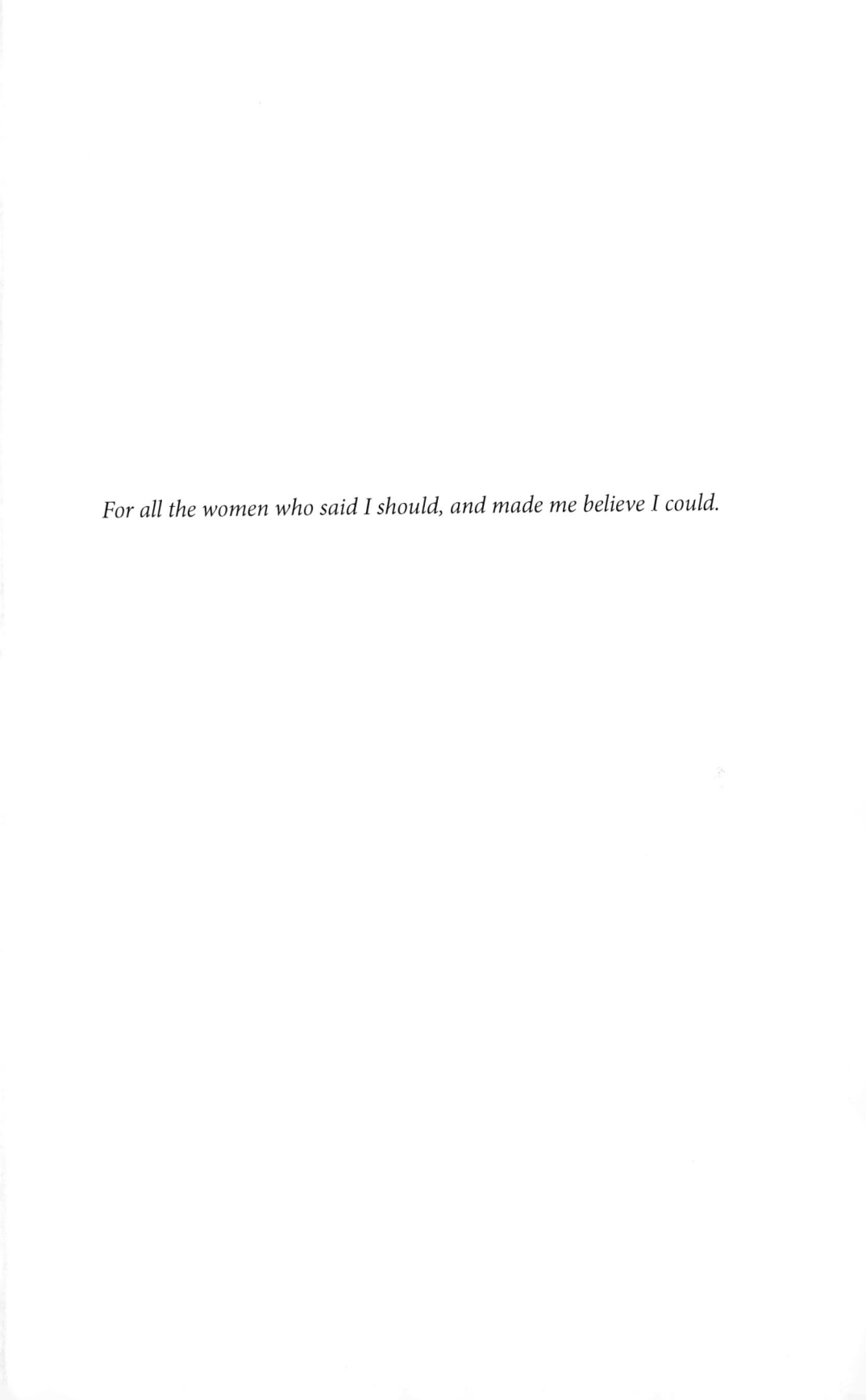

For all the women who said I should, and made me believe I could.

Emotions are immortal spirits trapped in mortal beings.

ONE

Girls Just Wanna Have Fun

Kensington Grace Roth was a princess. No, not an actual princess, but her grandfather had been governor, so almost. Demure, sweet, and dutiful: all the things a princess should be. Kensie liked being the princess, though she couldn't deny it was a lonely job—always on, always smiling. That's what princesses did, right?

What they didn't do, was wear red mini dresses that did little to contain their breasts, but there she was, standing in the middle of her bedroom, jersey spandex clinging to her body, and a tiny smile parked on her lips. Her best friend, Jamie, smirked at her handiwork. "Under boob is the latest wave, Kensie. Kylie Jenner wore something similar last weekend." It was payback for making Jam buy the burgundy Zanottis a few months back, when Kensie had used the other Jenner sister as a selling point.

"Great, because that's the look I'm going for." Kensie rolled her eyes at her blonde friend who was applying a final coat of bright red gloss to her pouty lips.

On the outside, she played it cool, but inside, she'd never felt so sexy. Too bad her hair and makeup would go to waste. "I just wish Trey were here to see me," she pouted, crossing her arms over her breasts.

"Well, he's not so you're stuck with me," Jam said, with an eye roll of her own.

Kensie and Jamie had been best friends since diapers. There was once a time the two were inseparable but growing up meant growing apart. With jobs and boyfriends keeping them busy, they rarely saw each other. In fact, if Trey weren't in Nevada for his brother's bachelor party, they probably wouldn't be going out in the first place; a thought that made Kensie frown. When had they become so disconnected?

"Hey, no frowning," Jam scolded. "This night is supposed to be fun."

"Fun for who? Slumming it at some dive bar with you and your boyfriend isn't my idea of fun." She sounded like a snob, but Kensie would rather not waste this dress on a grunge party in downtown Seattle. She wasn't even sure how she let her friend talk her into going in the first place. Kensie was more champagne and caviar than beer and chicken wings. "Remind me again how you met this guy? An interview or something?"

Jam's lips quirked up into a grin, the kind of grin that meant trouble. Jamie was a wild child—she lived life out loud, something Kensie admired. Being the princess wasn't always fun or easy but that was life, boring and hard. "Not exactly. We met before that, at the Rabbit Hole, the bar we're going to tonight. I was with Lo—"

"—so you were drunk," Kensie supplied.

She wasn't jealous of Lorena… Okay, maybe a little. Lo and Jam were so much alike, their friendship came easy, and Kensie couldn't help but feel like she'd been replaced.

"Yes, smart-ass. Anyway, I tried fighting my attraction to him all night, but there was something about him. His stage presence was electric. The entire crowd hung on his every word, his every note. Everyone in the room wanted him, and he wanted me. It was a high like you wouldn't believe. By the end of the night, we were practically dry humping at the bar; that was after I flashed him of course." She chuckled. It was trippy seeing Jam so happy, so light, so carefree. Love suited her.

"Of course." Kensie's voice came out breathier than she would have liked. Flashing and dry humping strangers wasn't really her style, but she understood the appeal. Raw, lust-fueled need taking over. An urge so strong that all caution and etiquette flies out the window. The type of chemistry she'd only ever read about in books. She'd never admit it, but she loved hearing all about Jam's conquests. Making love to Trey was nice—better than nice, it was great—but Kensie always wondered what it would feel like to be fucked. "So, then what happened?"

"I was so attracted to him—more attracted than I'd ever been to anyone before, there was no way I was walking away. I needed to feel him everywhere, ya know?"

Kensie nodded absently, her thighs pressed together, her cheeks flushed. Maybe it was the skimpy dress but listening to Jam's story ignited a fire in her core. Unfortunately, the only man who could extinguish the flames was doing God knows what in Las Vegas.

"I wanted him, but I didn't want the emotional connection. I didn't want the attachment. That's when I came up with the brilliant idea to have a threesome."

"A what?" Kensie shrieked. The blush spread across her entire body.

"It's insane, I know, but the bartender was hot, and in my fucked-up brain, I figured I couldn't get attached if there was another girl there—like a buffer. Plus, did I mention how hot the bartender was?"

"Okay, so you, Ry, and hot bartender had sex?"

"No, sweetie." Jamie shook her head slowly, like she was talking to a toddler. "We fucked in the back office."

"You had sex in an office in the back of a dirty bar?" Kensie shrieked. Who has sex in a bar? Jam. Jam has sex in a bar, that's who.

"Yup." She nodded, proudly, swinging her leather jacket over her shoulders.

"And this is the place you're taking me tonight?" Kensie followed her friend, flicking off lights as they went.

"Yup."

Oh my god, Kensie, thought. What was she getting herself into?

A jolt of fear skated through Kensie's veins as they exited the Uber. She couldn't tell if it was the cool breeze that greeted them as they stepped into the night or if it was how uncomfortable she suddenly felt in the red dress, riding dangerously high up her thighs.

Each step towards the small brick building with the blood-red awning, felt like a step into the abyss. Kensie reached for Jam's hand, lacing their fingers, and squeezed.

"Don't worry, babe, it's not as intimidating as it looks." Jam squeezed her hand back.

Intimidating was an understatement. The line wrapped around the building like moss on a tree. Hair dyed every color of the rainbow, flannel, and distressed t-shirts stared back, and suddenly Kensie felt ridiculous in her too tiny dress. "How long will we have to wait?" she asked, tugging at the hem.

"I'm fucking the lead singer. Do you really think we're waiting in line?" Jam snorted, walking right up to the largest man Kensington had ever seen, six-six and all muscle. His grim face lit up with amusement upon seeing Jamie.

"Hey, Kitty Cat." He smiled and waved them forward despite the groans from the crowd. "Who's your friend?" He eyed Kensie up and down, pausing at the strappy, black Louboutins on her feet. Apparently, he'd missed the *don't eye fuck the patrons* class in bouncer school.

"Kensie, this is Tee." Jam tried and failed to stifle her laugh. "Tee, this is my best friend, Kensington. I'm popping her Rabbit Hole cherry."

"Hurry the fuck up!" someone yelled from the line.

Heat crept up Kensie's neck. She was sure her face was as red as the dress painted on her body. This whole night was a mistake, but the Uber was gone, and Trey was in Vegas. "Nice to meet you, Mr.

Tee." She gave a hurried wave and rushed inside.

The bar was much bigger than it looked. Wooden panels covered walls painted the same blood red as the awning. Posters for live shows and upcoming events were scattered here and there. The noise overwhelmed her. The show was in full swing and a mass of bodies swayed in front of the stage, but Kensie's eyes trailed over to the bar. "I need a drink!" she yelled over the music.

"What would you like, princess?" Jam asked, snagging two empty stools.

Kensie thought for a moment. She hadn't been to a place like this since college, she was wearing a tight red dress that left little to the imagination, and she missed her boyfriend desperately. There was only one thing that could salvage this night. "Tequila."

"Tequila it is." Jamie smirked.

An hour and four shots later, Kensie was relaxed and curious to learn more about the men on stage. "The band is decent. What's their name?"

"Lithium Springs," Jamie said wistfully. Kensie could practically see hearts in her eyes.

"You're disgusting," Kensie teased.

"Fuck you, you're like that with Trey, and he's a douchebag."

"Hey—"

"No, we aren't having the Trey fight tonight. Let's dance." Jam pulled her from her stool and they shouldered their way through the crowd until they reached the front. There was no room to move—forget dancing—they were just trying to stay on their feet.

The music was intense, and Kensie understood what Jam had been trying to explain earlier. The way Lithium Springs commanded the stage, she couldn't keep her eyes off them, and it didn't hurt that they were all gorgeous.

The lead singer, Jam's Ryder, was tall and slim and covered in tattoos. He was shirtless, revealing the two shiny metal bars that pierced each of his nipples, and his black skinny jeans hung dangerously low on his hips. The bassist was equally handsome and equally tatted. His light-brown skin glistened with sweat as his deft fingers plucked at the strings on his bass guitar.

Behind them, partially hidden by a drum kit, was the most beautiful man Kensington had ever laid eyes on. If the other two men were kings, this man was a god. His face was perfection. The light-brown hair covering his jaw matched the curly, brown tendrils peeking out from under his black baseball cap. His corded arms were covered with brightly colored tattoos, intricately interwoven to tell a story, his story. But as sexy as all that was—and it *was* sexy—the best part of him, the part that had Kensie weak-kneed and breathless, was his eyes. Those mysterious blue orbs bore straight into her soul and left her feeling more exposed than the red fuck-me dress ever could.

She stood there, statue stiff, as the sounds of the final guitar riff crescendoed. The crowd swayed, a sea of sweaty bodies that propelled her forward until she was pinned against the stage.

She couldn't move.

She couldn't breathe.

The skimpy thong she wore under her dress was drenched; the tiny swath of fabric no match for her arousal.

"Kensie. Kensington! Let's go!" Jamie screamed, shaking her out of her daze. The music stopped and Ryder thanked the crowd for coming out, reminding everyone to download their latest EP. Kensie took a moment to regain her composure before turning to look at her friend.

Go?

Just as she was preparing to protest, Trey's face flashed in her mind. Yes, she needed to get the fuck out of there. She needed air. She needed to put some distance between her and her blue-eyed tormentor. She needed new panties.

Kensie followed Jam to the back of the bar. Her head spun. She was so preoccupied with trying to figure out what the fuck was back there, she didn't notice Jam following the large bouncer from earlier. She didn't question it when he led them out the side door, and she didn't question climbing into the waiting van. She didn't know when

Jam called the Uber but she was glad to see it.

"That was intense," Kensie breathed.

"I know, right?" Jam agreed, distracted, with her eyes locked on the door.

"Why aren't we moving? Where's the driver?" Kensie's heart pounded, erratic little *thump thump, thumps*. She looked to her friend, the friend who came here with every intention of introducing her to the lead singer of the band they'd just watched perform. "Jam?"

Even in the dark Kensie saw Jamie's eyes light up, and her breath caught in her throat as the side door swung open once again. She felt his presence long before she ever saw his face. Ryder exited the club first, then the bassist, and then him—the drummer with the eyes that caused her soul to shake.

"Jam?" she repeated. The van door opened and Ryder pulled Jamie up from her place next to Kensie and redirected her to the back row, winking as he gave her friend a firm smack on the ass.

The bassist was at the door next, looking at her like she was something to eat. "I'm Javi." He extended his hand, and his voice dripped with sex.

Before she could reply, she heard him, his deep voice just as intoxicating as the rest of him. "Back off, homie," he growled, grabbing Javi by the shoulders. "She's mine."

Kensie knew she should protest. They were fighting over who got dibs, like she wasn't even there, like she wasn't a person, just a snack to be devoured.

Javi looked at Kensie longingly and sighed, "You're lucky it's your birthday, motherfucker."

His birthday.

She committed the date to memory and instantly hated herself for it. She hated the way her traitorous body reacted when he'd called her his, hated the rush she felt as he climbed in the van and sat next to her, completely invading her personal space. Their legs touched, his arm draped lazily around her small frame and he pulled her into his side.

She fit perfectly—like she was made for him.

Jam giggled behind her. Javi jumped in the front passenger seat and the bouncer, Tee, got in the driver's side.

She knew she needed to break the contact, but his touch paralyzed her. His athletic body made her feel safe, and his bright tattoos were mesmerizing. He was like a calla lily—gorgeous, but toxic, and 100% likely to cause a rash. She needed to get the hell out of there before she did something she would regret, but instead, she looked up at the man absently rubbing circles on her knee and whispered, "I'm Kensie."

"CT." He grinned.

Her poor thong never stood a chance.

God, she was an awful person. Trey was loving, and kind, and he trusted her. Yet, there she was having illicit thoughts about a complete stranger.

"Everything okay?" CT asked, noticing the shift.

"I have a boyfriend." Kensie bit down on her lip. She hated herself for saying it, then hated herself for wishing she hadn't. She loved Trey.

She was in love with Trey.

"I'm not trying to be your boyfriend." He smirked, bringing his thumb to her mouth, gently wiggling her bottom lip free. His words stung, although she wasn't sure why. She was in love with Trey.

"Good." Kensie shifted, trying to put as much distance between them as the cramped space would allow.

"Not so fast." CT hauled her back under his arm. His hand ghosted up the hem of her dress, higher and higher. "This is short," he said, more to himself than to her. His face burrowed into the side of her neck, and his beard tickled the soft skin there.

"I have a boyfriend," she gasped as his teeth grazed her ear. The move sent her heart into convulsions.

"But tonight I'll be the one fucking you."

Kensie pressed her lips into a thin line. She couldn't let the small moan forming in her throat escape. She couldn't encourage him.

"Listen," she whispered once she'd forced the moan back to where it came from. "I know you're probably used to girls throwing themselves at you, but you're barking up the wrong tree. I have a boyfriend and he's the only one who gets to fuck me."

A smile danced on CT's lips. Amusement twinkled in his eyes. He was trying not to laugh and failing miserably. The cocky bastard had the audacity to laugh in her face and it pissed Kensington off.

Anger was good. The anger coursing through her veins helped suppress the lust that had nearly consumed her seconds ago. She wiggled out from under his long arm and gave him a hard shove. He fell to the side, laughing hysterically on his way down.

"Care to tell us what's so funny?" Javi inquired from the front.

"Nothing," CT croaked, regaining his composure. He righted himself and returned his arm to its home around Kensie's neck. "You're funny," he whispered, his mouth on her ear. His warm breath sent a chill down her spine.

"And you're a pig," she huffed, crossing her arms over her chest. She was going for incensed, but feared she came off as insolent.

"So, where is this boyfriend of yours tonight, and why was he stupid enough to let you out of the house in this?" He slipped his hand back up her thigh.

She should have moved it, but they were trapped in a moving vehicle, so it was pointless. He'd just keep coming back—that's what she told herself anyway.

"His brother is getting married. They're in Vegas for his bachelor party."

"I should send his brother a thank you gift then." CT gently massaged her leg.

Back and forth.

Back and forth.

His hand crept up, centimeter by centimeter, until it reached the edge of her thong. The arm around Kensie's shoulder pulled her closer until their foreheads met. "These are drenched."

There it was again, the moan threatening to break free. She bit down on her bottom lip, hoping to keep it at bay. This man was more intoxicating than the tequila she'd guzzled earlier.

She didn't mean to part her legs; it was her body reacting to the sensual torment. CT's fingers tugged at the useless material covering her, twisting and turning before releasing it with a soft thud. She was his instrument and he played her masterfully.

"I have a boyfriend." It was a plea and thankfully her prayers were answered. The car lurched to a stop and Kensie released a breath she didn't realize she'd been holding. The overhead lights sprang to life, illuminating the cabin of the van.

Slowly—so deliriously slow—CT withdrew his hand from between her legs. "Do you get this wet for him?" he asked, his voice low, garbled.

Don't encourage him, Kensington.
Don't encourage him.
Don't.

"No," she breathed.

TWO

Cool for the Summer

The van parked in front of a small, blue house at the end of a quiet cul-de-sac. Kensie wasn't sure what she was expecting—maybe a frat house or an apartment above a bar—anything but the modest single-family home in the working-class neighborhood. Most of the houses on the block were in desperate need of repair, others looked outright abandoned, but what was most striking to Kensie was how normal it felt, especially since what she was feeling was anything but normal.

She followed Jam, CT, and the rest of Lithium Springs around to a narrow walkway leading to the back of the house. Her heels caught in the cobblestone path, causing the typically poised woman to stumble. It was an omen, a sign she should get the hell out of there before she fucked her life up beyond repair, and yet her legs continued to push her forward.

Music and laughter billowed from the backyard, the party in full swing. "Your neighbors won't call the police?" she asked, curious to know how they tolerated the noise. A grunge band living at the end of the block probably didn't do much to drive up property values.

"Nah," Ryder said, turning his head in her direction. "Half of them are here and the other half were bought with beer and pizza."

"It's this douchebag's birthday," Javi added, playfully slapping CT on the back, "and we don't normally rage out here, so everyone is pretty chill about it."

A wooden fence ran the perimeter of the yard. The deck was furnished with mismatched lawn chairs, a card table, and a large, black grill rusted through on one side. To the left of the deck, in the overgrown lawn, sat a rectangular folding table with two large kegs flanking its ends. A white plastic cloth covered the table, loaded with liquor bottles, soda cans, and red, plastic cups.

To the right was a makeshift DJ booth, and as they walked through the gate, the DJ—a short man with jet-black hair—announced their arrival. "Yooooooo!" His voice bellowed out of the speakers. "It's the motherfucking birthday boy! Happy birthday, homie."

The crowd erupted into cheers and the thirty-plus people milling around the yard focused their attention on CT. He was greeted with fist bumps and high fives and birthday well wishes, effectively screeching an intense-looking game of flip cup to a halt.

"Alright, it's turn-up time!" the DJ yelled. Kensie watched as he retrieved a long black ski from under his table. There were four shot glasses glued to the top and he filled each with whiskey. He and the guys from the band lined up behind the ski and the crowd began to sing *Happy Birthday* in unison.

On the final word of the song, the guys adjusted themselves so everyone's mouth lined up with their respective glass and downed the shots in one gulp.

"Jam!" Kensie yelled to her friend over the music. "I need to use the restroom!"

Jam nodded and pointed towards the house. "This way."

Kensie followed her friend through the back door and into the kitchen. It was tiny and outdated, but clean. The walls were painted a faded yellow and the appliances looked as if they hadn't been replaced since the house was originally built. It reminded Kensie of something she'd seen in one of the '80s sitcoms she watched with her dad.

The restroom was at the end of a narrow hall. A small line formed outside the door. "Everything okay?" Jam asked as they took their place at the back of the line. The two girls in front of them were Snapchatting about being *"at a Lithium party"* and the guy ahead of them looked like he was drunk, or high, or some combination of the two.

"What the fuck am I doing?! He keeps…and I can't seem to… what the fuck am I doing?"

"I was going to ask you the same." Jam arched a brow.

"It's like I can't think straight when he's near me," Kensie confessed, running her fingers through her long brown hair. Between the hot, cramped club and the heavy petting in the van, what were once bouncy, beach waves had transformed into a tangled mess. "What am I going to tell Trey? I'm a terrible person."

Jamie rolled her eyes. "Jesus, Roth, loosen up. You're young and hot and most importantly, fuck Trey. What he doesn't know won't hurt him."

Kensie never understood her friend's hatred of her boyfriend. He'd always been polite to Jamie, and yet she barely tolerated him. "I love him."

The line inched forward. "Kensie, I love you, I really do. You're my best friend and as such, I feel like it's my duty to tell you this, Trey's an asshole."

"Jam!"

"No, let me get this out, just this once, and I promise I'll never say anything about it again."

Kensie nodded her agreement.

"He's turning you into this perfect little Stepford wife."

"No, he is not."

"You promised to let me finish."

"Fine, finish." Her words were tight. She knew where this was going.

"I get it. It's easier to fit in, and Trey is like a parents' wet dream. Honestly, I'm not judging you," Jam said, "but you know what I went through last year with Jared and my dad. I just want you to make sure Trey is what you want, not what your parents want for you."

Last year, Jamie's dad had tried to force her to marry the man who bought his company, despite her being in love with Ryder. Jared had wanted to mold Jamie into the perfect wife. They had been completely wrong for each other, but Kensie and Trey's relationship was different.

"I love him, Jam. He isn't Jared," Kensie said, not sure if she was trying to convince her friend or herself.

"Then what's the problem? CT's harmless. If you tell him to leave you alone, he will."

Kensie chose her next words carefully. "I…there's something about him."

"You want to fuck him." Jamie grinned, crossing her arms over her chest. It was more a statement than a question. Of course, she wanted to fuck him. Her body felt his absence since they'd exited the van. She missed his touch, she ached for it.

On paper, Trey was perfect. He went to the right schools, he had the right family name, and he was handsome. The total package. But one look from the scumbag covered in tattoos and Kensington was willing to throw all of it away. And for what? CT made it clear he was only looking for sex, and Kensie was the relationship type. It was as much a part of her DNA as her brown hair and type A blood.

"I don't know what I want," she huffed. The line moved again and the two girls in front of them went into the bathroom giggling at something on their phones.

"Stop overthinking this. He's hot, you're hot, and Trey is in Las Vegas. I've never seen anyone we know in this neighborhood and you literally never have to see CT again after tonight. Just relax, have fun, and let whatever happens, happen."

Kensie let out a long, cleansing breath. Jam was right. She could have fun and she could flirt, but she didn't have to have sex. She wouldn't have sex with him. After tonight, she never had to think about CT or Lithium Springs again.

After using the restroom, Kensie made her way back down the hallway, through the kitchen and into the backyard. Jam and the guys from the band were gathered around the flip cup table taking turns chugging beers and flipping cups.

"Just have fun, Roth," Kensie told herself.

Determined to ease her nerves, she walked over to one of the kegs. No more tequila for her tonight. She needed to be focused if she was going to keep CT out from under the hem of her tiny, red dress.

She hadn't tapped a keg since her days at USC. Kensie had loved her time at college. Being away from the Seattle elite had changed her, making her more aware of the world outside her small bubble. Being at CT's birthday party, with her very expensive heels sinking deeper and deeper into the mud, reminded her of the girl she had been back then. *Fuck this*, she thought kicking her heels off. She twisted her chocolate hair up into a topknot and began pumping the keg.

"You're good at that," CT said, coming up behind her and taking the faucet from her to refill his cup.

"Thanks. Happy birthday, by the way." Kensie dipped down to scoop up her shoes. She silently reminded herself of her no-sex vow, choosing to ignore the way her skin ignited when he was near.

CT followed quietly behind. Kensie felt his eyes on her, burning a hole through her dress. "Can you not stare at my ass, please?"

"I can't help it," he laughed, his voice dripping sex. "You have a very nice ass. I've been fantasizing about bending you over and licking you from here to here." CT dragged his knuckle down the small of her back, between her butt, and finally stopped at her core. Hooking his fingers around the back edge of her thong, he gently pulled and released, plucking at her panties as if they were strings on a guitar. Tiny jolts shot through her. She didn't even bother to see if anyone noticed his hand disappearing under her dress—she was too busy trying to remember to breathe.

Kensie wasn't sure why she was so drawn to him. At most, he was a self-indulgent asshole, and at the least, he suffered from a severe case of Peter Pan syndrome. He treated her like she was a piece of meat, something around solely for his pleasure, yet she reveled in it.

"Also, can you stop putting your hand up my skirt?" She was surprised at how strong her voice sounded, almost like she meant every word.

Almost.

"For now." He shrugged, removing his hand, and straightened her skirt. "But make no mistake, tonight you are mine."

CT was a bad influence. Kensie tasted his corruption on her tongue. Her inhibitions floated away during the second round of flip cup. By the fourth, he'd redefined her definition of French kissing. Trey's kiss was soft and gentle. He worshiped her, he loved her, but CT, he owned her. His kiss was rough, aggressive. It was as if he was staking his claim, driving the point home with each stroke of his tongue. He kissed her with an intensity so fierce, the rest of the party faded from existence.

As the night wore on, Kensie found herself on the couch, sandwiched between CT and Jamie. CT's arm planted firmly, possessively around her shoulder, as he and his friends reminisced about the time they accidently booked a gig at a biker bar. The bikers were pissed because Lithium Springs wasn't a Rascal Flatts cover band and things got tense.

"Bullshit, C," Ryder said, barely containing his laugh. "You almost shit your pants."

"I did not," CT countered, moving his hand from around Kensie's neck to point to his bandmate. "You were the one promising God to change your ways if we made it out of there alive."

It was nice. Laughing and drinking and talking. Kensie couldn't remember a time when she felt so carefree. She also couldn't remember a time where Jam looked happier. What she was doing was morally and fundamentally wrong, but Kensie also loved being able to see this side of Jam.

Their friendship took a hit when Kensie met Trey, but for the first time in almost a year, things felt right between them, even if every other decision she made that night was wrong.

"You two fuckers were both terrified," Javi added with a yawn. He looked up at the girl on his lap, Stacy or Tracy—Kensie hadn't bothered to remember—with lust shining in his eyes. "I'm beat." He kissed the girl on the shoulder, helping her to her feet. "Happy birthday, man." He nodded to CT before disappearing up the stairs.

The DJ popped his head in the living room. "Yo, I'm out." He jerked his thumb toward the back.

"I'm going to walk him out," CT said, kissing Kensie's forehead. He and Ryder stood and sauntered out the door, leaving Kensie alone with Jam.

"What the fuck am I doing?"

Jamie looked at her for a moment, assessing. "What do you want to do, babe? We can go home. It's not too late."

"I don't want to go home," Kensie admitted, heat rising in her cheeks. Once again, she couldn't bring herself to look her friend in the eye. "He's so intense, my brain turns to mush around him."

"Honestly, Ken, I think you have the same effect on him. I've never seen him look at another girl the way he looks at you and, trust me, there are always girls hanging around them. Usually, he ignores them until the end of the night, picks one to fuck, then he gives her the boot."

Kensie winced. "I'm just like them. He's only trying so hard because I told him about Trey. I think he likes the challenge."

"No offense, but you aren't putting up much of a challenge."

Kensie could always count on Jam to be honest—brutal—but honest nonetheless, and she was right. Kensie could have told CT to stop. She could have told him no, but she didn't. She wanted him, but she didn't want to lose Trey. "What should I do?"

"What do you want to do?"

Before Kensie had a chance to answer, the boys reappeared in the living room. The drummer stalked towards her like a lion to a gazelle. His bright tattoos swirled out from under the sleeves of the white Lithium Springs t-shirt stretched across his chest. He was lean, all muscle, the kind of muscles you can only get from working out every day. He raked his fingers through his overgrown brown hair; his tongue swept across his lips as he took her in.

When he bent over the couch, trapping her between his arms, his face was only inches from hers. "What do you want?" he asked, repeating Jamie's question. Kensie sat there, barefoot, legs tucked under her body, and hair pulled up into a messy knot, fully prepared to tell him she was going home. That she couldn't—that she wouldn't—cross that line. She was fully prepared to say and do all the things she should have said from the first moments in the van.

"I-I think-I want another beer."

CT's answering grin was panty-melting.

Coulda.

Woulda.

Shoulda.

Discarded cups and soda cans littered the grass. Kensie chugged the rest of her beer and quietly began to pick up the trash. She felt CT's eyes on her, but she ignored him, happy for the temporary distraction. After a beat, he joined her in clearing the yard. It took them about fifteen minutes to bag all the trash. Then, Kensie walked to the flip cup table and began to clean it too. She was stalling. She'd made up her mind; whatever was happening between them, was happening, but the cold beer and the few minutes of calm centered her.

CT sauntered up behind her, his hands on her waist. His head dropped to her neck and he placed small kisses at the base of her throat. One hand moved around to her front and the other pulled her dress up, exposing her little black thong. He palmed her pert rear end before continuing his journey around her body, pulling at the thong, balling the fabric in his fist, yanking it up. The friction against her clit made her knees wobble.

"You're so responsive. I've barely even touched you," he breathed into her ear.

A warm tingle trickled between her legs. "You've been teasing me all night," she moaned, grinding her ass against him. She felt him growing larger with every movement.

Her panties were bunched between her folds, as he stroked her. His touch electrifying her bare flesh.

"Me?" he asked, releasing her. "This fucking dress has had my dick hard all night, that plus all your lip biting. We almost didn't make it out of the van."

"You're a pig," she whimpered. Trey's face floated through the tequila-induced fog in her mind. This was bad, *really bad,* but she couldn't stop now—not with his erection pressing against her ass. She needed to feel him on the inside. She was dying for it.

Kensington was the perfect princess. Prim and proper, a classic beauty. Men worshipped at her feet, but not CT—CT with all his tattoos and muscles, he used her. He took from her body without permission. Not that he needed it. Kensie could be a good little slut, too.

CT hooked the strings of her thong with his thumbs and dragged it down her thighs. Kensie lifted one foot and then the other, helping him remove the useless garment, bending to his will, soft, pliable. She'd give him whatever he wanted, and in turn she'd take what she craved.

Kensie longed to be used, to be fucked.

A rush of excitement coursed through her veins as CT lowered to his knees behind her. His rough beard scratched her soft skin. He was the Big Bad Wolf and Kensie was his willing captive. He kissed and licked and bit her behind. His long arm reached up her back, pushing her forward, her stomach flush against the table, her bottom perfectly aligned with his face. "You have a very nice ass, Kensie," he growled, and she moaned in response, arching her back, granting him full access.

His strong hands pulled her cheeks apart, exposing her fully. Any awkwardness Kensie felt about being so bare in front of him disappeared as soon as she felt his wet, warm tongue stroke her opening with long, deliberate licks. He lapped at her greedily, slobber dripped down her crack; the sensation fueled her desire.

He was not soft.

He was not gentle.

But he was everything she never knew she needed. Kensie teetered on the edge of the mountain, needing one final push, shove, fucking drop kick, to send her, plummeting, spiraling, falling. She wasn't above begging for a release. "Please." Her voice cracked under the assault of his mouth. She ground her ass onto his face, seeking the relief her body so desperately needed. "Please." In that moment Kensie would give him anything just as long as he kept his mouth on her. "PLEASE!" she screamed, not caring who heard her.

CT stood, and Kensie nearly wept at the loss. He flipped her onto her back and the wobbly table dipped at the unexpected weight. His mouth was on her again, sucking her clit, while his finger slid inside her. He added a second finger as he dragged his teeth across the little ball of nerves at the apex of her thighs, pumping into her, driving her closer and closer to the edge.

Kensie writhed under him uncontrollably. "PLEASE." She dug her hands into his brown mane and pulled him into her, riding his face until an orgasm tore through her small frame.

CT bit the inside of her thigh and then he stood again, taking the heat from her body with him. Gasping, Kensie lifted up on her elbows and watched with unadulterated lust as he unzipped his skinny jeans, pulling them down enough to free his erection.

It was dark, well after 3 a.m. Kensie couldn't see him clearly, couldn't make out any distinguishable details, but she could tell it was big—like porn big. The way he stroked his length with long, firm tugs, she knew—she fucking knew—he was going to destroy her, and what sweet devastation it would be.

CT hit her clit with the head of his cock once, twice, three times. Her pussy spasmed. The squishing sounds his flesh made against hers as he rubbed his dick through her folds was euphoric. He smeared her wetness over his thick head before positioning his cock at her opening and diving into her, deep and without warning. Kensington's back arched off the table. Each thrust was more brutal than the last, so deep that his balls smacked the ass he'd just eaten like it was a five-course gourmet meal, in rapid succession.

Wrapping her legs around his waist, CT tilted Kensie so each stroke of his dick brushed against her g-spot. "Does he fuck you like this?" he grunted.

"No," she whined. The reminder of the boyfriend she loved made her body quiver. What she was doing was wrong, but the taboo situation only drove her desire for the tattooed man thrusting wildly inside her.

CT's thumb found her clit and he rubbed small circles on the little bundle of nerves, pushing her toward another release. Her muscles clenched around him as he continued pumping into her.

The table under them shook. Kensie vaguely registered sirens in the distance, but the sounds of the world quickly washed away as another orgasm ripped through her body.

"FUCK," he growled quickly, pulling out just as he started to come, pumping warm semen over the front of her dress. "Shit, sorry," he said pulling off his shirt. He cleaned the mess as best he could before shooting her a sheepish look.

"Oh my God!" she giggled, covering her face in her hands. "I'm on the pill, you jackass."

"You shouldn't be wearing shit like this anyway," he grinned, tugging her upright. He yanked up his pants, not bothering with the zipper, then wrapped her legs back around his waist, lifting her off the table. "I think there's merch in the garage, t-shirts, hoodies, sweatpants and shit. Something should fit."

Kensie nodded, biting down on her lip.

"Stop it," he groaned.

"Sorry," she giggled again. She wrapped her arms around his neck and nuzzled into him as he carried her back into the house, her ass still fully exposed and his semen staining that fucking red dress.

THREE

As We Lay

"Hello?" Kensie rasped into her iPhone, her voice thick with sleep. She was so exhausted she almost hadn't heard it ringing. She definitely didn't bother to check the name flashing on the display. She felt like she'd been hit by a bus.

"Good afternoon, sunshine," Trey's familiar baritone rang in her ear.

"Afternoon?" she mumbled, taking in her surroundings. Her dress lay crumpled in a heap. One Louboutin sat on the nightstand, the other thrown in the corner of the unfamiliar room. *Shit.* Everything came back to her in pieces, and the grogginess dissipated as the realization of her current situation washed over her. The dress. The bar. The van. The party. The strong tattooed arm draped around her body. One bad decision after another culminating in the biggest mistake of all—fucking CT on the folding table. How could she have been so stupid?

"It's one o'clock in the afternoon, Kensington."

"One?" Her life was turning into one big fucking cliché.

Trey chuckled. "I take it you and Jamie had a late night?"

"Ugh," she groaned. *If he only knew.* "Yes. She dragged me to some bar downtown and we guzzled shots of tequila like we didn't have any morals." She opted for a redacted version of the truth, no need to lie any more than necessary.

"I bet. Did you have fun?" he asked

"I guess. It wasn't really my scene, though."

"Oh really?" the man behind her grumbled as pain shot through her bottom. CT was awake and listening, and the fucker actually pinched her. She tried to stand, but his grip on her tightened.

"What time's your flight?" she asked, hoping Trey didn't pick up on the hesitation in her voice.

She could feel CT moving behind her, grinding his hips into her backside. His afternoon wood poking her ass made it difficult to focus on Trey.

"In about an hour. We just got to the airport."

"Good, I miss you." The truth, even if another man had been inside her mere hours ago. Even if she had to fight the urge to wiggle against his cock.

"I miss you, too. I could just come straight there?"

"No!" she yelped as the troublemaker slid his hand up her new "Lady Lithium" t-shirt. He twisted and pulled at her nipple, planting tiny wet kisses down the side of her neck. She bit back a moan, then silently counted to five before speaking. "Mmm…it's Sunday. I'll be at my parents'. You should go home and get some rest. Come to my place later tonight."

CT's hand slipped down the front of her body, his fingers gliding over her soft skin, igniting the need forming at her center. His nails grazed her clit and before she could stop him, two of his fingers found their way inside her still swollen vagina. "Stop it," she hissed, trying and failing to move his hand.

"Oh, that's right," Trey continued, thankfully oblivious to what was happening on the other end. "Maybe I'll swing by your folks' place. It's been awhile since I've seen your dad."

"Mmm…sounds great, baby." She hoped he'd confuse the need in her voice for sleep.

Please, God, let this be over soon.

Please.

"Baby?" CT growled, finally releasing her from his grasp. She scooted up into a seated position, shooting daggers in his direction, silently praying for actual daggers to fly out of her sockets.

What the fuck was his problem?

Her blood boiled. She was so angry she almost missed what Trey said next. "Okay, sleepyhead, we're heading through security. I'll text you when we land. I love you."

"I love you too," she replied, fighting the urge to stick her tongue out at the drummer. He sat back on his haunches at the end of the bed looking like a lion waiting to pounce. She triple-checked to be sure the call ended before gritting out, "What. The. Fuck. Was. That?"

"Me?" he asked incredulously. Like he wasn't just fondling her for her boyfriend to hear. "You're in *my* house, in *my* bed, naked from the waist down, and you have the balls to be talking to that cornball!"

"That cornball is my boyfriend. The one I never lied about. You knew what this was and you pursued it anyway. Like some sick and twisted game."

"Not a hard one either." Anger ricocheted from his body—still crouching—he looked like he wanted to swallow her whole.

He was a pig. She knew it last night, but lust and alcohol had temporarily convinced her otherwise. She didn't need this shit. This was supposed to be fun. She needed to get her stuff and get the fuck out of there, fast.

She moved to stand. "I fucking hate you," she growled, ignoring the moisture pooling between her legs.

"But you love fucking me," he spat, lunging towards her dragging her back onto the bed. He flipped her onto her stomach, smacking her hard on the ass. Kensie never thought she could feel this level of disdain for someone. She'd also never been so turned on. Ever.

As if on cue, the head of CT's afternoon wood pushed its way inside of her, balls deep and without warning.

"FUCK," she screamed, forcing her hips back to meet his thrusts. She concentrated hard on clenching and unclenching the walls of her vagina, not to please him, but to torment him the way he tormented her.

This wasn't the sweet lovemaking she shared with Trey, or the primal lust from last night. This was something different, something darker. She was hate fucking the drummer from Lithium Springs and she hadn't even bothered to catch his real name. The rage she felt for him in that moment grew like a cancer inside of her, fueling her lust. Each stroke drove her closer and closer to the edge. CT fisted a hand in her hair, her neck jerked back, and Kensie yelled out at the discomfort. Her body contorted as he pounded into her. It was pleasure and pain and lust and contempt all wrapped into one taboo and tattooed package.

Her body trembled—she was losing control. The orgasm that ripped through her body was hands down the most intense, most satisfying climax she had ever experienced.

CT shuddered behind her. His hips swiveled into her one, two, three more times before he collapsed on top of her. They lay there, limbs intertwined, and gasping for air.

Guilt washed over Kensie as she came down from her high. She'd known what it felt like to be betrayed and she swore she would never cause someone she loved that kind of pain. Yet, there she was in bed with a man she could barely stand.

Kensie wasn't risking a future with Trey for the great love of her life, she was risking it all for a drummer with a big dick.

"Do you like waffles?" CT asked, still trying to catch his breath.

"This was fun, but I think it's time for me to get back to my real life." He could stick those waffles up his ass for all she cared. Trey should be boarding his plane any time now, heading back to Seattle, back to her. She needed to get the fuck out of there.

"What about bacon?"

It was at that moment her stomach growled. The loud, angry roar reminding her that she hadn't eaten since before she and Jamie arrived at the Rabbit Hole.

"Bacon?" she asked. She couldn't remember the last time she'd had bacon, real bacon, the kind from a pig and not that turkey stuff everyone tries to pass off as the real thing.

"Bacon." His voice was smug. So smug she almost told him to go fuck off but the gurgling in her stomach convinced her to let it go. She would eat his bacon and never speak to his smug ass again.

Kensie should have known the promised waffles would be frozen and in a yellow box. She also should have known the useless drummer she let fuck her twice without protection couldn't manage to make bacon without giving himself a third-degree burn. After treating the big baby's wound, she took control of breakfast. At least she got a new Lithium hoodie and yoga pants out of the deal.

"Is that coffee?"

Kensie turned her attention away from the eggs she'd been whisking to find the owner of the sleepy voice, just in time to catch Javi stumbling into the kitchen, the last of their motley crew to awake. He looked like shit—well, as bad as a six-foot-three rock god could, but the red-rimmed eyes, floppy hair, and dried slobber around his lips, distracted from his otherwise flawless features.

"Yup," Ryder answered, lifting his mug. "Where's Macy?"

"Who?" Javi replied grabbing a mug of his own from the cabinet. He gave Kensie and Jam a, *"what's this guy talking about?"* eye roll, as if the girl he'd taken to bed last night was a figment of their collective imaginations.

She was trapped in Neverland, a place where the party never stopped and the boys never grew up.

"The girl who spent the night slobbin' on your knob," CT clarified.

"Oh. She had to go. She was a stage-five clinger."

These men were raised by wolves.

"Dude, turn that shit off," CT grumbled. That shit, Kensie

noticed, was Javi's phone buzzing wildly on the breakfast nook. A series of beeps and notifications illuminated the display. Whoever it was really wanted to get in touch with him.

"Is that the clinger?" Kensie asked, half-amused and half-curious. She made a mental note to ask what classified a girl as stage five.

"Nah, it's IG notifications. It's always like this after a show," Javi explained. "Mostly people tagging us in pictures and posts about the show and a few DMs from enthusiastic fans." His suggestive wink told Kensie everything she needed to know about those fans. "I'm in charge of the band's social stuff. We're verified on Twitter, Instagram, and Facebook," he finished proudly.

"Whatever that means." She shrugged, fighting the urge to roll her eyes. She didn't do social media, not since she went psycho stalker on her lying, cheating ex-boyfriend freshman year of college.

"What? Don't tell me you're too cool for social media, too," CT chimed. A look flashed in his eyes that she couldn't quite interpret, mostly due to the fact that they'd just met the night before.

"Too?" Kensie shot Jam, who was sitting on the counter sporting matching Lithium gear, a sideways glance.

"Ry thinks social media is going to be the downfall of our generation."

Kensie couldn't argue with that. She had firsthand experience on the subject. "No, not too cool." She returned her focus to breakfast, pouring the thoroughly whisked eggs into the waiting pan.

"Care to elaborate?" CT asked.

Not really.

Opting not to embarrass herself any further, Kensie went with her stock answer. The one she used whenever anyone asked her why she wasn't online. "I knew social media wasn't for me the moment my grandmother sent me a friend request."

The room erupted with laughter and Jamie grabbed her hand, giving it a light squeeze. Jam knew the real reason Kensie avoided social media like the plague and it had nothing to do with her nana, but everything to do with how she catfished her ex. Kensie figured sharing *that* would land her a permanent spot in the clinger hall of fame, not that she cared. She wasn't looking for love in that small house. She was looking for herself; she just wasn't sure she liked who she found.

"So, let's hear some of those DMs," Jam said, steering the subject into safer waters.

Javi's eyes lit up with amusement as he reached for the phone.

"Bro," CT and Ryder groaned in unison.

Ignoring his bandmates' protests, he opened his phone. "Okay, here's one: 'Hey, Ryder, I don't know if you will ever see this, but if you do, just know that I'll let you put it in whatever hole you want. Please Call ME,' I assume you don't want me to write this down?" He grinned looking from Jam to Ry.

"Dude, that's enough," Ryder growled.

"Here's one for you, C: 'CT, I want to taste your cum. CUM. XOXO.'"

"Okay, we're done." CT grabbed the phone from Javi and slipped it into his back pocket. He made his way to Kensie and snaked his arms around her waist. "Sorry about that," he whispered.

"It's fine." She finished the eggs and removed the pan from the heat. She was lying, but she didn't have the right to be upset. "I've got a boyfriend, remember?"

She could feel his body go rigid at the mention of Trey. Good. She wasn't the only jealous one. "So you keep saying." His voice was low, seductive.

Kensie knew where this was going and she needed to put a stop to it.

She needed to get back to the real world.

She needed to grow up.

She needed to leave Neverland.

FOUR

Lithium

Steam engulfed the bathroom. Kensie's head fell under the steady shower stream. The near unbearably hot water soothed her aching muscles. She never realized sex could be such an intense workout. Then again, she'd never had sex like *that* before.

Bath products of varying size and scents lined the shower ledge. Normally, she opted for the simple lavender wash she got from Whole Foods. The scent reminded her of the community garden near her college apartment in Los Angeles. When the lavender plants were in bloom, she could smell them from her bedroom window.

This time though, Kensie chose the Chanel shower gel she knew was Trey's favorite, and scrubbed her skin pink, determined to rid any trace of CT from her body. Soap ran down her slender frame. She watched the suds swirl down the drain, and foolishly wished the hot water could cleanse him from her mind as it did her body.

The weight of her recklessness consumed her. She was a liar, but what had her once again reaching for the Coco Mademoiselle shower gel was the realization that she didn't regret the night she'd spent in Neverland. What had Kensie lathering Trey's favorite scent onto her skin for the second time was the image of the bad boy rocker with the piercing blue eyes, driving wildly into her from behind.

She still felt him inside her.

Two days ago, Kensington was seriously considering moving in with Trey. She hoped taking the next step in their relationship would get her closer to the ring she desperately desired, but after last night, she didn't know if a ring from Trey was what she truly wanted.

Kensie wasn't naïve enough to think she had a future with CT. He wasn't husband material. He damn sure wasn't someone she could have children with, and her parents would die of shock if she ever brought him home for Sunday dinner. No, she didn't want a relationship with the drummer. She hadn't even bothered giving the asshole her phone number, but her lack of remorse for cheating on her boyfriend frightened her.

She never doubted Trey was her forever, but Jam's words from last night rang in her ears. *He's turning you into a Stepford wife.* Could it be true? Was she losing herself? Last night, she felt a freedom she hadn't felt since leaving college. She hadn't realized she'd stifled that Kensie, but she also knew she wasn't ready to give up on Trey. She was selfish and acknowledging it made her lather up the loofah one last time, willing the heat and the steam from the shower to quiet her inner thoughts.

Old Spice.
Grassy beaches.
'80s sitcoms.
Warm hugs.
Bright smiles.
Home.

Kensie repeated the list in her head over and over on the drive to her parents' house; a list of things that centered her. Things that reminded her of who she was—her values, what made her happy—what made her whole.

She loved growing up in Madison Park, loved spending her summers with friends at the beach, loved running around the country club driving their parents insane. She was at peace there. Most importantly, it was far enough removed from the city to offer solace from the atomic bomb she had detonated in her life. Coming home would put things into perspective.

Her parents waited arm in arm at the door as she pulled into the driveway, no doubt informed of her arrival by the security guard at the front gate. Before getting out of the car, Kensie took a moment to adjust the pearls dangling from her neck. The necklace wasn't really her style, but Trey had given it to her for Christmas, so she wore it in silent atonement.

"Hi, Mama, hey, Daddy." Kensie smiled, and hugged her parents tightly.

"Hey, baby girl," her mother cooed, ushering her into the house. "You look…different?"

"I'm just tired. Jam and I stayed out too late." Kensie's heels click-clacked on the marble floors, as they passed the formal living room and headed down to the den.

"Are you sure that's it, dear?" Jacquelyn Roth wasn't the type of woman to sweep things under the rug. She could smell bullshit from a mile away, a sense honed by growing up in a family full of politicians. Kensie wasn't sure why she thought today would be any different, but she definitely wasn't about to recount her exploits from the night before to her parents.

"Jacquelyn, give the girl a break. She said she's tired," Victor said.

Her mother pursed her lips but didn't push the subject. The three of them settled into their normal seats, her mom and dad snuggled on the sofa, and Kensie in the brown leather recliner. Her dad pointed the remote at the TV, the opening credits for *Three's Company* glowed on the screen. She didn't know if she should laugh or cry.

Irony, it seemed, had a morbid sense of humor.

They'd gotten through nearly two episodes of *Three's Company* before the guard alerted them to Trey's arrival. Kensie's breath hitched. Lying over the phone was one thing, but she didn't know if her poker face would hold up in person. Her mother sensed something was off with her in a matter of moments; how long would it take the man she loved?

"Are you alright, baby girl?" Jacquelyn asked.

Kensie fidgeted with the hem of her navy-blue dress. "I'm just excited to see him. It's the longest we've been apart since we started dating." She hoped her lie was convincing. Could her mother hear her heart pounding? Did she notice Kensie rubbing her damp palms down the front of her dress?

"Is that why you've been so wound up?"

Before she could answer, before she could add another lie to the growing list, she heard him. His voice was so happy and carefree it made her smile her first genuine smile since before her transgression. Kensie's eyes were glued to the entryway. Her heart stammered. Her breathing accelerated. Every bone in her body ached to run to him, to throw herself at his feet and beg forgiveness.

Seconds ticked by, then her father appeared with Trey just a few steps behind. His hands were dipped in the pockets of his khaki shorts. His posture was relaxed, his skin kissed by the Nevada sun, and his eyes shone with a love and adoration Kensie didn't deserve. "There's my girl." He grinned, his arms wide, waiting.

She was up in an instant, snaking her hands around his waist, burrowing her head into his chest. The tears couldn't be helped. What had she done?

"Hey, what's with the waterworks?" he asked, pulling her closer, inhaling her scent, the one she wore for him.

"I just missed you," she whispered.

"I'm here now, baby. It's me and you." She peeked up at him through her lashes, worried he would spot the infidelity written across her face. The invisible scarlet "A" permanently etched onto her soul. "Why don't you go get cleaned up and meet us out back," he suggested, brushing away her tears. She didn't deserve his tenderness. "Your dad said he was going to throw some steaks on the grill." She glanced around the now empty den. Her mother and father must have slipped out to give them privacy. Kensie nodded in reply. Still not trusting herself to speak, she tilted her head back and puckered her lips. Trey planted a chaste kiss in the middle of her mouth, groaning, "God, baby, I can't wait to get you back to my place."

Guilt pricked in her chest. Would he know? Would he be able to tell someone else was where only he should have been? She forced a smile and willed herself to relax. Releasing her grip on him, she said," I'm going to go fix my makeup. I'll meet you out there."

"Okay, baby, don't be long."

She turned to leave, but his hand on her waist halted her. "Babe?"

"Hmm?" she asked, turning back to look at the man she betrayed.

"Maybe you could do something with your hair too?"

Her hand shot up to feel around the messy top knot, confusion written on her features. "What's wrong with it?"

"Nothing, I mean, is gym rat chic a trend right now?" he mused, playfully tousling the bun.

"Oh… Umm no…I woke up late. I didn't have time to blow it dry."

"Ahhh, I see." Trey smiled, relief evident in his brown eyes. "I was worried this was a new look or something." He tilted his head down, pressing his lips to hers. "I'm going to go find your parents. Don't be too long."

Kensie stood there, watching as he walked away, oblivious to how his words made her feel. Lost in thought, a million different emotions coursed through her veins. Anger. Insecurity. Guilt.

Mostly guilt. Had she not been in Neverland she would have had time. She almost never wore her hair in a top knot—not since college. Could she blame him if he didn't like it? At least he was honest, that's more than she could say.

Grabbing her clutch off the chair, Kensie decided to forgo the downstairs washroom and, instead, journeyed up to her old bedroom, in the hope that something in there could help tame her mane.

Her parents kept her room the same, a time capsule of her adolescence. The walls were pale pink and covered with posters of her favorite boy band, and a heart-shaped mural comprised of photographs of her friends and family was mounted above her bed.

Kensie reached for the stuffed bear on her dresser. She had it for as long as she could remember, a security blanket of sorts, she even took it with her to college freshman year.

Sighing, she lay back on the full-size bed, the pink paisley print comforter surrounding her, and wondered what her teenage self would think of the woman she'd become. She was smart, had a job at Seattle's top advertising agency and she'd met the perfect guy, but inside she felt stagnate. Since leaving USC she lived her life on autopilot, always doing and saying what was expected. *What happened to the girl who wanted to inspire the world?* How could she have gotten so lost in the two years since she graduated? Last night, she had been reckless and selfish, but she had also been free.

Kensie put the bear back in his spot on her dresser and slinked into the attached bathroom. Her first mission was to fix the tear streaks in her foundation. Shuffling through her clutch, Kensie found her compact and started to buff away the damage. From the corner of her eye, Kensie noticed the screen of her iPhone come to life. *A text.* Probably Trey. She'd already been gone fifteen minutes. It was a wonder he only sent one. She debated on ignoring it. If he wanted her hair in something other than the messy updo, he was going to have to have patience.

Her phone pinged again. Irritated, she tapped the message

without a second glance.

Boyfriend#2: How's the cornball?
Boyfriend#2: Do you miss me yet?

She tried to fight the smile twitching at the corners of her mouth. CT was persistent, she'd give him that. She made a mental note to put a lock on her phone and then typed out a reply.

Kensie: If I wanted you to have my phone number, I would have given it to you.

Kensie tossed the phone back on the counter and stared at it like it might explode. She was playing with fire. She should block his number. They didn't have anything to talk about and she didn't plan on repeating the mistakes she made last night *ever again.*
Block his number, Kensington.
Block his fucking number.
The notification sounded again and again—against her better judgment—she checked the message. Why couldn't she seem to think like a logical person where he was involved?

Boyfriend#2: Then it's a good thing I took matters into my own hands.

Kensie: Look, I'm flattered, really, but I'm not interested. I'm sure there are a 100 other girls who would love the attention.

Boyfriend #2: 200 girls actually but none of them are the beautiful, messy-haired girl who made me breakfast.

Kensie: I have a BOYFRIEND!

Boyfriend#2: Your boyfriend won't let you have friends?

Kensie: You don't even know me. I could be a stage-five clinger.

Boyfriend#2: I know how good you taste so I'm willing to risk it. My dick is twitching just thinking about it.

Boyfriend#2: You wanna see?

Kensie: If you send me a picture of your dick I'm blocking your number!

Boyfriend#2: No dick pics, got it.

Kensie: I should get back. They're waiting for me.

Boyfriend#2: When can I see you again?

Kensie: In your dreams-xo

She silenced her phone. She needed to stop this. Trey and her parents were waiting, and she couldn't hide in her ivory tower forever. *Block him, Kensington.* She clicked into his contact information, staring at the **Block Caller** button. She knew what she should do but she couldn't bring herself to do it. Instead, she changed the display name from *Boyfriend#2* to *Peter Pan* and went to work on fixing her hair.

Kensie studied herself in the full-length bathroom mirror. She had somehow managed to transform the tangled and still damp bun into a stylish mermaid braid. The navy-blue dress she wore was just the right combination of sweet and sexy. The flirty hemline fell right above the knees and was much more modest than the red cutout dress Jam had convinced her to wear last night. Fingering the pearls dangling around her neck, two words swirled in her brain.

Stepford wife.

Kensie found Trey and her parents sitting under the covered deck. Their conversation seemed light, jovial. One of the things she loved most about Trey was how well he got along with her folks. Her family meant the world to her and the fact that he loved them as much as she did, made her heart swell. Trey grinned as she took her place next to him on the wicker sofa that cost more than the living room set in the apartment she shared with Jam.

"I was just about to send a search party," her dad quipped. He and her mom sat across from them, her dad's arm draped around her mother's neck, an easy smile plastered on his face. Even after thirty-plus years of marriage, they were still madly in love. Kensie hoped she would be so lucky.

She hoped she and Trey would be so lucky.

"I like this," Trey complimented, tugging lightly at the end of her braid.

"You better, it took me forever."

"Totally worth the wait."

Kensie beamed up at him, her teeth buried deep inside her bottom lip. She loved this man. They weren't perfect, but she could be content spending forever with him. It would be as easy as breathing.

"So, Kenny, Trey was telling us you two were thinking about moving in together?" her mother asked, breaking the moment. Kensie dragged her gaze from her boyfriend to her mother, her defenses rising immediately. She recognized *that tone*. Nothing good came of *that tone*.

"Umm...we've discussed it." Kensie's words were slow, measured, as she tried to control the sudden rage building inside of her. Trey brought up the idea of living together last week when he discovered her lease was up at the end of the summer. She had been considering it but told him she needed time to think about it, that *she* needed to talk to her parents. Nothing was set in stone and she certainly wasn't ready to tell her conservative parents that she was thinking about shacking up with her boyfriend, regardless of how well they got along.

"Don't be upset." Trey's voice was dismissive. He must have felt the anger radiating off her. "I know you were concerned about what your parents would think, so I asked them. The timing is right; it doesn't make sense to wait."

Her lips pressed into a thin line. She wanted to tell them in her own way, on her own time. "What do you guys think?"

"I think it's a wonderful idea, if it's what you really want." Her mom looked at her, the infamous Jacquelyn Roth's bullshit detector on full alert and trained at her daughter. "Is that what you want, baby girl?"

"I think," she turned to look at Trey, "I need more time to think about it. I think we have the rest of our lives to live together and I don't want to rush it because the paperwork would be convenient." Kensie crossed her arms over her chest. As far as she was concerned, this discussion was over.

FIVE

Trapped in the Closet

Kensie awoke the next morning engulfed in the pink paisley print comforter of her childhood bed. She had stayed in Madison Park out of spite. She was furious with Trey for ambushing her, at least that's what she told herself. A part of her wondered if she hadn't overreacted to avoid going home with him. She couldn't duck him forever, but her anger, mixed with the anxiety she felt about being intimate so soon after her betrayal, left her tap-dancing on the edge of sanity.

After showering, Kensie checked the closet to see if her teenage-self owned anything suitable to wear to work. "Of course not," she sighed. She had hoped to sneak out unnoticed. Her parents had given her space after their tense Sunday dinner, but she knew they wouldn't be as gracious in the morning.

She tiptoed down the hall to the master bedroom. With any luck, she'd be able to sneak in and out of her mother's closet and be on her way. The room was empty. Her father had left for work around six, but she didn't know where her mother was or when she'd be back. Careful, so as not to make a sound, she padded across the floor like the sly cat from one of those old-school cartoons. Was she being immature? *Yes.* Was it easier than admitting the truth? *Absolutely.*

Once safely inside the confines of her mother's closet, Kensie exhaled. The walk-in was massive; the word closet didn't do it justice. Mausoleum was more apt—a shrine of fashion and excess. The walls of designer clothes, shoes, and purses were great, but they paled in comparison to the mirrored island in the center of the oasis—her mother's ostentatious jewelry collection.

Kensie's fingers flitted over a rack of formal dresses. As a child, she'd spent hours tearing through the rows and rows of designer garments, playing dress up in Versace, Gucci, and Fendi, her own personal boutique.

Little Kensington couldn't wait to grow up. She couldn't wait to wear beautiful things and go to fancy parties. She'd enjoyed that life for a time, then everything had changed. *She changed.* College helped her realize there was more to life than beautiful gowns.

She'd still take the closet though.

Kensie put the memories of her past behind her. The uncertainty of her future could wait. She needed to be quick. A simple pair of gray slacks and a white button-down shirt would have to do. With the clothes in hand, she made her escape.

"Some things never change," Jacquelyn said, taking a sip from her water bottle. She was dressed as though she'd been running.

"Holy crap, Mom! You scared me!" Kensie squealed, slapping a hand over her chest.

"Serves you right for sneaking around my closet."

Kensie watched her mom pull the small, white towel from around her neck and dab gently at the moisture collecting on her brow. Jacquelyn Roth didn't sweat, she glistened. "I needed something to wear to work. I'll have it dry-cleaned and bring it back next week," she rambled, heading straight for the door. She was desperately hoping to avoid a rehash of the previous night.

"Not so fast, young lady. You aren't getting off that easy."

"Mom, I've really got to go. We can talk later." Kensie made it to the large oak door. She felt the cool metal of the knob. She was so close, and yet…

"We can talk now." Her mother's tone was final. "This won't take long."

"Fine," Kensie huffed. There was no use in fighting, so she plopped down on the California king bed and mentally prepared for the pending interrogation.

"Are you going to move in with Trey?"

"If you'd asked me that a month ago, I wouldn't have hesitated," Kensie confessed—since they were being blunt and all.

"What changed?"

"I changed. I know it sounds trite, the whole *'it's not you, it's me'* thing, but I'm not sure I can be the type of woman he wants."

"The dutiful wife?"

Kensie nodded. "I got so caught up in trying to play the part, I almost lost myself. I'm only just realizing it." *After having sex with someone else,* she added internally.

"I thought you were happy." Jacquelyn took a seat next to her daughter, her mother's warm eyes searched her face, no doubt looking for answers Kensie didn't have. She had thought she was happy too. Life was going according to plan, only it wasn't—not really.

"When did you realize Dad was the one?" Kensie used to think Trey was her future, that she'd finally found a man who lived up to the high standards her father set.

"Baby girl, it's been thirty years and I'm still debating on if I want to keep him around."

"Yeah, right. You two are perfect together. You may have set the bar a little *too* high."

"We aren't perfect. I couldn't stand your father when we first met. I still can't half the time. He pushes every one of my buttons and challenges me in ways no one ever has before. He drives me insane, yet, I'm so foolishly and hopelessly in love."

Kensie's chest tightened. The way her mother spoke of her father—love lacing each syllable—she wanted that. She longed for that, and the uncomfortable truth was she didn't have it—not with Trey, maybe she'd never have it. Falling back onto the bed with a groan she said, "Way too high, Mom."

Jacquelyn smiled, cuddling up next to her baby girl. "If you're looking for perfection, you'll never be satisfied. I didn't fall for your dad because he was perfect; quite the opposite. He was all wrong. He had no money, no family name, and your grandfather hated him. It wasn't easy—us being together—but we learned how to make it work. I never had a choice. He was it for me. It was always him. Only ever him."

Kensie didn't bother trying to hold back the tears.

The tires on Kensie's convertible screeched as she pulled into the parking lot of her office building. The clock on the dash read *9:07 a.m.* Traffic had been a nightmare and because she had an evil witch of a boss, there would be hell to pay for being seven minutes late.

Rachel Winston, also known as Cruella de Vil, was one of five senior advertising executives at Creative Marketing Corp and she made it her mission to make Kensington's life a living hell. Most days, she ran pointless errands, transcribed ad meetings, and cried in the ladies' room. Even so, she refused to give up. Being Cruella's bitch might not have been her dream job, but thanks to her father's connections, it was waiting for her as soon as she graduated from the University of Southern California.

Kensie skidded to a halt at her desk. Rachel stood there, hands balled into fists on her hips, and a scowl plastered across her overly botoxed face. Beth, Rachel's other assistant, shot Kensie a sympathetic look. "You're late," Rachel seethed. The little vein on her neck pulsed with anger.

"Traffic was horrendous," she explained rushing past, and shrugging off her purse with a spastic jerk. She missed the desk by an inch. The bag tipped over and its contents spilled out. Random tubes of lip gloss rolled here and there. Her cell hit the ground with an ear-splitting thud, the kind of noise that sounded like she'd be making a trip to AT&T on her lunch break.

"Everyone else seemed to make it to the office on time. Then again, we actually have to work for a living." And there it was—the reason Rachel never gave Kensie a chance to succeed. Nepotism may have gotten her the job, but talent and creativity kept her employed three years later.

Painting on a pleasant smile, Kensie ground out, "It won't happen again."

"It better not." Rachel turned, and shoved a piece of paper into Kensie's chest. "Also, these are awful. I've asked Brian from the art department to come up with something more suitable."

Kensie eyed the page. The designs she'd submitted for their latest campaign stared back at her. A Portland area grocery chain had hired them to do the branding for their new online subscription services and Rachel, in one of her rare moments of kindness, offered to let Kensie take a crack at the new logo.

"Why?" she asked, and her voice quivered. She had worked on her designs for hours, pouring her heart and soul into them, and they were good—better than good—they were amazing.

"They're garish and uninspiring. Better luck next time." Rachel's lips twisted into a smirk, but there wasn't an ounce of humor in her eyes.

"But—"

"I'll be unavailable for the rest of the morning. Hold my calls." Without another word on the subject, Rachel turned on her heels and stomped into her office, slamming the door shut behind her.

"Garish my ass. She wouldn't know taste if it slapped her in the face," Kensie fumed, looking down at her desk. It—like her life—was a mess. She began stuffing things back in her purse at random, mumbling obscenities under her breath.

"I don't know why you put up with her," Beth said. "It's not like you need the money."

"It's not about the money. I want to make my own way. All my friends have these big important jobs—Jam is a reporter, and Trey manages six figure accounts—I don't want to be *just another trust fund baby*."

Beth pushed her glasses up the bridge of her nose. "That's noble, Kensie, but seriously, Cruella treats you like shit, ten times worse than she treats me, or anyone else. Why not work under another exec?"

"Because everyone already thinks I'm only here because of my dad. What would it look like if I asked to move because my boss is mean to me?"

Beth's brows shot up. "Like you're sane and rational. Everyone here knows how she is."

"I'm stronger than that. I can deal." She sighed. In truth, Kensie was nearing her breaking point. She worked her ass off on those designs and it was all for nothing.

"You shouldn't have to deal. If you could do anything—you're dream job—what would it be?" Beth asked, her deep gaze penetrating.

Kensie stared at the printout of her designs one last time before tossing it in the trash. *What did she want?* Such a simple question, such a complicated answer. Who the hell knew? Twenty-five was old enough to know better. Young and dumb was starting to wear thin. Why was adulting so hard? "I don't know. Kids are cool, maybe I'd be a teacher or something."

"A teaching gig might be hard to find mid-year, maybe a sub, or…" Beth let the sentence trail off, her fingers tapping furiously over the keyboard.

"Or?"

"Safe Haven."

"Safe Haven?" Kensie asked munching on her bottom lip.

"It's a shelter for young boys. They're hiring."

"Email me the info, I'll think about it," Kensie said, opting to put a pin on her existential crisis. Bending over, she retrieved her cell, the screen was fine, but a new message awaited her.

Prince Charming: Are you still angry?

Kensie: I may have overreacted.

Prince Charming: Meet me at our spot for lunch?

Kensie: I'd like that.

At lunchtime, Kensie walked the two blocks from her office to Fonte Café. Fonte was a modern coffee bar that featured in-house roasted beans, freshly baked breads, and an extensive wine list. It was one of those places her dad, CEO for one of Seattle's largest coffee companies, often referred to as *"the hipster hell I'm forced to keep up with,"* as if anyone could compete with that ubiquitous white and green cup.

It's also the place where Kensie and Trey first met. After a particularly tough morning at the office, she'd decided on a lunchtime cocktail to help calm her nerves and prevent her from strangling her boss. Trey had been in line ahead of her and pre-paid her bill. She asked the server to send her glass of wine and chef's salad to his table and the two spent the entire hour talking like old friends. They'd bonded over the similarities in their upbringings and marveled at the fact that they hadn't met before that day. Of course, she'd heard the family name, *Knight*. Seattle wasn't that big, but he was a few years older and attended their rival high school.

Kensie spotted her boyfriend sitting at a table near the window, frowning at his tablet. She made her way through the bustling lunchtime crowd over to him. "Why the long face?" she asked, smoothing out the wrinkle on his forehead with her ring finger.

"Work stuff." Trey shut down the device and stood, placing a soft kiss on the corner of her mouth. He worked in risk management for a large financial firm and *work stuff* caused him to frown a lot. "It's nothing I can't handle. How's your day?"

"Miserable. Rachel was on a rampage this morning because I was seven minutes late." Trey pulled out her chair, and Kensie sat down gracefully.

"Hang in there, Kenny. It will get better, I promise."

"I hate it," she confessed, gnawing at her lip. Hate was a strong word, one she reserved for things like brussel sprouts and waiting in line at the DMV but working under Cruella was basically the equivalent of taking her driver's license picture with a mouth full of baby cabbages. "What if I got another job?"

"Mmm." Trey eyed her, lips pressed into a thin line. It wasn't the first time they'd had this conversation, or second, or even the third. It always ended in a lecture and Kensie pouting.

"I already know what you're going to say." She held up a hand.

"Then why bring it up?"

"Because, this time I actually know what I want to do." *This time.* Hard work had never been Kensie's problem, focusing was. She was artsy, she wanted to paint, and write, and change the world, but she had no idea where to start. "I think I've *finally* figured out what I want."

"And?" Trey asked, lifting a brow, a condescending little smirk on his face.

"You know what, never mind." She huffed, blowing a strand of hair from her face. Trey was the most practical man she'd ever met, and that's saying a lot considering who her father is. Shame colored her cheeks pink, her heart deflated a little with each passing second.

"I'm sorry, Ken. Please, tell me."

"There's an opening at a group home, young boys. I think... I don't really know."

"You don't know."

She wished she'd researched it more before bringing it up to Trey. It sounded like another one of her half-assed attempts at being an adult, but really... "I just...I'm unhappy," she blurted without thinking, "at CMC, I mean, and I think it would be a chance to do some good, a chance to make a difference, and I want to know what my boyfriend thinks."

"Fine." Trey's eyes snapped shut and he pinched the bridge of his nose, as if having this conversation was causing him physical pain, as if discussing her future was a nuisance. "If you insist we do this."

"I insist." She nodded.

"You think you're unhappy now, but what happens when the little angels you think you'll be saving become devils? You think working for Rachel is bad, try kids, but not just any kids, troubled ones. Kids who have a chip on their shoulder the size of Texas? You think you can save them, and that's sweet. It's one of the reasons why I love you, but you show up with your Gucci and your Chanel, and they'll chew you up and spit you out." A glass of water sat between them, she grabbed it, and chugged, giving herself a minute to think. *Why was he always so damn practical?* "See, this is why I didn't want to talk about it, you're pouting."

"I am not." She was too. Thankfully, the server chose that moment to bring their food.

"I hope you don't mind, I took the liberty of ordering." He'd gotten her usual salad, and even indulged her in a glass of wine. They sat in silence for what felt like an eternity, avoiding the twelve-thousand-pound mammal between them until Kensie couldn't bear it a second longer.

"I'm sorry about last night," she whispered.

"I'm sorry I ambushed you. I just don't understand what the hang-up is, Kensington. You seemed excited last week when I brought it up. Why the one-eighty?"

"It's just that the more I think about it, the more I don't know if it's such a good idea."

"Why?"

She hesitated, spearing a tomato with her fork. It was lunchtime. The café was bustling with activity, but everything in Kensie's mind was silent. Everyone else faded to black. *Why?* One little word held so much complexity.

"Baby, you need to talk to me. If we're going to do this, we need to communicate *honestly*."

"I'm afraid," she admitted.

Trey reached across the table and took her hand in his. His eyes brimmed with love and sincerity. "What are you afraid of?"

"That I'm too much, or worse, that I'm not enough. I don't want to disappoint you. I'm not perfect and I can't pretend to be anymore." She exhaled in a rush. The words burned her throat on the way out. The truth always tasted worse than lies.

"I'm not asking for perfection, Kensington. I'm asking you to try. I know you think I'm an elitist asshole—"

"I do not."

"You do, but it's okay. I am. *I can be*," he clarified. "But you fell in love with me anyway. You saw past that and took a chance. Don't give up on me now. I'll never be the guy who tells you to quit a great job to work at a failing company, no matter how much you want to do it. It isn't me. But I promise to love you and I promise to protect you. I'll never hurt you and I won't let you down. That must count for something, right?"

This was the man she fell in love with. He wasn't perfect, but then again, neither was she.

"Okay," she breathed.

"Okay?" he repeated

"I'll do it."

"Really?"

"Really," she giggled. His happiness was infectious.

"I promise you won't regret it." Trey could barely contain his excitement.

"Not so fast. I've still gotta tell Jam."

Trey's grin turned into a grimace. "Do you want me to come with?"

"No, I can't have her going and killing my new roomie, now can I?"

"No, I guess that would put a damper on things."

Kensie returned to work, happy about her decision to move in with Trey, though she dreaded the pending conversation she'd have to have with Jamie. Jam was the only person privy to Kensie's betrayal and Kensie could always count on her friend to give it to her straight, even if that meant telling her what she already knew deep down in her gut.

Her mother's words provided her some comfort. Her parents hadn't had the perfect start to their relationship, but they were the happiest couple she knew. Their love saw them through hard times and she loved Trey.

That would be enough.

It had to be.

She pulled her phone from her purse and tapped out a text.

Kensie: Are you home?

Jam: Yes, but I'm about to run out to pick up dinner. Indian. You want your usual? Is Trey coming over?

Kensie: Yes, please, and no, it's me and you tonight, Manning, but thank you for thinking of him.

Jam: Yeah, totally…I'm leaving something on the couch for you.

On the way home, Kensie stopped to pick up a bottle of Jamie's favorite wine. She wasn't sure how her friend would react to the news that she was moving in with Trey, but the wine couldn't hurt.

The short elevator ride up to their fourth-floor apartment did little to quell her nerves, and the soft music coming from behind the door let her know that Jamie had beaten her home. She let out a shaky breath as she unlocked the door. "It's now or never, Roth," she sighed pushing through the door. Her steps halted, as soon as her eyes found the *something* Jamie left for her on the couch. More specifically, a six-two someone, strumming an acoustic guitar.

Unruly brown hair, bright tattoos, and perfectly chiseled face that made her knees weak. His blue eyes locked onto hers, and his lips parted, giving way to the sexiest smile she had ever seen on another human being. She felt that smile deep in her core. She shivered as he set the guitar aside and rose to his feet. "Welcome home, Kensie."

Shit.

She needn't have worried about how Jamie would take the news that she was moving out because she was going to fucking kill her.

"I thought you were a drummer?" she asked, hoping the easy conversation would lessen the sexual tension threatening to suffocate them.

"I'm a man of many talents." His voice was low, seductive, as he stalked towards her. They weren't talking about music anymore.

"Stop!" she yelled. Her arm shot up, pushing against his hard chest. "Look, the other night was amazing…but I can't do this." She peeked up at him, biting her lip.

"Your body is telling a different story." His face darkened, his hand gently wiggling her lip free. "You're trembling, your cheeks are flushed, and I bet your panties are soaked. You want this as much as I do."

"It doesn't matter," she whispered. The heat of his touch threatened to weaken her resolve. "I can't do that to him again."

Annoyance flashed in his eyes. "He doesn't deserve you."

"You don't even know him. I'm the undeserving one."

He sighed, taking the wine from her shaky hand. His arm draped around her neck as he ushered her towards the kitchen. She knew she should have broken the contact, but she couldn't bring herself to do it. It was almost as if that was where she belonged, by his side. "I'm okay with a PG-13 night, we're friends, right?"

She stared up at him, sure they had different definitions of friendship. "Try G," she challenged, arching a brow.

He pulled her closer, bending down so that his lips hovered just above hers, so close she could feel his cool breath on her lips. "PG."

SIX

One Way or Another

Jam and Ryder arrived back to the apartment around the same time Kensie poured her second glass of wine. She'd bought it for her friend but seeing as Jam was on the top of her shit list, she unapologetically savored the crisp taste.

"You assholes drank half the bottle!" Jamie squealed. Kensie couldn't help the finger she lifted in her friend's face. It was the nicest gesture she could muster. "I see you found your surprise."

"Yup." Kensie drained the glass and slammed it on the breakfast bar. "A word, please." It wasn't a question and she didn't wait for a response. She grabbed Jamie by the hand, pulled her into the bedroom, and slammed the door behind them. "James Michele Manning, I swear to God I'm going to fucking kill you. I'm going to cut you up into tiny little pieces and scatter your remains across the Pacific Northwest," she seethed, pacing circles around her room, desperate to quell the rage building in her chest.

"You're being dramatic." Jamie rolled her eyes and plopped down on the bed.

"I am not!" Kensie shrieked. She stopped pacing and turned to look at her friend. Her fists flew to her hips and her eyes narrowed. "I just agreed to move in with Trey. I don't need CT complicating my life any further."

"What? Wait, when? What?" Jamie sputtered, raising up on her elbows. Shock, hurt, and disappointment flashed in her eyes as she stared up at her friend. Her light disposition was gone and tears threatened to spill down her cheeks.

"Our lease is up in September," Kensie added softly, regretting her bout of verbal diarrhea. Frustration had gotten the best of her, but Jam was her best friend and roommate for the past six years. They'd been through heaven and hell together, and now, because of her, all that was going to change.

"So, you're just going to up and move?"

"I'm not leaving tomorrow, but yeah." She nodded. It felt weird to say it out loud. She was moving in with Trey.

"But you're not happy with him."

"I am. I just…I got lost for a little bit. But I *am* happy. I'm not doing this for him. I'm doing it for me." Kensie wasn't sure if she was trying to convince Jamie or herself.

"Kensington, you are unhappy." Jamie's voice was raw with emotion. "This is a mistake."

"Trey is my future, Jam." Kensie always envisioned marrying a man like her dad. He had been the best example of what a man should be, and she was sure Trey was as close as she would get.

"If that were true, you wouldn't look at CT the way you do."

"What way would that be?"

"Like you can't see anything past him, like he's the only person in the room."

Kensie scoffed, "Now you're just reaching. He's a one-night stand who refuses to go away."

"Is he?"

"Look, I admit, CT and I have a really intense sexual chemistry, but I promise that's it. He's an arrogant asshole and we've never even had a real conversation. It's just sex with us. It *was* just sex," she clarified. "I've been with Trey for over a year. I don't even know CT."

"Uh-huh, if you say so," Jamie muttered skeptically. She fell back onto the bed and her blonde locks covered her face.

"You're just saying this because you hate Trey," she dismissed, walking into her closet. She needed to change out of her work clothes, but mostly, she wanted to steer the conversation back to safer waters.

"I don't *hate* him," Jamie called out. "I just don't think he's right for you."

"Why don't you let me decide that." Kensie peeled off her borrowed slacks and blouse and tossed them on top of a pile of laundry. They landed on the Lithium Springs t-shirt she'd worn the other day. As hard as she tried to suppress them, the memories of that night flooded her mind. She bit down on her lip—*really, really, really, really, really, intense sexual chemistry.*

She sighed, forcing the explicit thoughts to the back of her mind. She needed to focus on the task at hand. What should she wear? Pulling a pair of gym shorts and a USC t-shirt from a pile on the floor, she shook the clothes out and threw them on. Her hair went up into a ponytail on the side of her head and she briefly debated if she should take her contacts out. Casual, no frills, a far cry from the red dress she'd worn to the Rabbit Hole.

Jamie was sitting on the bed waiting for her to finish changing. Her eyes glistened with unshed tears and her voice was full of sadness. "I can't believe we won't be roomies anymore."

"I know," Kensie said, taking a seat next to her. "It's going to be strange not living with you, but you'll always be my best friend. That will never change, no matter how many times my address does."

"So…a few months, huh?"

"Yup."

They sat there for another moment, adjusting to the heaviness of the situation. Logically, Ken and Jam couldn't live together forever. They were both in serious relationships and cohabitation was the next logical step, but one of them moving out was always more of an abstract concept than an absolute. Now it was real. She'd said yes, her parents were on board, and she'd broken the news to Jamie. There was nothing left to do but pack.

The sound of the guitar stirred the girls from their misery. "We should get back out there before they eat all our food," Jam said and Kensie nodded.

CT and Ryder were in the living room huddled around the acoustic guitar. "This sounds so dope, dude," Ryder commented as CT plucked out the same tune he had been playing when Kensie found him on the couch. "Have you played it for Javi yet?"

"Nah," CT said, setting the instrument aside. "It's new. Just started working on it this morning. I've been feeling inspired lately." His blue eyes found Kensie's brown and he smiled shyly at her. "I think I've finally found my muse." He rubbed the back of his neck and she couldn't help but notice the bulge in his biceps as it flexed. The bright ink etched onto his skin danced around his toned arm with each movement.

"I'm sure you say that to all the girls," Kensie said, batting her lashes dramatically. Her tone was playful, even as a blush settled onto her cheeks. She couldn't let his words affect her. *He's just trying to fuck you—again.* "Who's hungry?"

Dinner conversation was light. The guys chatted enthusiastically about CT's new song. Kensie and Jamie smiled and nodded at the appropriate times, but Kensie's impending move was still in the forefront of both girls' minds.

"I'm hoping to have it done in time for the wedding," CT explained, before shoving a piece of tandoori chicken into his mouth.

"That works for me," Ryder mumbled, his mouth also full.

"Do you guys do a lot of weddings?" Kensie asked. Lithium Springs didn't strike her as the type of band to play the wedding circuit.

"Fuck no." Ryder's features twisted in disgust. "This is a one-time thing."

"It's a favor for my sister," CT added. His blue eyes shone with adoration at the mention of his sister. Kensie could tell he loved her. It was unnerving to see that level of affection from him. She'd only previously gotten the rocker sex god side of him or the unbearable asshole side, but she wasn't complaining. She liked it that way. Not seeing him as an actual person with actual feelings made it easier to avoid falling for his bullshit. It made it easier to draw the lines of their relationship. It had been just sex, mind blowing—sure—but sex nonetheless.

"That's very sweet." Kensie smiled at him. Their eyes met, and she could have sworn she saw a small blush creep across his face. She silently prayed for the asshole to rear his ugly head. This new, human version of CT was trying to blur the lines.

"So, *Friend*, how was work?"

"Awful," she admitted, suddenly losing her appetite. "My boss rejected all the designs I submitted for our latest campaign."

"Maybe they weren't as good as you thought?"

"No, they were great. She's just an evil bitch," Jam said.

"She hates me because my dad got me the job. She's had it out for me since day one."

"Sounds like a nightmare."

"It isn't ideal, but CMC is a good company, with a good reputation," Kensie said, but even she could hear the defeat in her tone. *A good job. A good company.* Who was she?

"If you could do anything in the world, what would it be?" CT asked. All of his attention was focused on her, what she was saying, how she felt. It was jarring, but what was more surprising was her eagerness to share her day with him.

"You know how when you're younger, people always want to know what you're going to be when you grow up?" she asked.

"Yeah," CT groaned, shoveling in more rice, "I fucking hated that shit."

"Me too! I would always reply with the standard, doctor or lawyer or whatever." Her eyes rolled involuntarily. "I didn't have a clue—I still don't, not really. I think I want to work with kids—there's this place, Safe Haven—but I also like to create things. Which is the problem, I never stick with anything long enough to make an impact. First, I thought—and Jam can attest to this—I was into photography, then it was pottery, and for an entire summer, I dressed in all black and spoke almost exclusively in iambic pentameter."

"You did not?" CT laughed.

"She totally did." Jam nodded.

"Yeah, I'm a total flake. I didn't declare a major until junior year: communications." She giggled. "I got to take classes with Diane Sawyer over here, and with advertising, I was able to have the 'practical' degree my parents pushed for, while still getting to flex my creative muscles. My dad knew someone, who knew someone, and I got hired at the largest marketing firm in the state."

"But you hate it," CT pushed.

"I can't just quit."

"Why can't you?"

"Because I'm an adult. You don't always get to do what you want. Sometimes you have to do what's best for your future."

"I doubt you need to worry about your future."

"I don't want to be just a socialite. I want to make my own way. I want to do something that matters."

"How does making rich, corporate asshats richer, matter?"

"You don't understand," Kensie sighed in frustration. She didn't understand why he was pushing her so hard. Why should he even care? This was supposed to be a one-night stand. CT could have any girl he wanted. Why was he so hell bent on derailing *her* life?

CT shot her an exasperated look. He turned to Jamie and Ryder shaking his head incredulously. "Am I the only one who thinks this is fucking ridiculous? I don't understand the problem. I mean, what's the worst that can happen? Your dad has to get you another job?"

"I don't want to have to go to my father every time I need a job," she seethed, throwing her fork down onto the plate. "I can do this on my own."

"I don't understand you rich people," Ryder said, rolling his eyes. "It's like you're running from your privilege."

"What's that supposed to mean?" Jamie asked defensively. The atmosphere was tense. What was meant to be a nice dinner with friends had turned into this ridiculous standoff.

"He's right," CT reluctantly agreed. A look passed between him and his friend as he continued, "You're lucky to be able to go to your dad when you need help. A lot of people don't have that. It isn't something to be ashamed of. It just is what it is. The shameful thing would be to continue working at a job you hate to prove your worth to people who will never think you're worthy."

Kensie exhaled deeply. The passion written on CT's face scared her. The weight of his words had her considering sending Safe Haven her résumé. Trey's advice had been logical and responsible, a stark contrast from the man sitting next to her telling her to take a leap of faith.

"Why spend another moment in misery when you could be somewhere that makes you happy?"

"I'll think about it," she conceded. Kensie's night in Neverland was impacting her life in more ways than she ever expected. She couldn't help but stare at the man she never wanted to see again, and for the first time, she wondered if it hadn't been a mistake.

※

"Well, this is awkward," CT chuckled, as the sounds of Jam's moaning grew louder.

Jamie and Ryder had disappeared shortly after dinner, leaving Kensie alone to entertain CT. They'd made it through about ten minutes of Netflix before the sex noises began. They did their best to ignore it, but even increasing the volume on the TV couldn't drown out the sound of her best friend's headboard banging against the wall. The spanking had been the final straw.

"Just go ahead and kill me now," Kensie groaned, her head falling back onto the black and white, upholstered accent chair. It wasn't the most comfortable seat in the house, but it was far enough away from CT that she could think straight.

"We can do better than that," he said with a wiggle of his brows.

"You wish," she mumbled.

"Is that a challenge?"

And just like that the playfulness of his tone was replaced with lust. He swept his tongue across his top lip and stood, eyes fixed on her as he walked the short distance to the chair. Before Kensie could protest, she was on her feet, her chest pressed against CT's. "PG, remember," she reminded him, or herself. Maybe they both needed the reminder.

"Yes, *Friend*, I remember," he responded before sitting down, pulling her onto his lap. Her heart pounded. His touch always managed to leave her breathless. His arms were like two steel bands wrapped around her middle, possessive, unyielding. Impossibly soft lips traced up her shoulder, then down to the base of her neck.

"I don't think friends are supposed to do that." Her voice was low and needy, completely at odds with her words.

"I'm the kind of friend who does that," he replied, gently biting the spot he'd just kissed so sweetly.

"And what kind of friend is that, exactly?"

"The kind who knows what you taste like." He kissed her again, and this time his hand slipped up the front of her shirt. Rough fingers tore at her bra, exposing her breast. His other hand settled around her throat tilting her head back slightly, granting himself full access. He continued to massage her chest, while his mouth alternated between small kisses and gentle nibbles on her neck. Jamie's moans turned to screams, heightening Kensie's arousal. "Can I have another taste?" CT groaned on her shoulder. She could feel his warm breath through the fabric of her t-shirt and she had to fight the urge to wiggle against him. She needed to stop this. She willed her body to listen to her brain.

"I can't do that to him again." She repeated her words from earlier. Kensie tore out of his grip and quickly scrambled to her feet. "I can't."

He sighed, releasing a deep and heavy breath as he struggled to mask the frustration written all over his face. "PG, right?"

"Right." She nodded, fixing her bra.

He blew out another breath and ran his fingers through his light-brown locks. "Well, then let's get to work on your résumé."

"What?" Kensie's head was still spinning from their close call. She wasn't sure how to keep up with his changing personalities.

"I can't sit here listening to that shit," he pointed at Jamie's door, "and pretend that I don't want to fuck you. That *you* don't want me to fuck you. So, let's do something productive."

"I *don't* want you to fuck me," she clarified, narrowing her eyes at him.

"Whatever helps you sleep at night, Friend."

"God, you're such a fucking asshole."

"Just go get your computer."

"Fine!" She stomped past him toward her room, and felt a sharp slap on her behind as she went. "You did not just slap me on the ass," she growled, pointing an accusatory finger in his face.

A smug smirk teased at his lip and it made her want to do him bodily harm. They only ever seemed to co-exist in states of extreme lust or extreme rage. Being near him was like being trapped on a never-ending seesaw, teetering between wanting to rip off his clothes and wanting to rip off his face.

"I couldn't help myself. You have a very nice ass." He shrugged. "Now, go get your computer." He didn't even pretend to be sorry. Smug bastard.

"If I thought I could handle the jail time, I would stab you without hesitation," she spat, turning on her heels. It was like he'd been sent into her life to drive her insane. Insane with need, with lust, with hate. No matter how hard she tried, no matter how much she wanted to, she couldn't push her blue-eyed tormentor away.

Her laptop was on her desk. As she unplugged it from the charger, she heard her phone ping. There was a new message from Trey.

Prince Charming : How'd she take the news?

Kensie: Not great, but she's still talking to me, so that's something.

Prince Charming : You want me to come over?

Kensie: No. Not tonight. I think we need some girl time.

Prince Charming : Fair. I'll have you all to myself soon enough

Kensie: I love you.

Prince Charming : I love you more.

The lies came easy. It was the aftermath—the guilt—that was the hard part. Sighing, Kensie put her phone back on the desk and made her way back into the living room. CT sat on the floor, arms spread wide across the couch behind him. He eyed her cautiously as she crossed the room. "You don't have a knife hidden behind that thing, do you?"

Kensie rolled her eyes. "I can do this myself, you know. I'm sure you've got more important things to do, groupies to bang, something." She didn't bother hiding the annoyance in her tone. She wanted him gone. If he stayed, she would end up killing him or sleeping with him, and she wasn't sure her conscience could handle either.

"He's my ride." CT pointed towards Jamie's room. From the sound of it, they were no closer to finishing than they were before she'd gotten her laptop.

"Whatever." She sat down crisscross on the floor next to him and opened her laptop. The blue Windows screen burst to life, and within seconds, a picture of Kensie and Jamie from graduation popped up. CT leaned forward to get a closer look at the screen. His chin rested on her shoulder, and she inhaled his woodsy scent. It was intoxicating and confusing. "I can't think with you constantly invading my personal space."

"How else am I supposed to see the screen? And trust me, when I invade your personal space, you'll know it, and you'll be screaming louder than that," he warned, nodding in the direction of the bedroom.

"You won't be invading my personal space ever again."

"If you say so, now stop stalling."

"I am not," she pouted. Kensie opened the file and pushed the computer between them. CT pulled the laptop onto his lap and began making changes to the layout. "Hey, what are you doing?" she asked, reaching for her computer.

He swatted her hand away. "I'm just cleaning it up a bit."

"So, now you are a professional résumé builder?"

"No, but having tattoos doesn't mean I'm an idiot."

"I didn't mean it like that," she said, feeling her cheeks heat. "Just curious to know how a drummer learned so much about formatting a résumé?"

A mischievous grin spread across his face, but his eyes stayed focused on the screen. "Juvie. They made us take a workshop."

"Juvie?"

"A juvenile detention center."

"Like jail?" she squealed.

He nodded. "Technically yes, but less *Oz*, more *Orange is the New Black*."

Kensie pulled her knees into her chest and watched with fascination as he transformed her boring résumé. "So, you're a criminal?"

He chuckled. "No, I was young and mad at the world. I did some stupid shit, but I don't regret it. It's how I met Ry. When did you start at CMC?" he asked, still working on the document.

"July, two years ago…what kind of stupid shit?" She couldn't help her curiosity. This man was a walking, talking contradiction.

"Felony vandalism. I trashed some kid's car the summer before my senior year of high school," he said nonchalantly.

"Why?"

"I don't even remember. I was a jackass when I was younger."

"You're still a jackass," she mumbled, picking at her nails.

"Touché, but now I'm a jackass who knows how to control his temper."

"Because of juvie?"

"No, because of the band. For the first time, I actually have something to lose."

"How many instruments do you play?" she asked, changing the subject.

"Only three: drums, guitar, and piano."

"*Only three?* Slacker."

"It's not that impressive." He continued typing. "I've played the piano for as long as I can remember. My mom insisted we all learn; me, my brother and sister. I started playing the drums when I was thirteen and the guitar just a few years ago. I'm not that great, but Javi and Ry are teaching me. Music is the only thing I've ever been any good at."

"You're good at this," she offered, pointing to the screen. He looked at her, mischief twinkling in his blue eyes. Kensie groaned, realizing her mistake.

"What else am I good at?" he grinned.

"I am not going to say it." She did her best to wipe the smile off her face.

He was impossible.

The worst.

"You know it's true," he teased.

Kensie pressed her lips into a thin line.

"Say it."

She shook her head from side to side, her ponytail slapping her in the face with each rotation of her neck.

"Say. It," he gritted, setting the laptop aside. His face was menacing, like a lion ready to pounce. "We can do this the easy way or the hard way."

"Nope." Kensie quirked a brow. She wasn't budging.

CT lunged forward so quickly she lost her balance. His hands found her midsection and he began tickling her mercilessly. Pinned between his thighs, she had no choice but to submit to his assault. "Okay… OKAY," she giggled, trying to wiggle herself free.

"I didn't hear you say it." He lowered his ear to her lips, waiting. His fingers poised to continue their attack.

"You're…you're good at…invading personal space, too," she panted. She didn't hate him so much when he was being playful.

"What was that? I couldn't hear you," he teased. CT brought his palms up, resting them on either side of her head. He rocked his groin into hers and his gaze focused in on the lip she didn't realize she'd been munching on.

"You heard me," she breathed, absently running her fingers through his hair.

His head fell forward and he ran his nose up the length of her cheek, murmuring, "Let me show you how good it can be."

"We're just friends," Kensie breathed.

"We both know that isn't true."

Her eyelids fluttered shut, a last-ditch attempt to shake off the intimacy. He'd been inside of her, he'd tasted her, and he'd seen every inch of her body, but she'd never felt as exposed to him as she did in that moment. Her mistake, her one-night stand, was shifting into something more, and she felt powerless to stop it.

SEVEN

Neighbors Know My Name

"That's it. I'm done. I can't watch another frame." Kensie yawned, untangling her limbs from CT's.

"Just one more," he pleaded, pulling her legs back across his lap.

"I've created a monster," she said, surprised the tatted-up drummer was into *Jane the Virgin*. They'd finished her résumé hours ago, but since Ryder and Jam never reemerged from behind her door, they decided to give Netflix another chance.

Kensie thought briefly about offering CT a ride back to his place, but she couldn't bring herself to say the words out loud. She wasn't ready to say goodbye.

"So," CT began, running his hand up her leg, his touch soft, teasing, "if you don't want to watch TV, what do you want to do?"

"Let's just talk," she suggested. "I'm curious to know more about the juvenile delinquent I let bang me on a folding table in the middle of the yard."

His eyes softened at the memory. Kensie could tell he'd thought about that night as often as she had. "I couldn't wait another minute. I didn't even use a rubber and I always use condoms, *always*."

Kensie blushed. "Honestly, it didn't cross my mind either, at least not until you ruined my dress."

He pulled her onto his lap so that she was straddling him. His hands moved down her back and onto her butt. She leaned into him, resting her head on his shoulder, inhaling his scent. The scruff growing over his jaw tickled her forehead as she traced the lines of the tattoo peeking out from under his tank. She'd given up the *"just friends"* pretense and was coming to terms with what she really was—a cheater.

Her behavior, she rationalized, was just a last hurrah, a last-ditch attempt to sow her wild oats. She'd made her decision. She was moving in with Trey and she had a sneaking suspicion *the ring* would follow shortly after her change of address went into effect. She'd take her place among the Seattle social elite as Mrs. Knight. In a few months, she'd have to grow up, but until then, her window would be open, and she'd wait for Peter Pan to take her to Neverland.

Kensie had only ever been in two serious relationships in her entire life: the ex who ruined her self-esteem with his cheating and lying, and Trey. The hypocrisy was not lost on her. Stephan's infidelity nearly broke her, yet here she was doing the same thing to the man she claimed to love. The difference—she reasoned—was that she would do everything in her power to ensure that Trey would never find out about her double life.

"I'm clean, just so you know."

She nodded, not wanting to dwell on the fact that they had been so careless. "So, CT? Is that like a nickname?" she asked, following the lines over his shoulder and down his bicep.

"Yeah. Ry started it and it just kind of stuck. Now, it's what everyone calls me. Everyone except my mom and sister, they hate it." He extended his hand to her. "I'm Carter."

She straightened her back, taking his offered hand in hers. "Nice to meet you, Carter. I'm Kensington."

"Kensington, I like that."

"Good, because I'm stuck with it." She smirked. "Also, I'm never calling you CT again."

"Just like the rest of the women in my life." He smiled, returning his hand to her ass.

There it was again, the love in his eyes as he talked about his family. Part of her was elated to be counted among the women he held so dearly, but a bigger part of her knew that wasn't enough to change their situation. She knew the truth. She belonged to someone else and she had no intention of giving up her relationship with Trey—a man who respected her triggers, a man her family had welcomed into their lives, and a man whom she'd come to love—for a drummer who would surely break her heart.

"I already know your birthday. What else should I know about you, Carter?"

"My favorite color is red, my favorite food is macaroni and cheese, and I'm fluent in French." His hands traveled up her shirt as he rattled off fact after fact. Kensie didn't realize he'd unhooked her bra until she felt the tickle of his fingers pulling the straps down her arms and out through the sleeves of her t-shirt. "Tell me about pre-juvie Carter."

"He was a total fuck-up." His voice was barely a whisper. His eyes were glued to her chest as his thumbs brushed against her protruding nipples.

"How so?" She raked her fingers through his hair to refocus his attention, the simple gesture eliciting a slight moan from his lips.

He leaned forward kissing each of her nipples before continuing. "I'm the middle child. I was pre-programmed to rebel against everything and everyone. It doesn't help that my brother is perfect."

"Nobody's perfect."

"You've never met my brother." He rolled his eyes, but Kensie could see the love in them, the same as when he spoke of his mother and sister. "He's good at everything. Every. Fucking. Thing. I spent my entire childhood living in his shadow. I wanted to hate him, but I couldn't. The bastard is even good at being a big brother. He never made me feel like a fuck-up, even when I got arrested. He was the person who got us our first paying gig."

Kensie stifled a yawn.

"Am I boring you?" he teased, slipping his hands down the back of her shorts and under her panties, resting them on her bare ass. Their presence against her skin sent a chill down her spine and a wave of moisture to her core.

"No." She yawned again. It was late, but she was too horny to be sleepy. "Tell me something else," she pressed.

"No, that's enough about me. What about you?"

"I'm also a card-carrying member of the total fuck-up club."

"How so?" he asked, repeating her words from earlier.

"Besides the fact that I'm a cheater?"

Carter tilted her chin down with his thumb and planted a soft kiss on her pouty lips. A mischievous smile played at the corners of his mouth. "We're just friends, remember?" He kissed her again. This time, his kiss was deeper, possessive. He pulled her closer, massaging her tongue with his, completely claiming her. She felt him growing underneath her.

"Maybe we should move this to my room," she panted.

"Nope, PG night, remember?"

She turned to look at the digital display on the cable box. "It's two a.m. so technically it's the next morning."

"Semantics." He smirked. She had a sneaking suspicion that this was payback. He was going to make her beg.

"I just want you to know that I hate you with every fiber of my being."

"You can talk dirty all you want. I'm not going to fuck you…yet."

"Yet?"

"I want to know more about Princess Kensington first."

She had to fight the urge to roll her eyes. "My favorite color is purple, I love bacon although I don't eat it often enough, and I spent a semester in Europe. My Spanish is passable, but my French is atrocious."

"Any siblings?"

"Nope. Lonely only."

"Is that why you're so concerned with disappointing your father?"

"My dad worked for everything he has. Literally everything. He came from nothing, worked to support himself through school, then worked his way up at his company. He helped turn it into the powerhouse that it is today. And here I am, his only child, complaining about my boss being mean."

"Is that why you refused to even try?" Kensie wasn't sure if they were talking about her professional life or her personal life.

"I'm just at this point in my life where I feel like I'm on autopilot. I graduated three years ago and I thought I would have it all figured out by now, but I second-guess every fucking decision I make. Taking the path less traveled is scary as fuck. What happens if I fail? I know how it must sound, *poor little rich girl*, but it's just hard letting go of the image of the person I thought I would be and accepting the person I am."

"Who are you?"

"That's the problem, I don't know."

"What is this?" he asked, motioning between the two of them.

She hesitated, knowing that speaking the words aloud would make everything real. There would be no going back. "I have a boyfriend. I don't plan on that changing."

He huffed in aggravation, "And yet you're here with me, for the second night in three days. How is that even possible? If you were mine—"

"I'm not though, Carter, I'm his. This is just sex."

"Your head is with him. Your heart… I'm not sure, but this," he grabbed a handful of her ass, "this is mine now, and I won't share that with anyone, not even him."

She nodded, even though it wasn't really a question. There was no point in arguing with him, he was right. For some inexplicable reason, her body craved him. She wasn't sure how long she would realistically be able to keep Trey at arm's length, but she'd cross that bridge when she came to it.

"I'll play second fiddle to the cornball for as long as you want. You can pretend to be in love with him, parade him around in front of your friends and family, but I know the truth and I've got time. I don't mind waiting for you to figure it out." He didn't bother to wait for a response.

Kensie fell back against the dresser, gripping the edge for support. Her knees wobbled as Carter yanked down her shorts, pulling her panties along with them. He forced her hands above her head as he tugged off her shirt. Her breasts sprang free and his rough hands were on her instantly. "Is this what you want, Kensington?" he growled in her ear.

"Yes," she moaned, writhing at his touch.

His hands moved from her boobs to her throat and his lips crashed into hers. He was rough, his tongue darting in and out of her mouth, his hands applied a slight pressure around her neck. It wasn't enough to restrict her breathing, but it was enough to make her quiver with anticipation. He wasn't going to show her any mercy.

"I'm going to ruin you for him," he gritted against her mouth. "He'll never compare. You won't even want him to touch you when it's all said and done." He was back on her before she could respond, before she could process the words. He bit her bottom lip, hard. His fingers flexed around her neck once more before traveling down her body. His mouth followed closely behind, his tongue, warm and wet on her neck, kissing and sucking and biting. She squirmed, attempting to break the contact.

"Don't," she pleaded. He was trying to mark her, trying to claim her.

"Your body is mine, Kensington."

"You have it, Carter. I'm here with you. I haven't been with him since you." It was what he needed to hear. It's what he wanted to ask her, but his pride wouldn't allow it.

It worked. He stilled, releasing a breath against her collarbone. He bit her once more before bending down, hooking his arms around her knees, and throwing her over his shoulder. He carried her the few feet to her bed and dropped her on her back. She tried scooting into a seated position, but he was on her before she could move, pulling her legs down, dragging her to the end of the mattress.

Carter dropped to his knees, bringing her legs up to rest on his shoulders. He hummed against her inner thigh, peppering the inside of her legs with kisses, deliberately avoiding her center.

Kensie bucked her hips, desperate to have his mouth on her.

"Please, Carter."

"Please what, Kensington?" he asked, inhaling her sweet scent.

"Kiss me." He brushed his mouth up her inner thigh once more; while the scruff on his face pricked at her sensitive skin. "Not there, jackass." Her hips buckled again, but this time, he wrapped his arms around her waist, pinning her to the bed.

"You're going to have to be more specific. Tell me what you want." He kissed the opposite thigh. "Tell me how you want it."

"You're really going to make me beg?" Carter's only response was a chuckle that reverberated through her body, nearly sending her into convulsions. "GOD. I HATE YOU!" she screamed.

"Wrong answer." He licked her thigh, biting and sucking over and over and over again.

"Carter," she panted, "don't."

"No." His voice left no room for further discussion. "He shouldn't be down here anyway," he commanded, before continuing his assault.

Biting.

Sucking.

Licking.

Kensie was on edge. She writhed underneath him, submitting to his punishment. He needed this. He needed to mark her. He needed to prove some part of her belonged to him, so she let him.

"God, I need to come. I need to feel your mouth on me, licking me, tasting me, please."

"Much better."

Finally, his mouth was on her, worshiping her center the same way he had her thighs. He licked and sucked her clit with such ferocity she felt her body tense. She was close, so close. She felt his fingers, his mouth, his tongue, the smattering of hair on his face, all of it was too much. "YES!" she yelled, fisting the sheets.

"We can do better than that, Friend." He stood abruptly, abandoning her.

"NO! FUCK, Carter!" She couldn't believe it. She was on the brink and just like that, it was gone. Kensie realized the angry purple bruise forming between her legs was only the beginning.

She glared at him as he stood over her, slowly unzipping his jeans. His blue eyes dark and stormy as he freed himself from the restrictive clothing. Their eyes met as the corner of his mouth pulled into a wolfish grin. He stroked his shaft leisurely, like he hadn't a care in the world, as if she wasn't a quivering mess lying half off the bed.

"Carter," she gritted.

"Yes, Friend?"

"If you don't finish what you started, I'll do it myself."

"Are you asking me to invade your personal space?" His brow quirked.

She hated this man.

She hated him, but lying there, body aching with need, watching him pleasure himself, drove her insane with desire. She knew what he wanted. "Fuck me."

"With pleasure," he growled, pushing her further back onto the bed. He stilled, hovering above her, searching her eyes. "Condom?"

"No, I want to feel every inch of you." In for a penny, in for a pound.

He grinned an, *I've got you exactly where I want you*, grin as he settled between her legs. He lifted one around his neck and slid into her wet folds with ease. His movements were slow and controlled. He was torturing her.

Kensie dug her nails into his shoulders, grinding into him, pushing him deeper. Two could play this game. "Make me scream. Make me scream so loud that it wakes them up, that it wakes up the entire building. Fuck me."

She could feel the smile against her cheek. She wasn't sure if she'd won or if he had. She didn't care. The only thing she cared about in that moment was how his hands felt around her wrists as he pinned her arms above her head. She cared about how each stroke pushed her back towards the Promised Land. The world was slipping away. Her head was spinning. She didn't know which way was up and which way was down. The pressure built inside of her like a time bomb, waiting to explode.

A garbled moan slipped through her lips as he swiveled his hips into her, pushing himself deeper than she thought possible. Her voice was unrecognizable, her words incoherent. She was no longer in control of her body, she was lost in sensation. Moaning and yelling and screaming, all nonsense. There was only one intelligible sound that escaped her throat that night.

One word.

One name.

Carter had promised to ruin her and he made good on his word.

EIGHT

Sit Still, Look Pretty

Kensie stared at her iPhone, willing it to ring. It had been two weeks and she still hadn't heard a peep. Not one single word. Her sanity slipped further and further away with each passing second. "Ring," she growled at the phone, hoping intimidation would work in her favor.

Knuckles rapped on the bathroom door in quick succession. "You okay in there?" Trey called from the other side. Kensie jumped at the sound of his voice, and her phone flew through the air, crash-landing on the marble countertop.

"I'm fine," she said, cursing under her breath. "I'll be out in a minute." Her shoulders sagged in defeat as she inspected her phone for damage. Thankfully, it was fine. Her nerves couldn't handle both rejection and a cracked screen.

"It's a quarter after, you're going to be late—again."

"Just finishing my makeup." It wasn't a total lie. She *had* been doing her makeup. She was doing her best to act normal. She *was* trying. Not anymore though, now she was sitting on the toilet manically bouncing her leg up and down, willing her phone to do something, anything. "Please ring, please."

A few more seconds of deafening silence passed, and she sighed, resigning herself to her fate. She needed to finish getting ready for work. She was being unreasonable; two weeks wasn't *that* long. Standing, she straightened the plush white robe embroidered with the letters TMK across the chest and finished getting ready for work.

Picking up her mascara, Kensie applied a light coat to her top and bottom lashes. Next, she reached for her blush, absently swirling the brush into the rose powder. It took every ounce of willpower she had not to pick up the phone, but she refused to let this ruin her day. She'd give it until Monday, then she'd take matters into her own hands.

Just as she began to make peace with the situation, the dark screen glowed to life. She sent up a silent prayer before checking the notification. Her heart sank. It wasn't the email or phone call she'd been waiting for. Instead, it was a text message. Huffing in annoyance, she snatched the phone off the sink.

Peter Pan: Hear anything yet?

Kensie: Nope, nada. They are never going to call, and I will be Rachel Winston's bitch for the rest of my life.

Peter Pan: You're being dramatic. Two weeks isn't an unreasonable amount of time to hear back for an interview.

Peter Pan: What are you doing tonight?

Kensie: Offering my blood to the interview gods.

Peter Pan: I think they only accept virgin blood, and well…

Kensie: Fuck you.

Peter Pan: I'm TRYING!!!!

Kensie: I don't know. I'll have to see.

Peter Pan: Come on, Kensington. He's had you for the last two weeks. It's my turn.

She sneered at the phone, "Pig."

They'd had a similar version of the same conversation every day since their X-rated night. He'd text her asking if she heard back from Save Haven—she'd say no. He'd ask if he could see her again—she'd say no.

It wasn't that she didn't want to see him. If she wasn't busy obsessing over Save Haven, she was fantasizing about the things he could make her feel, about the ways in which he would push her body to new heights. It was just that her boyfriend needed her too. Trey was her priority.

"What's the holdup, babe?" Trey asked, poking his head into the bathroom.

"Sorry, I got distracted," she explained, quickly closing the message app and tapping on the *Daily Mail* icon. She held the phone towards him, showing him the scathing headline of the day. "Actress busted for DUI."

Trey shook his head incredulously. "Whatever. I'm going to make some coffee."

Once he was out of sight, she tapped back into her messages and deleted the texts from Carter. Trey wasn't the type to snoop, but she deleted the forbidden messages anyway. Better safe than sorry.

With hair and makeup complete, Kensie slipped back into the bedroom. Trey's apartment wasn't a typical bachelor pad, but it was painfully impersonal, as if he'd bought the place furnished and never bothered changing a thing. After moving in, she'd need to inject some life into the space, make it feel like a home.

The coffee pot gurgled as Kensington entered the kitchen. The smell made her mouth water. Trey leaned against the kitchen island reading the *Seattle Times*. The sight of him also made her mouth water. The man did things to a suit that should be illegal. She couldn't help but stare. "Ah, there she is." He smiled, returning her heated gaze.

Kensie blushed, smoothing down the sides of her baby-pink shift dress. Even after everything they'd been through, he still gave her butterflies. "That smells amazing." She nodded towards the coffee pot.

"I picked up some of those beans you like from Fronte."

"Ugh, I love you," she moaned, throwing her head back in ecstasy. She didn't just like them; they were her favorite. The coffee those beans produced could bring about world peace.

Trey chuckled, setting the newspaper aside and pulled her into him. "That's the reaction I was looking for. How's the alcoholic starlet?"

"Heading to rehab." She smirked, lifting up on her tiptoes to give him a swift kiss on the corner of his mouth. "Thank you for the coffee."

"Anything for you, Kenny. What would you like for breakfast?" he asked, leaning in for another kiss.

"What are you having?"

"Bagel." Trey kissed her again, then walked toward the fridge. She watched as he pulled out a small container of cream cheese, two bottles of water, and cream for the coffee.

"Too many carbs."

"Umm, let's see. How about Greek yogurt?"

She scrunched her nose but held out her hand, taking it anyway.

"Kensie?" Trey called, grabbing her a spoon from the drawer.

"Hmm?" she hummed, refreshing her email browser once more. She'd officially gone off the deep end, but she didn't care. Patience was never her strong suit. She didn't consider herself a brat, not in the usual sense—never rude or ungrateful—she was just accustomed to getting what she wanted when she wanted it. Even her job at Creative Marketing Corp was waiting for her as soon as she'd graduated. This entire process was new to her. It unnerved her, made her feel uncomfortable, anxious, excited. It's how she knew she was making the right choice. How she knew she was finally living.

"Earth to Kensington?" She checked to make sure she had

service and then her Wi-Fi connection. She was so preoccupied with her phone that she didn't realize Trey was beside her until she felt it slip from her grasp. "What has you so distracted?" he asked, staring down at the screen.

"Nothing," she grumbled, dipping her spoon into the yogurt.

"Kenny, baby, tell me, what's going on? Is it something I did? This morning is the most affection you've shown me in two weeks, and even that was because I got your coffee. Are you still punishing me for that dinner with your parents?"

"No, baby, you're fine. We're fine. I'm just stressed."

"What could possibly have you so stressed? And what's with the phone thing?" he asked, holding it up. She noticed there was a red number one over the email icon. It felt like there was a jackhammer in her chest. It took every ounce of self-control she had to resist the urge to snatch the phone from his hand.

She hadn't told him about sending Safe Haven her résumé. She hadn't told anyone; not her parents, not Beth, not even Jam. Carter was the only person in the world who knew. "I've got to tell you something, but I don't want you to freak out, okay?"

"Okay." Trey eyed her cautiously.

"Seriously, promise you won't get mad."

"Ken, what the fuck is going on? You're scaring me."

"I sent my résumé to Safe Haven."

Trey sighed, relief washing over his face. "Jesus Christ, Kensington, that's it? That's why you've been so secretive? So distant?"

"I know you don't want me to leave CMC and that you think this whole thing is a disaster waiting to happen, but I really want this. Are you mad at me?"

"No, baby," he chuckled, tucking a stray hair behind her ear. "I mean, I think it's a terrible idea, but if it's important to you, I'll support it. Besides, it doesn't matter where you work, you'll be home full-time soon enough anyway."

She stilled, unsure how to process his words. "What's that supposed to mean?"

"I just mean when we get married, or if you'd like to wait until you're pregnant, that's fine too."

"Let me just get moved in first, okay?" Now it was her turn not to freak out.

"And when do you think that will be?" he asked, setting her phone down. He picked up his bagel and took a bite. He was eating his breakfast like everything was fine, as if they'd been talking about more *Daily Mail* nonsense and not the stay-at-home-mom-sized bomb he'd just dropped on her. She could barely breathe, and he was fucking eating.

She counted to five before answering, "In September."

"Why wait? You can start bringing your stuff over now."

"Why rush? I've already agreed to move in. Let me enjoy the rest of the time I have with Jam before I'm barefoot, pregnant, and trapped in this kitchen for the rest of my life."

"You say it like it's a bad thing."

"It's not a bad thing, it's just not a *Kensie thing*, which is something you would know had you ever bothered asking."

"You're being melodramatic," he dismissed, taking another bite of his bagel.

"ME?!" she squealed, throwing her spoon down. She didn't want the damn yogurt anyway. She pushed away from the breakfast bar with so much force the stool nearly toppled over. "You always do this. You get to decide everything. I was okay with it when the decisions involved where to eat or what to wear or what movie to see, but now you're making these huge, life-altering choices and you don't even bother asking me what I want."

"I'm ambushing you again, aren't I?" he said, pinching the bridge of his nose.

"Yeah," she snarked, going to the coffee pot. She grabbed two travel mugs from the cabinet and quickly filled each with coffee, then added cream and sugar to his, leaving hers black. Her mind ran a million miles a minute as she screwed the lids onto the mugs. She sensed him behind her. His big hands landed gently on her shoulders.

"I'm sorry. I don't want to fight. I feel like we've been at each other's throats since I got back from Vegas. I just want things to get back to normal. Have dinner with me tonight."

Kensie remained silent. Her answer would start another fight.

Trey's palms glided down her ribcage, his mouth hung just above her ear. "I'll take you anywhere you want, your choice."

"I made plans with Jam."

Lie.

"Cancel them," he whispered, planting a soft kiss on her neck.

"I can't just cancel on her."

Lie.

"She'll understand." He licked the shell of her ear, doing his best to change her mind. His fingers slid up her dress and inside her panties.

He was her boyfriend. It shouldn't have felt wrong—but it did. It shouldn't have felt like a betrayal to Carter—but it did. "I want to spend as much time with her as I can before I officially move out," she lied. "We can have dinner anytime."

Trey withdrew his hand from her underwear. He yanked his mug off the counter, and stormed out of the kitchen without another word, leaving her alone with her favorite coffee beans and mouth full of lies.

The next eight hours blew by in a haze. Between obsessing over her fight with Trey and obsessing over Safe Haven, Kensie barely got any work done. She tried calling to apologize, but he'd sent her straight to voicemail. Trey was right, all they did anymore was fight.

Was she subconsciously picking fights with him to assuage her guilt about spending time with Carter? Was she really that terrible of a person or was it simply that the honeymoon stage was over? Could it be the differences between her and Trey were becoming too much to ignore?

"Okay, what gives? You've been like a zombie all day," Beth asked.

Kensie glanced up at her friend's concerned face. "Sorry, I just have a lot going on. I can't decide if I need coffee, wine, or sleep," she confessed.

"Well," Beth said, throwing her coffee cup in the trash, "it's Friday and the wicked witch has vacated the premises, so I vote wine. You want to go grab a drink?"

Kensie shook her head and refreshed her email browser. "Raincheck. I'm afraid I wouldn't be very good company."

"Suit yourself, Debbie Downer," Beth teased, gathering her things. "If you change your mind or if you just want to talk, call me."

"I promise."

"Have a good weekend."

"You too. See ya Monday," Kensie said, and turned her attention back to the computer screen. *Three new messages.* The first one was spam, which she promptly deleted. The second, was a message from her stylist looking to change the time of her next appointment; she replied in agreement. The last, and most surprising, was from Trey's brother's fiancée, Reagan.

Outside of the fact that they were dating brothers, Kensie and Reagan weren't very close. It wasn't as though she disliked her; in fact, quite the opposite. What she did know about Reagan was great, it was just that they hadn't had much time to get to know each other. The only real time they'd ever spent together was during their Memorial Day trip to Napa, but even then most of the conversation revolved around wedding plans.

Kensie clicked on the message, an invitation for Liam's birthday party. She and Trey couldn't seem to go five minutes without arguing these days, so she wasn't exactly thrilled with the idea of spending a day with his family, yet she RSVP'd yes, and hoped like hell she and Trey were on speaking terms by next week.

Kensie shut down her computer and snagged her purse from the bottom drawer. She was halfway to the parking lot when her cell phone rang. Her anxiety bubbled into her throat as she looked at the display, a Seattle area code, but she didn't recognize the phone number.

"Hello?" she asked tentatively.

"Hi! May I speak with Kensington Roth?" a man's voice asked on the other end, and children could be heard playing in the background.

"This is she."

"Hi, Kensington, this is Tanner, Resident Director at Safe Haven. We received your résumé and were wondering if you'd like to come in next week to interview for the residential aide position?"

Kensie's steps faltered. Her voice shook. "I would love to."

"Great. I'll email you the details. See you then."

"See you then." She grinned, ending the call. Excitement jolted through her body, as she jumped and squealed as if they'd offered her a job. It was just an interview, one she could very well still blow come next week, but it was a step in the right direction; a baby step, but at this point, she'd take what she could get.

There was only one person she wanted to share the news with. She just wasn't sure how he would react. She dialed the familiar number and he answered on the first ring. "Hello."

"Daddy?"

"Hey, baby girl. To what do I owe the pleasure?"

"Can't I just call to say hello to my dear old dad?"

"You could…" Sarcasm dripped from his tone.

"How would you feel if I quit Creative Marketing Corp?"

"Quit? I thought you loved it there?"

There was a pause on Kensie's end. She may have exaggerated things a little for her parents, but she didn't want them to think she was ungrateful. "I kind of hate it." It felt good to finally admit it to her father. Like a weight had been lifted off her shoulders.

"How long have you felt this way?"

"Umm…three years."

Another pause, this time on her dad's end. "Why didn't you say anything sooner?"

"Because I didn't want you to think I was ungrateful."

"Kensington, sweetheart, I know you. I would never think that. What's the name of this company you're interested in? I'll make a few calls."

"I appreciate that, Daddy, I do, but no, thank you. I want to do this on my own. I need to know I got this job on my own merit, not because of whose daughter I am."

"Kensington?"

"Yes, sir," she mumbled, nibbling on her lip, as she waited for the lecture about how lucky she is to have a father who could help, but it never came.

"I don't think I've ever been prouder of you, kiddo."

A wave a relief washed through her. She was jumping and squealing all over again. "Thank you, Daddy. I won't let you down. I promise. Love you."

"Love you too, baby girl. We'll see you Sunday."

NINE

The Weekend

Kensie had only been home five minutes when Jam came bursting into her room. "Get dressed," she demanded, throwing a wad of black fabric onto her lap.

"What's this?" Kensie asked, inspecting the bundle. Confused, she looked at her friend, then back down to the black crop top with the words *Team Lithium* etched on the front.

"Check out the back." Kensie recognized the look on Jam's face from a mile away. Her lips were contorted into a mischievous grin and her eyes twinkled with sin. It was the same look she'd given her when she convinced her to buy that damned red dress—a look she shot Kensie whenever they were about to get into trouble. On the back, dead center, written in big, bold, block letters, was *CT*. Kensie chewed on her bottom lip, shaking her head at her friend as she absently traced the letters with her fingers. She couldn't deny how much she missed him, *and* she did need to tell him about her interview. "I thought you'd like it."

"I'm going to have to burn this when I move, you know that, right?"

Jam rolled her eyes, but otherwise ignored the mention of her moving. "It's our new uniform."

Kensie was so caught off guard by the intrusion she hadn't realized Jamie was wearing an identical t-shirt to the one in her hands. The only difference was the name on the back.

"Are you wearing Vans?" Kensie wrinkled her nose. "I think you're taking this grunge thing a little too far."

"When in Rome." Jam shrugged. "Anyway, get dressed. I already called the Uber."

"Uber? Where are we going and why do we need to be dressed like Mary-Kate and Ashley?"

"Just get dressed. I'll explain in the car."

"Fine," she huffed, "I'll be ready in five."

Kensie changed into the shirt, skinny jeans, and her white high-top Chuck Taylor All Stars. She studied herself in the mirror for a moment. The girl staring back at her looked the same. She had the same long, brown hair, same slender frame, same deep-set, coffee eyes, but underneath the clothes, she felt different. She felt alive.

"Time's up, Roth! The car's here," Jam yelled from the other room.

"Coming." Kensie grabbed her phone, credit card, and ID and slid them into her back pocket.

"Let's go, slow poke, I'm not risking my Uber rating for you."

"I got ready in five minutes, so screw you and your Uber rating." Kensie stuck out her tongue. They jogged down the four flights of stairs to meet the waiting car. As the driver pulled into traffic, Jam finally explained where they were headed. "We're meeting the guys at the Rabbit Hole. They have a show tonight."

"But it's only five thirty," Kensie whined. She did her best to subdue the pang of disappointment swelling in her chest. She was hoping for some alone time with Carter, but now it seemed as if she'd have to ignore the aching between her legs until the end of the night.

"Yes, but they've got to set up and do sound check and whatever else happens before a show."

"So, what's with the clothes?" Kensie asked, gesturing between them.

"Oh, right. They needed help with the merch table. Javi's brother normally does it but his kid is sick, so they commissioned us to hawk their stuff."

Kensie eyed her friend. It was still strange seeing Jamie so…monogamous. The old Jamie was a notorious commitment phobe, but the person sitting next to her was a proper girlfriend. A better one than Kensie, at that. "So, what's the deal with you and Ryder anyway?"

"The sex is outstanding, and he makes me laugh. Despite my best efforts, he loves me and I am head over heels in love with him."

"I'm really happy for you, Jam. You deserve it."

"What about you and CT?"

"It's just fun. I'm sowing my wild oats or whatever." Kensie grabbed Jamie's hand, her gaze focused out the window. Downtown Seattle passed by in a whirl of swirling colors and lights. "I know this is crazy and out of character and fucked up, but I'm not ready to let him go, not yet. It's selfish, but it's the truth. I won't make excuses for my behavior, I just feel like I need to do this."

"Just be careful, okay? Protect your heart."

Kensie chuckled at the absurdity. She knew firsthand the hurt that betrayal caused, and if her heart ended up shattered, she'd have no one to blame but herself.

※

The driver pulled to a stop in front of the bar. It looked different in the daylight, less intimidating. The first time they came here, Kensie had been completely out of her depth and she'd stuck out like a sore thumb. Now, she felt almost as if she belonged.

Javi stood in front of the bar smoking a funny-smelling cigarette. He smiled and waved them over as he flicked the roach onto the ground. "My saviors," he declared, draping an arm around each of their shoulders.

"How's it hanging?" Jam asked.

"Low and to the left," he joked, ushering them into the bar.

The place buzzed with activity as the staff geared up for a busy Friday night. Bartenders sliced lemons and poured buckets of ice into the drink well behind the bar while Tee, the bouncer from before, carried cases of booze up from the basement.

Javi directed the girls to a table set up just to the right side of the stage. Ryder was there, arranging CDs, t-shirts, hats, and stickers, all emblazoned with the band logo.

As they neared, Jam slipped out from under Javi's arm and jumped on her boyfriend. Ryder brought her legs up around his waist and his mouth found hers instantly. They didn't speak a word before he turned and carried her off towards the back of the bar.

"Sound check is in thirty minutes, Ry," Javi called just before they disappeared. He shook his head incredulously, looking towards the stage. "I suppose you're looking for him?"

Kensie's gaze shifted from the bassist and up to the stage where Carter stood, staring directly at her, and a slow, sexy grin crept across his face. Kensie's breath hitched at the sight of him. Goose bumps dotted her flesh, her body reacting to him from a single look. His loose-fitting tank provided her with a full view of the ornate tattoos that covered his arms and chest. His muscular frame oozed sex as he hopped off the stage and jogged over to where she was standing with Javi.

Carter pushed his friend's arm from around Kensie and pulled her protectively to his side. "You got it bad, bro, worse than Ry." Javi held his hands up in surrender.

"I've already got enough competition for this one." Carter grinned down at her. She rolled her eyes and elbowed him in the side with as much force as she could muster. "Ouch, what was that for?" he asked, rubbing the spot where she'd hit him.

"For being an asshole. I can't believe I was actually excited to see you," she teased, pulling away from him. She didn't get very far before he pulled her back, pressing his lips to hers. His tongue slid in and out of her mouth with long, wet strokes. She didn't care that they were making out in front of a room full of people. She'd been waiting for this moment for two weeks.

"Sound check is in thirty minutes, bro," Javi interrupted, prying them apart. "You've still got work to do." He pointed to the stage where Carter's drum kit lay scattered in a million pieces.

"Fuck," he whispered against her lips. "I just want to be inside you already." He kissed her again, then reluctantly tore his mouth from hers. Kensie expected him to get back to work, but he lingered, his hands exploring her body. His fingers slid down her arms, around her thighs, and back to her butt. "Your ass is perfect," he groaned before continuing his expedition up to her lower back and then around to her stomach. His eyes shone with lust as he tugged the hem of her crop top. "I love seeing you in my shit. It's such a fucking turn-on."

Kensie blushed. He was always so possessive, so intense, all-consuming. She wanted him inside of her just as badly as he wanted to be there.

"I should get back," he mused, tugging on her shirt one last time.

"Oh wait, I almost forgot." She jumped up and down, excited to share the news with him. He was the reason she took the leap of faith in the first place and she couldn't wait to tell him.

"What?" he chuckled.

"They called!" she squealed, throwing her hands up. "I've got an interview with Safe Haven!"

"I told you they would." He beamed at her.

"C," Javi's voice was a little more forceful this time, "down to twenty-five minutes, man."

Carter pressed his lips to hers one last time. "Congratulations, Kensington," he whispered sweetly before flipping off his friend and heading back up to the stage.

Kensie was grinning like an idiot, but she couldn't help herself. "So," she said turning to Javi, "what is it exactly that I'm supposed to be doing?"

"Mostly, just sit here and take people's money. Shirts are twenty, hats are fifteen, CDs are ten, and the stickers are free," he explained.

"They're kind of like our business card, hand as many out as you can." Kensie picked up one of the stickers. It was a simple black and white design with the band's logo. Their website and social media information were written in red along the bottom.

"The shirts are organized by size back here," he continued, pointing to a smaller table set up behind them. There were also two other boxes under the table that contained extra hats and CDs. "Once they're gone, they're gone, but they can check out the website for more gear. The address is on the stickers."

"Wow, this is pretty legit," Kensie said, taking a seat behind the table.

"Yeah, it was your boy's idea," Javi replied, taking the seat next to her. "Between shows and selling t-shirts and shit on our website, we're able to work on our music full-time."

"That's actually pretty impressive. I had no idea you guys were that successful."

"Things really started taking off for us last year. That's when I quit my job. Best day of my fucking life."

"I bet," Kensie mused. Hopefully with a little luck and a whole lot of fairy dust she'd soon know the feeling. Kensie looked back to the stage. Carter stood with his back to them, piecing together his instruments. It was finally starting to look more like a drum set and less like a jumbled mess of parts on the stage. She watched, fascinated by the way he moved, the care he took, his attention to detail. He wasn't the slacker she'd originally mistaken him for. The more she learned about him, the more she wanted to know. He was a mystery. Part of her wanted to keep it that way. It'd be easier when the time came for her to say goodbye.

"Hey, man, what's up?" Javi stood, greeting an older gentleman with salt-and-pepper hair. He, like everyone else in the bar, was covered in tattoos.

"Looks like you boys upgraded your sales team." He smiled, nodding at Kensie.

"Oh nah, man, my nephew is sick, so Los stayed home with him.

This is Kensie, she's CT's girl. Kensie, meet Dave, he owns the place."

"Hi, nice to meet you. I…uh…Carter and I are just friends so…yeah," she stammered like an idiot. She silently prayed for the ground to open up and swallow her.

Dave chuckled, "Well either way, welcome to the Rabbit Hole family."

"Thank you."

"Carter, huh?" Javi asked as Dave retreated.

"It's not that big of a deal," she defended herself. "We *are* friends."

"You sure he knows about the whole *'friends'* thing?"

Kensie glanced over to the stage. A brunette in tiny black spandex shorts and halter top had made her way up to where Carter worked. He was so focused on finishing his drum that he didn't notice her. Kensie's heart raced as she watched the woman run her fingers through his hair. He turned and smiled politely, mouthing something that Kensie couldn't make out. Whatever it was, it caused the woman to throw her head back in laughter. A flirty, obnoxious kind of laugh that Kensie heard loud and clear. "I think he's got it," she said bitterly, nodding in their general direction

"Tiff? That's nothing. She's not somebody you need to worry about."

"Who is she to him?" Kensie's focus stayed glued to the stage. She couldn't help herself. She was a glutton for punishment. Carter had gone back to building his drum but Tiff remained rooted to her spot.

Javi sighed, "Nobody."

"For nobody," she said, meeting his eyes, "she sure seems to touch him a lot." Javi rubbed his temple. She could practically see his wheels turning as he tried to think of some way to cover for his friend. "The truth, please."

"She's a *last call*."

"You're going to have to translate. I don't speak fuckboy."

Javi chuckled, shaking his head. "You know, like, it's the end of the night and there's no potential…"

"And?" Kensie was only half-listening. Her attention was back on the stage, back on Carter and Tiff. *What kind of name is Tiff, anyway?*

"So, like... Dios, Kensie, this sounds worse than it is, okay?"

"Just spit it out." *Tiff's* hands were now on Carter's chest and Kensie's face probably resembled a strawberry. She felt like a cartoon character whose head was about to pop off at any moment.

"You call a girl like Tiff to come through, no questions asked, no expectations, just sex."

"So, basically like me?"

"No, not like you. Look, there are groupies and then there are girlfriends. Groupies are for everybody, but girlfriends are off-limits. That's a groupie," he explained, pointing to Tiff. "She's up there practically begging him to fuck her and he's barely paying her any attention. You're his girl. He's obsessed with you. It's borderline creepy. Honestly, you should probably be worried."

"Okay, so first, that's the most disgusting thing I've ever heard. Second, I'm not his girlfriend."

He looked at her as if she was being deliberately obtuse. "Maybe not officially, but you're nowhere near groupie status. He's different with you."

"How?"

"Well for one, he almost ripped my arm off when he saw it wrapped around your shoulder, even though he knows I'd never cross that line." Kensie stayed silent. Carter being a possessive asshole was nothing new to her. "You know how he spent his morning?" *Silence.* "He had his sister come over at the ass crack of dawn to teach him how to make breakfast, to teach him how to make *you* breakfast. That ho...er...that girl or woman...whatever, couldn't even fucking tell you what our kitchen looks like."

That should have made her smile. It probably would have had she not looked back to the stage. She would have been elated had she not seen that bitch with her hand down the front of Carter's pants. Furious didn't even cover it. This was the exact reason she and Carter would never work. She had more than enough trust issues to deal with without adding the entire harem of women Lithium Springs had at their beck and call. She walked as fast as her legs would carry her towards the back of the bar.

"Kensie!" Carter yelled from the stage, but she kept going. She needed to find Jam and get the fuck out of there—fast. "Kensington, wait a minute."

"It's fine, Carter, you can do whatever you want. I just need some air," she threw over her shoulder, her tone clipped. She kept moving forward, searching for the back exit.

"That wasn't what it looked like...I should have shut her down from the beginning. I was just trying to be polite, but she wasn't taking no for an answer." Kensie ignored him. She knew the door was just ahead. She just had to keep going. "Kensington." She kept moving until, finally, she spotted her target. She pushed the door open and let it shut in his face. She didn't know where she was going, she didn't have a plan, but she needed a minute to regroup. "Kensie, will you stop and talk to me," he yelled, pulling her arm.

"I need a fucking minute," she snapped. She did her best to yank out of his grasp, but his grip was firm. He dragged her to him, her back to his front, and wrapped both his arms around her shoulders.

"No, not until you talk to me. I don't want this to fuck up our night. Who knows when we'll get another one." Kensie didn't trust herself to speak. She knew her voice would betray her. The silence seemed to drag on. Carter loosened his hold on her just enough to spin her around so that they faced each other. "Come on, *Friend*, I need to know we're good."

"It's fine, Carter. I'm being irrational. I don't have the right to be jealous." She sighed, refusing to meet his gaze.

Carter grabbed her chin, forcing her to look into his stormy blue eyes. "You can have whatever you want, Kensington." He pressed his lips to her forehead. "I'll give you a minute, if that's what you really need."

She nodded and watched as he retreated to the bar. What she needed was to end this madness. She was in way over her head. A relationship with him was never supposed to be an option. It was supposed to be sex. She didn't think he wanted anything else from her. She could handle it when it was just sex, but this—tonight—was the first time she realized that maybe there could be more and that scared her to death.

The slight buzzing in her back pocket distracted her from her pity party. She briefly considered letting it go to voicemail. She exhaled in frustration before pulling out her phone. Trey's face illuminated the screen. Great, just what she needed. "Hello."

"I've been a dick."

"Yup." Her voice was hard. Dick was an understatement. Not only had he stormed out this morning like a toddler—the irony was not lost on her—he had also ignored her several attempts at contacting him throughout the day.

"Are you going to Liam's party?"

"You're giving me a choice?" She was being a bitch, but he deserved it.

"Babe."

Kensie ran her fingers through her hair. She didn't want to do this right now. All she could think about was finding Carter. He was right, who knew when they'd get to spend more time together, and she didn't have the energy to be mad at him too. "I wouldn't miss Liam's birthday just because you're a controlling douchebag."

"Ouch. I guess I deserved that."

"Look, I should go. I'll see you tomorrow. We can talk then."

"I love you, Kensington."

She paused. The silence was immense, but in the end, she caved. "I love you." It was amazing how much could change in such a short amount of time. In the span of two weeks, Kensie had decided to quit her job and move in with her boyfriend. Then there was Carter. She still wasn't sure what to do about him, but she was determined to enjoy what little time she could spend with the tattooed deviant who had her questioning her future.

Kensie pulled the side door open and yelped in surprise. Carter was standing there, leaning against the wall with his head down and his hands in his pockets. "You scared the shit out of me!" she said, clutching her chest. "What are you doing lurking around back here, anyway? I thought you had sound check."

Carter cocked his head to the side, eyeing her for a moment. "Are we good?"

"We're good. I swear. I just needed some air."

He looked at her again, studying her face for any sign of residual anger. "You were jealous." It wasn't a question. He wasn't making fun of her, in fact, his voice was more hopeful than anything.

She knew what he wanted her to say, what he needed to hear. She walked up to him slowly, wrapping her arms around his waist, resting her hands on his ass. "This is mine now, and I won't share you with anyone."

"Is that so?" He smirked. Kensie nodded as her tongue darted across her top and bottom lip. The air was thick and the aching between her legs was becoming unbearable. "Jesus, Kensington, what are you doing to me?" Before she could answer, his mouth crashed onto hers, his tongue teasing her lips apart. His hands fisted in her hair and he tugged her head back, granting him full access to her mouth. His other hand feathered up her stomach, his fingers releasing her breast from the confines of her bra, then he twisted and pulled and rolled her nipple.

"Carter," she moaned, "don't you have to get back?"

He kissed her again and then once more before dropping to his knees. His mouth wet, warm against her navel. "Yes, but first I need to make sure we're good," he repeated as he unbuttoned her jeans. His nose ran circles across her pelvic bone. He inhaled her scent, sighing as if she were the sweetest thing in the world.

"Carter, stop it." Her voice was laced with panic as she looked up and down the hallway. "Someone could walk back here at any minute."

He looked up at her, a lopsided grin plastered on his face. "Then we'd better give them one hell of a show."

He tugged her jeans down just below her ass, just enough to allow him access to her clit. He kissed her through the fabric of her panties. "Silk?"

She couldn't speak, she was too busy trying to stay on her feet. Instead she leaned her head back against the wall, raking her fingers through the mess of deep toffee on top of his head, preparing herself for whatever it was he was about to give her.

He pushed her panties aside, and his teeth grazed her clit. Her knees nearly gave out from the sensation. She tried to spread her legs, tried to grant him greater access, but her jeans restricted her movements. She almost suggested he remove them altogether when a woman's voice called out, "CT? Are you back here?"

"Oh my God. Oh my God. Oh My God," she whispered, pushing Carter back. She did her best to shimmy her pants back up over her ass.

She'd barely covered herself when he pulled her back to him, her pants were still undone, but at least she was no longer exposed. He tilted his head so that his chin rested just below her navel. "Are we good?" He smirked, smugly.

"Yes, now get up," she gritted.

"There you…oh…umm…" Tiff stammered, unsure of what to make of the situation. Kensie almost felt bad for the woman. Almost. "They're ready for you."

"Cool," Carter said, jumping to his feet as if he hadn't been caught with his hand in the cookie jar. He tilted Kensie's chin up with his thumb. "Give me an hour, then I promise I'll finish what I started." He pressed his lips to hers and then turned, jogging past a shell-shocked Tiff and back toward the main bar.

TEN

No Angel

Patience was a virtue, at least that's what *they* say. Unfortunately, Kensie never could wrap her mind around all the *"good things come to those who wait"* and *"life's a journey"* nonsense her mother tried to drill into her head as a child. Delayed gratification just wasn't her thing. Her father dedicated his life to making sure she never wanted for anything and despite her mother's objections, he catered to her every whim.

Kensie released a shaky breath as she shifted uncomfortably in the chair. She was desperate for the friction, hoping it would help relieve the throbbing between her legs. Jam sat next to her, sipping a beer. Her lips were swollen, her clothes slightly askew, and her hair was a disaster. In truth, she looked well and thoroughly fucked.

Kensie pressed her thighs together.

She really hated waiting.

The guys spent the last hour tuning their instruments, adjusting the sound equipment, and making last-minute changes to their set. Honestly, it was kind of boring. "How much longer?" Kensie whispered, watching as Javi plucked out notes on his bass and then fiddled with the knobs on the amplifier.

"They should be about done," Jam answered, checking the time on her phone. "The bar opens at seven thirty, and it's seven fourteen now."

Kensie chugged the rest of her beer—her second. Alcohol was the only thing stopping her from dragging Carter off the stage and fucking his brains out.

When the guys finished their sound check, Carter hopped off the stage and sauntered over to her. "You hungry?" he asked in a voice that made Kensie's brain cells disappear. Every part of him, from his hair, to his eyes, and scruffy jaw, reduced her to the village idiot. Kensie couldn't think when he was around, she didn't want to. She only wanted to feel—feel that hair between her fingers, those eyes penetrating her body, that jaw tickling her cheek. "There's a taco truck down the street. The guys were talking about going before the show starts."

She shook her head. "I'm not hungry." *Not for food anyway.*

"It's going to be a long night. You should eat something."

She licked her lips and eyed him shamelessly. He'd taken his shirt off midway through sound check and his abs glistened under the neon lights of the bar. His muscles bunched with each movement he made. His shorts hung dangerously low on his hips, so low she wondered if he was wearing underwear. "Why don't *you* feed me then?" Her voice was breathier than she'd ever heard it before, needier, desperate.

Carter regarded her carefully. She could see the internal debate raging behind his blue eyes. She only hoped his need to fuck her was greater than his need to buy her tacos. Not wanting to leave it to chance, Kensie slipped her fingers in the waistband of his shorts and pulled him in between her legs. *Nope, no underwear.* "I seem to remember you promising to finish what you started earlier."

"Kensie." It was a plea. She could see his resolve crumbling before her eyes. It wouldn't take much to push him over the edge.

"I'm asking you to invade my personal space."

"How am I supposed to say no to that?" he asked, pulling her up from the chair. He slipped his hands into the back pockets of her jeans. If they were any closer, they'd be fucking. "I'm going to feed you, then we're going to the taco truck, deal?"

They were standing in the middle of the bar discussing her sex life. She was mortified, but oddly enough, it did nothing but fuel her need. "Deal."

They walked in silence back past the side door and further into the club, anticipation building with each step. Kensie's heart pounded. Wetness dripped from her sex. She finally understood the whole delayed gratification thing. She'd waited for this moment for two weeks, and now her patience was finally going to be rewarded.

Carter stopped in front of a door at the end of the hallway. She barely gave him a chance to lock it behind them before she started fumbling with his shorts. His lips found hers and they stumbled backwards into the room towards an old leather sofa that was across from a cheap desk. A large TV was mounted on the wall, along with various signed black-and-white photographs of local musicians. It wasn't anything special, but there was a door and a lock and she wouldn't have to worry about bitchy bartenders interrupting this time.

She pulled her lips from his, trying to focus on the task of unbuttoning his shorts. Carter kicked his shoes off and Kensie pushed his shorts down to his ankles, then pushed him back onto the couch. His dick was rigid, a thick vein ran along the right side of his shaft. Her mouth watered at the sight of it. She sunk to her knees. Biting her lip, she peeked up at him from behind mascara-coated lashes. She was going for sweet and innocent, knowing full well that what she was about to do was anything but. Kensie wrapped her fingers firmly around his shaft, slowly pumping her fist up and down. Her brown eyes stayed locked on his as she gently teased him.

Her tongue swept across her lips just before she leaned down and licked the tiny bead of pre-cum off the tip of his dick. She started slow, licking and sucking her way up and down his member, coating him with her saliva. Once he was thoroughly lubricated, she swallowed him further down her throat, so far her lips pressed against the base of his shaft. His eyes were hooded, his jaw tense.

Kensie massaged his balls as she bobbed up and down the length of his cock, hollowing out her cheeks to create a tighter suction. Carter inhaled sharply. "Jesus, Kensington."

Kensington Grace Roth may have been sweet and demure, and at times, a little flighty, but she knew how to give a blowjob. It was a skill she'd perfected. She loved the authority she felt in being able to render even the most powerful man a quivering mess, all from the comfort of her knees. It didn't hurt that her gag reflex was non-existent. The rest was easy.

"Baby," he moaned. It was the first time he'd ever used the epithet. She wasn't sure how it made her feel. Sure, she loved the way it sounded slipping from his lips, especially while she worked him over with her mouth, but it also reminded her of how much the lines of their relationship had blurred.

Carter fisted her hair and yanked her back. Her mouth made a small popping sound and a string of spit trailed from her lips to his penis. She couldn't help the frown that contorted her face. Her eyes found his. She was pouting. "Don't look at me like that," he admonished, pulling her hair again. He leaned forward so that his mouth was directly on her ear. His warm breath sent a chill down her spine. "You're really good at that—too good. Trust me, I'm going to have a lot of fun with that mouth of yours, but right now I need to be inside of you."

His words sent shock waves through her body. She could do nothing but nod her agreement. He stood, pulling her up with him. He unfastened her jeans and roughly tugged them down over her hips, dragging her panties along with them. He kneeled, taking a moment to untie her shoes, then pulled them off and tossed them over with the other garments. Next, he unhooked her bra and pulled it out through the sleeves of her shirt. She started to take off the *Team Lithium* crop, but he stopped her. "Leave it," he growled. "I've been daydreaming about fucking you in this since you walked in the bar."

He was a narcissistic asshole and she had every intention of telling him that, but he never gave her the chance. He spun her around and pushed her over the arm of the couch. Pain shot up her back as his palm landed squarely in the middle of her ass. "Ouch!" she yelped.

"That's for not telling me you could deep throat." He pulled his hand back again, and again he spanked her. "That was for making me wait two fucking weeks to have what's mine." He slid his fingers through her wetness, slowly swirling them around inside of her. She pushed her hips back, grinding up against them, needing more. "Uh-uh," he scolded, withdrawing his fingers from her, spanking her a third time.

"What was that for?" she breathed.

"Because I know you wanted me to do it again." She didn't bother arguing. Instead she wiggled her ass, silently asking for another. He chuckled, his voice low, gritty. "You're not as sweet and innocent as you want everyone to believe."

"I was. You ruined me, remember?"

He didn't respond, instead, he pushed her legs apart, spreading them wide. The tip of his cock slipped through her folds and he pushed slowly into her, filling her totally, then stilled, giving her time to adjust to the intrusion. "This is going to be rough, Friend," he growled.

She moaned, wiggling back against him. She needed it rough. She needed him to fuck all the worry and doubt and anxiety out of her body.

Carter pulled back, drawing out his length, then slammed back inside of her. His nails dug into her flesh as he plowed into her over and over, thrusting faster and harder each time until he was pumping into her so wildly she could barely stay on her feet. The noises that escaped his mouth were animalistic. He was lost in her and she was completely at his mercy.

Her arms were all but useless as she struggled to hold herself up. Her head jerked back as Carter pulled her up into a standing position, then quickly slipped his erection back inside her warmth. One arm circled her waist and his other hand rested firmly around her neck. "Do you trust me?"

"Yes." Totally, madly, implicitly.

With knees bent, Carter thrusted into her pussy. The movement forced Kensie onto her tiptoes. He was deeper than anyone had ever been before, so deep she teetered on the line between pain and pleasure. Each thrust sent a wave of vibrations to her core. The pressure built. A layer of sweat coated her body. The pleasure tore through her like lightning across the night sky. Carter's hand flexed around her throat and her eyes shot open. Panic mixed with unmatched passion woke every nerve in her body as she clawed at him. "Relax, baby. Just let go."

And she did. His words were her undoing. She fucking lost her mind. She was lost in him, *lost to anyone but him*. Her body shook violently. She came long and hard, gasping for air. His grip loosened and she slumped back against him. The hand that was around her neck slid down the front of her damp body and found her clit. Carter rubbed small circles over the tiny bundle of nerves as he continued to fuck her.

She vaguely registered Carter tensing behind her as he came. He pulled out and warm liquid ran down her thigh. "You good?" he asked, steadying her. Her head bobbed up and down, and she used the wall to brace herself. Carter swiped a few tissues from the box on the desk and kneeled before her, gently cleaning up the mess between her legs. Kensie fiddled with the hem of her *Team Lithium* shirt, embarrassed by the intimacy of his actions. "Stop," he reprimanded.

"Stop what?"

"Stop overthinking this."

"I'm trying. I just…this was supposed to be sex and here I am helping out at your show and wearing your name on my back like I don't have an entire life outside of you, like I don't have a boyfriend."

"Look, I understand that your being happy with me feels like an added layer of betrayal to him, but you can't shut down every time I fuck you. It isn't fair to me."

"I know and I'm sorry. This is really intense and unexpected, and

I get overwhelmed and I don't know how to feel."

"Do you want to be here with me or not?" She nodded, chewing on her bottom lip. She was exactly where she wanted to be, but that was the problem.

"Then *be here* with me."

ELEVEN

Waves

Trey merged onto I-90 eastbound. Kensie sat in the passenger seat, her forehead pressed against the tinted glass. Mile markers and speed limit signs whizzed by in a blur as Trey drove them seventy-miles-per-hour towards Bellevue. The drive was a quiet one. If it weren't for the radio playing softly in the background, there wouldn't have been any noise at all.

The silence provided Kensie with time to think. She loved Trey, she would never deny that. When he came into her life she had been broken, and he'd helped heal her heart. He helped restore her faith in happily ever after, but what if he was never meant to be her Prince Charming?

This thing with Carter was spiraling fast and she was powerless to stop it. Their one-night stand somehow morphed into a full-blown affair—an affair that had her questioning the fate of her relationship. Carter wasn't supposed to get the boyfriend perks. He was her sex friend and Trey was her boyfriend. That was the line. There wasn't supposed to be feelings or emotions involved. That was how she justified her actions. It's how she could look in the mirror and not hate the person staring back.

Last weekend, she hopped, skipped, and jumped so far over that line, she feared she'd lost herself on the other side.

Would she ever find her way back?

Did she even want to?

Being on Team Lithium was fun. Being with Jam was fun. Javi and Ryder were fun. And if she were being honest with herself—truly honest—she loved spending time with Carter. Things were so different with him. They were like magnets, naturally drawn to each other. She could talk to Carter about anything, and he'd listen as if what she was saying was the most important thing in the world. He had a passion for life that inspired her, and the sex was divine—a Holy Trinity, born again kind of sexual awakening that Kensie had only ever read about in books.

On the other hand, there was Trey. He was analytical. He didn't do anything unless it made sense, unless it made money. He would provide her and their future children with everything they'd ever want. He was dependable, stable, and most importantly, she knew he'd always protect her heart. Their relationship would never be intense, but it would be everlasting.

Kensie had a choice to make. Was for now with Carter worth risking forever with Trey?

"Do you plan on ignoring me for the rest of the day?"

She sighed, picking her head up off the glass. Going to this party with him was a mistake, but it was too late to back out now.

"No, I'll smile and do the whole Stepford wife thing once we get there, just let me sulk for a little while longer."

Trey's jaw tensed and his grip on the steering wheel tightened perceptibly. He was one of the most controlled men she'd ever met. This was only the second time she'd ever seen his composure slip. The first time was last week, in his kitchen. "What's going on with us?" he gritted. His expression was impossible to read behind his dark Ray-Bans.

"I don't know," she said as she fiddled with the pearls around her neck. *Pearls to a pool party.* They didn't match the tiny purple bikini she wore under her yellow sundress, but she put them on anyway. It was a ritual now. She'd worn them after every night spent in Neverland.

"You're still moving in, aren't you?"

"I don't know," she sighed. Her eyes drifted back out the window. Bellevue was just across Lake Washington. They were getting closer and closer with each passing moment. The city long behind them, as they crossed the East Canal Bridge.

"You're giving up after one fucking fight?"

"No, I'm not giving up. We still have a lot to learn about each other, about what we want out of life, and where we see ourselves in the future. I don't know if it's a good idea."

"I get that all the marriage and children talk freaked you out, but it isn't like we haven't discussed the possibilities before."

"We've talked about *one day* getting married and *one day* having children. Me quitting my 'silly little' job and staying home full-time was never part of the discussion. You make it sound as if this time next year I'll be Mrs. Knight and we'll be expecting our first child. So yes," she admitted, "it freaked me out. I just want it to be Trey and Kensie for a little while longer."

"I never called your job silly."

Kensie's eyes bulged out of their sockets. She was trying to have a serious conversation about the future of their relationship and that's what he chose to focus on? "Are you really fucking arguing semantics with me?"

He bristled at her tone. His knuckles turned white as snow. "Language, Kensington," he warned, and she had to bite her tongue until she tasted blood to refrain from exploding. If they kept this up, she wouldn't be able to pretend to be the happy couple they were supposed to be. "Baby, I don't want to fight. You can work if you want, you can stay home, you can even work from home. I don't care, I just don't want to fight with you anymore. I want us to be happy."

Kensie released a shaky breath and tears welled in her big, brown eyes. His sincerity almost knocked the wind out of her. That was all she'd ever wanted from him, only now she feared it was too little, too late.

Ring

Ring

Ring

Trey's phone blared through the speakers, just the distraction Kensie needed. This conversation was getting too heavy for a day meant to celebrate Trey's little brother turning twenty-five.

"Hello."

"Hey," Reagan's hushed voice wafted through the car, "are you at my parents' place yet?"

"No, we're almost to the gate," Trey answered. Kensie looked out the window then. She recognized the neighborhood. Trey's parents lived here too.

"Hurry, we're finished with brunch and we should be there in fifteen. Grant's home, so just go around back to the pool house…shit… he's coming. See you soon!"

Kensie couldn't help the smile that played at her lips, her first genuine smile of the day. Reagan's energy was infectious, even over the phone she felt her warmth. It was like she'd been thrown a life raft. The one bright spot on this otherwise dismal day. "I don't want to fight either, not today. Let's just try to get back to Trey and Kensie, okay?"

"I like that. I can do that," he agreed.

"Babe, what are you doing? We're going to be late," Kensie asked as Trey parked in his parents' driveway.

Trey smirked at his girlfriend. "The party is right next door. Reagan sent out a mass text this morning telling everyone to park here so the cars wouldn't tip Liam off. There's a path out by the boathouse that connects to the Thayers."

"Oh," she said in surprise. She'd known Liam and Reagan had been high school sweethearts, but she had no idea they literally grew up together. Kensie followed Trey around the estate and back down to the boathouse. The view from the yard was stunning. The afternoon sun danced off Lake Washington, filling Kensie with an overwhelming sense of calm.

She reached for Trey's hand as he led her down a narrow path and through a smattering of evergreen trees. He smiled down at her, bringing her fingers to his lips. "What's going on up there, Kensie?"

"I was just thinking about how awesome it must have been to grow up here," she said as they strolled leisurely through the woods.

Kensie studied his profile as they traveled the worn path between the two properties. His sunglasses were pushed up on top of his head, providing her with her first glimpse of the brown eyes she'd fallen in love with. His body was relaxed, much more than it had been just moments ago. For the first time since she'd met Carter, things were starting to feel almost normal between her and her boyfriend.

"It definitely didn't suck. We spent so much time in these woods when we were younger, running back and forth between our house and the Thayers'. We drove our mothers crazy." A myriad of emotions passed through his eyes as he recalled his childhood, joy, adoration, contentment, then finally, sadness.

She wasn't sure what caused the sudden shift in his mood, but she decided not to push it. This is the first conversation they've had that hadn't ended in a fight in days and she wanted to savor it.

The Thayer estate was massive, and the view was equally impressive. The large brick and stucco house sat back from the water. There was a boat docked down by the lake, a tennis court and a deck overlooking the yard. A tall blond man with blue eyes greeted them as they approached. There was something vaguely familiar about him, like she'd met him before, but she couldn't place him.

He extended a hand to Trey, pulling him in for a hug. "Haven't seen you since Vegas, dude." The man grinned. "Thought you might have died from alcohol poisoning."

Trey groaned, "I'm never going anywhere with you guys again."

Kensie shuffled awkwardly at the direction of the conversation. She couldn't help the nagging feeling in the pit of her stomach when she thought about Trey's trip to Sin City. It was the same weekend she met Carter and, yes, that made her a hypocrite. She knew her flaws, she was jealous, immature, and a cheater, but she was still human.

"Oh, I'm sorry," Trey said realizing himself. "Grant Thayer, this is Kensington Roth. Kensie, Grant. He's Reagan's oldest brother."

Grant smiled at Kensie and, again, she couldn't help feeling as if they'd met before. "Hi!" she greeted, wrapping her arms around Trey's waist. "I hope you guys didn't have *too* much fun in Vegas." Her tone was playful, as she tried to suppress the angry little green monster bubbling inside of her.

"He was on his best behavior," Grant assured her, ushering them up towards the pool. "Scout's honor."

Trey draped his arm around her shoulder, pulling her forehead to his lips. He looked at her, really looked at her for the first time in months. It was as if he could sense the shift and he was trying to remind her of why she fell in love with him in the first place. She could do this. She could get through this party with a smile on her face. She needed this. *They needed this.* She needed to know if her relationship with Trey was worth fighting for, or if she should jump out the window and fly off to Neverland forever.

The backyard was a circus—literally. Unicorns floated in the infinity pool and game stations were set up throughout the yard. There was a popcorn machine, cotton candy, and even face painting. It was like a child's birthday party, well aside from the fully stocked bar and the thirty or so twenty-somethings milling around in swimwear.

Grant's phone chimed, Reagan letting him know she and Liam were pulling onto the street. He directed everyone to get into position. Kensie and Trey ducked behind a lounge chair, their eyes focused on the French doors. Her heart pounded. Time seemed to stop as they waited patiently for the doors to open. She felt like a kid waiting for Santa.

"They're coming," someone whisper-yelled from across the patio.

The door creaked open and Liam's face peeked into view.

"SURPRISE!" the small crowd yelled in unison as Liam and Reagan walked out onto the patio. Shock and surprise flashed in his eyes before he turned to his fiancée. There was so much love, so much adoration, and so much intimacy in that one look that Kensie had to turn away.

Liam and Reagan made their rounds, politely thanking everyone for coming and answering questions about their upcoming nuptials. They looked so blissfully happy, Kensie couldn't help but wonder if she'd ever feel that way. She glanced at Trey. He was busy chatting with Grant and one of Liam's frat brothers about last week's Mariners game. She racked her brain trying to recall if he'd ever looked at her with even half the intensity that his brother looked at Reagan.

Sure, Liam and Reagan had known each other their entire lives, and maybe she and Trey had only been together for a little over a year, but they were supposed to be moving in together. They'd discussed marriage and children and spending the rest of their lives together, yet Kensie couldn't recall a single time when Trey looked at her like that.

"I'm going to grab a drink, baby, do you want anything?" Kensie asked, shaking off the depressing thoughts. She was going to enjoy herself if it killed her.

"A beer would be great. You guys good?" Trey asked his friends.

"I'd love a beer." Liam's frat brother nodded.

"I'll come with," Grant offered.

Kensie gave him a small smile as they turned and headed towards the cabana.

"If she can pull all of this off last minute, I can't wait to see what the wedding looks like," Kensie marveled. Even the bar was decorated in the circus theme. There were special labels over the liquor bottles and clown faces on the napkins and plastic cups.

"Liam hates clowns," Grant chuckled, shaking his head. "I'm just grateful she only uses her evil powers to torture her fiancé." He held up a bottle of vodka with a picture of Liam's head photoshopped onto a ringleader's body. The sight of it caused Kensie to double over in laughter.

"What's so funny?" Reagan asked as she and Liam approached. Reagan was gorgeous. Her body curved in all the right places and she had a face that looked like it belonged on a runway.

Grant turned the label toward Liam, raising his brow. "It's not too late to back out you know," he said, ducking as his sister took a swing.

Liam laughed. Although he was two years younger than Trey, they could have passed for twins. The only real difference between them was that Trey was two inches taller. "No such luck," Liam lamented, smiling at Reagan. "She had me at hello. I never even had a choice."

Reagan stuck her tongue out at her brother and then leaned up on her toes to press a small kiss on Liam's mouth. They lingered for a moment until Grant started making gagging noises. "Ugh, you two are hopeless," he teased, his face wrinkled in mock disgusted.

They *were* hopeless and Kensie thought it was adorable. It was the kind of love that endured. It was the kind of love that her parents shared, the kind she saw on Jam's face when she looked at Ryder, and the kind she wished to one day find for herself. "You really outdid yourself with this party, Reagan," she said, looking around the yard.

"She sure did." Kensie's heart stopped upon hearing the familiar voice. It came from somewhere behind her. She felt him as he approached. The hair on the back of her neck stood at attention. She couldn't breathe, couldn't move. His voice alone was enough to send her into a catatonic shock. "Too bad my invitation must have gotten lost in the mail." Carter came to a stop at her side, but she didn't dare look. If her stupid legs would work, she'd turn and run back out the door.

What is he doing here?
Why the fuck is he here?

"It's Liam's birthday. These are his friends," Reagan explained.

"But you invited this motherfucker." Carter grinned, pointing to Grant. As he spoke, his body shifted so that their arms touched. To everyone else, the movement seemed harmless, accidental, but she knew better.

"Give me a break, Cart. Grant is Liam's best friend and one of his groomsmen. Plus, I knew you wouldn't come because *he's* here," Reagan countered. "Not to mention, I had to beg you to play at the wedding, AND you're making us pay!"

"You can afford it." He smirked. Kensie felt his eyes trail down to her but she refused to meet his gaze. Suddenly the clown decorations were the most interesting thing in the world. "We were together last week, little sister, you could have at least mentioned it."

That's when it happened. That's when her world stopped.

Holy Shit.

HO-LEE SHIT!

Shit

Shit

Shit

Carter and Reagan were brother and sister. Kensie was fucking her boyfriend's-brother's-fiancée's-brother. There had to be an episode of *Jerry Springer* in there somewhere. Her knees wobbled. She turned and grabbed one of the bottles with Liam's face on it and poured herself a double shot. *What the fuck was happening?* Her worlds were colliding, and she could only hope to contain the fallout.

Reagan rolled her eyes. "Why are you even here?"

Carter looked back to Kensie. She silently pleaded with him not to blow her cover. "I didn't realize I needed a reason to come home." He was talking to his sister, but his gaze stayed trained on Kensington. "But if you must know, I need dad to look over some contracts and stuff for the band. He told me to drop it off whenever," he explained, shaking the manila envelope in his hand to drive the point home.

Kensie discreetly tipped her cup of vodka back. The liquid burned going down her throat, but it did nothing to quell her anxiety, so she poured another.

"Oh, well you're more than welcome to join us, you know that."

"Maybe I will." Carter eyed Kensie like she was a treat, a tasty morsel to be devoured. Her cheeks were on fire.

"Oh no. Absolutely not. Don't even think about it, big brother," Reagan said looking from Carter to Kensie and back again. "You're barking up the wrong tree, in the wrong forest, on the wrong planet."

He reluctantly tore his gazed from Kensington to shoot his sister a questioning look.

Before anyone could utter another word on the subject, an arm wrapped possessively around Kensie's neck and she peeked up to see Trey glaring at the drummer. The air surrounding them was impossibly thick. Everyone sensed the shift.

"Back. The fuck. Off," Trey seethed.

Confusion, anger, then sudden realization washed across CT's features. He chuckled to himself, shaking his head, finally putting it together. "The cornball."

"What the fuck is that supposed to mean?" Trey asked, as he brought his other hand around Kensie's front, forcing her back into his chest. He was staking his claim, letting Carter know that she belonged to him.

"Who's your *Friend*?" His words were intentional. He was talking to Trey, but the hidden message was for her.

"Don't worry about it," Trey snipped. "She's out of your league."

"I don't know, man," Carter said scratching his head, "chicks dig the tattoos." His eyes traveled back to Kensie. She glared at him, willing him to let this go.

"Stop eye fucking my girl," Trey growled. Kensie had never seen this side of Trey before, and she'd rarely ever heard him say fuck. His anger unnerved her. She could feel the rage rolling off him in waves.

"Or else what?" Carter smirked. His face was smug, like he knew something that Trey didn't. Everyone else must have assumed it was bravado, but Kensie knew, she was his ace in the hole.

"We can settle this right now if you want," Trey threatened, releasing Kensie from his hold. He took a step forward.

"Because that worked out so well for you last time," Carter said, also stepping forward.

"Yeah, well, this isn't last time and we're not nineteen anymore."

"Will you two stop it," Reagan shrieked. "This stupid rivalry is getting old. Liam and I are getting married in a couple of weeks and we are all going to officially be family. I'm sick of this shit. Come on, Kensie, let's go." Reagan grabbed Kensie by the hand and pulled her back towards the house.

"What the fuck was that?" Kensie asked, releasing the breath that she'd been holding ever since Carter arrived.

"Intense, right." Reagan nodded.

"So intense."

"Can you believe they used to be best friends?"

"Trey and your brother?"

"Yup."

"Best friends?"

"Yup. Crazy, right?"

Shit.

TWELVE

Jealous

Kensie needed a minute—no, she needed a fucking month. It was bad enough Carter turned out to be Reagan's brother, but the fact that he and Trey were mortal enemies, that was catastrophic. "Are they always like that?" Kensie asked. She'd done her best to keep it together, but her voice betrayed her true feelings.

"They never used to be." Reagan shook her head. "When we were younger, they were like each other's shadow, they were inseparable. You'd never see one without the other."

"But they're so different! I mean…they seem so different."

"Not really. Physically, yes, my brother takes the black sheep thing to a whole new level, then again, he never does anything halfway." She smiled, her expression softening ever so slightly. "But appearances aside, Carter and Trey are cut from the same cloth. They're both selfish assholes. Trey's just better at hiding it."

Kensie considered it for a moment. She thought back over the previous few weeks. She hadn't noticed it before, but Reagan was right. They were both arrogant and stubborn and possessive. Apparently, Kensington had a type. "So, what happened? How did they go from best friends to archenemies?"

"That's the thing, nobody knows." Reagan shrugged. "Whenever you bring it up to either one of them, they just shut down. It's like we aren't supposed to talk about it. Like we're supposed to pretend that them going from being joined at the hip to not being able to stand the sight of one another was normal."

Of all the men in Seattle, what were the chances that she'd fall into bed with the worst possible one? She exhaled and raked her fingers through her hair. It was karma. Kensie was the cheater. The hurt and pain that was sure to come from all this was her fault. She wasn't the damsel in distress, she was the villain. She didn't deserve happily ever after with either of them.

Kensie glanced over towards the cabana. Carter and Grant had disappeared, and Trey stood there with his little brother. His handsome face was marred with tension as he lifted a red clown cup to his mouth. He tilted his head back, swallowing whatever it was. She only ever saw the man nurse more than one or two drinks, and now he was taking shots.

She wasn't sure when the music started playing. She hadn't noticed people in the pool until that moment. The party raged on, unaffected by Carter and Trey's little showdown.

Kensie followed Reagan in silence toward the yard and over to the makeshift game station. The warm summer breeze blew Kensie's hair all over, causing the chestnut strands to tangle in the clasp of her necklace. She tugged on it, hard, but karma wasn't letting go. "Can you show me where the restroom is?" she asked, pointing to the hair knotted in her pearls.

Reagan inspected the damage. "Ouch, that's really stuck. Yeah, here, use the one in the guest house. It's easier than walking back up to the main house."

Kensie nodded, following as Reagan led her around to the other side of the yard to the smaller building. The guest house was simple, quaint. If Thayer Manor was Cinderella's Palace, this place was Snow White's Cottage. There was a small eat-in kitchen, a fully furnished living room, two bedrooms, and a master bathroom. "Thanks." Kensie smiled politely as Reagan pointed her down the narrow hallway.

"You take care of that and I'll get us some shots!" Reagan grinned. "We're not going to let their ridiculous rivalry ruin the party, are we?"

Kensie shook her head enthusiastically. "No, we aren't." She smiled. Alcohol was probably the last thing she needed but there was no way in hell she was getting through this day sober.

Once she was safely inside the bathroom she pulled out her phone.

Kensie: Holy shit, Jam. I'm freaking the fuck out!

Jam: What's wrong? Are you ok?

Kensie: I'm at a party for Trey's brother and you'll never guess who just walked in.

Kensie stared at her phone, waiting for Jam's reply. She tugged nervously at her necklace, ignoring the pain caused by pulling out the hairs at the nape of her neck. "Fuck," she grumbled, snatching the damn thing off, nearly breaking it.

Ring.

Her phone chimed. "Jam," she groaned.

"What's going on?" Jam's voice was laced with concern.

"Oh nothing, you know, just hanging with my boyfriend at his brother's surprise party and the guy I'm cheating on him with just so happens to walk in," Kensie quipped.

"No way. No. Fucking. Way."

"Fucking way, Jam, and that's not even the most fucked-up part. Trey's brother is marrying Carter's sister."

"WHAT?!" Jam yelled so loud that Kensie had to pull the phone away from her ear.

"Their parents live next door to one another. They all grew up together. Carter and Trey had some huge falling out years ago, and now they hate each other. They almost got into a fist fight."

"Shit. Ken, he did say he was from Bellevue, but he never really talks much about his life pre-Lithium. I can't believe I didn't put it together," Jam said, and Kensie could practically hear the wheels spinning. Jamie was a reporter and curious by nature. If Jam didn't see it, then she didn't feel like as big of an idiot—an idiot—just not as big a one.

"Yeah, well, now I'm hiding in the guest house bathroom, praying for a miracle."

"Do you want me to come and pick you up?" Jam asked.

She could hear keys jingling in the background. If nothing else, she could always count on Jamie to rescue her.

"No, I think Carter left. The party is at Reagan's…well Carter's too, I guess…it's at their parents' house. He just came by to see his dad. He didn't even know we'd be here."

"You don't think…he didn't know about you and Trey, right?"

"No. He seemed just as shocked to see me as I was to see him, and even so, how could he? They go out of their way to avoid each other. Trey's never even so much as mentioned his name, and you said yourself he's never talked about his life before Lithium Springs."

"Yeah."

Knock.

Knock.

Knock.

"That's probably Reagan," Kensie whispered into the phone. "I should go, but I promise to catch you up to speed as soon as I get home."

"Okay. Just please call if you need me."

"I will. I promise."

Kensie hung up the phone and shoved it, along with her necklace, back into her wristlet and opened the door. If there were ever a time when she needed a drink, now was it. "Reagan, you're a lifesaver…ugh," she groaned, rolling her eyes at the sight of the other Thayer. Against her better judgment, she pushed open the door, allowing him access to the confined space, before locking it behind him.

"You shouldn't be here, Carter," she said, still facing the door. She couldn't bring herself to look at him. She couldn't get sucked in, not with Trey just a few yards away.

"Trey fucking Knight?" he barked, placing his hands on either side of her head. His body warm against her back as he surrounded her. She couldn't think when he was this close. The logical side of her brain knew that him being in there with her was a terrible idea. If someone found them it would be a disaster, yet there she was, body trembling from his close proximity, reminding herself to breathe.

"Carter fucking Thayer?" she countered, once she regained her composure. "You never once thought to mention your last name?"

"You never asked," he whispered, leaning into her. He reeked of whiskey and bad intentions, but he was right, she'd never asked. She never wanted to know. She had done her best to keep him at arm's length, a fact she had since grown to regret.

"Did you know?"

"You walked into *my* life, Kensington. You turned *my* world upside down. I didn't tell you my name because that's not who I am anymore. I don't fit in here. I don't belong. I love my family, but this world isn't for me. I'd much rather be in my little house with friends who have my back unconditionally than here, surrounded by everything I could ever want, with vultures like Trey Knight. I'm not Carter Thayer, I'm CT, and I never lied to you about that."

She let his words marinate. Jam never picked up on it. Trey never picked up on the fact that Jamie was dating the front man of his arch nemesis' band. If two of the smartest people in Kensie's life hadn't seen it, then she had to take Carter at his word. "What are we going to do now?" she asked, turning to face him.

His stormy eyes were trained on her. His jaw tensed as he searched her face for answers to unspoken questions. "Let's get out of here."

"I can't."

The noise that escaped his mouth was raw, primal. He grabbed her leg and wrapped it around his waist, digging his fingers into her hip. "You. Are. Mine," was the last thing he said before his mouth found hers. She parted her lips, granting him full access. Their tongues danced wildly.

"Carter. We can't do this here," she breathed. "They could—"

"Fuck Trey," he growled, tugging hard at her bikini string until it came loose. He pulled back, just enough to unbutton his shorts, the head of his erection probing her entrance.

"He's my boyfriend," she moaned as he rubbed his tip through her folds.

"Do you think I give a fuck about that title?"

She gasped as he pushed inside of her. God, she wanted him, but she knew she needed to stop him now, while she still possessed a shred of willpower. "I get it," she squirmed, "I do. I was like this the other day when I saw you with Tiff, but we can't do this. Go home. I'll come over after the party and you can have me any way you want me. You can bite me, and spank me, and choke me until you feel better. You can take all of your jealousy and anger out on me, you can lose yourself in me, you can fuck me until you can't feel anything but me, just not here—not now."

"I'm not leaving without you. I can't stand the thought of him touching you," he whispered into her neck, forcing her back into the door. He pulled her other leg around his waist, as he ground his hips into her.

"Carter, you have nothing to worry about," she moaned, clawing at his shoulders. She was barely keeping it together. If she couldn't think straight when he was near, then she completely lost all brain function when he was inside of her. "He and I aren't even having sex."

He laughed, but there was no trace of humor in the sound. "I'm sure you've made similar promises to him, and I bagged you the night we met."

Kensie stilled. His harsh words hit her like a bucket of ice. "I'm such an idiot." She pushed him back, fighting hard to untangle her limbs from his. "You don't get to treat me like a whore because you're mad at him."

He ran his fingers through his hair, tousling his brown locks. "I'm sorry." Guilt flashed on his face. "Shit, Kensie, I didn't mean it like that. I just…"

She hastily tied her bikini before checking her appearance in the mirror. Her cheeks were flushed, and her lip gloss was smudged. She looked like shit, but it would have to do.

"Kensie, please," Carter begged, grabbing her arm.

"Look, just go home. Nothing good can come out of this if you stay."

"I'm not leaving without you."

"Where'd you go, Kensie?" Trey asked, shifting her on his lap. Much to Carter's annoyance, he'd kept up some form of physical contact with her for the past two hours. If she wasn't on his lap, his arm was around her neck, and if his arm wasn't around her neck, then his fingers were laced with hers. If he wasn't touching her, he was kissing her.

She did her best to plaster a huge grin on her face. "I guess I must have zoned out. All the sports talk." She shrugged.

Trey smiled, kissing her shoulder. "Sorry, babe."

"It's fine, but I think I'm going to need a drink if I have to sit and listen to one more stat."

Trey's smile faltered as he glanced towards the bar. Carter was there flanked by two bikini-clad bimbos. They cheered him on as he chugged from a champagne bottle. "You want me to come with you?"

"No, it's fine. Talk to your friends. I'm sure there's some arbitrary aspect of this season that you have yet to cover," she teased.

"Are you sure?" he asked looking back at Carter. The girls were jumping and clapping as he slammed the now empty bottle back into the table.

"Babe, I think it's safe to say, he's moved on."

Trey nodded reluctantly as she slipped out of his arms. She threw one more smile over her shoulder before storming over to the bar. Her happy façade was slipping, her anger boiling over. Carter was goading her, she knew it—but seeing him with other women made her irrational.

Carter eyed her smugly as she approached. "Susie, Emily, why don't you ladies go for a swim?" he said dismissively, nodding in the direction of the pool. They pouted but begrudgingly obliged and trotted off.

"Why are you doing this?"

"It's a party, Kensington." He crossed his arms over his chest. She couldn't help but notice his biceps flex with the movement.

"And Emily and Susie?"

"Options."

"Options," she repeated. She was so angry she couldn't see straight. "Are you intentionally trying to hurt me or do you just not give a damn?"

"You don't get to have your cake and eat it too, Friend. You've gotta choose, it's him or me, but I can't do this," he motioned between them, "anymore."

"I think I already have—" Just as she started to speak, a man and a woman walked up to the bar. They stood in awkward silence while the couple poured their drinks. Carter swallowed hard, his expression unreadable.

"CT, we saw you play last month at the Coliseum. You guys are killing it," the man said.

"Thanks, bro." Carter nodded.

The man looked to Kensie. "You're Trey's girl, right?"

Kensie gave the man a tight smile. She didn't need to look at Carter to know his eyes were focused on her response. "Kensie," she said, extending her hand.

"Nice to meet you, Kensie. I'm Jensen."

"Alright, J, I guess I'll see you at the wedding." Carter's voice was rough, and there was no mistaking his meaning, *go the fuck away.*

"See you around. Nice to meet you, Kensie."

She exhaled, watching them as they walked away. "I think I'm falling in love with you." The words tumbled out of her mouth so fast that she wasn't sure if he even understood her.

"What?"

She shook her head, looking around. "Are you really going to make me say it again?"

"Come home with me." He stepped towards her.

"I can't do that to him," she said, taking a step back.

"Why not? You don't owe him anything." *Another step.*

"He deserves better than that."

"What about me?"

"Carter, you won. I'm yours. What would humiliating him in front of his friends and family prove?"

His jaw tensed as his eyes darted over her shoulder. Trey's arms wrapped around her body and his hand slipped up the front of her sundress and inside her bikini bottoms.

"Babe, stop," Kensie protested, trying to remove his hand from between her legs.

"I don't know how many times I have to tell you, this is mine," Trey sneered.

"Trey," Kensie gritted as she tried to wiggle herself free. Her eyes pleaded with Carter. "Just one more day," she mouthed.

Carter shook his head, snatching a whiskey bottle off the bar. He brushed past them, storming toward the pool.

"Trey, get off me. You're drunk." Kensie pushed him back, causing him to stumble.

"Why is it okay for him to act like a drunken idiot and not me? Why does he constantly get chance after chance and I make one mistake, one time when I was fucking seventeen, and I'm the asshole?" Trey's eyes were glossed over. He wasn't talking about the party anymore.

"Tell me what happened? Help me understand."

"It's nothing. Never mind." He leaned down and kissed her. She allowed him to pull her into his arms. This had gotten way out of hand and she was the only one sober enough to put a stop to it.

She pushed Trey back. "I need to use the restroom, then let's get out of here." The lie came easy, she didn't have to pee, but she needed another minute alone with Carter. She needed to make sure he was okay. She needed to tell him that she was going to end things with Trey.

Kensie scanned the yard. She'd nearly given up when she spotted him, dragging Susie into the guest house. "Go tell your brother goodbye, I'll just be a few minutes."

With each step towards the guest house, her heart pounded. Her subconscious begged her to turn around, but her legs continued pushing her forward. She wanted nothing more than to walk away. Ignorance was bliss, right?

It felt like she'd been walking forever and, yet, when she reached her destination, she wasn't ready to face whatever it was she might find.

"Hey, Kensie, what's wrong?" Grant asked as he exited the bathroom.

She didn't bother answering him. She was focused on her mission. It didn't matter that Trey was just a few yards away. It didn't matter that there was a party raging on just outside the walls of the guest house. It didn't matter that Carter's brother was staring at her as if she'd lost her mind. The only thing that mattered was finding Carter.

"Kensie, what's going on?" Grant asked as she stormed through the living room. She turned down a narrow hallway, opening the first door she saw, a linen closet.

"If you tell me what's wrong, I can help you," Grant pleaded.

She headed for the door at the end of the hallway. Her stomach sank as an uneasy feeling flooded her body. He was there, she could sense him. Her body always knew when he was near.

Turn around, Kensington.

Turn around and go find Trey.

She steeled herself, pushing the door open, Grant hot on her heels. Carter was sitting on the bed, lying back on his elbows, as Susie kneeled before him, her head bobbing up and down.

Kensie froze. She knew what to expect. She knew what she was in for, but seeing it made something inside of her snap. She stepped forward, lunging at them, but was yanked back, before she knew what was happening.

Grant mumbled an apology, pulling her out of the room. Carter's eyes snapped opened at the sound of his brother's voice. The last thing she saw before Grant closed the door was the regret that flooded his blue eyes.

She couldn't help the sobs that tore through her chest

"Kensie?" The panic was evident in Grant's voice.

"I'm such an idiot," she whispered.

The door swung open and Carter and Susie came tumbling out. Kensie sneered at the woman as she scurried out of the guest house.

"Kensie…"

"Your zipper's down," she growled. She didn't want to hear his bullshit. She needed to get the fuck out of there.

"Baby, I'm sorry."

"Baby? What the fuck is going on?" Grant asked, looking from Carter to Kensie, confusion written all over his face.

"Ask your brother," Kensie bit, brushing past him, swiping angrily at her tears.

"Carter, tell me you didn't."

"Grant, it's not like that. Kensington, wait a goddamn minute!" he yelled, grabbing her arm.

She spun around and slapped him across the face. "You don't get to touch me, ever again."

CT grabbed her wrists and pulled her closer, his eyes flashed with something Kensie couldn't read. "You don't get to be mad at me. I've had to sit here and watch him fucking grope you all day. You think that was easy for me? Yes, I fucked up, but you're not innocent!"

"What did you want me to do, Carter? He's my fucking boyfriend."

"So, fuck my feelings then, right?"

"Yes! Fuck your feelings and fuck your half-ass apology. You know I'm not sleeping with him. I told you I loved you, and you turn around and let that bitch suck your dick."

"Look," Grant said, stepping in between them, "I'm not sure what's going on, but I think it's time to end this conversation unless you're looking to start World War three."

"You're right." Kensie nodded. She inhaled and exhaled slowly, desperately trying to check her emotions. She turned and headed for the bathroom.

"Kensie…" Carter's voice cracked.

"Bro, just give her a minute," Grant ordered, pushing his brother back.

She needed to get out of there. She couldn't stand the sight of Carter and she couldn't face Trey in her current state, so she called the only person she could think of, her true knight in shining armor. She answered almost immediately.

"Jam." She only got the one word out before collapsing onto the floor, overcome with grief.

THIRTEEN

Advice

Rain dropped from the sky like a thousand tiny shards of ice prickling Kensie's skin. After spending the weekend in the fetal position, she relished the pain. Physical pain was always easier to manage than emotional. Her personal life may have been in shambles, but that didn't mean she had to tank her personal life as well. It took courage to step out from under her father's shadow, and she wasn't going to let Carter, or Trey, or random pool house skanks ruin the one thing she had left to cling to.

Safe Haven was located in West Seattle. The large brick home looked like every other house on the block. Older, slightly run-down, but so full of life and history, she knew almost immediately, she had made the right choice. Being there, seeing the kids run and play and laugh, meeting Tanner, the resident director, and one of the kindest men she'd ever met, felt as natural as the sun on her skin.

She'd nailed the interview, answering each question he threw at her flawlessly. For the first time in her life Kensie knew exactly what she wanted. She knew exactly who she was. Helping people, and not in a $5,000 a plate charity dinner way—but actually getting her hands dirty—that was who she wanted to be.

Biting back a shiver, Kensie crossed her arms over her chest before darting out towards her car. A man dressed in all black leaned up against the side of it, hood up, head down, hands shoved into the pockets of his jeans. Though she couldn't see his face, she could feel him. His presence warmed her even under the assault of the cold rain.

She skidded to a halt, debating her next move. Logically, she couldn't avoid him forever, but she wanted to ride the high of her interview for a while longer. Puffing out her chest, she continued walking, breezing past him without so much as a second glance.

"How'd it go?" he asked as if Saturday had never happened. She ignored him and continued her journey to nowhere, but Carter fell in step beside her. "Talk to me."

"What are you doing here?" Her voice cracked on the last word. God, why did she have to love him? Stupid heart.

"You wouldn't answer any of my phone calls or text messages. I needed to see you. I need to make this right."

"How did you know where I was?"

"I knew your interview was today." He shrugged. "I've been here all morning. I watched you walk in." CT was usually all swagger, all bravado. He took what he wanted, when he wanted it, but the man beside her seemed lost.

"What do you want from me?" she asked, turning to look at him. The rain blurred her vision, or maybe it was the tears she was holding back that made it hard to see.

"You said you were falling in love with me." He unzipped his hoodie and draped it around her shoulders. "You said you chose me."

"Momentary lapse of judgment. I was hypnotized by your devil dick." Kensie pulled the jacket from around her and held it out to him. She'd rather the rain soak her down to the bone than wear anything that belonged to him.

"Baby—"

"No," she seethed, stabbing a finger into his chest. "Don't baby me, Carter. I don't want your apologies. I asked you to give me one day. One fucking day. I was willing to throw everything away for you and you tossed all that to the side because of jealousy and pride."

"I know. I fucked up and I'm not going to give you some bullshit excuse because you deserve better than that. I just…" He ran his fingers through his wet hair. "Seeing you with anyone would be fucking unbearable, but seeing you with him…I couldn't handle it."

"Why do you two hate each other so much?"

"It's complicated," he said. His eyes were the darkest she'd ever seen them.

"Complicated how?"

"Are you still with him?" he asked, changing the subject.

Thunder roared high above them as the rain continued to pour. A couple brushed past them, umbrella held high, as they moved forward. Forward. Everyone's life moved forward, while Kensie stayed stagnate—umbrella-less—under the cold summer rain. "That's none of your business."

"The first sign of trouble and you run back into his arms?" Accusation infected his tone. Like *she* had betrayed *him* and not the other way around.

"I watched some skank give you a blowjob," she reminded him.

"And I had to watched Trey maul you all fucking day."

"So, what, you thought you'd make yourself feel better by destroying me? What did you think would happen here?"

"I told you, I didn't think. I just needed to see you."

"Well, I'm sorry you wasted your morning, but we don't have anything else to talk about."

"That's it then, you're just giving up?"

"Yeah." She nodded. "I knew this would happen. I just didn't think it would happen before we got the chance to try."

The hurt in his eyes was quickly replaced by anger. "This wasn't worth the fucking headache. I should've just fucked you and left you alone. That's all you wanted anyway, right?"

She laughed, though there was no humor in the sound. "You can't be serious? After all this, waiting outside for hours, that's how you want to end it?"

"Yeah, I guess." He shook off the residual pain. Kensie watched as he retreated inside his head. She could see it happening. A flip of a switch and his self-preservation mode kicked in.

Kensie shoved the sopping wet hoodie into his chest. "Goodbye, Carter."

It was almost five o'clock when Kensie finally found the strength to drag herself out of bed. Jam would be home soon and Kensie did her best to put on a brave face. She ordered pizza from their favorite pizzeria and prayed that a hot shower would help rinse Carter from her spirit. Their breakup left her reeling. It felt strange calling it that—a breakup. They'd only known each other a short while and she had a boyfriend throughout the duration of their relationship, but that's what it was, a breakup.

She'd certainly felt broken.

"Get it together, Roth," she reprimanded. Her interview couldn't have gone better. Safe Haven was everything she'd hoped it would be. She should be celebrating.

A faint knock at the front door pulled Kensie from her misery. She grabbed her robe and wrapped it around herself, securing it tightly before jogging to the living room. She pulled the door open to greet the pizza delivery person, only to find Trey standing there in business casual, holding her pizza hostage.

"Hi," she said meekly. She didn't know if her psyche could handle two breakups in one day.

"May I come in?" he asked. She couldn't decipher the look in his eyes.

Anger?

Pity?

Hurt?

"Sure." Kensie stepped back, granting him entrance. She followed quietly behind as he walked into the living room and set the pizza boxes on the coffee table. They stood awkwardly, him staring, her fiddling with the ties of her robe.

"What's going on with you, baby?" Trey asked. The pleading expression in his eyes would have broken her had Carter not already done so.

"Maybe we should sit?" she suggested. Trey nodded and pulled her down onto his lap so that she was straddling him. It was the most intimacy they'd shared since before Trey left for Vegas.

"What happened Saturday? We were supposed to be getting back to Trey and Kensie. You left Liam's party without so much as a fucking goodbye."

"I texted you," she murmured, avoiding his gaze. She'd been so devastated that day that she couldn't bring herself to face him. She'd stayed hidden in the guest house until Jam arrived. Grant had reluctantly helped run interference.

"You texted me once you were already on your way back home," he argued. "I was going crazy when you disappeared. Grant and Liam had to drag me out of the party. Then yesterday, I called you a million times. I was so worried about you that I went to CMC to make sure you were okay, and Beth told me that you took a personal day. Do you know how stupid I felt, standing there lying to your friend like I'd gotten the days mixed up?"

"I get it," she croaked out. Kensie was such a nervous wreck that she gnawed on her poor lip until she broke the skin. "I've been selfish and immature, I just…I know what I need to do but…it's hard."

"Then don't do it," he pleaded, running his hands up her thighs. God, why did she have to be naked under her robe?

"I think…I need a break." She said it, finally, but instead of relief, she felt crushing heartbreak. She'd loved him once. She loved him still, but she was *in love* with Carter.

"Don't, Kensington. You can't just throw this past year away."

"I'm not, but I can't do this anymore," she sobbed, resting her forehead on his. She still couldn't look him in the eyes. She didn't want to risk it, she'd surely cave. She never wanted this to happen, she never wanted to hurt him, but she couldn't pretend anymore. "I'm not happy."

"Tell me what to do? I'll do whatever it takes."

"Trey, that's just it, there isn't anything you can do. You didn't do anything wrong. You've been the same this entire time. I'm the one who's changed. Somewhere along the way, I lost myself and I need to figure out who I am and what I want."

"I can fix this," he promised, pressing a kiss against her cheek. "You've got to let me fix this." Another kiss, this time on the corner of her mouth.

"Trey, please don't make this any harder." She cried endless tears as her body shook uncontrollably. Life would be so much easier if she could just love him the way he loved her.

Trey's mouth hovered over hers. "Let me fix this." He kissed her again, his tongue gently begging for entrance.

"This doesn't change anything between us," she whispered. Her body softened, her lips relaxed, and she granted him access to her mouth.

Taking advantage of her newly wrecked resolve, Trey flipped Kensie onto her back, rising above her. He pulled the ties on her robe loose and his hand traveled down her body. "I can fix this," he murmured, trailing kisses down her neck.

She arched her back as he kissed his way from her neck, down between the valley of her breasts. Kensie never stopped crying. There was no passion or pleasure. She wasn't going to change her mind. Sorrow punctuated her every movement. She was broken and selfish enough to use Trey to make her feel whole one last time.

"Ahem."

Kensie stilled, her eyes snapped opened to find Jam and Ryder standing in the entryway of their apartment. Dread filled her body as she scrambled to cover herself. Her eyes locked on the door, waiting…for him.

"It's just us," Jam mouthed, as if she could read Kensie's mind.

Relief flooded her. She was awful at this whole double life thing. "Sorry, he was just leaving."

Trey swallowed hard. "Come with me."

Kensie shook her head. She didn't trust herself to speak.

Trey sighed, his own resolve crumbling. "I'll give you space, if that's what you need, but I'm not giving up on us yet," he promised, bringing her hand to his lips. He lingered for a moment longer before turning to leave. It wasn't until then that he really looked at the man standing behind Jam. Confusion flashed in his eyes as he turned to look back at Kensie.

"Oh…uh, that's Jam's boyfriend, Ryder. Ryder, this is Trey," she stammered. She knew introductions were probably pointless, but she didn't know what else to do. As far as Trey knew, yesterday was the first time she'd ever met Carter.

"Knight," Ryder spat. "I thought I smelled pompous asshole." His jaw flexed, every muscle in his body tensed.

Trey laughed bitterly. "Jesus, Jamie, I know you love a good project, but you're really scraping the bottom of the barrel with him."

"Trey," Kensie reprimanded.

"I thought you were leaving," Jam seethed.

"I am," he said, leaning down, kissing Kensie once more before heading towards the exit. "Hide your valuables around that one," he called over his shoulder as he slipped out the door.

Ryder slammed it behind him, punching it, before Jam put her hand on his arm. "Babe, relax. He's not worth it."

He sucked in a breath, then released it. "Why is he even here?" he gritted, spinning around to face Kensie. "CT is home losing his shit over you and you're here with him?"

"Ry," Jam warned.

"No, Kitty Cat. I haven't seen him this bad in years. You can't keep flip-flopping back and forth."

"Me?" Kensie shrieked incredulously. "I told him I was falling in love with him and he responded by letting some bitch blow him."

"I'm not trying to excuse what he did, but he doesn't think

straight when it comes to Trey. He's his trigger. CT's got some serious trust issues, and most of them are because of that cocksucker!" Ryder yelled, pointing towards the door.

"He's not the only one with trust issues," Kensie countered.

"He's not the only one to blame either."

"Ryder," Jamie's voice was cold as she turned to face her boyfriend, "back the fuck off. CT did this. Kensie can do whatever the fuck she wants."

"No, it's okay, Jam, he's right. I'm no angel. I know what my part was in all this, but that doesn't mean that he gets a free pass to treat me like shit. I never lied to him. He knew what he was getting into."

"I'm just saying you have a bigger effect on him than you realize. I know he can be a dickhead, trust me, I get it. Just, don't let him push you away. He needs to know that someone is willing to fight for him."

"Who's going to fight for me?" She understood triggers. She could deal with trust issues, and she knew the pain of betrayal, but she was sick of managing everyone else's expectations.

She was Victor and Jacquelyn's princess, and Rachel's errand girl. She was Trey's perfect little wife, and she played Wendy to Carter's Peter, but that was all going to change. She made a silent vow, as she grabbed one of the pizza boxes off the table. From that moment on, she would be unapologetically Kensington Grace Roth.

FOURTEEN

Fidelity

"Bless you," Beth grumbled, tossing a small packet of tissues on Kensie's desk.

"You're a lifesaver," Kensie thanked her, runny nose, bloodshot eyes, raw throat, and all. She'd been nursing a cold all week, first blaming it on her allergies, but as time wore on her symptoms only worsened.

"Leave it to you to catch the flu in the summer," Beth observed as she squirted hand sanitizer onto her palms. "No offense, Kensie, but you look like a zombie. You probably should've stayed home today."

Kensie sneezed again. "I couldn't," she sniffled. "I was out Monday. Rachel would have a meltdown if I missed another day." That was only partially true. The real reason she insisted on coming to work, even though she felt like she'd been hit by a bus, was because she wanted the distraction. Being home provided her with an unlimited amount of time to think about the mistakes she'd made and the pain she'd caused.

"I think she'd understand," Beth said shaking her head. Kensie watched as her co-worker pulled a disinfecting wipe from the tube sitting on the corner of her desk. She wiped down her phone and keyboard before tossing it into the trash bin.

"Maybe so, but it's Friday and I plan to spend the entire weekend lying on the couch in a NyQuil-induced coma," Kensie said, holding back another sneeze.

"Whatever, but if I get sick, this friendship is over."

Just as Kensie was about to tell her she was being ridiculous, her cell phone rang. Reagan's name flashed across the screen.

"Hello?" Kensie answered tentatively. She hadn't spoken to Reagan since the disaster that was Liam's surprise party, and now that she and Trey were broken up, she could only think of one reason that she would call. Grant wouldn't have spilled the beans, would he?

"Hey, Kensie, it's Reagan." Her voice was sad, like she'd been crying.

"Are you okay?"

"No, not really, are you busy? I mean, can we meet for lunch?"

Kensie glanced at the clock; it was getting close to break time anyway, and she was curious to know what Reagan wanted. "Sure, I'm free in about an hour?"

"Okay, great. There's a little coffee shop downtown, Fonte, have you heard of it?"

She cringed. "Yeah, I know it."

"Great, see you then."

Steam rose from her mug of green tea she'd ordered five minutes ago. It was still too hot to drink. She preferred the coffee. Fonte's coffee was the stuff over-caffeinated pipedreams were made of, but her raw throat begged for the soothing relief of mint, tea, and honey.

"You look like shit," Reagan blurted out, as she slid into the booth across from Kensie. "I'm sorry, it's just—"

"It's okay," Kensie brushed it off with a wave of her hand, "I feel like shit."

"I take it now isn't the best time to ask for a favor?"

Kensie arched her brow as Reagan placed a small, blue Tiffany's box in front of her. She hesitantly removed the lid, revealing a dainty silver necklace with an infinity pendant dangling from the chain. Along with the jewelry was a note that read:

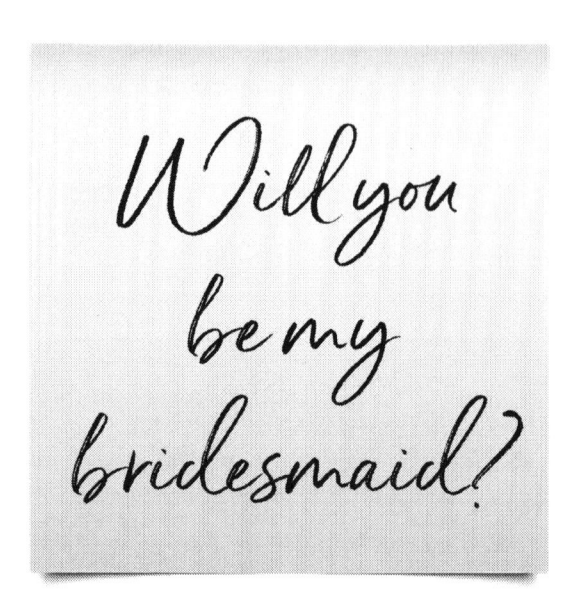

Will you be my bridesmaid?

Kensie shook her head, ignoring the dizziness. She couldn't be in Reagan's wedding. The last time she was in the same room with Carter and Trey it ended in disaster. Her one saving grace from this entire fiasco was that she no longer had to worry about the wedding.

"Please, Kensie?" Reagan begged. "I'm desperate. Susie backed out on me last minute. Apparently, she hooked up with my brother at Liam's party and now he won't answer any of her phone calls. Like, what did she expect? Now she's too embarrassed to face him and I'm down a bridesmaid—a week before my wedding." The lines and planes of her delicate features contorted into a grimace, and Kensie did her best not to wince as the thought of Susie on her knees threatened to consume her.

"That's awful, really, but—"

Reagan continued, ignoring Kensie's meek attempt at protest. "I was having a panic attack, but then Trey suggested I ask you. He said it made sense. You're going anyway, you and Susie are practically the same build, and we're going to be sisters eventually. It's the perfect solution."

"This was Trey's idea?" Kensie asked, again doing her best to mask her emotions. She was going to kill him.

"Yeah, he was with Liam when I called freaking out about Susie."

"Today?"

"Yes, about an hour before I called you. Please say yes. You don't have to do anything but walk down the aisle."

"Reagan…" she began but was interrupted by the ringing of her cell phone. The screen display read Safe Haven. "I'm sorry, I have to take this." Kensie excused herself from the table, pressing the green receiver icon as she walked outside the café. "Hello?" she sniffed, doing her best to hide the stuffiness in her voice.

"Hi, Kensie, it's Tanner, from Safe Haven."

"Tanner, how are you?"

"I'm doing well, thank you. I was calling to see if you were still interested in the resident aide position?"

A small grin crept up Kensie's cheeks. Her professional life was going as planned, now if only her personal life would catch up. A cough formed in her chest, but she choked it back. "Yes, of course."

"Great. Welcome to the Safe Haven family. I'll email you the details. I assume you need to give your current employer notice, so I'll set your orientation date for two weeks from Monday."

"That sounds fantastic. Thank you so much!" She ended the call and went back inside the café.

"Everything okay?" Reagan asked as she returned to her seat.

"Yeah," she said, sipping her now cold tea, "amazing. I think I just got offered my dream job."

"That is amazing, Kensie! I'm so happy for you!"

"Thank you. I'm in shock. I mean, I nailed the interview, but you just never know, ya know?"

Reagan nodded. The sounds of the espresso machines filled the silence. People filed in and out of the café grabbing lunch or coffee. Everyone wore smart business suits and bleak expressions, but for the first time all week, Kensie felt like everything would be okay.

"So," Reagan began, sending Kensington crashing back down to earth, "since you're in a good mood and everything…"

"I'd love to help you, I really would…"

"Please, Kensie, I'm desperate." Tears welled up in Reagan's big, brown eyes. Kensie could see her heart breaking. She couldn't say no—she wanted to say no—but she couldn't. She'd been far too selfish for far too long. This wasn't about her or Carter or Trey, it was about Reagan, and Reagan had never been anything but kind. This was a test. She'd vowed to be a better Kensie, and now it was time to put up or shut up.

"Fine, I'll do it."

Kensie threw in the towel after lunch. She'd pushed herself past the limit, and as a result, her body staged a coup. Rachel was surprisingly understanding, though Kensie had a feeling her graciousness was more about not wanting to get sick and less about Kensie's health and well-being. Either way, she gladly accepted the reprieve from Cruella's normal bitchiness and decided it best to wait until Monday to drop the bomb about her new position at Safe Haven.

Stopping by the drugstore on the way home, Kensie bought enough medicine, cough drops, and tea to hibernate all weekend long. She set up her own mini pharmacy on the coffee table and settled in on the couch. Jam was gone, and her bedroom felt lonely. *His* presence lingered there.

She thought she'd never see *Him* again, at least not until Ry coerced Jam down the aisle, but thanks to Trey, she'd be forced to deal with the drummer a lot sooner than expected.

After an hour on the couch and a dose of cold medicine, Kensie was calm enough to tap out a text message to Trey.

Kensie: I had lunch with Reagan today.

Prince Charming: Oh really? That's nice.

Kensie: She asked me to be a bridesmaid in her wedding. She said you gave her the idea. She seems to think we are still together, something about us being sisters one day. Why is that?

Prince Charming: I miss you. I wanted to see you and I knew you wouldn't say no to her.

Kensie: Manipulating me is not the best way to go about winning me back.

Prince Charming: I'm sorry. I just don't understand why you are doing this.

Kensie: I told you. I need to figure out what I want and YOU need to tell your family the truth BEFORE the wedding.

Prince Charming: I will. I promise.

Kensie: I won't pretend like we're a couple.

Prince Charming : I'll tell them.

Kensie didn't bother responding. Instead, she dropped the phone back on the coffee table and pulled the covers up to her neck. She was snoring in a matter of minutes.

"Hey, I'm home."

"Hey, Jam."

"Jesus, Roth, you look like shit."

"Thanks," she grunted before sleep stole her away again.

"How do I look?" Jam asked. She stood in front of the TV, twirling around in a flirty, white lace, halter dress with a low-cut back. James Michele Manning was twirling—in a dress. Her blonde hair was pinned back in a loose, braided updo that looked like it took hours to perfect, and her makeup was soft and dewy. In short, she looked flawless.

"Wow," Kensie rasped, as she attempted to sit up to get a better look at her friend. *Big mistake.* She felt like she was on a Tilt-A-Whirl. "How long have I been asleep?"

"Hours. You barely said two words to me when I got home. I sat there rambling on for ten minutes before I realized you were asleep."

"My cold got worse."

Jamie pressed the back of her hand against Kensie's forehead. "Jesus, Ken, you're burning up." Jamie disappeared into the bathroom and returned moments later with a digital thermometer and sanitizing wipes. "Orally or rectally?" Her tone was teasing, but Kensie could see the worry etched across her perfectly made-up face.

"I'm fine," Kensie moaned. "I mean, I will be just as soon as the room stops spinning."

"Just open your mouth."

"That's what she said," Kensie coughed.

Her attempt at humor fell on deaf ears. "Kensington, now," Jam scolded. Kensie did as she was told. "Holy shit, your temperature is 104!"

"I'll be fine. One of those should be a fever reducer," she said, pointing to the medicine bottles strewn all over the table. Jamie found the right one and poured the recommended dose into the little plastic cup.

There was a knock at the door. "Shit, that's probably Ry. Drink. I'll be right back."

Kensie swallowed the grape-flavored liquid and strained to hear what they were saying. Jam sounded apologetic and Ryder was pissed.

"I'm sorry, babe, but I can't leave her like this."

"James, if this is you changing your mind—"

"Don't be so dramatic, I'm not. We can go next week."

"I'll be fine, Jam," Kensie yelled as best she could from her spot on the couch. She could feel the medicine's effect. Darkness threatened to take her yet again. "I'll probably be asleep for the rest of the night anyway," she yawned closing her eyes. The voices continued, but sleep was within reach.

"What if I call him to come and sit with her?" Ryder suggested. "You know he wouldn't let anything bad happen."

"That sounds like a fucking terrible idea."

Somewhere in the land between sleep and awake, the sounds of a guitar roused Kensie into consciousness. The living room was dark, the sun had long since set. She scanned the room, seeking out the source of the music while her eyes struggled to adjust to the darkness. The faint outline of a shadow caught her attention. Carter sat in the upholstered chair, his instrument draped over his lap while his fingers danced along the strings. She recognized the melody, the same tune he'd played before when he sat in that chair and unknowingly stole her heart.

He hummed softly, in tune with the beat, as Kensie watched, mesmerized by him. Even though she couldn't see the unruly, brown hair or piercing blue eyes through the blackness of her living room, the impact his presence had was no less significant.

They hadn't seen each other or spoken since Monday. She replayed their last encounter over and over again in her mind. Her interview, him standing in the rain, the tears she'd shed, the hurtful words they'd hurled back and forth. His betrayal and then hers. In a perfect world, she'd be able to sever ties with the drummer. He'd get tossed into the pile of men who'd wronged her and she would move on. The only problem was their two best friends were madly in love. They'd be forced to interact sooner or later and the mature thing to do would be to confront the shit-storm they'd created head on.

Kensington was a lot of things, however mature wasn't always one of them. Naturally, she did the immature thing. She played dead. Her breathing evened out as she channeled Sleeping Beauty and a post-apple Snow White. Her eyelids fluttered closed and kept still, willing her body to shut down.

Go back to sleep.

Sleep, Kensington.

Sleep.

A tightness burned its way through her chest, but she fought like hell to suppress the scratchy, irritated feeling. In the end, her body won out and she surrendered to the uncontrollable coughing fit.

The music stopped and the shadow stood. Carter set the guitar aside and stomped into the kitchen. Kensie heard the refrigerator opening and closing. The light switched on and Carter was by her side with a bottle of water, the thermometer, and cough medicine.

"Open," he demanded, holding the thermometer to her lips. She complied, unsure of what else to do or say.

They waited in awkward silence for the probe to beep and when it did, she snuck a peek. The display read 100 degrees. Carter yanked the thermometer out of her mouth and set it aside. He poured a dose of the fever reducer and thrust it at her, watching with thinly veiled anger as she swallowed the purple liquid.

"Drink," he grunted, replacing the medicine cup with the bottle of water.

"You'd make a shitty doctor," she mumbled, bringing the bottle to her mouth.

"And you're an ungrateful brat."

"I didn't ask you to take care of me."

"I'm not here for you. I'm fucking pissed at you," he seethed, snatching the bottle from her hand. Water sloshed from the brim and he cursed under his breath. "I'm here so that Kitty Cat could go on the date Ryder spent the last two weeks planning."

"You're pissed at me?" She was going for incredulous, but it came out as more of a squeak than anything.

"You think I don't know about you and the cornball? I want to fucking burn this couch." His eyes were twin pools of rage.

Trey was his trigger and Kensie didn't have the energy to fight. "Do we really have to do this now?"

"Yes, we really have to fucking do this. If they hadn't walked in, what would have happened?"

"I don't know," she whispered.

"You don't know?" his voice cracked. His ass hit the ground with a thud and he leaned back against the couch. His hands raked through his overgrown hair and tugged. "Do you still love him?"

"No!" There was no hesitation, no doubt. "I'm in love with the tattooed asshole who broke my heart."

"Why'd you do it?"

"Because I did, at one point, love him. I can't erase that. I can't take back the year we spent together. It wasn't lust, or love, or passion. It was closure. It was goodbye."

"I wait for you all morning. I stand in the pouring rain and the only closure I get is a 'fuck off.' Why does he deserve a goodbye fuck?" A mixture of anger and sadness laced his tone. His jaw clenched and unclenched. Carter was hurt, but so was she.

"Trey didn't let Susie blow him in the guest house."

"I apologized for that. I tried to explain where I was coming from, but you pushed me away and then fell into bed with Trey. Did you do it to get back at me?"

"No… Yes…partly, I guess. I don't know. I'm not explaining this right."

"No shit." The pain was evident in his voice and his body. His back was straight and he stared straight ahead, refusing to even glance in her direction.

"I know you hate him and I get that you don't want to talk about what happened between you two, but Trey was there for me when I needed him. He taught me how to trust again. I was broken, and he fixed me. Maybe that's co-dependency, but I felt like I owed him something for not loving him the way he loved me." Kensie ran a hand through Carter's hair. His shoulders slumped, and he leaned into her touch. "I guess I felt guilty because he did all that work and you'll get to reap the benefit."

"You don't owe anyone anything, least of all that rat bastard."

"I know, it was a mistake. I'm sorry that it happened but I can't change it any more than you can change what you did."

"I'm royally fucking pissed at you."

"I don't know if we could ever work," she confessed.

It was quiet for a beat, and in that time, Kensie felt the tides shifting. She was the moon and he was the earth, their attraction as natural and as true as the ocean. Fighting it was stupid, but hurt people, *hurt people.*

"How do we get past this?"

"I don't know. We did everything backwards. Our entire relationship—if we can even call it that—was based on sneaking around, lying, and having sex."

"Great sex," he chuckled. "Amazing."

Kensie swatted him on the shoulder. "We should start at the beginning. We have to learn to trust each other."

"So, are you saying you want to be my friend?" Carter asked. His tone was light.

It amazed her how he could go from deep, dark, and sad, to laughing and playing. If her head weren't already spinning, it would be now.

"For real this time. Just friends—no benefiting, because us screwing like rabbits without taking the time to get to know each other is what landed us in this mess in the first place."

"That sounds like a terrible idea, Kensington."

"It's the only way I'm willing to try. I need to know that I can trust you and you need to trust me."

"How long?"

"Until it feels right."

"Until it feels right for me or for you?" he asked.

"Until we both feel like it's right."

"Fine," Carter huffed, "but one condition. Trey fucking Knight is a hard-fucking limit." Kensie sighed. She needed to drop the bridesmaid-size bomb on him. "That's non-negotiable."

"I agree, but there's one small problem, Reagan's wedding."

"You don't have to go."

"I kinda agreed to be a bridesmaid. Something about Susie never wanting to see your face again." Her voice was laced with sarcasm, and if she was honest, residual anger.

"God, I really am a fuck-up." Carter's head fell back against the couch.

"Yes, yes, you are, but it also means that we need to keep our friendship quiet for a few more weeks. Your brother won't say anything, will he?"

"Nah, I mean he's livid with me, but he wouldn't snitch, especially if it would fuck up Reagan's day."

"Good," Kensie yawned.

"You know Reagan is the only reason I'm agreeing to this, don't you? I couldn't care less about Trey's feelings."

"I understand," she yawned again.

"Go to sleep."

Kensie smiled to herself. "I will, just one more thing."

"I don't think I can handle anything else from you tonight, Friend."

"This is a good one. I promise," she mumbled. Her medicine was starting to kick in and she was barely hanging on. "I got the job."

"No way."

"Yep."

"I didn't doubt you for a second."

"Mmm." Her eyelids fluttered.

"Sweet dreams, Friend." She could feel his lips pressing gently against hers as she drifted off to sleep.

FIFTEEN

Sex with Me

*S**ex complicated things.*
   Kensie certainly wasn't going to win a Nobel Peace Prize for her revelation. Nothing groundbreaking or Pulitzer worthy about it, but there was something to be said for clichés. They're relatable, that's how they became cliché to begin with.

Sex complicated things.

A truth, universally acknowledged, that sucker punched Kensington Grace Roth right into the friend zone. It's what she wanted, of course, but Carter didn't have to be so goddamned agreeable.

He remained by her side for most of the weekend, catering to her every whim. When she was cold, he got her a blanket. When she was thirsty, he got her a drink, and when she was bored, he read from her favorite novel. He only left her once in the span of three days, and only because Lithium Springs had a gig at some bar Kensie had been too drowsy to catch the name of.

Without the distraction of sex, Carter and Kensie got the chance to get to know each other. They talked about everything, philosophy, politics, music, food, and art, and when the words ran dry and her throat was too raw to continue, he pulled out her collection of Disney movies and they lost themselves in fairy tales.

Carter stayed true to his word. He was the perfect gentleman. His hands stayed above her waist but below her chest. His kisses were sweet little pecks dotted across her face, and his penis stayed safely tucked away in his pants. It didn't even make an appearance Saturday night when he came stumbling into her room after his show, reeking of whiskey.

A tiny part of her wished it had.

A tiny part of her missed it.

Sex complicated things, but this new side of Carter—the kind, funny, and smart man hiding beneath the tattooed asshole—threatened to crumble her resolve.

Kensie stepped out of the shower and onto the plush bath mat. Though the hot water helped rinse away the residual cold, she still felt a little like death and sounded a lot like a man. She dried off and made her way into her bedroom. Bacon, coffee, and something distinctly cinnamon, scented the air. A violent growl emanated from her belly. After two days on the chicken broth and cold medicine diet, solid food was high on Kensington's list of things to do, but first she needed to get ready. It was the Fourth of July and Lithium Springs had a show.

She pulled on the waiting red and white tank with a smirk. Lithium Springs on her front and Carter on her back. They may not have been having sex, but that didn't stop him from claiming her, and it didn't stop her from basking in the attention.

Sex complicated things, she reminded herself as she finished getting ready and made her way through the apartment. Carter was in the kitchen, standing with his back to her. He wore a pair of loose-fitting camo shorts and a shirt identical to hers. The bright tattoos on his arms danced as he divided scrambled eggs onto three separate plates.

Kensie leaned on her elbows, admiring the view. Carter's body was a work of art. The muscles in his back flexed as he moved clumsily around to the toaster, plucking the golden-brown bread up and dropping it onto the plates. When he bent to pull the pan of bacon from the oven, Kensie lost it. His ass in those shorts! "Mmm," she groaned, the sound, vulgar and objectifying.

Carter threw a glance over his shoulder, grinning wildly as their eyes met. "Are you staring at my ass?"

"I can't help it," she shrugged, "you have a very nice ass."

That earned her a hardy laugh. "I thought we were practicing abstinence?"

"We are, but I'm not blind."

"Does that mean it feels right?" he asked.

Kensie shook her head slowly, only vaguely registering the sound of his voice. The way the vein in his biceps pulsed as he piled slices of bacon—real bacon—onto plates rendered her speechless.

"What about…other stuff?" He was renegotiating the terms of their friendship.

She exhaled her consent. "I'm okay with other stuff."

Carter lifted two of the plates off the counter and sauntered over to her. The closer he got, the more her resolve weakened. "Bon appetit." His husky voice was deep, rich, and manly. Kensie suddenly felt lightheaded and it had nothing to do with her cold. "I only had one lesson, so it might not be perfect," he cautioned as worry crept into his blue eyes.

Kensie giggled nervously, shaking off the spell Carter seemed to cast simply by being near. Tearing her eyes from his, she glanced down at the plate. Her first solid food in three days consisted of undercooked bacon, soggy French toast, and charred eggs. She had beaten the common cold, only to be taken down by salmonella.

There were a million ways to describe Carter: rocker sex god, loyal friend, unbearable jackass, but in this moment, the only one word that fit—adorable. "I'm sure it's great," she said. She was going to eat the damn eggs, even if it meant her being back on the couch for another week. He was trying. He'd done everything she'd asked; surely she could suffer through this for him.

Crunch.

Crunch.

Crunch.

"It's...great..." she lied, doing her best to plaster a smile on her face. In truth, it was quite possibly the worst thing she'd ever tasted, but a small price to pay to see the look of pure joy stamped on his handsome face as he watched her eat.

"Cool." He grinned, brimming with pride. "Coffee or juice?"

"Coffee, please." She gulped, forcing down the crunchy eggs.

Carter poured them each a cup and came around to sit on the stool next to her. He grabbed his fork and dug into the eggs. His face contorted in disgust. "This is fucking awful," he spit. "God, why didn't you tell me this was so bad?"

Kensie couldn't help her laughter. She laughed so hard her chest started to burn and her giggles turned into a coughing fit. "I'm sorry," she sputtered. "You just looked so proud of yourself. I didn't have the heart to tell you."

"Aww, Friend, you'd risk food poisoning for me?" he joked, pulling her off her stool and between his legs. His arms swallowed her whole, the warmth of his embrace made her knees weak, and when he kissed the tip of her nose, the butterflies returned. The sun shone, the birds chirped, and somewhere, tiny mice dressed in tiny little hats danced with glee. Peter Pan had a little Charming in him after all.

"Apparently." She blushed. Her teeth sank into her bottom lip as she tried to make sense of her emotions. Can there be love without trust? Did she trust him? Did he trust her? Then there was Reagan's wedding and the inevitable reunion with Trey. But even with all the fucked-up shit standing in their way, being in his arms felt right.

"Stop biting your lip," he rested his forehead against hers, "unless it's my turn next."

Yes! she thought. Oh God, how she wanted him to bite her lip. In truth, she wanted to feel his teeth nip at every inch of her flesh. She wanted him to bite his way down her body and lose himself inside her thighs. She wanted to run her fingers through his unruly hair as he drove into her mercilessly, but the only way they could work is if they took things slowly.

No sex.
No sex.
No sex.
"Carter."

"I thought other stuff was allowed," he murmured, running his hands down her ribcage and around to her ass.

"I just don't want to get so caught up in the other stuff that we lose track of what we're trying to do."

"What are we doing?" he asked into her neck.

Kiss.
Bite.
Lick.
Repeat.

"Building forever," she breathed. She wasn't sure where it came from, but now that it was out there, floating in the space between them, she couldn't take it back. Instead, she braced herself for his reaction.

"I'm not a fairy-tale kind of guy, Kensington."

"I'm not asking you to be. If that's what I was looking for I would have stayed with Trey." She could feel him wince at the mention of her ex, but she ignored it. She couldn't erase her past any more than he could erase his. "I like being so wrapped up in you that I let you fuck me on a folding table in your backyard. I don't want any of that stuff to change. I'm just asking for other stuff, too," she said, using his words against him.

"Other stuff," he repeated, testing the weight of it on his tongue.

"I want it all—one day—and I'd like to have it with you."

"No pressure," he teased. His hands flexed on her ass and he buried his nose deeper into the crook of her neck.

"I'm not trying to pressure you, but you need to know where I stand. I'm not cool like Jam. I don't do casual well, but I'm also not willing to lose myself in the men I love anymore. I can't pretend to be someone I'm not to please you. I don't need a ring tomorrow, but I will need one someday, when it feels right, so if that's not where this is heading, then maybe it's good things happened the way they did."

"Do you remember the night we first met, and I said that I didn't want to be your boyfriend?"

Kensie swallowed. She remembered those words and they weren't what she wanted to hear, especially now with her heart on the table. "I do."

"Do you know when I changed my mind?" he asked, and she shook her head. "That same night. You and Kitty Cat were sitting on the couch talking. Your hair was a disaster, your makeup was smudged, and your feet were dirty from walking around all night barefoot. It was kind of gross, but also kind of perfect. You want everyone to think that you're this pretty pink princess, but that night, you weren't playing dress up. You weren't slummin' it with your friend. You belonged there just as much as Kitty Cat. The only problem is, I'm not Ry. I'm not good. You told me you had a boyfriend and I should have left you alone, but I'm selfish and impulsive. Seeing you on my couch, wild and carefree, I knew—questionable hygiene aside—I was a goner. One night with you would never be enough. I could never put you in a cage. I don't want to change you. I want to soar with you."

Water pooled in Kensie's eyes as she swatted Carter in the chest. "Not the fairy-tale kinda guy, huh?"

"I'm a quick learner."

The Pike Market Music Festival was a big deal in Seattle. The entire city converged at Gas Works Park to listen to live music and binge eat deep fried food. Kids ran free, bouncing back and forth between games and rides, hyped up on powdered sugar and adrenaline. It was a community effort. Local breweries sampled craft beer, and even companies like the one Kensie's father ran donated food, money, and resources to ensure the festival was a success.

They'd arrived at the venue a little before eleven. The sun glinted off the lake. The sky a mosaic of blues and white. The grass as green as Kensie had ever seen it. Every experience was heightened in Carter's presence.

She watched in awe as crews worked together to prepare for the start of the festival. The park buzzed with activity. It was hectic, but everyone moved with a singular purpose. A wall of food trucks lined the perimeter of the park, game stations to the west, craft vendors to the east, and in the center of it all, like a beacon guiding them home, was the main stage. Kensie and Jam followed the band as they made their way through the chaos and to the security table. There was a small line comprised of other bands, crew members, and fans looking to score the coveted VIP lanyard. Kensie recognized one of the faces in the crowd. She shifted uncomfortably as Carter's older brother approached them wearing khaki shorts and a black Lithium t-shirt.

This was a mistake.

Kensie had been so excited to get out of the apartment that she didn't think about the potential repercussions. This wasn't a dark grunge club on the wrong side of town. This was the Fourth of July at Gas Works. It would be nearly impossible to keep a low profile and even if they could, she had his fucking name on her back. What if Reagan was there with Liam? This was a big deal. Why wouldn't his family be there to celebrate in his success?

"Creed couldn't make it so he sent me," Grant explained, handing everyone their credentials. A look passed between the brothers, a glance really, lasting mere seconds. If Kensie weren't already so hyperaware, she'd have missed it. The older Thayer was uncomfortable with her presence. Carter dropped a heavy arm around her neck and pulled her into his side. The act reeked of defiance and possession. It said, "*she's with me now, get over it or get lost.*"

Grant turned to Ryder and Javi. "Fifteen minutes for sound check, then you guys have press, then a meet and greet. After that, you'll have a few hours to enjoy the festival and we'll meet back here at five thirty. Showtime's at six, and then we're done."

They guys nodded in agreement and made their way up the stairs onto the stage. The air was thick with nervous energy. The normally lighthearted aura that seemed to surround Lithium Springs was gone as the three men got down to business.

Kensie watched them prepare from the side of the stage. Jamie stood to her left, snapping pictures of the guys on her smartphone, and Grant, to her right, with his hands in his pockets and his shoulders relaxed. "I hear you're going to be a bridesmaid?" he asked, quirking his brow.

Kensie groaned. "I couldn't say no to your sister."

"None of us can," Grant chuckled.

They stood in an awkward silence for a beat. Javi plucked a few notes on his bass. Jamie snapped a few more pictures. CT tapped on his snare. The world kept spinning, but the unasked questions lingered on.

"Just say it."

"My brother has made it abundantly clear that it's none of my business, but…"

"You want to know how?"

He nodded. His eyes were so much like Carter's that Kensie felt compelled to confess. She laid out every sordid detail of how she met his brother, how they hooked up, and how she fell in love. Their story wasn't pretty. It wasn't a fairy tale, but it was real. She was finally being honest and that counted for something.

"Are you two officially a couple?" he asked once she finished.

"No…" She shook her head. "It's complicated. I never wanted to hurt Trey. I never intended for any of this to happen, but I fell in love with your brother. We aren't perfect, you witnessed firsthand just how fucked up we can be, but I'm willing to try because the alternative hurts too much."

"He seems to feel the same. I've never seen him in love before. It's nice," Grant conceded. "Liam and Trey are two of my best friends, and as much as I hate this for Trey, as much as I try to stay neutral in this bullshit feud, CT's my little brother. I will always root for him. It's just fucked up, you know?"

She tried not to take it personally, but the harsh reality was starting to set in. This was what they'd be up against. No matter how happy she and Carter were, no matter how long their relationship lasted, it would always come back to how they began. Even now that she and Trey were broken up, she'd always have to deal with the fact that she cheated. There was no way around it, Carter and Trey's lives were too intertwined. They were practically family.

"Do you know what happened between them?" Kensie asked, she couldn't help herself. Trey was the root cause of Carter's trust and insecurity issues. If she could just understand why, then maybe it would be easier to forgive him for Susie, easier to move forward.

"No." Grant shook his head. "I was away at school during my junior year at Cornell. I was so excited to come home. Carter was back, and it was supposed to be the best summer of our lives, then all hell broke loose."

"How old was he?" Kensie asked, trying to put the pieces together.

"Uh…let's see…he would have been nineteen or almost nineteen."

"After he got into trouble?"

"Yeah," Grant answered. His eyes shifted downward and he shoved his hands into his pockets. "He just pushed us away. I think he felt like we betrayed him for not picking a side, but he won't talk to us, not really. Not anything of substance. I miss my little brother. That's why I do this. I'm not a manager, but if it's the only way to spend time with him…"

"I get it," was all Kensie said in response, because she did get it. She'd do just about anything to spend time with Carter. He was a charismatic jackass who she couldn't help but fall in love with.

She never even had a choice.

SIXTEEN

Firework

"I don't understand the point of this?"

"The point, Kensington, is to catch them all," Jamie explained as she flung red and white balls across her phone screen. They had been walking around Gas Works for nearly thirty minutes, waiting for the guys to finish their meet and greet. Around the ten-minute mark, Jam had decided that the best way to kill time would be to teach Kensie about her new obsession, Pokémon GO.

"But why?"

"Because it's fun. Look!" Jam took Kensie's phone and tapped onto a nearby Pokémon. She tossed little balls at the squirming creature until it landed on its head.

"Remember when your idea of fun was getting drunk and trying to see how many guys would send you dick pics on Tinder? I think I like that Jamie better."

"Okay, first, fuck you, and second, just try it. It's addicting, plus cardio."

"Fine," Kensie huffed, snatching her phone from her friend. There was a Bulbasaur standing in front of a funnel cake vendor. She caught it with one throw and smiled, despite herself.

The two women wandered around the park, laughing and catching up, while they collected as many little monsters as possible. Playing Pokémon GO was like stepping into a time machine that catapulted Kensie back to when she was a young girl, running around the Gas Works with her best friend. Life had been simple then. There hadn't been any ex-boyfriends. No drummers. No cheating. She'd been carefree, so full of life and adventure, drunk on the prospect of a real-life happily ever after.

"There you two are," Ryder grumbled as he and Carter approached. "We've been trying to call you for the last twenty fucking minutes."

"Oh, sorry," Jam giggled, "we got caught up in this silly game."

"What game?"

"Pokémon!" Kensie said proudly, holding up her phone. She'd made it to level ten.

"You've been on your phone this entire time and didn't bother answering our calls?" Ryder chastised.

"Sorry, baby." Jamie smiled wrapping her arms around her boyfriend's waist. "We were in the middle of an intense battle."

"Whatever, I'm hungry." Ry pouted, rubbing his nose against Jam's.

"Let's get you some food and if you're good, you can have a Shirley Temple," she teased. "You guys want anything?"

"Nah," Carter replied, looking to Kensie, "I think we'll go hang out in the van. I don't want her to overdo it."

"Overdo it. Riiiggghhht."

Carter flipped his middle finger at their friends' backs as the sea of people swallowed them, leaving Kensie alone with her sort of rockstar boyfriend. "How was the meet and greet?" she asked. Small talk. Carter had quite literally fucked her stupid on multiple occasions, he'd spent the weekend taking care of her, and yet, she couldn't shake her nerves around him.

"It was good. Lots of thirteen-year-olds," he said as they linked hands and he led her towards the parking lot. The sun sat high in the afternoon sky. People milled about here and there while kids ran wild. It had all the trappings of a perfect Fourth of July.

Kensie should have been happy, but there was still so much left unsaid. Her talk with Grant lingered in the recesses of her brain. She had doubt, big, abrasive insecurity plagued her thoughts, but it was his day, so instead of voicing them, she took the path of least resistance. "Wanna play?"

"Why not?" He smiled, taking the phone from her hands. If he sensed her unease, he didn't show it, and for that she was grateful.

After a quick overview of how to play the game, Kensie relinquished control to Carter, who promptly wasted ten Pokéballs in as many second. "You're supposed to hit the Pokémon," she quipped.

"They won't stop moving and what the fuck does this mean?" Carter tilted the phone down so Kensie could see.

"Oh! We hatched an egg!" she squealed. Jigglypuff jumped out of the egg, the same time a text message flashed across the top of the screen.

New message from *Prince Charming*.

Carter white knuckled Kensie's phone. The happy Carter from a moment ago was gone, and all that remained was bitter and cold.

Prince Charming: Happy Fourth of July, Kensington. I miss you. I love you. I want you back. Please call me.

He scrolled through the messages, reliving the last few months of her and Trey's relationship. There were I love yous and I need yous, sweet exchanges and sexy banter. Then there were the pictures, at least fifty. Pictures of Trey, ones of them together smiling, pictures of their bodies intertwined, and of Kensie with stars in her eyes. Carter poured through every detail, every dinner plan, every good morning, every how was your day. With each message, his body grew more rigid, his anger, more palpable.

"It means nothing, baby, not anymore," she insisted, reaching for her phone.

"Then why did you keep this?" he growled, pulling just out of reach.

"It wasn't intentional. I just didn't think to delete it." That was the truth. She only ever had to worry about deleting Carter's texts, not Trey's. The thought had never even crossed her mind.

Carter shook his head and stormed off into the parking lot. Kensie had to jog just to keep up with his pace. She weaved through groups of friends and families, trying desperately not to lose sight of her target. "Will you slow down and talk to me?" she yelled. "Why are you doing this? We had such a great weekend, don't do this."

He kept walking and didn't stop until he reached the van. "I want you to block his goddamn number," he seethed, yanking the door open.

"You do know that you don't have to act like a fucking toddler and throw a temper tantrum every single time his name comes up, don't you? I don't understand why it has to be a fight."

"You don't understand? You almost fucked him on your couch! That's not reason enough for me to be pissed?" he roared.

"We were broken up," she yelled, jabbing her finger in his chest, "which is a lot more than I can say for you when you let Susie blow you in the guest house."

"I told you I was sorry about that. You can't keep throwing it in my face."

"But you're allowed to throw Trey in mine?"

"That's different. Trey and I have a history and we weren't broken up, not really. You've been mine since the day we met. You'll always be mine," he seethed, inches from her face. "You might as well tattoo my name on your cunt."

"Fuck you," she said, slapping him hard across the cheek. Her hand stung and her blood boiled. This wasn't love, or even pain. This was retaliation for something she had nothing to do with. "You told me not to talk to him and I won't, but you can't get mad at me when he seeks me out. If this is your reaction to a text message, what's going to happen at your sister's wedding?"

"I'm sorry, okay? Just get in the fucking van," he said with a grimace.

He was so full of shit, Kensie almost hit him again.

"No, I won't keep doing this. You don't get to treat me like shit because of something that happened before we met. I deserve better than that." They were causing a scene, but she didn't care. She was done riding this roller coaster.

"I know I don't deserve you. You think I don't know that?" His anger transformed into sadness, and the pain in his voice nearly weakened her resolve. Whatever had happened between Carter and Trey all those years ago affected him as much today as it did back then.

"That's not what I said," she insisted, cupping his face in her hands. "Please, talk to me. Please, I'm begging you. Don't shut me out and don't push me away."

"Can you please just get in the van?"

"You have to tell me why he makes you act this way."

"Fine, just get in."

Kensie relented and followed him into the van. They sat in the middle row. It was more poetic that way. Their relationship began there and depending on the outcome of this conversation, it would either end or flourish in that same place.

Carter pulled Kensie onto his lap and buried his head into her neck. He inhaled and exhaled slowly, her body rose and fell in time with his. His hand slipped up the back of her shirt and he tugged on her bra. "No," she said, pushing him away, "we're talking, not fucking."

"I don't even know where to start."

He swallowed hard and Kensie watched as his Adam's apple bobbed up and down. She leaned in and kissed the little knot on his throat, mumbling, "Start at the beginning."

"Do you remember what I told you about juvie?"

"That it's where you met Ryder and where you learned how to design a killer résumé?"

"Yes," he chuckled, "but do you remember why I told you I was there?"

"You trashed someone's car."

"Only I didn't. Trey did."

"Wh…wait, what?" she sputtered in shock. She did her best to process what he was saying. "He blamed you?"

"No, it was my idea," he murmured, brushing a strand of hair behind her ear. Despite the heat inside the van, Kensie shivered. "It was right before our senior year. We were at a party and this kid was talking shit about how he fucked Trey's girlfriend and Trey snapped. They fought, and the kid's friend jumped in. Then, I jumped in and it turned into a brawl. The cops showed up and we all ran.

"I thought that was the end of it. It wasn't until the next day that I found out about the car. After we got home, he called his girlfriend and she confessed to cheating. It set him off. He was so angry that he took a baseball bat and fucking wrecked that Benz. The kid's dad was livid. He called the police, filed a report, the whole nine. Trey came over to my house later that night and told me everything.

"He was trying to get into Harvard and a felony would ruin that. He was the good one and I was the fuck-up. I was planning to take a gap year anyway. Trey was my best friend, my brother, and I would have done anything for him, so I turned myself in.

"My dad was able to delay my sentencing until after graduation and I served a year in a juvenile facility. When I came home, I thought things would go back to normal, but Trey stopped returning my calls. At first, I chalked it up to him being busy at school. But when summer rolled around, and he was still ignoring me, I decided to confront him. I walked over to his house and I asked him point blank if he was avoiding me. Do you know what that cock sucker said?"

Kensie shook her head. She could feel him shaking. His pain and anger reverberated through her and she absorbed it like a sponge. His hurt became her hurt.

"He said, '*I can't be friends with a felon,*' like he wasn't the sole reason I was in there. I lost it. I swear I tried to kill him. If it weren't for my brother running outside and pulling me off, I might have."

"I'm so sorry, baby." It all made sense. Trey's betrayal was so profound, more than just high school bullshit or two people growing apart. It was unforgivable.

Her heart ached for the man she loved. She finally understood why it was that Trey affected Carter so intensely, why his reactions were so extreme. It didn't absolve him of guilt, but at least now she knew where his insecurity issues stemmed from. The swagger, the cockiness, it was all a carefully crafted act designed to protect what was left of his heart.

"Hey," he shushed. He comforted her. He was reliving one of the most traumatic experiences of his life, yet he was worried about her. "I'm fine, and like I said, it's where I met Ryder. If it weren't for him and Javi, I don't know where I'd be."

"I know why he won't tell anyone what really happened, but why won't you? He doesn't deserve your silence. You've given him enough."

"What does it matter? I already did the time."

"I'm not saying send him to prison, but I'm sure if your family knew—"

"—they'd hate him. I know. I thought about it. I thought about it a million times but taking away his family didn't seem right."

"You still care," she said in awe.

"I don't know. I hate him, and I want him to pay for what he did, but I couldn't take them."

He couldn't take them from him, so he left. She didn't think it was possible to love him any more than she already did. Kensie pressed her lips into his neck. Her voice was timid. "Carter?"

"Hmm?" he murmured, absently stroking her back.

"Will you be my boyfriend?"

She could feel his smile on her forehead. She couldn't help but giggle, as the smattering of hair on his jaw tickled. "Does that mean I get to invade your personal space again?"

She grinned, nodding. "I thought you'd never ask."

"Kensie?"

"Yes, boyfriend?"

"I love you."

"I love you too, forever."

"Mmm, baby, we should stop," Kensie moaned against Carter's lips. Despite her words, her fingers curled in his hair as she yanked his mouth back to hers. She ground her hips into his, desperately seeking the friction.

They'd been like that for nearly twenty minutes. Twenty minutes of going back and forth between kissing and touching and teasing each other. The windows of the van were covered in a thick fog, a physical representation of the lust that crackled in the air. "No," he murmured, "I need to fuck you."

Need—not want. They'd long since surpassed whatever it was that drove people towards intimacy. This wasn't desire. It was primal. They were a tangled mess of limbs and tongues and slick bodies. Her hair clung to her skin, her bra was slung over the back of the seat, and her red Lithium tank had been pushed up over her chest, leaving her exposed to him. Carter took advantage, palming her breasts with his hands, rough and calloused from hours of gripping wooden drumsticks.

"What if someone sees us?"

"No one can see in here, the windows are tinted and there's enough fog to keep you modest." It was good enough for her, as she pulled his head back into her chest. His mouth found her nipple and he tugged on it with his teeth. Pain and pleasure mixed and she was lost in him, in his touch. Her skin vibrated with lust and she arched into him, desperate to be closer. Desperate to become one. One body, one mind, one heart. She missed this. She missed him.

Carter lifted his head. "Don't. Please don't stop," she mewled in protest.

"Don't pout," he said, expelling a breath in the crook of her neck. He trailed hot kisses up one side of her throat and down the other. "I'm going to fuck you senseless, but first, I need you to tell me how you want it. How do you want me to fuck you, Friend?" His teeth sank into her earlobe and she bucked in response. "Do you want it hard and fast?" *Another kiss, another bite.* "Do you want me to fuck you from behind while I pull your hair?" Carter wrapped his hands around Kensie's ponytail and tugged, hard. Her head snapped back and he licked her collarbone. "My girl likes it when I'm rough, don't you, baby?"

"Mmm," she moaned wiggling on his cock. "I love it."

"Oh, I like that, Friend. Do you want to be on top? Do you want to ride my dick while I suck on your tits?"

Kensie pushed Carter into the seat and attacked his mouth with hers. She sucked on his bottom lip, biting and licking her way inside. The heat inside the van made her chest tight. It was sweltering, but only served to turn her on more. It was like Carter, with hands around her neck, times a hundred. She liked when he was in control and she loved when he was rough, but this time, this time, *she* wanted to own *him*. "I want to ride you. I want to see the look in your eyes when I make you come."

Carter smirked, then flipped her onto her back. He yanked her shirt up over her head and her shorts down her legs. Kensie lay on the hot van seat in nothing but a pair of thin cotton panties. "Cupcakes?" He grinned, planting a kiss smack dab in the center of her cupcake-print-covered pussy. He pinned her to the seat with his forearm, while he hooked his other thumb in the side of her bikini briefs and peeled them down her legs. "Such a perfect pussy," he hummed, as his tongue probed her entrance. "Do you know how many times I've fantasized about this?" he asked, licking her up and down tantalizingly slow. "That first night, God, you smelled so sweet, better than cupcakes."

He continued his delicious torture, slowly increasing in speed, licking and swirling up and down and in and out. Her body was wet and sticky. She could barely breathe, forget thinking. Kensie didn't need air or food, the only thing she needed was Carter's mouth and fingers on her, inside of her, fucking and sucking every inch of sensitive flesh. Her body quivered, and her internal muscles clenched and unclenched around him. "So tight." *Lick. Pump.* "I can't wait to get my dick inside of you." *Lick. Pump.* Kensie clawed at the seat desperately trying to anchor herself as he pushed her higher. Her back arched and her legs stiffened as an orgasm tore through her body.

She scooted back against the side of the van, trying to catch her breath. Carter dug inside the pocket of his shorts and fished out the keys to the van. The first wave of air hit Kensie, cooling her pink skin, but did nothing for the fire in her belly. She was greedy. He promised her a ride and they weren't leaving until she got one.

With hooded eyes, Kensie watched Carter lift his shirt over his head. He was as close to perfection as they came, strong arms, chiseled abs, and a face as gorgeous as any male model, but it was those mysterious blue eyes that pierced something deep in her chest. Before she could stop herself, she was up kissing him, tasting herself on his tongue. She fumbled clumsily with his shorts, pushing them down over his ass. "Do you even own a pair of underwear?" she groaned, spurred on by his bare skin.

He chuckled, twisting them so that they were back in a seated position with her straddling him. "Makes fucking you that much easier, Friend." Kensie raised up on her knees, hovering above his erection. She licked her lips as he fisted the base of his cock. He positioned himself at her entrance and she slowly sunk down, enveloping him in her warmth.

Carter's eyes rolled back and his hand gripped her waist, his nails biting tiny crescents into her skin. "So fucking perfect," he growled, bucking up into her. His mouth found her nipple again and she began to move, grinding her hips onto his. Slow and deliberate at first, but once she adjusted to the intrusion, her pace quickened.

He was rough with her, grabbing and biting and slapping her breast in sync with the movement of her hips. It was the mix of passion and pain that she'd grown to love. It sent her into a frenzy as she bounced up and down, taking her pleasure and milking him of his.

He tilted his hips so that with each thrust, his cock stroked her g-spot. "Come with me, Carter," she moaned, resting her forehead on his. Their eyes locked, brown-to-blue, and they both came undone, sweat dripping, limbs tangled, and utterly spent.

"How are you feeling tonight, Seattle?" Ryder drawled into the old school microphone stand. The stage lights were so bright, Kensie had to squint to see him. He looked at Javi on his right and the crowd erupted in cheers. The deafening sound nearly knocked the wind out of her. "Javi, introduce yourself to the people." The bassist grinned and plucked out a few notes. "CT?" Ry looked over his shoulder as Carter banged on his drums and Kensie's heart swelled with pride. "As for me..." His words inspired another roar from the audience. There had to be tens of thousands of people in attendance and Ryder had them all enthralled. "I'm Ryder, but you can call me *Sex God.*" CT went wild on the drums, pounding out the beat, then Javi joined in on bass, and Ryder with guitar. The crowd lost it. Even Kensie found herself jumping up and down, sucked into the Lithium vortex. Nothing else existed outside of the three men on stage. They were as good as any band she'd ever seen, a thought that both excited and terrified her.

"They're really fucking good," a man said coming to stand next to Grant. "You their manager?"

"Kind of." Grant shrugged.

"I'm Lawrence. I'm the road manager for The Unburned. Wiley is a big fan. Lithium's making waves in the underground music scene. We are putting together a fall tour and I'd love to talk to them about it."

"That…that would be…amazing."

"Cool. We'll link up after the show. I'll give you my info."

"Awesome, enjoy!" Grant shook Lawrence's hand.

The mood shifted. They all sensed it. Things were changing and Kensie only hoped her budding relationship would survive.

SEVENTEEN

Write on Me

Kensie traced the outline of her bottom lip with her fingers. She tasted him there. She felt him on her skin. Her body was on fire and it had nothing to do with the temperature of her shower, and everything to do with being in love.

Love was an intense and soul-searing tornado of emotion that overturned trees and uprooted lives. Sometimes love was the eye of the storm, a false sense of calm right before a final act of devastation. Other times, it was the peace after, the quiet stillness that comes with knowing you survived.

In the days that followed the Fourth, they were practically inseparable. Carter laid his secrets at her feet, and she fell harder than she'd ever thought possible.

"You scared the shit out of me!" Kensie yelped as the shower door swung open and Carter slipped in behind her.

"You should see the look on your face. Who'd you think it was, a serial killer?" he teased, pulling her into his chest, biting the back of her shoulder.

Kensington believed in fairy tales.

She'd always imagined marrying a handsome prince, one who would sweep her off her feet and carry her off into the sunset. She never dreamed of falling for a Lost Boy. Carter was loud and vulgar, and he pushed and pushed and pushed until she wanted to scream. He made her face herself and all of her shortcomings. He inspired her to chase her dreams. He didn't treat her like this breakable thing who needed protecting. He loved her hard. He loved her possessively, intensely, and maybe a little wrong—but like a thief, he stole her heart.

"I'd almost prefer it," she retorted, settling into his arms. His erection pressed against her backside, the thickness of it sending a chill down her spine. The veins pulsated against her flesh. His hands trailed down her stomach and his mouth found her neck. He sucked and he licked and he bit at the sensitive spot just below her ear. "Baby, stop or I'm going to be late," she moaned in protest. The man was relentless. His need to claim her, to possess her, even now, even after she'd given herself to him, mind, body and spirit, that need was always there. He insisted on marking her.

"I'm sure your parents won't mind."

"You've never met Victor and Jacquelyn Roth."

"Well, when do I get to meet them?"

"Who? My parents?" Kensie blinked at his question. It wasn't that she didn't want him to meet her folks, but Carter didn't strike her as the "meet the parents" type, especially parents like hers. "You want to?"

"They mean a lot to you," he said lifting a shoulder.

"Of course, they're my parents."

"It's more than that. You value their opinion, it matters to you, and you matter to me, so yeah, I want to meet them."

"Okay." She nodded carefully. He had a point. She wanted forever, and him meeting her parents was inevitable. "But can we just get through this wedding first?"

"One disaster at a time, I can do that. Now, let's get you cleaned up." Carter brushed his lips against her shoulder before turning to eye the products arranged along the shower ledge. With an easy smile, he plucked the tube of Coco Mademoiselle and brought it to his nose.

"This shit smells awful," he grimaced, tossing it out the shower door. Next, he chose the lavender wash. This time, he was cautious, slowly bringing the bottle to his nose as if any sudden movements would cause it to explode. A content hum emanated from his chest, and the corner of his lips tipped up in a lopsided grin. It was her favorite grin. A secret smile that was equal parts playful and mysterious.

"Why that one?" Kensie asked, her old foe curiosity besting her once more. The subtle lavender scent filled her nostrils as he worked the suds onto her skin.

"It smells like you." His answer was simple, his voice, reverent, and yet those four little words caused Kensie's heart to skip a beat. She'd thought it was a euphemism, an old wives' tale, a proverb, or a psalm. He spoke as if it were obvious, as if him figuring out in just a couple of months what Trey still hadn't known after a year, was nothing. He explored her body, his fingers teased her nipples, floated down her stomach, and over her hips, then he sank to his knees and rubbed up and down her legs and between her ass. He lingered there, he touched her there, kissed her there. "Mine," he whispered in the same reverent tone. He made her feel loved, cherished, desired.

"Yours, forever," she moaned, simply because she was his. No matter what happened, no matter how their fairy tale ended, Carter Thayer would always possess her heart.

El Gaucho's was one of those old-meets-new fine dining establishments. Coltrane drifted through hidden speakers, candles flickered on tabletops, and the scent of generational wealth perfumed the air. Servers buzzed around the dining room in pristine white oxfords and coal-black slacks, while bartenders mixed Manhattans and poured fingers of fifty-year-old Scotch.

Kensie followed the hostess to the back, each step sent a delicious sting to her sex. After washing her, Carter fucked her on the bathroom floor until her knees were raw and her limbs were putty. She had to rush to get dressed, and had only made it to the restaurant in time by the grace of God.

El Gaucho's was her father's favorite. They'd eaten there for birthdays, anniversaries, and her graduation, but tonight, as she weaved through tables en route to her parents, Kensie couldn't shake the feeling that she was walking into the lion's den. There was something about her dad's voice when he'd called and invited her to dinner, a tightness to his words, that catapulted Kensie back to when she was ten and had broken the vase her mom flew in from Milan.

"Hey, baby girl." Her mother smiled brightly as she neared the table.

"Hey, Momma, hey Daddy," she said. Her father nodded in return and her heart sank. She hadn't seen her parents in almost two weeks—unusual for them—yet Victor only offered a polite nod.

"How are you feeling?" Jacquelyn asked.

"Much better, thank you." Kensie took the seat across the table from her parents.

"It's been awhile."

"I know, Daddy, I'm sorry. I've just had a lot going on."

"Hmm," was his reply, a noncommittal noise that was a mix between a grunt and a sigh. Her mother launched into a tirade about a charity event she'd been planning with Jam's mom. Their server brought the wine and they placed their orders. All in all, the evening progressed in normal fashion, but something was off. Somewhere after the first course, but before the second, Victor broke his silence. "Do you remember Mark Lebowitz?"

"He works at your company?" Kensie guessed, unsure of what Mark had to do with anything. Her eye darted to her mother who sat up a little straighter—too straight. This was it. Whatever *it* was.

"He's head of public relations. He's also in charge of organizing local community efforts, for example, the Pike Market Music Festival."

"Is he?" Kensie yawned, feigning boredom. She was twenty-five years old and had been self-sufficient since she graduated college. What she did and *who* she did it with was her business, not her parents', and certainly not Mark fucking Lebowitz's.

"He also told me he saw you backstage, VIP access and everything."

"Jam's boyfriend is the lead singer of one of the bands." *And my boyfriend is the drummer.*

"He didn't mention James kissing anyone, just you."

And there it was. "Daddy—"

"I had lunch with Trey the other day."

"Daddy—"

"He said the last time he saw you, he had hoped this little split of yours was temporary, but then you stopped taking his phone calls, and I'm wondering if that boy in that band has anything to do with it?"

"Trey and I aren't together because we aren't compatible," Kensie gritted.

"I think that's a cop-out."

Kensie turned to her mother. "Do you feel the same?"

"Your father and I have differing opinions on Trey, sweetheart. I think you're better off, but," Jacquelyn added, taking a sip from her wine glass, "I don't like the idea of you jumping into another relationship so soon. You lose yourself in these boys, Kensington."

"Carter is different."

"Trey *was* different, and before that, you were so in love with Stephan that you followed him to Los Angeles, and I don't need to remind you how well that turned out," Jacquelyn sighed. "I just think you need some time alone."

"And I don't want to see you throw something good away for something fun and exciting," Victor added.

"What about what I want?"

"I know who we raised, and I know you have a good head on your shoulders, but I also know you wear your heart on your sleeve."

"Daddy, I'm just—"

"Baby," a familiar voice called from behind.

"Please tell me you didn't," Kensie sighed, rubbing her hands over her face as the chair beside her screeched backward and Trey sat down.

"Victor," Jacquelyn warned.

"Don't be mad at him, Kensie, it was my idea. You won't talk to me."

"So, you thought ambushing me in front of my parents would be a better way to get me to talk to you?"

"I didn't think."

Her dad spoke up, "We can go. You kids talk."

"No." Kensie stood. "There isn't anything to talk about—"

"Baby—" Trey's voice cracked. The sound gnarled and mangled. She almost caved. Hearing him so broken, seeing him so desperate, ate away at her. She had loved him once and those feelings didn't just disappear, but they were nothing compared to what she felt for Carter.

"I told you I don't want this, you need to accept that. And, Daddy, I'm really disappointed in you." Kensie yanked her bag off the side of the chair and stormed out of the restaurant. She was furious—at Trey, at her dad, and at herself.

Her mother followed quickly on her heels. "Wait, Kensington, I'm sorry. I didn't know he was coming. I would have warned you."

"Oh, so *you* were okay with ambushing me, just not with Trey doing it. Got it."

"It wasn't meant to be an attack. We're just concerned about you. You're our only child. We have a right to worry when we hear about you dry humping someone in public, on the same day we find out you broke up with the man you were supposed to be moving in with."

"You weren't young once, Mother?"

"I was, and I've done a lot worse than that, but it's my job to keep you from repeating my past mistakes."

"Grandpa and Grandma didn't like Daddy in the beginning and that turned out okay."

"I'm not saying this drummer can't make you happy. I'm only saying you need to learn to find happiness outside of him."

"I have. I am happy, and I'd like it if you and Daddy were happy for me, but if not, I've got to live my life on my own terms."

"I know, and I'm sorry if we overstepped."

Kensie sighed, "I'm really mad at your husband right now."

"He means well."

"Yeah, well so did Grandpa."

EIGHTEEN

Coffee

Carter dropped a plate of eggs in front of Kensie as she sat down at the breakfast bar. She eyed the plate suspiciously. It looked better than his first attempt, and his second, and his third—but not by much. Reaching for her fork, she stabbed into the eggs and lifted the fork to her mouth, taking a small bite. "Uh-uh. Nope," Kensie said, shaking her head, spitting the eggs into a napkin. "Too salty and still crunchy."

He grabbed the plate with a huff and tossed it into the sink before reaching into the cupboard, swiping a Pop-Tart from the box. He'd bought them after yesterday's disaster of a breakfast, referring to them as *Plan P*. Kensie tore into the silver packet and pulled out one of the frosted pastries. She bit into it, closing her eyes and moaning with pleasure. When was the last time she'd eaten a Pop-Tart?

Carter chuckled. "And here I thought I was the only one who could make you moan like that."

"Not so special after all, Thayer," she mumbled with her mouth still full.

He rolled his eyes in response, grabbing the other pastry and dropping it into the toaster. "You're eating it wrong," he commented.

She peeked up at him, raising the rectangle to her mouth and bit into it. "How so?" she asked between bites.

"This guy made this thing way back in the 1800s that allows you to make toast. Toast, which elevates otherwise boring bread or pastries into glorious breakfast delicacies. It's like a slap in the face of science and innovation to eat a raw Pop-Tart."

"A raw Pop-Tart?" she repeated, arching her brow.

"You'd be better off eating the eggs." He grinned lifting his coffee mug.

Kensie did her best to keep a straight face as she lifted the pastry to her mouth again, this time shoving in as much as she could manage, so much that her cheeks puffed out and she could barely close her mouth. "I happen to like them raw." Crumbs fell from her lips.

"You look like a squirrel," he chuckled, grabbing his breakfast from the toaster.

"A cute squirrel?"

"The cutest."

They ate in a comfortable silence. With Trey, Kensie had worried about how she looked, if she was eating too fast or too slow, or any of the other million insecurities she felt around him, but with Carter it was as natural as breathing. "So, boyfriend, what have you got planned for today?"

"Gym, a meeting with Creed, and then we've got some studio time later."

"Creed's your manager, right?"

"Yeah, he's based in LA, so Grant helps out when he isn't here."

Kensie nodded and took another bite of her Pop-Tart. "I'm meeting your sister today. I've got my first and last fitting."

"Are you going to tell her about us?" Carter asked.

"I don't know. I don't think it's a good idea to tell her about us yet, not until after the wedding." She paused, wondering if she should continue. "He Who Must Not Be Named still hasn't told anyone that we're broken up."

Carter growled, setting a mug of coffee down in front of her a little too forcefully. "He hasn't told them because he thinks he still has a chance."

"I don't think that's it. I've made it clear that we're done."

"Trey doesn't give up on anything…well, except for me." Sadness flashed briefly in his eyes. "He probably thinks spending the weekend in Napa, at a wedding no less, will soften you up."

"It won't," she insisted.

"I know, baby. Plus, you'll be too busy with my devil dick to fall for his bullshit."

"Never gonna let me live that one down, are you?"

"Nope."

"I'm going to tell Reagan that we broke up. I still need to sort out some place to stay since the hotel is booked. Maybe I can bunk with one of the other bridesmaids."

He looked at her like she'd grown a second head. "You'll stay with me, obviously."

She shook her head. "Share a room with you, Ryder, and Javi? No, thanks."

"We've got our own rooms."

"That's perfect! You can bunk with one of them and I can take your room."

"Why would I sleep with one of those smelly bastards when I can sleep with you?"

"And how would we explain that?"

"I don't fucking care."

"Carter, what's the point of keeping us a secret until after the wedding if we're going to be sharing a room?"

"I don't want him sniffing around you." He crossed his arms over his chest.

"He's going to, you said it yourself, but you have to trust that I won't fall for his bullshit."

"I trust you, I don't trust him."

"Baby, we've got to be on the same page. This is your family, your sister. If you want to announce our relationship at her wedding, then I'll be sure to pack all my Lithium merch, okay?"

He sighed. "Fine, I'll share a room with Ryder, but only if Kitty Cat comes too. She hates Trey as much as I do."

"That works for me," she agreed. She was basically going to be alone the whole weekend anyway. Without Trey, she was an outsider.

"This whole thing is going to be a fucking disaster, isn't it?" he asked.

Kensie stayed quiet. She knew the answer, but refused to say it out loud.

After work, Kensie made her way to Dolce Bleu, the swanky, by appointment only, bridal shop located in downtown Seattle. "Kensie!" Reagan squealed as she approached. "Thank you so much for doing this. I know it's totally last minute, but you really are saving my life right now."

"Don't mention it." The two women linked arms and pushed through the doors of the shop. Cream, bone, ivory, and every other shade of white imaginable greeted them. A cluster of mannequins in the center of the room, each modeling a trend for the current season. The floors, the furniture, and even the employees were cloaked in black, making the dresses the focal point.

Reagan led Kensie back to the dressing rooms. A curvy redhead greeted them as they approached. She eyed Kensie for a brief moment before a slow grin creeped across her face. "She's perfect."

"I know, right?" Reagan said, pushing Kensie forward a little. "The dress shouldn't need much, maybe just hemmed a bit. Oh, Kensie, this is Melissa. Melissa, this is Kensie."

"Nice to meet you," Kensie said, extending her hand.

"You don't know how happy I am to see you," Melissa said, pulling her in for a hug. "I almost had a nervous breakdown when Reagan called and told me about one of her girls dropping out. These dresses were handmade and it took months to finish them. There is no way that I could have remade, or even heavily altered, the dress in a week."

"I'm happy to help."

Melissa ushered Kensie behind the curtain and helped her into the gorgeous sequined gown hanging in front of her. The dress was stunning. The floor-length column number fit like a glove and sparkled with every move she made. The short cap sleeves and boat neck made the dress appear modest from the front, but the back told a different story. Turning to look in the full-length mirror, Kensie gasped. The loosely draped scoop dipped so low that it exposed the dimples on her lower back. Kensie smiled at her reflection. Images of Carter and his strong tattooed hands pressed against her soft, creamy skin as he helped her out of the dress danced in her mind.

"Ready to show her?" Melissa asked, breaking her from her naughty thoughts.

Kensie nodded. She could feel her cheeks heat as she followed her out of the dressing room to the couch where Reagan waited, sipping on a glass of champagne. "Holy crap!" Reagan croaked, nearly choking on the bubbles. "It's perfect!"

"Should we try it with shoes?" Melissa suggested.

"Please." Reagan nodded. Kensie told the woman her size before she disappeared back into the main gallery. "Trey is going to freak when he sees you."

"Actually, Reagan, Trey and I…we aren't…we sort of broke up."

Guilt flashed in Reagan's eyes. "We sort of thought so. Liam said Trey's been moody and on edge and when you didn't show up on the Fourth, well…" She trailed off.

"I won't flake on the wedding. I just thought you should know."

"Thank you, and you never know, a weekend away might do you two some good." Reagan winked.

"I don't think—" Kensie started.

"Here we are," Melissa said, interrupting. She handed Kensie a pair of strappy heels that were the same color as the dress. Kensie sat and let the tailor help her into the shoes before standing again.

"I think I'll hem it just a bit, but other than that, it works."

Reagan smiled, reaching for her glass, watching as the woman quickly pinned the bottom of the dress.

"Okay, that's it," Melissa said with a clap of her hands.

"That's it?" Kensie asked, relieved.

"Yup."

Kensie changed back into her clothes then went to find Reagan. "Thank you again, you really saved the day." She beamed and handed Kensie a glass of bubbles. "Susie was supposed to be one of my best friends. I didn't think she was stupid enough to fall for Carter's crap. I swear, he's banged half of my friends. As soon as they find out he's in a band, they lose their freaking minds. I think he's slept with everyone in my bridal party that we aren't related to. Well, except you, of course." She giggled. "They all think they can change him," Reagan scoffed. "Do you know how many friends I've lost because of it? They get mad at me when he doesn't call them back. At me! Not themselves, not Carter, me. I can't even be mad at him. He tells them up front and they still think he'll miraculously change his ways. I can't wait to meet the woman who finally gets him to settle down."

"Yeah," Kensie added weakly. Carter had a past. He was a bad boy drummer with abs that made women stupid. She was one of them, but she tried not to let his past affect their present. She really, really tried. She'd chosen to forgive the Susie thing, but she was only human, and spending a weekend surrounded by women, whom he'd known intimately, was going to be a challenge. Kensie chugged the champagne.

This wedding was going to be a fucking disaster.

"Jam, please. I'll love you forever," Kensie whined as she and Jamie rode the elevator up to the third floor of Glenn Sound Studios. They'd planned to crash the guys' studio session and on the way over Kensie caught her bestie up to speed on the last few days.

"You know weddings aren't my thing, especially a wedding for people I don't even know."

"But your boyfriend will be there, and me, your favorite person in the world."

"I see him every day, and I've lived with you since college. I could use a break," she teased.

"Okay, well then you've forced my hand."

"What's that supposed to mean?" Jamie asked. The elevator doors swung open and Kensie stepped out into the hardwood floors of the studio lobby.

The walls were covered in gold, silver, and platinum plaques from artists like the Smashing Pumpkins, the Kings of Leon, and the Dave Mathews Band. There was a seating area in the middle of the room, with a couch and two reclining chairs surrounding a coffee table. "Oh nothing," Kensie sang, "I'll just have to ask my boyfriend to talk to your boyfriend."

Jamie rolled her eyes and followed her friend down the hall. "I wear the pants in that relationship."

"You once told me that he could get you to agree to anything when you guys were having sex. I'm sure he won't mind persuading you."

"You're such a bitch."

"I love you too, Jam."

A thick haze of smoke covered the dimly lit studio. A brown leather couch was pushed up against the back wall, and a coffee table was nestled in front of it. Disposable cups, a bong, and a handle of Jack Daniel's sat on the table. Javi and Ryder sat behind a board covered with hundreds of buttons and knobs and levers. Next to them was a man who looked to be in his late forties, with long white hair and a longer beard. Kensie assumed it was Creed, the guys' LA manager.

"Hey, Kitty Cat." Ryder grinned as Jam slipped onto his lap. He gave her a long, almost sad look before briefly pressing his lips to hers.

Kensie's eyes found her friend. "Everything okay?" she mouthed.

Jam nodded, flashing her a *we'll talk later* look, before resting her forehead on her boyfriend's. Kensie nodded, not quite satisfied, but dropped it for the time being.

"Thanks for letting my boy off his leash long enough to come to work." Javi grinned, pushing the empty chair next to him out for her to sit.

"That doesn't smell like a cigarette," she teased, pointing to the skinny black metal pen dangling from his lips.

"Because it's not. Take a walk on the wild side, princess," he said, handing it to her.

"I don't know why you guys think I'm this sheltered prude, I've gotten high before," she huffed.

"I know you're not a prude. I share a wall with him," he said, tipping his chin to the booth where CT sat behind a drum kit.

"You're such a perv," she squealed, pushing his hand away.

"Okay, CT, let's do it one more time, then I think we can move on," Creed said. Carter nodded, then banged his sticks together three quick times, before tapping the snare. Creed hit a few buttons on the board and the sounds of a piano filled the hazy room. Slow. Melodic. Hopeful. Kensie watched, mesmerized, as CT played along in time with the music. It was so different from anything she'd previously heard them play, operatic at times, beautiful. Tears welled in her eyes.

"It's good, right?" Javi whispered, attempting to pass her the vape again.

"It's amazing," she breathed, pushing his hand away.

"It's about you." Reluctantly, Kensie tore her gaze away from her boyfriend to look the bassist in the eyes. "He wrote and arranged the whole thing himself. Wait until you hear the lyrics. He's got it bad," Javi chuckled, "but he's never been better. This album is going to be next fucking level. Perfect timing with the tour and everything."

"What?"

"Yeah, it's official as of today. The Unburned tour manager called Creed the day after our show at Gas Works. We hit the road in September," he explained, handing her the vape pen once more. This time, she took it and inhaled deeply. "I'm surprised he didn't mention it."

Kensie exhaled. "Yeah, weird," she said, pulling in another puff. Her chest felt like it was on fire, her lungs filled with smoke, and she couldn't contain the coughing fit building in her chest.

"Take it easy, lightweight," Javi said, taking back the vaporizer.

Kensie's heart was pounding, but it had little to do with the weed and more to do with the million and one questions swirling around in her head.

Why hadn't he mentioned it?

A tour? A different city every night, different women throwing themselves at him.

Could their budding relationship survive the distance?

Would he even want to try?

"How long?" Kensie croaked, her voice still raspy from inhaling too much of the vapor.

"Three months," Javi said handing her back the device.

"No, thank you," she said waving it off. "I think the room is spinning. I'm going to go take a walk."

"You good?" he asked.

"Yeah, I'm fine," she lied as she stood to make her escape.

"I'll go with you," Jam said, eyeing her from Ryder's lap. His face was in her neck and his arms wrapped tightly, possessively, around her midsection, and suddenly, Kensie understood the sad looks from earlier. "Baby," she chuckled, prying her boyfriend's arms off her body.

Ryder kissed her, his lips lingered over Jam's. "I'll miss you."

"I'll be right outside the door."

"You know what I mean."

"I know." Jam kissed him back. Kensie turned away, watching them made it real. If they were struggling with it, what hope did she and Carter have?

It felt good to get out of the cramped studio, to breathe fresh air. Kensie wandered back down the hall and into the lobby. Jamie appeared a few minutes later, a sad smile on her lips.

"They're really going on tour?" Kensie blurted out.

"Yeah." Jam sighed, plopping down next to her. "He didn't tell you?"

"No, and neither did you."

"I assumed you knew, and then you launched into the family dinner from hell and Carter banging all the bridesmaids—it kind of slipped my mind."

"Ugh," Kensie groaned, resting her head on Jamie's shoulder. "What am I going to do?"

"What do you mean?"

"He isn't going to want a girlfriend while he's on tour. It's probably why he didn't tell me and he's trying to figure out a way to break up with me."

"You're overreacting."

"That's easy for you to say. Ryder adores you. I'm surprised he hasn't asked you to go with them."

"He has." Jamie laughed. "Like a million times."

Kensie shot up. "You can't leave me too. Jam, please."

"Ken, relax. I have a job that I actually love. I can't leave for three months. And Carter isn't going to break up with you, he's obsessed with you. It's borderline creepy. You have nothing to worry about."

"Ugh," she groaned again. Jamie wrapped her arm around Kensie and they sat still, listening to the faint sound of music drifting from each studio. Jamie's words helped ease a bit of Kensie's anxiety, but her mother's words from a few days ago haunted her. *"You lose yourself in these boys."* Was that what this was? Was Carter just another mistake?

"I can hear you overthinking," Jamie teased.

"Was my mom right?"

"I don't know," Jamie answered honestly. "I mean, it doesn't feel like it did with Stephan or with Trey, but I just want you to be as happy outside of a relationship as you are when you're in one."

"Ouch, Jam." She was right, of course, and so was her mother, but that didn't lessen the sting of their words.

"There's my little stoner." CT grinned, appearing in front of them. He wore all black. His tattoos glowed in contrast. God, she loved him.

"Hey," Kensie whispered.

"That's my cue," Jam said, jumping up from the couch. She whispered something to Carter on her way back to the studio. Whatever it was, he dropped his head, and nodded.

"What was that about?" Kensie asked.

"She told me to fix it."

"Why didn't you tell me?"

Carter shrugged, then fell onto the couch next to her. "It wasn't official until yesterday. I was going to tell you this morning, but I didn't know how to bring it up." He lifted her leg across his lap and pulled her on top of him, slipping his finger in the tear just below her butt. "I know you still don't trust me completely—"

"It's not that I don't trust you."

"It's okay, babe. I fucked up, I know that, but there won't be any more blowjob-gates. I swear." Kensie nodded, biting her lip. "It's you and me, Friend, forever. We'll figure it out."

"Okay," she breathed.

"Good. Oh, I got you something."

Kensie ran her fingers through his curly brown hair, unsure of what to expect. "You didn't have to do that."

"It's not much," he explained, lifting them up so he could pull a small bag from his pocket. "I know the cornball probably bought you all sorts of flashy shit, but I saw this and had to buy it. I don't know, this just seemed like you, seemed like us." In the bag were two silver necklaces, each with half of a heart-shaped pendant. Held together, they read *Best Fucking Friends Forever*.

"It's perfect. Put it on me, please," she breathed, shuffling off his lap.

"I don't know. It seems silly now. Maybe I can have you one made with platinum and diamonds or whatever."

"Carter, it's perfect," she repeated, reaching for the other necklace and clasping it around his neck. She pressed a small kiss on the pendant sitting on his collarbone before snuggling into his side. "I don't need that stuff."

"I can give you everything he could and more. My trust is just as big as his."

"I can buy my own damn jewelry. I wasn't with him for money and I'm not with you to rebel. I'm with you because I feel most like myself when you're around."

"Promise me you'll tell me if that ever changes, okay?"

"Promise."

"C," Javi called, coming from down the hall.

"What's up, man?"

"Creed needs an hour to mix the track, then he wants you to lay down the reference."

Carter nodded. "So, what do you want to do for an hour?" He grinned, grabbing hold of Kensie's backside.

"Oh no, you two aren't ditching me, too, no fucking way," Javi pouted, sitting next to them on the sofa.

"Where'd they go?"

"I don't know, off to some empty studio probably. I think his plan is to fuck her until she can't walk."

"Hey," Kensie said, slapping Javi on the back of the head.

"What?"

"You guys are pigs," she giggled.

"What are we going to do for an hour?"

"Wanna get high?" Javi grinned, holding up a bag of gummy bears.

"Edibles?" Kensie asked.

"What do you know about edibles?" CT asked incredulously.

"Dude, this isn't the first time she's gotten high," Javi clarified, handing Kensie one pink and one blue gummy.

"Just take it easy, babe, this isn't like smoking. It takes a little longer to kick in but it's way more potent," Carter cautioned, before grabbing a few for himself.

45 minutes later…

"What's a reference track?" Kensie giggled.

"I sing the song how it's supposed to be so Ry can hear the cadence, then he records the final version."

"Oh. You can sing?" She giggled again. She wasn't sure what was so funny, but she couldn't help herself.

"I'm in a band, baby."

"What about you?" she snickered, pointing to Javi.

"I'm in the same band, baby," he mocked, ducking a swing from CT.

"You guys are silly. Sing something." She clapped. "Please sing. I've never heard you sing." Kensie smiled. She was as high as a kite.

"What do you want to hear?"

"My song?" she offered.

"No, not until it's finished."

"Know any Beyoncé?"

Javi and Carter exchanged glances. "We might know the words to *Bootylicious*," Javi confessed.

"Yes," Kensie squealed, "do that."

"It'll cost you." Javi grinned.

"What?"

"Show us your boobs," he said, straight-faced.

"I'm going to fucking kill you," Carter growled, lunging at his friend as Kensie burst into a fit of laughter.

She was happy.

She was in love.

NINETEEN

Paper Planes

"We should have just gotten on the fucking jet," Jamie huffed, falling back onto the plush king-size bed.

Kensie rolled her eyes at her friend. She wouldn't be saying that if it were her ex-boyfriend, Jared, on a private jet surrounded by a gaggle of Ryder's groupies. Granted, they had to wake up at five to catch a 7 a.m. flight from SeaTac to SFO, and then drive the hour into wine country, but really, it wasn't so bad. Not as bad as being trapped in a tin box with women who had been up close and personal with Carter's devil dick.

Kensie plopped down next to Jam, snuggling into her side. "I'm sorry," she said, without any real remorse. "At least the bed is nice."

Nice was an understatement. Magnificent was more appropriate. Everything in the small, sixty-room luxury hotel screamed understated elegance and romance. It was the perfect place for a wedding. Soft lighting, subtle rustic charm, and a view to die for. The back wall in the two-room suite was made up entirely of floor-to-ceiling mirrored glass windows that framed the beauty of Napa Valley. Vineyards stretched out as far as the eye could see, lush and green and vast.

"At least," Jamie grumbled.

Kensie ignored Jam's attitude and, instead, opted for a change of subject. "It's kind of romantic isn't it? I could totally see myself getting married here."

"Uh-huh." Jamie yawned an incoherent response and snuggled further into Kensie's side.

Strange, Kensie thought. Jamie had strong opinions on marriage, and jet lag aside, the fact that she didn't launch into her usual tirade about marriage being a business deal struck Ken as odd. "What about you?"

"What about me?"

"You, Ryder, wine country?" Her implications hung thick in the air between them. Jamie inhaled, then exhaled deeply, shifting her focus from Kensie to a spot on the wall behind her. Alarm bells rang out in Kensie's mind. Kensie knew Jamie better than she knew herself and she could practically hear the *be patient. Be mindful. Be kind,* playing on a loop in Jamie's brain. "James Michelle Manning, what is it that you aren't telling me?"

"Nothing."

"Bullshit. Jam, spill."

"Okay, I'll tell you but you have to promise you won't get mad?" Jamie asked, lifting up on her elbow.

Kensie's chest huffed up and down. "I promise," she said, though she had no intention of keeping said promise. How could she possibly predict her reaction to news that would probably make her upset? People don't say, *"promise you won't get mad"* when they have good news, only when they are about to throat punch you with their words.

Jamie sighed and scrambled off the bed. Their luggage lay discarded by the door. By the time they convinced—bribed—the man at the front desk to let them check in early, neither of them had much energy left for unpacking. "I kind of did a thing," Jamie began as she rummaged through her suitcase.

"What kind of thing?"

Jamie pulled a small velvet bag from the mesh pocket inside her case and ambled back over to the bed. "Hold out your hand," she instructed and Kensie complied. Her heart beat wildly as Jamie dumped the contents onto her palm. Water leaked from her big brown eyes as she stared at two diamond and gold rings. "Two," she whispered. Her voice garbled and broken. "I'm going to fucking kill you."

"You promised not to get mad."

This was worse than a throat punch. It felt as if Jamie had reached inside Kensie's chest and ripped out her heart. "I would be pissed if you got engaged and didn't tell me, but this—you getting married," she lifted the dainty gold eternity band, "this fucking hurts. I'm your best friend."

"I know." Jamie slipped the rings on her finger. Her gaze dropped to her lap, a shy blush crept up her neck. "If it makes you feel any better, aside from our mothers, you're the only one who knows. We just sort of did it."

"When?"

"Remember when you were sick and CT had to come and take care of you?"

"You're a heartless bitch," Kensie sniffled. Was she being dramatic? Possibly, but Kensie had been there for every major milestone in Jamie's life, and vice versa. First periods, first crushes, first heartbreaks, you name it and they had endured it together. Jamie was Kensie's heart. At the end of the day, when boys with tattoos and overbearing parents let her down, Jamie was there to pick her back up. Kensie wanted to be that for Jam—she thought she was, but now...

"Stop looking at me with your big Bambi eyes, Ken. I swear I didn't think you would react this way. It's really no big deal."

A pillow lay to Kensie's left. It wasn't a brick, but she could use it to smother Jamie—maybe then she'd get it. "I know things were off with us last year, but we were both to blame for that," Kensie growled. She wasn't going to let Jamie talk her way out of this one. They were bonding if it killed her. Hell, Kensie hadn't completely abandoned the pillow idea, anyway. "You can't keep pushing me away. I'm trying to fix it, but you're still keeping shit from me—*big*—life-changing shit. It isn't fair." Kensie hit Jamie in the head with the pillow. "I should have been there." She enunciated the words with another *whack*. "I hate that I wasn't. Also, I'm telling your brother."

Kensie lifted the pillow again, but Jamie yanked it from her hands. "Kensington, I'm sorry I didn't tell you…I just…I don't know…I don't want him to regret it," Jamie breathed.

Kensie hadn't expected those words. Jamie was the strong one. The self-assured one. "Regret what?"

Tears shined in Jam's greens. "Loving me."

"Jamie, do you know how amazing you are?"

"I thought I was a heartless bitch?" she chuckled sadly.

"Where's the pillow? I'm being serious. You're smart and funny and one of the bravest people I know. You inspire me every day. Ryder is lucky to have you, cold heart and all."

Jamie sniffled. "Fuck you for making me cry, Roth."

"You're welcome," Kensie said, brushing away Jamie's tears with the pads of her thumbs. "Now, let's take a nap, and when we wake up, you can tell me how you got your mother to agree to attending a shotgun wedding."

"Oh God, you have no idea," Jam groaned, snuggling back onto the bed. Kensie wrapped her arms and legs around her friend, clinging onto their past, their present, and their future with everything she had. They lay in silence for a few minutes. Kensie had already begun to drift to the land between sleep and wake when Jamie's voice pulled her back to reality. "I suppose now would be a good time to tell you I'm late."

It took a full sixty seconds for Kensie to process her words. "You're…late? Like late-late? Like pregnant-late?"

"I don't know. I haven't taken a test or anything. You know after everything happened, I'm kind of scared shitless…"

"Oh my God." Kensie jumped up on her knees.

"Kensie," Jam said, holding her arms out, "don't make this a big deal."

"Oh. My. God."

"Calm down."

"OH. MY. GOD."

"You can't say anything. I haven't told Ry yet." Without another word, Kensie snatched the pillow from the bed and threw it at her friend. "I know, heartless bitch; now can we please take a nap?"

Bang!

Bang!

Bang!

Startled, Kensie's eyes popped open. "What?" she mumbled sleepily. It took a few seconds before she registered what was happening. Fists reigned blows on the door of their suite. Muffled voices yelled in the distance, voices she'd know anywhere.

"OPEN UP!"

"OPEN THE DOOR!"

"LET US IN!"

"God, they're so immature," Kensie groaned. She threw the covers back, rolling her eyes at a still sleeping Jamie as she shuffled to her feet. Their voices got louder the closer she got to the door. It was a wonder no one called security.

"Party's here," Javi exclaimed the moment she swung the door open. The guys spilled into their room and headed straight for the mini bar, slamming down not one, but two liters of Jack Daniel's on the wooden tabletop. "Who's ready for shots?"

"Dude, we just got here," CT chuckled, pulling his girlfriend into his arms and kissing her sweetly on the nose. "Hey, sleepyhead."

"Hey yourself." Kensie wrapped her arms around his neck, her ire at their rude awakening long forgotten. Lifting up on the tips of her toes, she pressed her lips to his. "I missed you."

"I missed you more, Friend."

"Where's my girl?" Ryder asked glancing around the suite in confusion.

"Don't you mean wife?" Kensie couldn't help the venom in her tone. She was still pissed about the secret wedding. Though judging by the looks on CT and Javi's faces, Jamie was telling the truth, they really hadn't told a soul.

"Wife?" the drummer and bassist said in unison.

"She told you?" Ry asked. He ran his fingers through his curly blond hair, a shy grin plastered on his lips.

"Wait…what?" CT released his hold on Kensie, and he and Javi cornered their friend. "Married? When?"

"A couple of weeks ago." Ry shrugged as if it were no big deal. Like marrying her best friend in secret and then knocking her up was just another day in Lithium Land. He and Jamie really were made for each other. Kensie would have found it adorable if she didn't want to rip his fucking head off.

Javi made a face at CT before turning back to Ry, his signature smirk in place. "How the fuck did you convince her to marry your broke ass?"

CT nodded. "What he said."

Ryder responded by lifting a middle finger into his friends' faces. "Where is she?"

"Bedroom." Kensie tilted her head in the direction of the room. Apparently, she was the only one bothered by this little revelation.

"Go get her. We need celebratory shots," Javi said, lifting up a handle of whiskey.

"Umm…I…don't think she's feeling well."

Concern creased Ryder's brow as he made his way to the bedroom. Blurting out the secret marriage was one thing, but the baby news was on Jam.

"I still can't believe he got a ring on that finger," CT said to no one in particular.

"SHOTS," Javi repeated, a little more forcefully this time.

"Fine, one," CT huffed, dropping his arm from around Kensie's shoulder. The three of them made their way over to the mini bar while Javi poured three shots into tumblers with the name of the hotel etched in the glass.

"Don't *fine* me," Javi said, handing them each a shot. "It's the least you could do considering we could have been sipping Dom on a PJ, but noooooo, because you couldn't keep the peace for two fucking hours, we flew Southwest."

"What's wrong with Southwest?"

"Nothing, but who turns down a private jet?" Kensie almost raised her hand but thought better of it. "Whatever, dude. It's shot time. ¡Arriba, abajo, al centro, pa' dentro!" Javi raised his glass up, then down, then out, before tipping it back and swallowing the liquid in one gulp. Kensie and Carter followed suit. The whiskey burned away any remaining tension and apprehension in the air.

The three of them spent the next two hours drinking and laughing and watching *HBO*. Jamie and Ryder eventually emerged from the bedroom to join the party. Judging by the way Ryder kept at least one of his hands on Jam's stomach at all times, it was safe to say the cat was out of the bag. For a moment, locked away in her suite with her friends, Kensie felt at ease, almost as if they weren't in the eye of the storm.

A phone buzzed in the distance, a harsh reminder of the hurricane that brewed outside. Wiggling off Carter's lap, Kensie went to retrieve her cell. There was a message from Reagan.

Reagan: We're going to meet in the lobby for dinner around eight, Jamie is more than welcome to join us if she'd like, and don't forget to wear red!

Kensie: Awesome. See you soon, Mrs. Knight. ;)

Mrs. Knight.

There was a time when she'd wanted nothing more than to be that person. It seemed like so long ago. Hard to believe how many things could change within a month. Boyfriends. Blowjobs. Babies. Life sped forward down a bumpy highway and Kensie barely had time to strap in. *Mrs. Knight. Mrs. Thayer. Miss Roth?* Who knew where she'd be this time next year. She hoped she would be with Carter. Playing house maybe? Babysitting for Jam and Ry. Kicking ass at work and taking names.

"Everything okay, Friend?" Carter asked, coming up behind her. His hands ran up the length of her torso, his breath, lightly scented with whiskey, warm on her neck. Heat radiated off his body. The way he said *Friend* made every muscle in her body clench.

"Yeah," she gulped, swallowing back her desire, "your sister."

"What did she want?" he asked, inhaling her scent. His right hand continued its journey up and between her breasts, settling around her neck. He tilted her head back to rest on his shoulder while his left hand slipped down the front of her yoga pants.

"Babe," Kensie protested, vaguely aware their friends were just a few feet away.

"Yes, *Friend*," he said again in that voice that made her knees weak. Slipping two fingers inside her panties, he moaned in her ear, "Always so wet for me." All the fight drained from her body as he pumped in and out of her slowly. "You want to see what my room looks like?"

It was too risky. The rest of the bridal party had arrived, which meant Trey was lurking around somewhere, but the whiskey and his fingers and Jam getting married was all too much. She needed the release. "Yes, please."

"Yo, we'll be back," Carter called over his shoulder as he pushed Kensie out the door in front of him.

"Which way?" she panted. Would she ever get used to the effect this man had on her?

"Down the hall, room 200," he said, grabbing her by the hand and tugging her in the right direction. Desperation and need and lust guided them. They practically tripped over each other en route to their destination.

"Shit, I forgot my phone," she hissed, stopping in her tracks.

Carter tugged her forward. "Leave it."

"I can't. I'm officially on bridesmaid duty so as much as I'd like to hide away with you all night, I'm on a tight schedule. You'll need to make this quick," she teased. "I'll run back and grab it and I'll meet you there. Room 200, right?" Carter's lips jutted out into a pout. "I'll be right there." She swatted him on the behind.

Kensie turned and headed back to her room. They'd left in such a rush she'd even forgotten the key card. Knocking, she waited for one of the drunken idiots to let her in.

"Hey," Ryder's lips tugged up into a lopsided grin, "I almost didn't recognize you without CT's mouth attached to some part of your body."

Kensie blushed. "I could say the same thing about your hand and Jam's belly."

Ry beamed. "Still a little pissed that she told you first."

"Still a little pissed that I wasn't invited to the wedding," she retorted.

"Touché." He shrugged, opening the door wider so she could slip past. She grabbed her phone, rubbed Jam's tummy, and was back out the door in seconds. There was a text from Carter.

Peter Pan: Hurry up or I'm coming to get you.

He was such an asshole, but she loved him hard. Grinning at the screen, she began tapping out a reply, when her arm hit something. "Oh, I'm sor—"

"Baby, there you are." Everything about Trey—his tone, his eyes, his posture—begged for her to listen. Dropping his duffel, he pulled her into his arms.

"Stop," she said, pushing him back. "We don't have anything to talk about. I can't believe you'd ambush me like that."

"What the fuck was I supposed to do? You stopped answering my phone calls and text messages. You just cut me out without so much as a goodbye." His face was inches from hers. He was so close she was forced to take a step back and then another, and another, until she felt her back hit the wall behind her.

"We broke up."

"That's bullshit, Kensington. The last time we were together, we almost made love," he reminded her, tucking a strand of hair behind her ear. "What changed?"

"Everything."

"It doesn't have to. I still love you. I still want you." He brushed his fingers over her lips. The longing in his gaze nearly broke her. "God, I've missed you so much."

Carter. Carter. Carter. She reminded herself. It wasn't that she wanted Trey, but she couldn't turn off her emotions. She'd loved him once, and seeing him so broken was gut-wrenching, but she couldn't lead him on. "I can't do this with you anymore," she said, wiggling out of his grasp. "I've got to go."

Kensie made it all of three steps before Trey wrapped his hand around her bicep. "Will you fucking stop running away and talk to me?"

"Let go."

"Not until you talk to me." His grip on her tightened. He was frantic, desperate.

"You're hurting me," she hissed. She didn't want to cause a scene, but she didn't want this either. Her decisions brought them here. Her impulsiveness and immaturity were to blame, she knew that, but she didn't know how to fix it. "Trey, please, let me go. Maybe we can talk when you calm down."

"She said let go," Carter growled, appearing from nowhere. He shoved Trey, hard, pulling Kensie away from him.

"This is between me and my girl," Trey roared, pushing him back, "mind your fucking business."

Rage boiled in Carter's eyes. "Your girl?" They were face-to-face, nose-to-nose.

"My girl," Trey repeated, "*mine*. I don't know what your obsession is with her but get the fuck over it."

"Stop it." Kensie panicked, stepping between them. "Both of you, just stop." She could feel the tension rolling off Carter's shoulders. He was about to say something they'd all regret. "Trey, I'm not yours. We broke up, so you need to stop this. Thank you, Carter," she said, her eyes pleaded for him to let it go, "but I'm fine. You can go."

"Him first." Carter's face was set in a hard line, his jaw locked. His hands hung by his sides as his fists clenched and unclenched with each ragged breath he took. He wasn't budging.

Kensie turned to look at Trey. "Please, just go."

"Fine, I'll be the bigger man. I'm staying right down the hall, room 210, whenever you're ready to talk." He dropped a kiss on her forehead, and Carter yanked her back. Trey's eyes narrowed, but he continued down the hall. They didn't speak again until Trey disappeared behind the door of his room.

It was Kensie who broke the silence. "You've got to do a better job of keeping it together."

"What about him?"

"He's hurt."

"You don't think it hurts me to see you with him? To know everyone here thinks you're his?"

"I know who I belong to, and in three days, they will too. You've just got to keep it together until then."

TWENTY

What Lovers Do

> Roses are red.
> Violets are blue.
> It's time for us to say,
> I Do!
>
> I'm writing this email to thank you all again for being a part of our special day. I can't believe we are less than a week away from #KnightNuptials! Enclosed is an itinerary of events for the weekend to help you pack accordingly.
>
> I love you all and I promise not to go all BRIDEZILLA on your a$$es! Well, I'll try not to. ;).
>
> Xoxo,
> The Future Mrs. Knight.

Kensie scanned the email printout once more, fingering the half-heart pendant around her neck. She contemplated taking it off but fuck it. Carter was insecure enough about this weekend, she didn't want to add another reason for him to go all—*me Tarzan, you Jane*. She was going to wear it, consequences be damned.

"I can't believe you brought this thing," Jamie snorted, tugging on the hem of the now infamous red dress. Well, it wasn't *the dress*.

That dress was ruined, but she did find an identical one online.

"The email said, *'please wear your sexiest red dress'* and well..." She shrugged, the *"this is the sexiest dress I own,"* was implied. Plus, the dress was special, a lucky charm of sorts. A talisman to ward off evil skanks and cornball ex-boyfriends.

"If you say so, Roth." Jamie smirked, unconvinced.

"Okay, maybe also—just a tiny bit—I want to look hotter than the rest of those bitches," Kensie admitted, blushing. Was it fair to call women she'd hardly known bitches? No, but all was fair in love and war, right?

"No contest, babe," Jamie assured, falling backwards on the bed. "Does he know that's what you're wearing to dinner?"

"Not exactly. I wanted it to be a surprise."

Jamie rolled over on her tummy and tucked her hands under her chin. "He's going to blow a fucking gasket when he sees you."

Kensie rolled her eyes and smeared a layer of red lipstick across her lips. "He loves this dress."

"He loves that dress when you're on his arm, not when he has to pretend like he doesn't know you."

Kensie pursed her lips. Jamie had a point, especially after the showdown he and Trey had in the hallway. Maybe she should have thought this through a little more. "You don't happen to have a red dress in your suitcase by any chance, do you?"

"Nope," Jamie responded, popping the "p."

"What should I do?"

"It's too late to change."

"Are you sure you won't come with me?" Kensie whined.

Jamie yawned. "No. I'm exhausted, plus I'm pretty sure Ry has my ass on lockdown until he finds a stick for me to piss on."

"Wait, he's not going either? You guys are like the voices of reason."

"Javi will be there," Jamie offered.

"Javi would probably throw the first punch."

"Probably," Jamie snorted.

"Alright, well how do I look?" Kensie asked, twirling around.

"Even hotter than you did the first time you wore it. Give 'em hell, Roth."

Kensie sighed and took one last look in the mirror. Smoky eyes, red lips, and dewy skin. Her hair was porn star big. Loose waves cascaded down her back. Then there was *the dress*. The fabric clung to her, hugging every dip and curve on her body. Flashes of tan skin peeked out from underneath the band around her chest. Jam was right, she looked like sex.

Grabbing her clutch off the dresser, Kensie slipped her phone and lipstick inside and gave Jamie's still flat tummy a good luck rub, before heading to the elevator. Anticipation and dread filled her belly. She wanted Carter to see her in the dress. She wanted him as jealous and needy as she felt, but what about Trey? Could they really pull this weekend off?

The elevator pinged, and the doors slid open. Reagan and another woman stood inside giggling. "Holy smokes, Ken, you look…" Reagan trailed off into a low whistle.

"Me?" Kensie shrieked, stepping into the elevator. "You don't look so bad yourself, Mrs. Knight." Reagan looked stunning in an ivory sequin wrap dress that accentuated her every curve. It dipped down low in the front and was cut so high, Kensie assumed double sided tape was the only thing keeping it in place.

"It's not too much?"

"It's perfect," the woman in the red halter dress said. "I'm Emerson, by the way."

"Kensie. You were at Liam's birthday party, right?"

"Yes. You're Trey's girlfriend."

"Umm, not anymore." Kensie blushed. She did her best to keep her expression neutral, but she was sure the smile she'd forced onto her face resembled a grimace more than anything.

"Oh, bummer." The blonde frowned. She was slightly taller than Kensie, but not quite as tall as Reagan. Her medium-length blonde hair was swept over her left shoulder and her red dress was exponentially more modest than what the other two women wore. Kensie wondered if Emerson was a part of the family or a part of the harem.

"It's fine." Kensie shrugged.

"Well, I haven't given up on you two yet, and I know Trey hasn't either." Reagan winked. The elevator doors slid open and Reagan and Emerson stepped out into the lobby, but Kensie stood, frozen into place.

She breathed and then counted to ten; she was stalling. It took everything she had in her not to ride the elevator back up to the second floor and hide out in her room. It wasn't until the doors pinged, signaling that they were about to close, that she finally found the courage to step out of the car.

The hotel lobby bustled with activity. By Kensie's count, most of the twenty-member bridal party, including Trey, and the two tattooed degenerates, had already made their way down.

"What the fuck are you wearing?" she heard the familiar voice growl. Kensie chuckled, hidden behind the large potted plant in the lobby, as she watched Carter approach his sister.

"What's wrong with it?" Reagan asked, defensively.

"Half of its missing," Carter said, half-teasing, half-serious.

"You do realize I'm getting married in a couple of days, right?"

"Liam," Carter asked, flinging his arm around his sister's fiancé's neck, "tell your wife she needs to go upstairs and find more clothes."

"I think she looks amazing," Liam replied blushing shyly. This earned him a resounding *aww* from the small crowd gathered around the bride-and groom-to-be.

"She's really got you whipped," Carter chuckled, releasing the younger Knight brother from his hold.

Kensie frowned. While it was nice seeing this side of Carter, the protective big brother side, she was sad that they had to hide their relationship. This entire weekend should be about love and happiness and the wonders the future will hold, yet, for her, it was about lies and deception and, as much as she hated to admit it, guilt.

Trey was an ass, of that there was no denying, but it didn't change the fact that he was in love with her and she had cheated on him. Her eyes scanned the crowd for her ex. He was smiling, talking to his cousin, a fellow groomsman. Everyone seemed so comfortable, so relaxed, and here she was hiding behind a plant, watching like an outsider, as the men in her life interacted with their family.

"Why are we hiding?" Grant whispered, coming up behind her.

Kensie rolled her eyes at the eldest Thayer. "Wouldn't you, if you were me?"

He scrunched his nose, as he took in the sight in the lobby. Carter and Javi were talking and laughing with Reagan and Liam, while Trey sat in the opposite corner of the room, laughing with yet another groomsman, chugging from a bottle of champagne.

"Well, they don't seem to want to kill each other as much as normal, but I'm sure that will change once they see you, so yeah, I guess I'd be hiding too."

"If I sneak back upstairs, will you tell Reagan that I've become violently ill?" she asked.

Grant's eyes softened. "It'll only be awkward at dinner, after that the guys are going one way and the girls another. You'll be fine."

Kensie nodded. She could handle dinner, right? She looked over at Grant, but his gaze locked on his brother. Carter, on the other hand, focused solely on her, his body rigid, his eyes glazed over with lust, and the corners of his mouth tipped up into that patented Carter Thayer smirk.

The cocky bastard stalked over to where they were standing, extending his hand to his brother as he opened his mouth. "I don't know if I'm more pissed off or turned on that you're wearing that dress." He was looking at Grant, but the message was for Kensington.

"I didn't have anything else appropriate for the occasion," she whispered, her cheeks flush.

"Baby, this dress is far from appropriate. It's taking every ounce of self-control I have not to fuck you right here, right now."

"Okay, this is getting weird." Grant cringed, dropping his little brother's hand.

"Bro, you gotta keep him far the fuck away from her. I'm not kidding. If he touches her, I will fucking annihilate him."

"I'll do what I can," Grant agreed, his lips pressing into a tight line.

"And you," he said, turning to Kensie, his eyes roaming the length of her body, taking in the sight of her in the dress. His tongue darted out, sucking in his bottom lip, as he dragged his hand through his wavy brown locks. Eye fucking didn't even cover the way he was looking at her. An adequate phrase had yet to be discovered. The look was equal parts possession and promise. A warning. "You're lucky I can't touch you because if I could, I'd fuck you until you couldn't walk, and then I'd keep fucking you until I couldn't."

"I'm standing right here," Grant said, breaking the spell between them.

"Later," Carter whispered, slowly retreating backward. Kensie released a shaky breath, one she'd been holding from the moment he smirked at her. One word never held more promise.

TWENTY-ONE

Drunk in Love

Magic was the common theme among all the princess movies Kensie grew up on. Fairies and spells and potions helped the princesses chase their dreams. Too bad Kensie's fairy godmother was knocked-up and taking a nap, and the only potion in her possession had an eleven percent alcohol content.

Despite her lack of magic, dinner went smoother than Kensie could have hoped. The bridal party sat around a large table in the private dining room of one of Napa's most prestigious restaurants. Food and drinks flowed freely as the Thayer/Knight wedding party kicked off their weekend-long celebration. Much to Kensie's surprise, Carter held it together well, managing to pretend as if she didn't exist.

Mostly.

Small glances, secret smiles, and dirty text messages sustained her. He was discreet, never lingering on her longer than a moment, but enough to make her feel secure, to feel loved, even while being trapped at a table filled with women who'd known him in the biblical sense.

Then there was Trey. His sad brown eyes roamed her body every chance he got. She felt the longing in his stare, the weight of it, how unapologetically he yearned to be near her. Guilt prickled at her skin when he looked at her like that, like he'd lost his best friend. But despite his staring, Trey seemed to be on his best behavior as well, only telling her she looked beautiful as they boarded the party busses.

All in all, the atmosphere in Napa was light. Kensie didn't know whether to attribute it to the copious amount of alcohol or the fact that everyone was content to put their feelings aside to celebrate Reagan and Liam. A little magic would be nice, but she couldn't deny that she enjoyed seeing Carter with his family. She enjoyed their subtle flirting. She enjoyed listening to everyone tell stories about Reagan and Liam and about how they'd been best friends since they were in diapers.

They'd been lucky. They didn't have to search through the muck to find their other half. Reagan never had to kiss any frogs, her Prince Charming was right next door. Reagan didn't have to endure the pain of heartbreak or the devastation of finding out the person she loved wasn't who she thought they were.

Kensie's cell phone pinged, and she chewed on her lip in anticipation.

Peter Pan: You are by far the sexist person in the room.
Peter Pan: And stop biting your lip.

Her eyes found his, and with deliberate, measured motions, her lips parted, and her tongue darted out of her mouth as she licked her top lip, before ever so slowly sinking her teeth into the bottom one.

Kensie: I can't help it, it's like my body's natural reaction to you and your teasing.

Peter Pan: I'm not teasing. I mean every word.

Kensie: That's not helping.

Peter Pan: I bet your panties are soaked.

Kensie: Wouldn't you like to know…

Peter Pan: Go take them off.

Kensie: What?

Peter Pan: Go take them off and give them to me.

Kensie: You've lost your mind. We are supposed to be keeping a low profile.

Peter Pan: I'm not asking you to take them off at the table and throw them across the room. Go to the restroom and take them off.

Kensie: NO.

Peter Pan: By the end of the night, not only will I be in possession of your panties, but you'll be begging me to fuck you.

Kensie: So far, you're the only one begging.

Peter Pan: Care to make it interesting?

Kensie: What did you have in mind?

Peter Pan: The first person to initiate sex loses.

Kensie: What do I get if I win?

Peter Pan: Me.

Kensie: And if you win?

Peter Pan: I get you.

"God, he is so fucking hot," the brunette to her right slurred into Kensie's ear.

"Huh?" she asked nervously, covering her phone.

"Reagan's brother," she slurred again. Kensie's eyes darted across the room.

Please be talking about Grant.
Please be talking about Grant.
Please.
Pretty please with sugar on top.

"The one with the tattoos." *Of course not.* "…but I'd take Grant too. Hell, I'd take them both at the same time." If she was trying to whisper, she was failing miserably. Her eyes had that glassy, far-off look in them. It was obvious that she was tiptoeing on the line of sobriety.

Kensie frowned. She'd been so preoccupied with sexting her boyfriend, she almost forgot about the loose-legged bridal party.

"Gross, Cameron, that's my cousin," the woman on the other side of Kensie groaned.

"Your cousin is a sex god, Quinn," Cameron stated unapologetically. "I know from experience," she mumbled to Kensie.

"Still not whispering." Quinn rolled her eyes.

Kensie shook her head. She didn't know how to react, so she just smiled and picked up her glass of wine, fighting the urge to throw its contents at the brunette named Cameron. What kind of stupid fucking name was Cameron, anyway? Breathe, Kensie, just breathe, she willed herself, turning to look at the woman on her left. Red hair, bright green eyes hidden behind thick-rimmed tortoise shell glasses, and a look on her face that said she wanted to be there about as much as Kensie did.

Quinn.
Quinn was family.
Quinn was safe.

She decided in that moment to attach herself to Quinn for the rest of the night. It was pathetic, but as she glanced over her shoulder at the drunk girl shooting her boyfriend bedroom eyes, she knew it was her only option for surviving the night.

"You're Reagan's cousin?"

"Yup, Quinn," she introduced herself, extending her hand. "Our dads are brothers. You're Kensie, right? Trey's…ex?" Her tone was questioning. She, like everyone else in the wedding party, seemed unsure of their official status.

"Yes, ex," Kensie confirmed, bracing herself for the inevitable, maybe you guys will work it out. "Good for you. Trey's an asshole."

"You have no idea." Kensie grinned, raising her glass.

Quinn lifted her own, bringing it to meet Kensie's with a clink.

Kensie was liking Carter's cousin Quinn more and more.

The party bus pulled up in front of Silo nightclub at around 10 p.m. CT and Javi crashed the girls' party, opting instead to go with them rather than chance CT and Trey getting into a drunken bar brawl. Kensie was happy to have her boyfriend close by even if she still couldn't touch him, and even if half the women in their party were eye fucking him.

She peeked out the tinted window of the bus. A bright red, neon sign hung above the entrance of the club, illuminating the night sky. She sat and stared at it, waiting. That was all she ever did anymore, wait. She waited for her dream job. She waited for the day she could finally go public with her boyfriend, and now she waited for eight other women to exit the bus.

She felt his gaze on her, but she stayed in her seat, her eyes focused out the window until she felt the brush of his leg against hers. "You coming?" he whispered, looking ahead. One by one the bridesmaids exited, until they were finally alone.

"Yes," she said, finally tearing her gaze from the sign. She straightened her dress as she stood. Their bodies were close, so dangerously close that she felt the heat radiating off him.

Reaching for his hand, she pressed the tiny swath of silk into his palm. "Game on, Thayer." She winked, sinking her teeth into her bottom lip. Her hand brushed over the bulge in his pants as she made her way to the front of the bus.

The low, throaty, "Fuuuuuck," that escaped his lips made her stomach flutter.

Score one point for team Kensington.

Once inside, the group made their way towards a long bar situated to the left of the dance floor. The place was a far cry from what the less than sober bridesmaids were expecting. In fact, Club Silo wasn't really a club at all, more an upscale lounge. Soft jazz pumped through the speakers and the dim lighting cast a soft blue haze throughout the room. Not exactly a place where a group of drunk twenty-somethings could rage.

"This place is dead," Cameron said, looking around the mostly empty dance floor. There were two older couples swaying to the music and a few more people milling near the bar, but Club Silo was otherwise dull.

"We're in Napa, what did you expect?" Quinn retorted. "It's not like it's the spring break capital of the world."

"I know, but I thought at least there would be some eye candy. It's nothing but old married guys."

"Uh, what are we, chopped liver?" Javi asked, motioning between himself and Carter.

"Look, it's still early and Mr. Thayer already pre-paid the tab, so let's just make the most of it."

"See? Thank you," Carter said winking at Emerson, "that's the spirit. Come on, little sister, let's get you wasted." He dropped his arm around Reagan's neck and she beamed up at her brother.

"What about us?" a blonde whose name Kensie didn't know pouted at Carter. She stood up a little straighter, thrusting her chest towards him.

Reagan rolled her eyes at her friend. Apparently, she liked them flirting with Carter just as much as Kensie did.

"Drinks for everyone. Order whatever you want, it's on my dad," Carter responded smoothly. He shoved his sister towards the bar, throwing an apologetic look over his shoulder. Kensie added two more names to her list—Emerson, harem member number two and the Blonde Slut, number three.

"Javi, make sure she's good."

"I got it, bro." Javi nodded, sauntering over to where Kensie and Quinn stood. Kensie glowered at him. "You already know what it is, relax," he whispered, before dropping one arm around her shoulder and the other around Quinn. "What are we drinking, Ginge?"

Quinn blushed. "You know I don't drink."

"Come on, it's a celebration, just have one."

"Fine, just one," she giggled.

"Tequila," Kensie grunted, annoyed by Javi and Quinn making heart eyes at each other. Quinn was this smart, snarky, self-assured girl, but one look from Javi, and she dissolved into a giggling, blushing mess. Fucking Lithium Springs and the affect they had on the opposite sex. Wherever they went, women threw their panties at them, but could Kensie blame Quinn or anyone else? Hell, she'd literally just done the same.

"Tequila?" Quinn shuddered. "That didn't end well for me last time."

Javi's gaze dropped down to the swell of her chest. "That's not how I remember it, Ginge." There was something raw and honest in his tone. Javi and Quinn had a past, and judging by the looks they were exchanging, Kensie had a feeling whatever had happened between them was only the beginning.

"Okay, one more shot and then we dance!" Kensie yelled to Quinn.

After two hours and too many shots to count, Silo was starting to feel more like a party and less like a funeral. They talked the DJ into playing music from the current decade and more and more people in their age range began to arrive.

Carter handed them each a shot glass full of Patron. "Maybe you should slow down," he said, eyeing the two warily.

"It's a party." Kensie shrugged, tipping the glass back.

He narrowed his eyes at her, gearing up for an argument, but a heavy hand on his shoulder stopped him. "Bro, chill." Javi handed him a shot glass. "This is supposed to be fun."

"Yeah, Cart," Quinn added. "We're totally sober."

"Totally," Kensie added with a snicker. "OHMYGOSH, I love this song!" Kensie squealed, grabbing Quinn by the hand. "Let's dance before the party police throw us in jail."

The two girls stumbled out onto the dance floor, joining Reagan, Emerson, and the rest of the bridal party there. The opening chords of Beyoncé's *Drunk in Love* blared through the speakers as Kensie's hand's found Quinn waist. "I think my cousin has a crush on you."

Kensie shook her head. The room spun, her vision blurred, her lips numb. She was officially, totally, and completely wasted. "I'm drunk," she yelled over the music.

"We're all drunk, and I don't even drink."

"I love this song," Kensie said, as her hips swayed in time with the beat. Quinn flung her arms around Kensie's neck and the two girls danced and swayed, letting the music take control.

Kensie pulled Quinn's hips in closer, her forehead resting on the other woman's, their limbs intertwined, their hands exploring each other as their bodies moved as one.

"Can we cut in?" The girls turned towards the sound of the voice. Two men stood behind them, lust shining in their eyes.

Kensie looked to the bar. Carter was there, handing shots to Cameron and the Blonde Slut. "Sure," she nodded, "why not?"

The shorter of the two men wrapped his arms around her small frame, pulling her to him, her back to his front. His hands gripped her waist tightly as he rolled his hips into her backside.

Time ceased to exist. Common sense and rational thinking had long since vacated her body, leaving only jealousy and anger and resentment. She was lost in the music, buried deep under a tequila-induced fog. Her eyes closed, her head fell back on his chest. It wasn't until she heard the familiar low baritone growl, "Get the fuck away from my girl," that she realized where she was. Carter stood in front of her, his blue eyes almost black, anger rolling off his body.

The man behind her quickly released his hold. "My bad, dude. I didn't know."

"Well, now you do," he grunted, pulling Kensie into him. She vaguely registered Javi glaring at the man behind Quinn, but was too focused on the angry man in front of her to see the man behind her retreating.

"Are you trying to get me arrested?" His voice was deadly.

"I was just dancing."

"Is that what you call it?"

"I didn't even think you would notice. You seemed pretty preoccupied with the Blonde Slut earlier."

"That's what this is about? You're trying to make me jealous?"

"I don't like you flirting with women you've slept with."

"They mean nothing to me. I'm just trying to show my sister a good time."

"By fucking her friends?"

"I fucked Emerson in high school," he gritted, tugging hard on her hair, causing her head to snap back, so she couldn't look anywhere but him. His mouth found her neck and he bit kisses up the side of her throat. "Cameron came to a show and practically begged me to fuck her, so I did. And the blonde? I don't even remember her name. I don't give a shit about them, only you. I didn't forget who I belong to."

"You didn't?"

"No, baby. I don't care where we are or who's watching, I'm yours, forever." His voice was thick with lust, love, and longing. "And you're mine."

"I know."

"Do you? Because it seems like I need to remind you." He bit her earlobe and his hand slid up the back of her dress, cupping her bare ass.

"No, Carter," Reagan shoved her brother back, "leave her alone. You've already fucked enough of my bridal party."

Carter pulled Kensie back to him, kissing and then biting the place where her shoulder and neck met, narrowing his eyes at his sister.

"Babe," Kensie whispered so only he could hear, "I'm fine. I'm sorry. You don't have to do this."

"You're lucky you're getting married, little sister."

She glowered at him. "Go, there are plenty of skanks here. Please leave my friends alone."

"I'm going. I'm going," he said raising his hands in surrender.

"Sorry about him, Kensie," Reagan apologized.

"It's fine," she breathed, running her fingers through her hair. "He's harmless."

"Tell that to Cameron," Reagan snorted.

Kensie's phone buzzed. She discreetly pulled it from her bra, checking the message.

Peter Pan: Meet me in the bathroom.

Carter's words rang in her ear, *I don't care where we are or who's watching, I'm yours, forever.* He loved her, only her. "I gotta pee, Reagan," she yelled over the music.

"Want me to come with?"

"No," Kensie shook her head, "stay, dance, have fun. I'll be back in a flash."

Reagan grinned at her, then turned back to the circle of drunk girls clad in red dresses swaying to the music.

Kensie made her way to the back of the club as quickly as her legs would carry her. She felt his presence even before she saw him, even before she felt his long fingers wrapped around her wrist. His touch seared her skin. Every nerve ending in her body stood at attention.

"I'm going to fuck you," Carter spoke softly, as he pushed the door to the men's room open. He quickly scanned the room. They were alone, but Kensie knew it wouldn't have mattered either way. She could tell by the way he looked at her as he walked her backwards into the last stall. He was going to fuck her because he knew she needed to be fucked. She needed him to claim her, and as she was quickly learning, he'd do anything for her.

"I win." She grinned.

"Are you ready for your prize?" he asked, locking the door behind them.

"I think I've earned it." Kensie ran her hands down his hard chest, and tugged the hem of his t-shirt, pulling it up over his head.

Unhooking the button on his jeans, Carter unzipped his pants, revealing the base of his swollen member. "Is this what you want?" he exhaled, freeing his erection. He wrapped his hand around his shaft and gently began stroking himself, back and forth, and back and forth and back and forth.

Kensie nodded slowly. Her gaze traveled from his eyes down to his lips, then to his sculpted shoulders, rock-hard abs, and further down still until she reached her prize. The sight of him pleasuring himself drove her wild with lust. The whiskey from earlier, mixed with the wine at dinner and the tequila from the bar, eviscerated her inhibitions.

It didn't matter that they were in the men's room. It didn't matter that Carter's sister was waiting for her to return. It didn't matter that someone could walk in at any moment. Nothing mattered but the man in front of her. She dropped to her knees without a bit of shame or hesitation.

"Jesus, I love your mouth," he groaned, his voice strained, as the tip of his dick hit the back of her throat, "so fucking much." His words spurred her on as she pulled her head back, hollowing out her cheeks. She sucked further and further until he fell from her lips making a small popping sound. Her hand lifted to cup his balls, and she licked the underside of his shaft again and again, before slipping him back into her mouth, taking him deeper and deeper. "Fuck, baby. If you keep it up, I'm going to come."

"Is 'at a chawenge?" she gurgled around his cock.

"There's my girl," he chuckled, pushing her head back down until her nose was buried in his pelvis. He pumped his hips in and out of her mouth slowly, savoring the warmth and wetness. "I love you so much it hurts, do you understand that?"

"I know," she moaned around him.

"It fucking kills me that I fucked this up." His blue eyes aflame as he yanked her to her feet and slammed her back against the stall. Kensie could see the pain and the hurt and the regret marring his beautiful features He lifted her legs around his waist, positioning himself at her center. "I don't even look at other women the same way," he confessed as he pushed his way inside of her. "It's only you for me, baby. No one will ever possess me the way you have. You're etched onto my heart and my brain. You own every part of me. No one else will ever compare."

His words pierced her mind, his dick penetrated her body, and his eyes, all blue and sad, seeped into her heart. He owned her, that she already knew, but there, in the men's room of Club Silo, he made it clear to her that she owned him too.

"Mine," she growled, kissing the pendant around his neck.

"Forever," he murmured as he thrust in and out of her.

Her heels dug into his backside as he pushed them both closer and closer to ecstasy. He fucked her hard against that bathroom stall. Fast, and relentless, just what she needed to take the edge off. It wasn't sweet or romantic or the fairy tale she once thought she wanted, but neither was their relationship.

Carter never was her Prince Charming and he never would be, but he loved her and he understood her. He never judged her or tried to change her. He wasn't perfect, but then she was no angel either.

"I love you. I love you. I love you. I love you. I love," he chanted, burrowing his head in her neck as he drilled into her mercilessly. It wasn't long before she reached her climax, biting down on his shoulder to muffle her cries. He followed shortly after, shooting his semen deep inside her center.

They stood there for several minutes, her back against the stall, his cock still buried in her warmth, basking in the afterglow of what they'd just done. His tongue explored her mouth with long possessive strokes. Her fingers ran through his copper locks, comfortable in his embrace. Comfortable in her skin. Comfortable with him in her skin.

"We should get back," she sighed ruefully. She wasn't sure how long they'd been gone, but since no one came to look for her, she'd assumed it wasn't too long.

"Are you okay now?" he asked, unwrapping her leg from around his waist. He held on to her while she steadied herself, then he pulled up his pants, stuffing his semi-erect penis back inside.

She ran her fingers through her hair, hoping she didn't look as thoroughly fucked as she felt. "I'm more than okay." She smiled shyly at him.

"That's not what I mean, Friend." He quickly cleaned up the mess between her legs before pulling her panties from the pocket of his jeans and helped her into them.

"I know and I'll do a better job of keeping the jealous girlfriend thing in check."

"No more dancing with random dudes."

"Now who's being jealous?" He shrugged. "Well, I won't dance with anyone and you don't flirt with anyone, and maybe we'll make it through this night without killing each other."

"Deal. So, how do you want to do this?" he asked.

"Me first," she whispered, pressing a kiss onto the scruff on his chin.

She slipped out of the stall, only to find a round older gentleman standing in front of one of the urinals. Their eyes met briefly, the heat rising in her cheeks, as she darted out of the men's room.

She burst out of the door, giggling at the absurdity of the situation. The humor quickly evaporated when she ran smack into the tangled ball of limbs she recognized as the bride and groom. Apparently, they had the same idea as she and Carter.

"Did you just come out of the men's room?" Reagan squealed, unwrapping her arms from around Liam's neck.

"Umm… I…" she stuttered, trying to come up with a good excuse as to why she'd just come busting out of the door marked *Gentlemen*. "What are you doing here, Liam?" she asked, opting instead for a diversion.

"Hey… Kensie." Liam smiled sweetly at her. His face was red, like he'd just been caught with his hand in the cookie jar. "The other bar was a bust, so we decided to crash your party."

"Oh, well then, I'll leave you two to it." She was hoping to flee before the drummer emerged from the door behind her. No such luck.

"Carter?" Reagan shrieked.

Shit

Shit

Shit.

"What's up, Li," he said, extending his hand to his future brother-in-law. Kensie did her best to slip past them, but Reagan wasn't having it.

"Don't what's up him, Carter. What the fuck? I asked you to stay the fuck away from her. And you," she screamed, turning towards Kensie, "I warned you. I fucking warned you." Prim and proper Reagan Thayer had left the building.

"Reagan, it's not what it looks like," Kensie tried to explain.

"It looks like you just fucked my brother in the men's room." Reagan crossed her arms over her chest. A look that said, *I dare you to lie*, settled into her delicate features.

"Well, technically…I mean we did but…" Before she could finish, the older man walked out, smiling knowingly at Kensie before giving Carter a pat on the shoulder.

"Gross," Reagan yelled.

"Calm down," Carter reprimanded his sister, "and what do you mean, warned her about me?"

"You'll have sex with anything that has a vagina," she said to her brother. "And what about Trey?" Reagan turned to Kensie, a million questions flashed through her brown eyes.

"Fuck Trey," Carter growled, wrapping his arms around Kensie's waist nuzzling into her neck. He was done pretending.

"Baby, if Liam's here, Trey's here," Kensie reasoned, shrugging out of his embrace. "The wedding is in two days, we've made it this far."

"Baby?" Reagan scoffed.

"Baby," Carter repeated, arching his brow. He pulled the pendant from under his shirt, dropping it over Kensie's shoulder, it landed just inches away from the matching one around her neck. "As in *my girl.*"

Liam's eyes shot up. "What the fuck, man?" he roared. Kensie never even heard the younger Knight brother raise his voice at a Seahawks game, and here he was screaming at Carter. "Tell me you didn't? Please tell me you didn't, CT. He's in love with her."

"So am I, and she loves me."

"Is this true, Kensie?" Liam asked.

"I never meant for it to happen. I just couldn't stop it. I tried my hardest to love your brother, but Carter's my soul mate."

"How long?" he asked.

"Does it matter?"

"I have to tell him," Liam huffed. The determination in his voice was unnerving.

"No, you can't," Reagan cried. She turned to plead with her fiancé, her expression grim. "I have been dreaming about this day since I was five. I've planned everything out to perfection. Telling him will ruin everything."

"Reagan, I love you more than life, but I can't keep this from him."

"I'm not asking you to keep it from him forever, just two more days, please," Reagan begged.

Kensie could see the internal struggle raging behind Liam's eyes. He had a choice to make, his brother or his new family. "Liam," she began, "Reagan's right, two days and then I'll tell him myself. I owe him that much."

"No, you don't," Carter grunted.

"Baby, I know how you feel and I get it. If he did to me what he did to you—"

"Wait," Reagan interrupted, "you told her? I've begged you for years to explain it to me and you told her?"

"I tell her everything."

"Look, this isn't the time or the place to have this conversation."

"Liam's right," Kensie said, "we should get back."

"You two go on," Reagan frowned, tilting her head towards the bar, "I need to talk to my brother."

Carter rolled his eyes but nodded his agreement as Kensie and Liam headed back into the main room.

"I'm sorry," Kensie said as they made their way back.

"I'm not the one you should be apologizing to, Kensie. You destroyed him and you're off running around behind his back with CT. How's that fair?"

"We weren't right for each other, Liam. CT or not, it wouldn't have worked."

"I guess we'll never know now, will we?" he said, eyeing her with disdain. She didn't deserve his empathy, but she wasn't expecting this level of hate. Not from him, not from Trey's shy little brother.

As soon as they reached the main room, Liam made a beeline for the bar. Kensie searched the crowd for a friendly face, Quinn or Grant or Javi, anyone who wouldn't make her feel like a monumental fuck-up.

She spotted Quinn and Javi making out in the corner. Grant was at the bar, ordering drinks. He was flanked by Emerson and Liam. She sighed, wishing that Jam and Ry were there. They'd know what to do.

Resigning herself to her fate, she went and sat at an empty table off to the left of the dance floor. She didn't have enough energy to pretend to be social, and the tequila was starting to make her head spin.

She'd been sitting there, her head propped up against the wall for about ten minutes, when Trey walked over, setting a bottle of water in front of her. "I know you're pissed at me, but it looked like you could use this."

She regarded him for a moment before picking up the bottle and taking a drink. She hated to admit it, but the cold liquid was just what she needed. "Thank you."

"Can I sit?" he asked, shoving his hands into the pockets of his slacks. He was impossibly handsome, but there was grief in his brown eyes, grief that she'd undoubtedly put there.

She looked around the bar. Javi's tongue was planted firmly down cousin Quinn's throat, Grant was doing shots with Liam and the groomsmen, and Carter hadn't reemerged from the back with his sister. "Ten minutes," she said, pushing a chair out with the bottom of her heel.

"I miss you," he began.

"Trey, if that's what this is about, you can save it."

"Why?"

"Why what?"

"Why, suddenly, did you shut me out? I thought we were in love."

"We wanted different things. It wasn't fair for me to hold on to you when I knew in my heart it wasn't going to work."

"You didn't even try. Why wouldn't you try?"

"I...tried... I did, but then..." She struggled for the words. There wasn't a nice or polite or kind way to say it so she just did. "There's someone else."

"What?" His voice cracked, as a series of one-word questions spilled from his lips. "When? Who? Why?"

"I met him while you were in Vegas," she confessed.

"While we were still together?

"Yes," she nodded, "I'm so sorry."

"Who?"

"It doesn't…you don't know him," she lied, figuring the truth would come out soon enough.

"You're willing to throw this past year away for someone you've known for a few fucking months."

"It's not…"

"I don't care," he growled cutting her off. "I love you. I'm willing to try again," he said, pulling something from his pocket. "I saw this a while ago and I knew it belonged on your finger." He sat a small red box on the table. "I was planning to do this in November, for your birthday."

"Trey," Kensie breathed. She used to dream about this moment, with this man. How would he do it? Would her family be there? Would he get down on one knee? What would the ring look like? Never once in any of her fantasies were they in a dark corner of a club, alcohol clouding both of their judgment, and certainly not after she'd just confessed to cheating on him.

"I don't expect you to answer right now. I know this isn't the grand gesture that you deserve, but I need you to understand that I'm not giving up on us. I'm willing to fight for you. My heart's on the table. It's yours if you want it." He stood, bending down to plant a kiss on the top of her head, before retreating to the bar.

Her eyes stayed glued to the box in front of her. She couldn't breathe, she couldn't think. Reluctantly, she tore her gaze from the table only to find Carter standing there. The look on his face, the utter devastation in his eyes, as he glanced down at the red Cartier ring box sitting in front of the girl he loved, nearly destroyed her.

TWENTY-TWO

Dangerously in Love

Light seeped out from under the bathroom door, the soft yellow glow the only sign of life in the otherwise dark room. The shades were drawn over the floor-to-ceiling windows canceling out the romantic view. The alarm clock on the nightstand read 8:37 a.m. Kensie sighed and rolled to her back, the haze of last night's party lingering on. The unruffled pillow on his side of the bed taunted her.

Where he went was a mystery, one that niggled at her subconscious. After everything they'd been through, he still couldn't talk to her. That hurt more than his absence. She tried convincing herself where he was didn't matter. He was back—hiding out in the bathroom—but back. The door creaked open and Carter's shadow glided across the room. The bed dipped and strong tattooed arms encircled her small frame. His skin was damp, warm. A shower? *Don't freak out. Don't freak out.*

"Where'd you go?" she choked.

"Out for a run."

"Kind of early for a run, isn't it?" They got back to the hotel around three, she could barely move, let alone run.

"Every time I tried to close my eyes, I saw the look on your face when he put that fucking box on the table. I can't get it out of my mind. I damn sure couldn't sleep."

Kensie turned to face him. Dark rings shaded the skin around his sad, blue eyes. He looked…tortured. "Baby, you have nothing to worry about. I told you last night, the ring doesn't change anything. I'm exactly where I want to be."

"Hmm," he muttered. His chest rose and fell with each breath. His clean scent invaded her nostrils. His warmth was comforting. "Can I see it?" His voice was easy breezy, but his body told a different story. It was rigid, like he'd been preparing to take a hit. Maybe in a way he was. Carter was handsome, talented, and one of the most charismatic bastards Kensie had ever met. He exuded confidence in nearly every aspect of his life, but on the inside, he was just as insecure as she was.

Trey was his Achilles heel, the source of his resentment and abandonment issues. It had been ten years since Trey's betrayal, and still, Carter felt like second best. In his eyes, he'd never measure up to Trey Knight. Carter was the fuck-up, the black sheep.

Kensie threw a leg over Carter's waist, lifting to straddle him. Their foreheads touched. "See what?" she asked, nibbling on his bottom lip. He was hurting. She tasted the doubt on his lips.

"Do you like it?" His hands gripped her ass tightly, so tightly she was sure there would be little purple bruises in the shape of fingertips on her behind.

"I love you," she murmured, trailing kisses from one corner of his mouth to the other, his overgrown beard scratching at her soft skin.

"Do you like it?" he repeated, guiding her over the growing bulge in his pajama pants.

"I didn't even open the box," she confessed, grinding down on him. This was their love language. Carter needed actions, not words. He needed her to show him. He needed to feel her love.

The air in the room crackled. Kensie felt the tides turning. The earth shifted as she pulled her night shirt over her head. This time would be different. They'd spent the last few months fucking on almost every surface of Seattle. He claimed her wherever they went. Their attraction was raw—primal—but in their Napa hotel room with that damn Cartier box hidden away in the nightstand, they would share an experience foreign to their union—slow, passionate lovemaking.

"I don't care what it looks like." She tugged down his pants just low enough to free his erection. "It doesn't change anything, I know who I belong to," she said, reciting his words from the night before. They belonged to each other, neither Trey nor the harem could change it. Her parents couldn't change it. The tour couldn't change it. Pushing her panties to the side, she hovered over him, her brown eyes meeting his blue. "The only ring that I want on my finger is the one that you give me. Until then," she lowered herself onto him, "this is all I need. You are all I ever need."

The groan that ripped from his throat in that moment made Kensie's heart constrict. It was both sad and hopeful, like he couldn't believe her words, but maybe, just maybe, she'd choose him anyway. "He's better for you than I'll ever be. He'd never hurt you the way I did. Your parents love him. If I were a better man, I'd give you up, I'd let you be happy."

"Then I'm glad you're not a better man," she said on his lips. "I don't want a better man, I want you. That ring doesn't change how I feel." Her hips swirled. Her body rose and fell. She rode him slow, her pace languid, her intent clear, she wasn't going anywhere.

"You seemed so…speechless. The look on your face…I just figured."

"He caught me off guard. I'd just told him that there was someone else and he said he'd fight for me. I was expecting anger or disappointment, hurt—not a marriage proposal. I was in shock." Her lips found his, their tongues dancing, as their bodies collided.

"Do you want him to fight for you?"

Her back straightened, her hands found her chest and she played with her nipples as she ground into him. "No, I want you to accept that I love you. I want you, forever, *Friend*." Her words seemed to soothe him. For the moment, all seemed right in their little world, in their little bubble. They were two imperfect beings in an imperfect relationship, but somehow, for them, it worked.

"Forever," he groaned. His eyes ran down the length of her body, zeroing in on the place where their bodies connected. Every time she moved, it revealed a little of his length, glistening with her arousal.

"I love you so fucking much," she cried, enveloping his mouth in hers. She placed her forearms on either side of his head and lifted her hips and let them fall. Her muscles clenched around him, squeezing everything out of him. They were all hands and lips and hearts as they clung to each other, falling together.

"Can I see it?" he asked again, hours later as they lay in bed, sated, content. He wasn't letting it go, and Kensie wasn't going to argue. If he needed this, then she'd let him have it.

Reaching over to the nightstand, she pulled open the top drawer. "Here," she said, handing it over without so much as a second glance.

He held what could have been her future in his hands, eyeing the thing like it might explode. His sucked in a sharp breath, bracing himself as he opened it. Inside was a three-carat, pear-shaped, solitaire diamond ring. It was beautiful. A month ago, you would have had to pry it off her finger, but now it was just another pretty thing.

He quickly shut the box and handed it back to her. "He's an ostentatious bastard, isn't he?" Kensie tucked the red leather box back into the drawer and snuggled up to her boyfriend. Carter brought her hand to his mouth, kissing her ring finger. "I thought about it."

"About what?" she asked, resting her head on his chest.

"How I'd do it. How I'd ask you." His voice was soft, quiet, as he continued to fiddle with her finger.

"How?" she breathed.

"Nice try," he smirked. "Although, I wasn't planning on doing the ring thing."

"No ring?" She arched her brow.

"Nah, I was thinking of something a little more…permanent."

"Such as?"

"Tattoos."

"Of course," she giggled. Her hand traveled down his chest, down, down, down.

"As much as I'd love to spend the rest of the day inside of you, we should probably eat something before you go."

"I'm not going," she said, falling back on her pillow.

"I thought it was a part of your bridesmaid duties."

"I'm barely a bridesmaid, and I'm pretty sure Reagan hates me, so it's best I skip it."

"You're being dramatic. Reagan doesn't hate you. She was pissed at me, but we talked. She understands."

"You told her about Trey?" Kensie asked, resting her chin on his chest.

"No."

"Why?"

"I told you why."

"You don't want to take them from him."

Carter stayed quiet. He kissed her ring finger again, and then again.

"You're a better man than he could ever hope to be. I just wish everyone knew the truth."

"Don't worry about it, baby. I'm happy. I have you. I win."

"But—"

"All I want you to worry about is what you're going to eat for breakfast."

"Bacon," Kensie huffed pulling herself out of bed. "I'm going to shower." She had a spa day to get ready for, after all.

TWENTY-THREE

All the Stars

Kensie inhaled deeply, pulling open the heavy metal and glass door to the hotel spa. Lavender and vanilla scented the air of the large modern salon, making her feel instantly at ease. She had a love affair with lavender, one that began during her freshman year of college. It grew wild in the field behind her dorm, soft and feminine and whimsical. She'd sit with the window open on crisp spring days while the scent wafted in, wrapping her in its warmth.

It was home.

She smiled, walking up to the sleek steel receptionist desk. Carter was right, this was exactly what she needed. "Hi, I'm Kensie. I'm with the Thayer/Knight wedding party," she said, extending her hand to the lady standing behind the desk, dressed in all black. The woman's blonde hair was pulled back into a low bun and her red lips spread into a wide grin as she gave Kensie her hand.

"Brittany," she greeted before dropping her eyes to the computer screen in front of her. "Looks like everyone else has gone back. I can show you if you'd like?"

Kensie nodded eagerly and followed Brittany through the reception area, back to a large dressing room. A row of mahogany lockers lined the wall, and a large, plush bench sat in front.

"So, you're dating Ry?" Quinn's voice drifted over the lockers.

"I kinda married him." Kensie heard the smile in Jam's voice and made her way around to her friends. "There you are," she said. "I didn't think CT would let you out of his sight after last night."

"I'm lost," Quinn said, looking from Kensie to Jamie and back again.

"She's boning your cousin, babe," Jamie said dryly.

"JAM!" Kensie groaned. This was quickly becoming the worst-kept secret in the history of secrets.

"I knew it! I mean, I didn't know, know—but I knew—ya know? The way he went all alpha on that guy who was dancing with you. It was way more than the protective older brother bullshit he likes to pull with me and Rea. He was so caught up with you he didn't even get pissed about me and Javi. Last time, they didn't speak for a week."

"Wait, you fucked Javi?"

"Yes…no…this isn't about me. This is about you and Cart. Does Trey know?"

"Trey proposed," Jamie blurted out.

"Jam?! Keep your voice down," Kensie squealed, glancing over her shoulder. "It wasn't a proposal, he just kind of set the ring on the table and said it's mine if I want it. I panicked. I was drunk, and Carter was pissed, so I just grabbed it before anyone else saw. Now I have this fucking ring, Carter is still pissed, and I'm so beyond screwed."

"So, are you two like a legit couple?"

Kensie nodded and pulled her shirt over her head. Her pants went next, then her bra, and Jamie tossed her a towel.

"And Trey has no clue?"

"I told him I was seeing someone else—"

"But not who?"

"No."

Quinn's eyes widened, and she looked to Jam for confirmation. "Holy. Shit!"

"I know," Kensie groaned, banging her head on her locker. The shit had ascended from hell, passed through purgatory, and settled in heaven.

"You're fucked."

"I know." Sideways, diagonally, and crisscrossed fucked.

"They're going to kill each other."

"I know." It was bad, and it would only get worse as long as she held on to that ring.

The door opened again. Kensie, Jamie, and Quinn turned their heads as Annabelle Knight strode into the locker room. Her brown eyes were expectant as she looked to Kensie's left hand. "It seems as if we've got another wedding to plan," Annabelle said, settling in next to Kensie. "Would you girls mind giving us a minute alone?"

Jam and Quinn exchanged a glance, then pushed their way into the massage room, leaving Kensie alone with her ex-future mother-in-law. Annabelle Knight was the definition of Stepford wife. Not only was she tall and blonde and gorgeous, she was smart and calculating. She had a degree from Yale that she never used. Her background in corporate law made her wholly over-qualified to be a housewife, but her husband, Thomas, was more interested in her looks than her mind.

Kensie always marveled at how someone as clever and business savvy as Annabelle Knight ended up as arm candy for one Thomas Knight. Trey's dad was as ruthless and calculating as they came. Annabelle had given up any possible career to cater to Thomas's, Trey's, and Liam's every whim. She was fiercely protective of her boys and she'd do anything to ensure their happiness.

It had taken three months before Annabelle acknowledged Kensie's existence, another two before she uttered her name. In fact, they'd only had their first real conversation a few months ago, once Annabelle realized that despite her best efforts, Trey was hopelessly in love.

"I don't think either of us want that," Kensie confessed.

Annabelle's eyes bore into Kensie's. "You're right, but he thinks he's in love with you."

"I thought I was in love with him, too."

"You two are all wrong for each other. He still thinks you're the one. The more I try to convince him otherwise, the more he clings to you. He's always been a fool when it comes to girls. He nearly flushed his entire future down the toilet over some tart who only cared about his money. At least we don't have to worry about that with you," Annabelle said as if it were a compliment.

"At least." Kensie bit her tongue, desperately trying to remain respectful, but Annabelle was no longer a factor in her life and her patience for the nitpicking was wearing thin.

"Thankfully, it worked itself out. Trey stayed out of trouble and I was able to convince him to cut the trash out of his life for good."

Time stopped ticking. Kensie's heart stopped beating. "What is that supposed to mean?"

"He needed to focus on his future, not some misplaced sense of loyalty. Anyway, that's in the past. Now, I need to figure out what I'm going to do about you. All that pedigree, all that beauty, wasted."

"Lucky for you, I prefer the company of trash over selfish, self-serving assholes like you and your son. Enjoy the spa, you cold-hearted bitch," Kensie seethed, before yanking her towel up and storming out.

She was fuming. Part of her felt bad for Trey, having to grow up with the Wicked Witch of Seattle, but a part of her didn't. Liam grew up in the same house, with the same parents, and he was as sweet and selfless as they came. He'd never do what Trey did, no matter what Annabelle wanted.

Kensie's hands were shaking as she wrapped herself in the towel. It was time for her massage, but it took everything in her not to go back in there and tell Annabelle exactly how she felt.

She sucked in a sharp breath as she headed through the locker room over towards the room where the masseuse was waiting. She was still trying to process what had just happened. Kensie always knew Trey's mother would do anything to protect her children; hell, she'd spent the better part of last year as the sole recipient of her malice, but she never in a million years could have guessed that Annabelle was behind Trey's dismissal of Carter.

Annabelle loved Reagan like she was her own daughter. The Thayers and the Knights seemed to be like family, so why would she counsel her son to abandon his closest friend?

Kensie sighed, willing her anger down. "This is supposed to be relaxing. Breathe, Kensie," she told herself, "just breathe." She repeated her little mantra four times before she was calm enough to enter the massage room. "Hi." Kensie smiled tightly at the woman in white.

"Hi! Kensington, right?" the masseuse asked.

"Yeah, that's me," she responded, looking around the dimly lit room. Her voice was laced with confusion as she noticed the older woman sitting on the second massage table.

"Kensington?" the woman asked. Kensie recognized her instantly; she had the same dark-brown hair as Reagan, and the same blue eyes as Carter and Grant.

"Mrs. Thayer? Hi, I don't think we've met," she said, extending her hand to Carter's mom.

"No, we haven't, but I hear you're sleeping with my son."

Nope, Kensie thought to herself as she retracted her hand.

Nope.

Nope.

Nope.

She didn't have the energy to deal with another crazy mother. One was enough for today. And unlike Annabelle, this was the one she'd be stuck with.

"Kensington, wait."

"With all due respect, Mrs. Thayer, yesterday was rough and today isn't shaping up to be much better. I can't do this right. I know I'm a terrible person who's all wrong for your baby boy, but lucky for me, he loves me anyway."

"Well, I wasn't thinking that exactly. I'm curious to get to know the woman who has my son and his best friend so deeply captivated that one is proposing marriage and the other is professing his unwavering love."

"Carter and Trey are not friends."

"Reagan tells me you know why."

"Maybe if you were less concerned with keeping the peace and cared more about your son, he'd tell you, too."

Kensie didn't bother to wait for a response. She turned and got the hell out of there before she buried herself in a deeper hole. She'd never changed so quickly in her life. On the elevator back up to the second floor, she tapped out a text to Jamie briefly explaining where she went, then headed to her room to retrieve the ring.

"You're back already?" Carter asked in surprise. He was standing in front of the mini bar with a cold bottle of Corona pressed against his lip. His shirt was stretched out around the collar and his knuckles were purple.

"What happened?" Kensie gasped. All thoughts of past and potential monsters-in-law vanished as she took in her boyfriend's appearance.

"You should see the other guy," Carter said, wincing slightly as he popped the cap off the beer and took a long swig.

"Trey?" she asked, gently touching the corner of his mouth.

"Javi," he grunted, pulling her into his arms. He trailed light kisses down the side of her throat, his lips cold from the beer.

"What happened?"

"Family is off-limits."

She pushed him back slightly; he had to be joking. "You guys got into a fist fight because he hooked up with your cousin?" Her voice was incredulous. Quinn was a grown woman and Javi was one of his best friends, surely this could have been settled with a simple conversation. "Is he okay?"

CT scoffed, "He's fine."

"Are you guys okay?"

"Yes, baby, guys aren't like girls. We don't hold grudges. We fought and now it's over."

"Boys are stupid," she snorted, rolling her eyes.

"Why aren't you getting a massage?" he questioned, picking her up and setting her on the mini bar. He spread her legs as far apart as they'd go, his eyes trained at the apex of her thighs.

"I met your mom."

"Thanks," he grumbled, pushing her legs back together.

"The first thing she said to me was, *I hear you're sleeping with my son.*"

"Yikes." Carter cringed, as he picked the beer bottle back up and took another sip.

"Yeah, and that was after Annabelle told me that my looks and pedigree were wasted on me."

"Annabelle is a bitch."

"That's not the worst part." She grabbed the beer from his hand and drained half the bottle. She knew the next part would be hard for him to hear, but she couldn't keep it from him.

"It gets worse?"

She nodded, trying to think of the best way to tell him. How was she supposed to say it? How was she supposed to twist the knife that was already planted in his back? "She's the reason Trey did what he did. She told him to cut the trash out of his life—her words—not mine."

Carter swallowed so deeply his Adam's apple bobbed up and down. His gaze seared her. She could see the gears turning and clanking in his mind. They'd known each other for such a short time, but Kensie could read him like a book. She saw past the tattoos, and zero-fucks-given attitude, down to his heart. "Don't!" she sighed, running her fingers through the messy brown locks sitting on top of his head.

"Don't what?" he whispered, leaning into her touch.

"Don't start thinking that maybe Trey isn't an asshole after all. He was nineteen years old when this happened. He was old enough to know better."

"I know, baby…I just, fuck—" He took the beer back from her, and chugged what was left of it. "I think I need to fuck you," he said, pushing her legs apart again.

"I think I can handle that, but I need five minutes."

"Why?"

"I need to give the ring back," she whispered.

"Bring it to the rehearsal dinner." He kissed her cheek.

"I don't want to do it in front of everyone."

"I don't want you alone with him." He didn't say it, but she could see it in his eyes, the memory of the last time she was alone with Trey haunted him still.

"You have nothing to worry about," Kensie assured him. She wrapped her arms around his neck, forcing him to look at her. "I'll be gone for five minutes and then I'll come back, and you can fuck me senseless."

"Five fucking minutes, Kensington, and then I'm coming to get you."

"Okay," she said, pressing a kiss to his lips. Grabbing the ring, she made her way down the hall. Each step towards Trey's room felt like a mile, and yet, the closer Kensie got, the heavier the Cartier box felt in her palm. *It's yours if you want it.* How many times had she fantasized about him proposing? Maybe some big romantic gesture, in front of their friends and family, or a quiet evening in, just the two of them. Mrs. Knight, she had wanted that once. She had wanted to be that person, or at least she had thought she did.

Trey was Prince Charming, after all. Perfect on paper, successful, safe. Carter would never be the safe choice. He'd never be the perfect guy or work a nine-to-five job. There would always be women throwing themselves at him, but she found solace in something her mother said months ago.

We aren't perfect. I couldn't stand your father when we first met, I still can't half the time. He pushes every one of my buttons and challenges me in ways no one ever has before. He drives me insane, and yet I'm so foolishly, hopelessly in love.

She'd never be happy with Trey. She'd never be happy with anyone other than the heavily tattooed drummer who, in such a short time, had broken down all her walls and inserted himself into her heart. Kensie rapped on the door three times.

Knock.

Knock.

Knock.

The door swung open, relief shined bright in Trey's eyes. "Baby, you came."

"I'm not staying. I just wanted to give this back," she said, holding up the ring.

"Come inside. Talk to me, please."

"That's not a good idea."

"You cheated on me. You broke my heart. Now you're telling me that you don't even have enough respect for what we had to come inside and fucking talk to me?"

His voice was broken. Kensie could hear the pieces of his heart rattling as he spoke, but she had to stay strong. "Neither one of us were perfect."

"Maybe not, but I never cheated. I'd *never* do that to you." Trey's jaw ticked as he took a step forward.

"No, you just tried to turn me into someone I'm not."

"Come inside. I don't want to do this in the hallway."

"I can't," she said, and once again tried to hand him the ring.

"Jesus fucking Christ, Kensington, just talk to me, please."

"It's not a good idea." She met his gaze, imploring him to understand that it was over—that they were over.

"Because of him?" The rattling was back. The broken man was too. This was harder than Kensie thought. She had loved Trey once, somewhere, deep down. It may not have been hopelessly or foolishly, but it was love.

"Trey, this isn't about me falling in love with someone else. You and I were wrong for each other."

"No, we aren't. We hit a rough patch and you gave up on us, like you do everything else, but I won't let you do this. Just give me a chance to prove that I'm the guy for you. Give me a fair fight. I only just discovered I'm competing for your heart."

"But that's just it, you aren't. There is no competition. It isn't even a choice. It's him. It will always be him for me."

"Does he even know you? Does he know about your past, about your trust issues? Does he know what kind of coffee you like? Your favorite color? Hell, does he even know when your fucking birthday is?" Tears and vulnerability spilled from his eyes. "Please. Please. Please." He begged.

Five minutes had come and gone, and Kensie didn't doubt Carter would be there soon. Pressing the ring box in his palm, she said, "I'm sorry I couldn't be what you need." She spoke softly as she closed his fingers around the box and pressed a kiss on his knuckles before turning her back on him for the last time. "Goodbye, Trey."

TWENTY-FOUR

Setting the World on Fire

Time was a matter of perspective. It could either move at the speed of light or it could drag on for eternity. It all depended on the person, their place in life, their distance from a situation, and their ability to look past themselves and see things as they really were.

To Reagan, this day had been a lifetime in the making. Liam had waited for this moment, for this girl, since he was thirteen years old. The Thayers and the Knights were like family for over thirty years and today's ceremony would make it official.

To Kensie, this was the day she'd been dreading since Reagan asked her to be a bridesmaid. Time flew into hyperdrive and fate threw her to the wolves. She was the outsider. The interloper meddling in family business. The harlot who had jumped from one lost boy of Bellevue to the other. The one who broke Trey's heart, and the one making Carter choose between family and loyalty.

Now that the day had arrived, the flowers, the dresses, the decor, every detail planned to perfection, the pendulum shifted. Perspectives switched. "Oh my gosh, I can't believe it's already one o'clock," Reagan squealed as she fanned herself with her hands, desperately trying to quell her nerves. "I think I'm going to throw up."

Reagan's maid of honor and best friend handed her a glass of pink champagne. "Just breathe, and have a drink," Emerson coached, sitting her down in the makeup chair.

Kensington watched as the scene played out in front of her in slow motion.

The nine women—Kensie, seven other bridesmaids, and one very nervous bride—converged in the bridal suite of the Villa Terre Hotel and Spa. The team of hair and makeup arrived at ten, and one by one each girl was transformed into a princess for Reagan's big day. Reagan was the last in the makeup chair, the artist taking special care to ensure the bride looked like a queen. Her eyes were soft brown and smoky, her lips creamy and nude, and her cheeks flushed with a soft pink hue. Her sleek black bob was styled in loose waves and a blush-colored rose pinned back the left side. She was whimsy and elegance personified.

Just when Reagan drained the glass of champagne the door to the suite swung open and Annabelle and Penelope fluttered in with a large white garment bag. "It's time!" Penelope cooed. Pride swelled in her eyes as she looked upon her daughter. Absently, Kensie wondered if the day would ever come that Penelope would look at her with the same adoration. If she'd take the same care in unzipping her dress from its bag. If she'd share the same small glances with her mother that she did with Annabelle.

There was an audible gasp in the room as Reagan stepped into the strapless cream-colored dress. Her curvy frame was engulfed in layers of chiffon and lace. She was stunning, and everyone told her so. The tears and the champagne flowed freely as the nine women finished getting dressed. Kensie reluctantly took off her *best fucking friends forever* necklace and donned the mandatory infinity charm.

She did her best to stay out of the fray, to keep her head down and blend in with the crowd. Despite their beginning, despite her past with Trey, Carter was her present and if she was lucky, he'd be her future—*they* would be her future. He'd assured her that they'd come around; Reagan was already beginning to, but Kensie knew there'd be a mountain to climb.

The women raised their glasses once more, as Annabelle gave an emotional speech about Reagan being the daughter she'd always wanted. Her eyes focused on Kensie as she told the room how perfect Reagan was for her son and how she could only hope Trey would be so lucky. Her sweet words were laced with venom but the rest of the bridal party was either too caught up in the moment or too polite to acknowledge the slight.

"Alright, ladies," the wedding coordinator announced with a clap of her hands, "the groom is in place. It's time to make our way down to the gardens."

One by one the women made their way out of the suite. Kensie felt a tug on her elbow, Reagan. Her face was serene, her earlier nerves all but forgotten. "He loves you," she whispered.

Kensie couldn't help the confused look that stretched across her face. She wasn't sure which *he* Reagan was referring to.

"My brother."

"Yes, he does." Kensie smiled back.

"I've never seen it before, but last night, after the rehearsal dinner, he pulled me and my mom aside and told us, in his words, to leave you the fuck alone. He's never cursed in front of Mom before, never."

"I don't want to come between you guys," Kensie said, shaking her head.

"We lost Carter ten years ago," Reagan said sadly. "He barely comes around and when he does it's like he can't wait to leave."

Kensie had to literally bite her tongue to keep from saying something that might upset the bride. Inside she was screaming, *because you threw him away,* but instead she went with, "It's not you. He just can't get past the betrayal."

"How bad is it?" Reagan questioned.

"It isn't my secret to tell."

"Girls," the wedding planner said, popping her head back into the room, "time to go."

"I guess we'll still be sisters." Reagan grinned, lacing her arm with Kensie's.

Kensie did her best to control her emotions. "I really hope so." She smiled. "Let's get you married."

The intimate ceremony took place in front of a hundred of Reagan's and Liam's closest friends and family. White lights and blush-colored roses were dotted throughout the garden, as soft and as feminine as the bride herself.

A hundred faces in the crowd and Kensie found Carter's from across the room. He stared at her with lust and love and adoration and she stared back at him with matched intensity. It was like they were in their own world, listening as the minister recited the vows.

"Do you, Liam, take Reagan as your lawfully wedded wife, to have and to hold, from this day forward, for better, for worse, for richer, for poorer, in sickness and health, until death parts you?"

Carter mouthed, "I do," and it nearly knocked the wind out of her.

"Do you, Reagan, take Liam as your lawfully wedded husband, to have and to hold, from this day forward, for better, for worse, for richer, for poorer, in sickness and health, until death parts you?"

"I do," Kensie mouthed back to the tattooed rocker who made her knees weak. In that space, in their bubble, neither time nor perspective nor past nor present existed. They were frozen, lost in each other's eyes. Bound by their unofficial promise, for better or for worse.

"You may now kiss your bride."

The minister announced the newest Mr. and Mrs. Knight and the crowd erupted in cheers as two by two, the wedding party made their way back down the center aisle. After pictures, everyone made their way back to the garden for the reception.

"My little brother has been in love with the girl next door for as long as I can remember," Trey's speech began. He paused, loosening his bow tie. Kensie wondered if everyone else could see the sadness hiding behind his eyes. She did that, she broke him. Guilt prickled at her scalp. Trey may have been a lot of things, but it didn't rinse away the blood on her hands. She could have told him she was unhappy. She never wanted to hurt him and, in the end, she destroyed him. She'd have to pay for her sins, just like Trey was paying for his. Karma had a long memory, and there was no statute of limitations on infidelity.

"They were fourteen when he finally found the nerve to ask her out. He'd been in love with her since infancy. Everyone could see it but you, little sister," he teased, looking down at Reagan. She blushed before turning to her new husband, love pouring out of her every cell.

"He found out some jerk from the football team was planning on asking her to homecoming. He spent the entire day working up the courage to ask her first. I thought he was going to wear a hole in the carpet, he was pacing so much." This elicited a low rumble of laughter from the crowd who hung on Trey's every word. "He worried about how he'd do it, or if she'd say no, or if he was too late, then Carter," Trey paused, regret, anger, and sadness flashed on his face, as he recalled the memory, "Carter threw a book at him and said, go get your girl before I kick your ass. Suddenly, it was like a calm washed over him, and he marched over there, and he did it. Reagan never stood a chance."

Kensie smiled from her spot at the end of the main table. The garden, deep in the vineyard behind the hotel, looked like it was ripped out of a fairy tale. She scanned the rows of round tables and beautiful people, all who screamed wealth and privilege, looking for her other half.

The three tattooed guys in suits were easy to find. Even off stage, their presence was electric—they drew you in—hard and soft, perfect and flawed, clean and dirty, all at the same time.

Trey's voice faded into the background as Kensie watched them. Ryder's arm was draped lazily around Jamie's shoulder, his burgundy suit tailored to fit his long lean body like a second skin. He looked every bit the unaffected rockstar that he was. With the smoking-hot blonde on his arm, he was king.

Javi, The Joker, the playful one, wore a gray pinstriped suit and his signature grin. The jacket hung over the back of his chair, and the sleeves of his shirt were rolled up midway to his forearm, exposing the black and white ink on his arm. His gaze, intense despite his smile, trained on Quinn.

Then there was Carter, *her Carter*, dressed head to toe in all black. The only visible colors were those of the reds and blues and greens that swirled on his hands and peeked up through the collar of his dress shirt. The sight of him in a suit made her feel things for him she didn't think were still possible. His presence had been such a constant in her life this past month that she'd almost become numb to how handsome he was. She'd grown accustomed to it, but seeing him all cleaned up, looking as dapper as any one of the Ivy League-educated groomsmen in attendance, sent a shiver down her spine and a rush of moisture to her panties.

Her teeth found her bottom lip, and her thighs pressed together as heat pulsated through her body. She was staring, unabashedly so, taking comfort in the fact that everyone's attention was focused on Trey as he spoke fondly of his little brother.

Just when she finally convinced herself to look away, his head turned, and his blues found hers. It was as if he could sense her arousal from the other side of the garden, because she certainly recognized his. She'd know that look anywhere, from any distance. That face haunted her dreams, the one he wore when he spotted her in the crowd at the Rabbit Hole that night and the one he wore as he fucked her against the bathroom stall at Silo. He looked at her like she was a cool drink on a hot day, shelter from the storm, and Christmas morning all wrapped into one. It was pure lust, all physical, all sexual. His gaze made her core spasm.

Carter tipped his head toward the exit. She nodded her agreement ever so slightly. He stood first, bending down to whisper something into Javi's ear. The guitarist grinned and looked over at Kensie, before extending his hand to his friend, his brother. Carter shook it, pulling Javi in for a quick hug, before he stood and walked back towards the hotel, disappearing into the shadows.

Kensie counted to fifty in her head, before leaning over and whispering to Quinn, "I'll be right back." Then she stood as gracefully as possible and followed in the same direction.

The garden was bigger than she remembered, or the lust was clouding her judgment, she wasn't sure. Her legs pushed her forward, looking for the man in black. She kept going, further and further, until finally, she spotted him in the courtyard. He was sitting on the edge of the fountain. His elbows rested on his knees, his hands were steepled in front of his lips, as he watched her approach.

"You look amazing. I want to rip that dress off you and fuck you right here." He swallowed hard, his voice strained as he took her in. The sequined dress shone in the setting Napa sun. She was a goddess placed there for him.

"You don't look half-bad yourself." She grinned. Her fingers raked through his hair, eliciting a low growl from his throat.

"I love when you do that," he moaned, wrapping his arms around her waist. He pulled her in between his legs, resting his forehead on her midsection.

"And I love you," she said, bringing her other hand to his head, tugging gently. They stayed like that for a few minutes, soaking in the beauty of their surroundings and of the moment. She played with his hair, he caressed the exposed skin on her back, neither in a hurry to break the spell.

"Is this how you picture our wedding?" he asked after a few minutes.

"No," she replied, scratching behind his ears. In truth, she'd never pictured her wedding. She knew she wanted to get married, but she always figured that's what wedding planners were for.

"No?" Carter's brows shot up in surprise. "How then?"

"I don't want the circus."

"Every princess wants the fairy tale."

"How do you picture it?" she asked, amused. She didn't take her rockstar boyfriend for the romantic type, but then again, weddings brought out the inner romantic in even the coldest hearts.

"Just me and you. Maybe Vegas?" His eyes glazed over like he could see the day clearly in his mind.

"Sounds good to me."

"Yeah, right," he snorted, "what about Kitty Cat? Your mom and dad?"

"Well, maybe our parents can come, provided they have their shit together by then."

"Mine will, but yours," his head tilted back, and his face scrunched up, "I don't know."

"They'll come around," she assured him, tracing his bottom lip with her tongue. "I don't think anyone can resist you."

"You tried," he said, catching her tongue with his teeth. He bit her gently, then kissed her sweetly.

"Ha," she scoffed, "you fucked me the first day we met."

"That's because you liked this," he pointed to his face, "not because you liked me."

"Maybe a little, and your body, your body's pretty hot too," she giggled.

"But you couldn't stand me," he challenged, arching his brow.

"I fucking hated you."

"When did it change?"

"Liam's party."

Carter winced, pulling her down on his lap. "I'm sorry."

"Water under the bridge." She shrugged. "But *that* wasn't when it changed. Being in the same place with both you and Trey made me realize I had to make a choice and I knew it was you. I think I always knew. I'm stubborn, just like my daddy."

"Why me?"

"The entire time Trey was kissing me and touching me and holding me, I wished it were you. I hated that you had to see that. I wanted nothing more than to leave with you. I thought it was guilt keeping me there, but it was fear. Fear of the unknown, fear of getting hurt."

"But I did hurt you."

"Yes, and it sucked. Don't ever do that shit again," she warned, holding his gaze.

"I swear it. You're it for me, Friend."

"I realized something. I was holding on to Trey so tightly because he was safe, but I couldn't let fear control me anymore. I've spent my entire life dreaming, and then you came along, and those dreams became reality. Perfection is a fallacy. I'm not perfect, I'm insecure and needy. I like messy buns and sleeping in and I fucking love bacon. I can't be Trey's perfect little wife. I don't want to be. I want you, with your tattoos and your devil dick and your dirty mouth. I want to soar with you."

"Marry me."

"Yeah, right," she giggled, doing her best to ignore the swell in her chest.

"Marry. Me."

"You're serious?" He couldn't be, could he?

"Before the tour."

Kensie's heart stopped. Time stopped. Life stopped. Part of her was crazy enough to marry him tomorrow, but she didn't know if that part was co-dependent Kensie or madly-in-love Kensie. "Let's just get through *this* wedding."

"I think I know a way to make you more agreeable," he whispered into her collarbone.

Ahem. The clearing of a throat pulled them back to reality, back to the wedding. Kensie stood, putting distance between her and Carter. They were getting careless. "I don't mean to interrupt, but they're almost ready for you," Penelope said, looking at her son like she was trying to solve a mystery.

"This isn't over," Carter murmured.

"You're out of your mind." She smiled at the ground. His mother's presence made her nervous, especially after their run-in at the spa.

"No, I'm madly in love," he corrected, lifting her chin. His mouth found hers and she opened to him.

Ahem. Penelope cleared her throat again.

Reluctantly, he pulled away from Kensie and went to his mother. Wrapping her in his arms, he lifted her off her feet and swung her around. "Carter, put me down!" she laughed.

"Protect my heart, Mother," he said, looking back at Kensie.

"Always, dear, always. You just have to talk to me." Love and adoration shone in her eyes as he set her on her feet and retreated back through the grapevines.

"I want to apologize for yesterday," Penelope began. "It's just, the only thing I'd ever heard about you was in connection to Trey. Then my daughter calls me devastated about how Liam is so angry with her for making him lie to his brother and, well, it wasn't the best first impression."

"I don't mean to be rude, really, but it isn't anyone else's business. I'm here because Reagan needed a favor. We're doing our best to be discreet."

"Are you really? Because I just walked in on the two of you in a very compromising position."

"It's hard for him, putting on this show to protect Trey's feelings. He only agreed to keep us a secret for your daughter, but we *are* trying."

"What happened back then?" Penelope asked, her eyes imploring.

"It isn't my place to say."

"Please help me understand. I just miss my son." Desperation infiltrated every surface of Penelope's face. Her son, her baby boy, could barely stand to come home for holidays. After ten years, the distance was starting to take its toll.

"I can't."

"Is it over a girl?"

"No."

"Money?"

"No, Mrs. Thayer."

"Kensington, please. I'm begging you."

"Okay," she said, taking a seat on the edge of the fountain. Kensie hated to betray Carter's trust, but she also didn't think it was fair that everyone suffered because of Annabelle and Trey. "Do you remember why Carter got into trouble?"

"Of course," Penelope said, sitting next to her. "He destroyed his classmate's car. The damage was in the thousands. It was all John could do to keep him out of jail until after graduation. It was a really tough time for us."

"Sure, but do you know why he did it?"

"No. He was always getting into fights. He used to have such a short fuse that anything would set him off. We were at our wits' end with his behavior. Nothing surprised us. But what does one thing have to do with the other? Was Trey involved?"

"More than involved," Kensie nodded, "Carter wasn't even there."

"But that doesn't make sense. Carter confessed. He had the bat in his room."

"He confessed because he was protecting his friend. He knew no one would question him being responsible, he was the fuck-up and he was taking a gap year anyway."

"So, why the fallout?"

"Because after Carter spent a year in jail so that Trey could follow his dreams, his mother decided that Carter wasn't good enough. The woman who you think is your friend, told her son to cut the trash out of his life, and he listened."

"Annabelle? Why?'" Horror took center stage as Penelope searched through her memories looking for clues.

"You'd have to ask her."

"Why didn't Carter say anything to us? We all assumed…"

"That he did something wrong," Kensie finished, her tone

harsher than she intended it to be.

"I know how it sounds, but you didn't know him when he was younger." A myriad of emotions shone in Penelope's eyes, regret chief among them. Regret for not recognizing the self-loathing that haunted her middle child. Regret for perpetuating those insecurities, regret for being closer over the last ten years to the people who'd wronged her child than she was with her son.

"I know his heart and I know he's still hurting. It's easier for him to stay away. Deep down, buried under all the anger and resentment, he misses his friend. He told me he couldn't take his family from him. That's the man you raised. That's the man I fell in love with."

The sound of a piano in the distance caught Kensie's attention. She recognized the faint melody as the one she'd heard that day in the studio. "I'm going to head back."

"He's lucky to have you, Kensington. We all are."

Kensie smiled sadly, leaving the woman alone to process.

Reagan and Liam stood on the dance floor, their arms wrapped around each other as they swayed to the music.

There were three stools up on the stage. Carter sat in the center, flanked by Javi and Ryder. His hands clung to the microphone stand as he sang her song for his sister and her new husband.

You walking into the bar with stars in your eyes, I knew I was in trouble then, brown-haired girl, red silk hugging your thighs

One night,

It's what I told myself.

One night with you

It was never supposed to last you and I, we were meant to crash, you took my world by surprise, in one night, you opened my eyes.

Kensie watched through blurry eyes as the man of her dreams, her Peter Pan, professed his undying love in front of his friends and family. Her heart was full as the tears fell uncontrollably. Nothing else mattered. The snare kicked in, then the bass, then the horns, and finally the three men on stage sang out,

You're the place between sleep and awake I dream of you always, my happiest thing, you gave me wings.

I spent my entire life chasing Neverland,

Found it in the brown-eyed girl who makes me so high I fear I'll never land.

Was a lost boy before you, Wendy,

You inspired me to be a man.

You're the place between sleep and awake

There I'll wait for you

My best friend

My lover

My Forever.

"It's him, isn't it? Carter?" Trey asked. He was standing in front of her, a tumbler of something dark and strong in his hand. "You left me for Carter fucking Thayer."

TWENTY-FIVE

Losing Control

"I...I don't...I don't know what you're talking about," Kensie stuttered, shaking her head. This wasn't happening. This couldn't be happening. She closed her eyes, willing herself to breathe. She needed to stay calm. They'd been careful—mostly—there's no way he could know.

"Don't treat me like an idiot, and for fuck's sake, stop with the lies," Trey seethed, inches from her face. His brown eyes narrowed in on her, his rage so palpable she felt it bone deep. Gone was the hopeful man who proposed to her just two days prior, and in his place stood a bitter, jilted ex-lover looking for revenge.

"You're being ridiculous," she huffed, "and this isn't the time or place to have this conversation." Her heart was in her throat as she scanned the crowd for a lifeline, a friendly face, to help diffuse the situation before it escalated, or worse, before Carter saw. But there was no one. The longer she stared into those soulless chocolate pools, the more panic began to settle in her stomach. It became clear that she needed to put as much distance between herself and Trey as possible before their hushed tones turned into a full-blown shouting match.

"Carter Thayer is Peter Pan," he mused, more to himself than Kensie. His body shook so violently the ice in his drink rattled.

"What did you say about Peter Pan?" she asked. Her subconscious screamed at her to get the fuck out of there, but her curiosity won out in the end.

How?

How could he know about Peter Pan? There was no way, she never even spoke the name in his presence.

"That morning in my apartment," he shook his head, recalling the memory, "you got up to make coffee and left your phone sitting on the breakfast bar. You were so pissed and I was trying to get you to calm down. I barely even remember. There was a message from Peter Pan. I only caught a glimpse of it out of the corner of my eye. I didn't think anything of it. I just assumed it was a work thing, like how you call Rachel, Cruella de Vil. It didn't even cross my mind again until now, watching you, watching him sing about Neverland. God," he finished, downing the contents of his glass, "all this time he's been fucking you and laughing at me."

"I'm not doing this here," she insisted, brushing past him. He had her and judging by the look on his face, he knew it. Months of secrets, lies, and deleted messages and phone calls. Taking every precaution to keep her infidelity a secret, and he had the key all along, he just didn't realize it opened Pandora's box. Now that he figured it out, now that he'd opened the box, all the ugly things hidden inside had flown out, along with whatever fleeting hope he had of ever getting his girl back.

There was nothing she could say, no way to spin this in her favor, and quite frankly, she didn't want to. She was sick of the lies and the hiding and putting everyone else's feelings above her own. She'd done her part. She donned the dress and smiled as they all judged her, and now she was done. Who said she had to stick around for the party? Getting drunk in her room and talking to Jamie's belly would be more fun than being here with these people anyway.

"No," Trey gritted, grabbing her elbow, "you're going to fucking talk to me." He pulled her forward, guiding her away from the dance floor, away from the sanctuary of the crowd and back towards the path she took when she snuck away to meet Carter before. His strides were long and quick, and soon, she was stumbling to keep the pace.

"Trey—" she yelped, her foot tangled in the long gown, the one that was custom made for another woman, a woman who was two inches taller. Kensie fell forward landing on all fours, a garish ripping sound pierced her ears as angry tears pooled in her brown eyes. "Stop this right now," she pleaded, looking up at him, completely at his mercy.

"That's not going to work this time, sweetheart." His voice dripped with venom as he wrapped his fingers around her forearm and hoisted her to her feet. He regarded her for a moment, sadness and anger battled for dominion. His love for her—his hate—both left invisible scars on his handsome face.

"You're causing a scene." She was hoping to appeal to the rational man she'd known for the past year. To the man who looked before he leaped, the man who thought through every decision before choosing the best possible outcome. But one look at his hard face told her that man was gone. The Trey she knew had vanished, and in his place, was the teenage boy who committed felony vandalism over a girl who never really loved him. It was déjà vu, high school all over again.

Trey looked around, most of the wedding guests were standing in a semi-circle surrounding the dance floor. They watched Reagan dance with her father, unaware of the conflict raging on behind them.

Kensie took his temporary distraction as a chance to break free, but his grip on her was tight. "You are going to talk to me, so we can do it here, in front of everybody, or you can come with me."

"I don't owe you anything."

"Always so fucking stubborn," he snapped, bending down and throwing her over his shoulder. That's when it happened. That's when her blood ran cold. She didn't need to look to the stage to know he was watching, she felt his gaze. "Please, just put me down." She fought, digging her nails into his back.

Trey tutted, dismissing her attempts to break free. His hand grazed her bottom, holding her to him as he carried her away from the reception. The last thing she saw before they exited the garden was Carter's face as he threw the mic stand down and hopped off the stage. The fury and resentment that had been slowly simmering these past ten years finally boiled over.

"Is that what you like?" Trey growled, pushing forward through the vineyard. If he was aware that Carter was following them, his voice didn't betray it. "You like being treated like a whore, don't you? You could have just told me. I can fuck you like a whore too."

"You're being an asshole." She pounded her fists into his back, but he only squeezed tighter. Almost as if he could just hold on tight enough, everything would go back to normal, his world would be right.

"And you're an idiot if you think he really loves you."

"I was an idiot to think I could ever love a man like you. You don't know him the way I know him. Now put me down and I'll try to convince him not to fuck up your face, much," she added with a sneer.

He laughed, a cold and hollow laugh, dropping her on her feet. "I know him better than anyone. You forget there was a time when we were inseparable. I know all his deep dark shit and he knows mine. Just because you've given him a few blowjobs doesn't mean that he's been magically transformed into a good person."

"I get that I hurt you, I do, but fuck you. You're the last person I'd look to for advice on someone's character. Especially when you're acting like a jerk." She was sorry for the pain she'd caused, and maybe she deserved his anger, but she wouldn't stand for the name calling and slut shaming, and she certainly wouldn't let him reduce her relationship to a petty revenge plot.

"I thought that's what you wanted? A jerk, like Carter? I can be that. We perfected it in high school." He grabbed her ass and pulled her to him, his mouth crashing down onto hers.

"Get off me," she growled, biting his tongue. She was going to tell him to go fuck himself. She was going to tell him that if he ever put his hands on her again, she'd cut off his balls, but before she got the chance, a tattooed fist went flying into Trey's jaw.

"Are you okay?" Carter asked, looking her up and down, panicked. She could only imagine what she must look like. Tear stains streaking her makeup, lipstick smudged from Trey's kiss and a rip in her dress that ran up the length of her leg. "Baby, did he hurt you? I swear I'll kill him if he hurt you."

"I'm fine. I just want to get out of here." She said it because it was true. She wasn't hurt, not physically, not emotionally, even her pride was still intact. She had already shed all the tears that she ever would for Trey Knight. He ruined any sympathy she had left for him when he forced himself on her. She was done, and she wouldn't make apologies for her happiness any longer.

"No, stay," Trey sneered, wiping at the blood on the corner of his mouth.

"Carter, tell our girl to stay." He was a man possessed, driven mad by betrayal.

"Back the fuck off, Knight." Carter's voice was deadly, as he took a protective stance in front of Kensie.

The air under the setting Napa sun was impossibly thick. The two men stood almost nose-to-nose, both mentally preparing for a bloodbath in one of the most serene places on earth. The lights from the courtyard twinkled, a spotlight showcasing the main event.

"Or what? You won. You stole my girl and got your revenge, congratulations," Trey boiled, giving CT a round of applause. "Ten years too late, but hey, I deserved it, right?"

"It isn't like that," Kensie said from behind Carter. She looked to him for confirmation, but he was focused solely on Trey, some unnamed emotion flashing in his eyes. "This isn't about you."

"Oh, come on, Kensington, you went to USC, you aren't that fucking stupid."

"Call her stupid again, I dare you." Carter's fist clenched at his side. That emotion, the one she couldn't decipher, it was still there.

"You're taking this a little far aren't you? You fucked her. You proved your point. I get it. We're even."

"That's enough." Kensie, Carter, and Trey all turned, finding Penelope standing in the courtyard, flanked by her eldest son and daughter.

"What the fuck?" Reagan cried. There was only one word to describe the look on her perfectly painted face, devastation. Her big day, her moment, ruined. They promised their shit wouldn't spill over onto her, but there they all were, knee-deep in it.

"What on earth is going on?" Annabelle huffed, coming from behind. "John and Thomas are doing what they can to contain the situation. Hopefully your felon won't embarrass us any further."

"Annabelle," Grant warned.

"No, son, please let me," Penelope said in a voice so controlled it made Kensie wince. This moment was ten years in the making and neither Carter nor Trey nor Annabelle knew that the cat was out of the bag. Hell, the cat was halfway to Mexico.

"The only embarrassment here is you and *your* felon," she said, cutting her eyes to a shocked Trey. "Kensington could never be happy with an opportunist like you, get over it."

"Excuse me?" Annabelle gasped, looking to her friend of thirty-plus years.

"You heard me. I know all about what really happened all those years ago, and I see right through you, down to your nasty, narcissistic core. You're lucky my daughter loves your son, or else, I'd make it my personal mission to destroy you. But make no mistake, if you or your evil spawn over there ever speak to Carter that way again, you'll regret it for the rest of your miserable life."

"Mom?" Reagan questioned Penelope with wide eyes. "You know?"

"Yes, it seems as if your brother went to jail for a crime he didn't commit."

"What?" Reagan and Grant shrieked at the same time.

"His only sin was being loyal to that selfish...asshat." The word didn't sound right coming from Penelope's mouth. It was so out of character that it made Annabelle take a step back, unsure of how to proceed.

"Dude, is this true?" Grant barked, taking a step towards Trey. His mother caught his wrist, and with a slight nod towards Reagan, reminded him of where they were.

Silence befell the courtyard, as everyone gaped at the two poised women sizing each other up. No, they wouldn't throw a single punch, nor would they raise their voices above an acceptable octave. Years of ingrained manners wouldn't allow for them to behave so commonly, but they would wage war; one fought at charity events and in social clubs. One fought with power and prestige. Their battle would be epic, and Kensie wasn't sure Seattle was large enough to contain the fallout. But for now, the masks were firmly in place, they had a wedding to host after all.

"Carter, dear," Penelope called.

He swallowed, misty-eyed, looking at his mother, his protector again, for the first time in a decade. "Yes, Mother."

"I'm sure Ryder and Javi can perform without you, right?" He nodded slowly. "Good, enjoy the rest of your night with your gorgeous girlfriend." She smiled, twisting the knife further into Annabelle's chest, before heading back to the reception.

"That was intense," Kensie said after a long, uncomfortable silence. They'd ridden up the elevator in it. They changed out of their wedding clothes and bathed in it, her in yoga pants and a white tee and him in a pair of gym shorts. Now they sat on the couch in the two-room suite stewing in it.

It was maddening. She couldn't read his stoic face. He was lost in his thoughts, no doubt replaying the events of the day.

"How's your hand?" Kensie asked. It was bleeding, split open from the force with which it had connected with Trey's jaw. She got up to retrieve a damp towel from the bathroom, then returned to clean the wound, split for the second time in as many days.

"Thank you," he murmured, pressing a kiss to her temple.

She shrugged, unsure if he meant thanks for cleaning his hand or thanks for telling his mother the thing he never could. "Does it hurt?" she asked. She wasn't talking about his hand.

"No, it looks worse than it feels."

It was quiet, again. Eerily so, like the end of days. She didn't know what to feel or think or even what to say. Everything was out in the open, everyone knew and what would happen next, she wasn't sure.

The rational side of her brain knew that these secrets and lies had been left to fester for far too long, but she couldn't help thinking that she'd opened this can of worms. Had she kept her mouth shut and her legs closed, none of this would have happened.

"Hey," Carter said, taking the blood-stained towel from her hand, "don't do that."

"Do what?" she asked averting her gaze. How did he always know? He could read her like a book and, yet, she still felt wholly out of depth when it came to him.

"This shit isn't on you, baby."

"I should have never said anything to your mother. I just couldn't tell her no. I know what it's like to be absent from you and we were only broken up for a short while. I can't imagine the pain she must have felt."

"No, I'm glad you told her. I'm glad it's out. I almost feel like I can breathe again."

"Almost?" she asked. What else could there possibly be?

Now it was his turn to look away. He tossed the towel on the table and grabbed her hand, before pulling her onto his lap. She rested her forehead against his, waiting for him to speak, unsure of what he might say.

"I don't deserve you," he whispered.

"You deserve more than me."

"I will love you forever."

"Ditto," she smiled, kissing the tip of his nose, "but we aren't getting married yet," she teased, needing to lighten the mood. They'd spent enough time in the shadows, and despite the chaos that raged on under the Napa Valley stars, they were finally free. No more heavy shit. No more secrets. No more lies.

"Yet?" His lips touched hers. His scent, masculine with a hint of whiskey, invaded her senses.

"Eventually." Another kiss, this one tasted of desperation. Sad, blue eyes found her brown. "Let's just be happy."

"There isn't anything I want more in this world, but first I have to tell you something and I'm scared shitless."

"Anything," she assured, although the look in his eyes told her this wasn't going to be a good something. In fact, she regretted the word as soon as it escaped her lips.

"I knew who you were." His voice was a whisper.

"What?"

Confusion.

Another kiss.

More sadness.

"The night we met, I recognized you from a picture on Reagan's Instagram. You and Trey and her and Liam, on Memorial Day."

"What?" She stood, raking her fingers through her stiff hair, sticky from the hair spray the stylist had used. She knew the picture well. It was taken downstairs at the onsite restaurant, when they'd visited in the spring. The trip was the turning point in her and Trey's relationship. It was also when Annabelle finally accepted it. She was the one who had snapped the picture. That trip meant so much to her, she had it framed and kept it on her desk at work.

"I knew who you were and I fucked you because of it." Finally, he breathed. His final confession released into the atmosphere like a noxious gas.

"You knew the entire time," she coughed, choking on his words.

"Yes."

"Now what, you're breaking up with me? Or were we really ever together?" That was the million-dollar question. Did he ever really love her or was this all some elaborate scheme gone too far. Was she a casualty of their war? Or did she hand herself to the enemy on a silver platter?

"I love you, you know that." He stood, stalking towards her. The pain was there, the regret, but also, the determination. That unnerved her.

"When?" she barked, pushing her palm into his bare chest. His heart pounded beneath her, a frantic rhythm that reminded her of her favorite Lithium song. It would have been poetic had it not been so tragic.

"When, what?" His knuckle grazed her cheek as he took another step forward, and then another and another until he closed the space between them. He clutched his hand on top of hers, pulling it from his heart, eliminating the last of her defense.

"When did it stop being about revenge?" Kensie croaked. Her voice sounded as broken as she felt.

"My attraction to you was real, my feelings for you *are* real. It's just my motives then weren't as pure as they are now." He made it sound simple. Like ABCs and 123s. Like his confession hadn't shattered what was left of their trust. Like it wasn't the iceberg that sank their unsinkable ship.

"Okay, but when did it stop being about revenge?" she repeated. "When I told you I was falling in love with you? When I was sick, and we decided to try again? In the van when you spilled your soul to me?" she yelled.

"I don't know, but the thought of leaving made it real. Us going on tour, and the possibility that you might not want to wait for me, that gutted me. I knew then that you were the most important thing in my life and that losing you would be the hardest thing I'd ever done. Harder than the year I spent in jail and harder than the ten I spent keeping my family at arm's length. I knew I had to let that shit go because you deserve better. Baby, I love you." His lips found hers, his tongue prodding at her mouth, begging for entrance, for forgiveness.

"But not enough." She had to be strong. She refused to lose herself again, not when she'd just found the real Kensie.

He swallowed her words like a bitter pill. "Don't say that. It isn't like that and you know it. What we have is real."

"How?" she asked, ignoring him. "How did you even know I would be at your show or did you plan that too?"

"No, I swear it was a coincidence. I didn't even know you and Jamie were friends, but when I saw you on my birthday, I thought it was a gift, a reward for ten years of loyalty."

"What was the plan?" A debate raged on in her head. She needed to know, but his answer, regardless of what it was, would destroy them.

"Kensington."

"Tell me how you planned on ruining my life," she insisted.

"I took a picture of you in my arms after you fell asleep. I was going to send it to him."

"Why didn't you?"

"Because, baby," he cried, placing a palm on each of her cheeks, "I wasn't ready to lose you."

"Because you wanted to fuck me again." Tears rolled down her cheeks fat and warm, the dam broke. Her façade shattered.

"Yes, I wanted to fuck you again, and I wanted to hear you laugh again, and I wanted to taste you again, and I wanted to hold you in my arms again. I wanted more. I was falling for you even then. It's just I've been carrying this vendetta around for years and you fell into my lap and I just thought…"

"You thought since you couldn't take his family, you'd settle for me." It was more a statement than a question. All the dots connected in her mind. Suddenly, his possessiveness made sense. God, she really was an idiot. She fell for his bullshit, hook, line, and sinker.

Carter's hands roamed her body, his touch searing her skin. He explored her, seeking redemption in the only way he knew how. Down her shoulders, around her chest and then up and under her shirt. "It's not settling. I was stupid and impulsive, but I never once lied about how I felt."

"Just about everything else." She leaned into him, relishing the contact. Their time was nearly up. Their story almost done, but damned if she didn't want to stay.

"What can I do?" *Kiss.* "Tell me." *Kiss.* "I'll do anything."

Kiss.

Kiss.

Kiss.

"You can't fuck me and expect me to forget that you lied and manipulated me," she cried into his mouth.

"I know, I fucked up. I'm so sorry, please give me another chance," he pleaded, burying his head into her neck, his tears dampening her skin.

"You're not a man of your word. You're not a good person. You're no better than him. And you and I are done, forever, *Friend*."

TWENTY-SIX

Resentment

It had been four weeks since the wedding from hell, and Kensie felt like a *Walking Dead* reject. She'd spent the last thirty days wandering around life like a zombie. Undead. Stuck. She wasn't living, not really, not for the past month, but she wasn't dead inside either. Numbness would be welcomed, but no, she felt every ounce of the pain and the heartache and the resentment she deserved. Karma was a heartless bitch.

Kensie hoped that she would be over it by now. They'd only dated for a few months, so why did it still hurt? The breakup rule, per *Sex in the City*, stated that it took half the total time you went out with someone to get over them, but Kensie felt as crushed today as she had felt that day in Napa.

If only it were that easy. If only love and heartbreak could be quantified by a simple equation. But the problem with the breakup rule was that it didn't account for anomalies. It didn't account for Carter Thayer.

A few months was all it took. Months of guilt and shame and pain and blowjob gates, and still she fell so helplessly and completely in love. *In love with a man who only wanted to destroy your world,* she reminded herself bitterly. She'd set out to find herself and had ended up even more lost than ever before.

Her day-to-day life had become monotonous. Work. Home. Sleep. Repeat. Work was the only thing that lessened the agony. Her new job at Safe Haven was the only good that came out of her time with *Him*.

Kensie glanced at her watch, five thirty on a Friday afternoon, and her weekend off. Weekends were the worst. Those were the times when she felt most alone. With no work to distract her, she was forced to deal with the harsh reality.

She shook her head, willing her brain to focus on the six boys running around the backyard. "You're still here?" Tanner asked, peeking his head out the door. His kind blue eyes assessed her. He was too polite to prod, but even a blind man could see the devastation hidden beneath her irises.

"Oh, I'm just telling the boys goodbye," she said, forcing a smile onto her face. She'd stayed late every night that week, helping with dinner, or cleaning, or just hanging out with the kids and playing. She was still learning the subtle nuances of her new role, part-caregiver, part-administrator, and part-consoler, but she loved every minute of it. Currently, there were nine boys living in the safe house, but they could shelter up to fifteen. Some days were hard, some of the stories were brutal, but Kensie finally felt like she was making a difference.

"Good. Go home, have fun. You're too young to be a workaholic. It's going to be a beautiful weekend, so get out and enjoy it, kiddo. See ya Monday."

"See ya," she whispered sadly as she watched him disappear back inside the house. She said goodbye to her boys and headed out to her car. The drive from Safe Haven to her and Jamie's apartment was torture. Traffic moved at a snail's pace as she navigated her Mercedes through the city. "DRIVE!" she yelled, laying on the horn. "Green means go, asshole!"

Relax, Kensie, she coached herself, because if not, she feared she wouldn't make it through gridlock without committing a felony. *She'd be a felon, like Him.* Her brain, when left up to its own devices for too long, always strayed back to Him. She shook the thought out of her mind and turned up the radio, praying the noise would be a welcomed escape.

Welcome back to Power 93, Seattle's number one hit music station. You're listening to Big Mike and this is Big Mike's Rush Hour Mix. I have a treat for all you commuters out there this evening. Today in the studio, I am joined by three of the most handsome dudes I've ever seen. Please give it up for Seattle's very own Ryder, Javi, and CT. Lithium Springs, ladies and gentlemen.

"No. No. No. No," Kensie chanted as tears prickled in her eyes. She'd had a good week. No lunchtime crying fits in the bathroom, and no drinking until she passed out, and this is how fate decided to reward her. The evil bitch was almost as bad as her sister, karma.

She should just turn it off. She really wanted to turn it off, but she was a glutton for punishment.

"Welcome, guys," Big Mike greeted.

"Thank you," the three men said in unison.

"So, the tour starts next week. How does it feel to be opening for The Unburned?"

Ryder took that one. *"I think I can speak for all of us when I say it's a dream come true. I mean, Wiley White. He's a pioneer, a legend."*

"I take it you guys are fans of The Unburned?"

"Hell yes," Javi chimed in, *"I think every kid growing up in the Pacific Northwest has at one point or another wanted to be in a grudge band. It's a sound that is so uniquely Seattle and it helped bond us. We came from different backgrounds, but the one thing we had in common was that we felt out of place. We were three misfits looking for somewhere to belong."*

"Tell me about your next project. I gotta say, I listened to it earlier and it's out of this world, but it's a new sound for you guys. What inspired it?"

"CT, you wanna take this one, bro?" Ryder purred into the mic in that voice that made women's panties melt.

Kensie felt the tightness in her chest as she prepared herself to hear his voice. She had the same reaction every time she heard it since the wedding. He called her every night, and every night she'd send him to voicemail. Her subconscious told her to delete the messages, or better yet, block his number, but she couldn't. She wasn't strong enough. She wasn't brave.

Some nights, he'd leave messages apologizing for his wrongdoings and he'd beg for forgiveness. Other nights, he'd tell her about his day or sing songs that reminded him of her, and sometimes he'd just wait. Those calls were the hardest. The ones where all she heard was his breathing, all she felt was his pain. It was on those nights that her resolve waned. She had the power to ease their suffering, but the price was too great. Her self-worth came at a higher cost than a few sympathetic words left on her answering machine.

"*My girl inspired it,*" he said in a scratchy voice, far from the cocky bastard she'd known. "*I wrote most of it about her, our love, our breakup...*" He trailed off, leaving that last part hanging thick in the air.

"*Aww, dude, you just broke a million hearts,*" Big Mike teased, cutting the tension.

"A million and one," Kensie muttered sadly. Traffic continued to crawl as Big Mike asked the guys more questions about the album and the tour. Kensie only half-listened while they played a silly game of would you rather. She was so lost in her thoughts that she didn't realize she was crying until she felt the hot tears roll down her chin. She missed him, but there was just too much to forgive, too much to forget.

"*Alright, this has been fun, but let's give the people what they want, a Power 93 exclusive. You guys want to do the honor?*"

"*Yeah, this is the title track and first single off our upcoming album. It's called Neverland.*" Ryder introduced the record in that too cool rockstar voice of his.

Kensie turned the radio off. She couldn't listen to that song, her song. She'd rather the silence consume her than to drown in the memories. Memories so tangled up in deceit that she couldn't decipher what was real and what was fake.

Was it all fake? That was the question that kept her up at night. He said that his feelings were real, that his love was real, but how could it be when he had an ulterior motive?

The day after his birthday party, when Trey called her, he knew who was on the phone the entire time. *Is that why he got so angry?* He fingered her while she talked to her boyfriend. He wanted Trey to hear her moaning. God, she was a fucking idiot. He told her over and over that Trey didn't deserve her. Why didn't she see it then? Why didn't she pay attention to any of the signs? In hindsight, everything was so blatantly obvious. Was she really that stupid or was she blinded by lies?

She spent the last four weeks picking apart their time together. She questioned everything, every word, every action. She hated him for what he did, but the worst part was that she let him. She opened her legs willingly, knowing she had a boyfriend, and now she was suffering the consequences. As much as she hated him, she hated herself more.

Finally, after nearly forty minutes in gridlock, she made it home. All she wanted was to drink the bottle of red wine she had stashed in the kitchen and sleep for the next two days. She flipped on the light switch and as expected, Jam was M.I.A.

Though she hadn't officially moved out—Ryder didn't want her to be alone while the guys went on tour—Jamie was rarely at the apartment. She was either on assignment or with her husband. Kensie didn't begrudge her, though. Of course, she wanted to spend time with Ryder before he left for three months, and as much as she missed her friend, seeing Ryder only reminded her of Him.

That was her life post-apocalypse. Drinking in excess and avoiding anything and anyone who conjured up *His* memory.

Him, Douchebag, Asshole, and Fuckface were the only acceptable pronouns to describe the man who set out to destroy her life.

Kensie made a beeline for the kitchen to retrieve her wine. The stress and tension of having a nervous breakdown in rush hour traffic had taken a toll, but she was home alone, and after a long week of pretending, she was exhausted. Her body was finally starting to relax. She looked forward to putting on her pajamas and drinking straight from the bottle. As much as she hated being by herself, it was nice to just be sad.

With her wine in hand, she went to the bathroom to run the water for a bath. As she stripped out of her clothes, she wondered if it would always be this way. If this unhappiness was her new normal. She wore her depression like a badge of courage. She'd gone through something horrific and, somehow, she was still standing. Well, sort of...not really. Either way, she was going to indulge in the decadence of sadness and grief. *Fuck the breakup rule*, she thought. She was miserable, and she wasn't going to apologize for it.

The bath products were neatly aligned on the ledge. She'd gotten rid of both the Coco Mademoiselle and the Whole Foods lavender wash. They went out the window the day she got back from Napa. Add her favorite shower gel to the ever-growing list of things that Fuckface had ruined for her.

Showers.
Pop-Tarts.
The radio.
Peter Pan.
Sex.
Sex.
Sex.

She hated that he'd ruined sex for her. She couldn't even climax without thinking of *Him*. One night, she masturbated to his voicemail. After she came, she spent the rest of the night sobbing.

"You're pathetic," she said to herself, reaching for the LUSH bubble bar to crumble under the stream.

"I wouldn't say pathetic," Jamie offered, leaning against the doorjamb. She looked as gorgeous as always. Her blonde hair pulled up into a high ponytail and her white blouse unbuttoned at the top.

"Hi, what are you doing here? I thought you'd be with Ry." *I hoped you'd be with Ryder so that I could get drunk and ugly cry in solitude.*

"Nope," she chirped pushing up off the door. "I think my bestie needs me more."

"I'm fine, Jam. He's leaving soon and you'll be stuck with me for three months. You guys have already spent enough time apart," she added sadly. After Napa, Jam went on a rampage. Pregnant Jamie was even scarier than normal Jamie. She and Ryder got into a huge fight over them, even though neither he nor Javi had any idea what Fuckface was up to, but he was his best friend, Kensie was hers, and lines were drawn in the sand. "He'll be able to survive without me for one night."

"I'm fine, really. I'm just going to take a bath and go to bed. I probably won't be very good company."

"Kensie, I know how it feels to want to drink the pain away—trust me, I get it—but you can't keep doing this. Let's go out."

"Jamie," Kensie groaned shutting off the water, "I'm not in the mood for people." Translation, she wasn't in the mood to pretend. People looked at her funny when she wasn't pretending, when she wore her heartbreak on her sleeve. It made them uncomfortable and if one more person told her to smile, she was going to fucking snap.

"Kensington Grace Roth, you've got to get it together."

Kensie shot her a look, one that said, *my boyfriend confessed to sleeping with me to get revenge on his childhood best friend and I'll cry if I want to.*

"I don't mean you can't be unhappy," Jam raised her hands in surrender. "What I'm saying is it's time to rejoin the land of the living. All you do is go to work and come home. The only excitement you get is Sunday dinner in Madison Park, binge watching eighties sitcoms with your dad."

"What's wrong with that? All you do is work."

"I have a life outside of work. I go out. I have fun."

You have a husband, Kensie added mentally. "I just want to sulk."

"I already called Quinn. I'm going to change."

"Jam," Kensie called after her friend.

"Get dressed!"

"Jam!"

Silence

"James!"

She was going to strangle her.

Forty-five minutes later, Kensie was dressed and found herself sitting in front of a blank canvas, regretting her decision to leave the house. Paint night, it sounded like a good idea. There was wine, and for once, she wasn't drinking alone, but now that she sat around the large rectangular table, she wanted to die.

They were in a small art studio in downtown, The Station. There was an adjoining gallery next door where the staff, comprised of local artists, sold their original works. On the studio side, they taught couples and drunk girls how to recreate classics, and hosted children's birthday parties. The walls of the studio were lined with paintings of varying shapes and sizes, showcasing the many different options to choose from. Tonight, they were painting dandelions. A weed. A visual reminder of the sun's power during the darkest days. A symbol of hope. *Of course, even the painting was screaming at her to move on.*

Aside from Kensie and her friends, there were about ten other people at the table, two couples, a pair of sisters, and another group of women sporting Lithium Springs gear. Among them was one Rabbit Hole bartender and Fuckface's former friend with benefits.

"I can't believe Tiff is here," Kensie whisper-hissed to Jam.

"I swear I didn't know." The blonde looked appropriately contrite.

"I just wanted to do something I thought you'd enjoy, something different."

Tiff smirked at her, whispering something to the girl to her left. The girl turned to look at Kensie and sneered.

"So did they," Kensie snipped, grabbing the glass of wine the instructor set in front of Jamie and downed it. It wasn't like Jam could drink it anyway.

"Welcome to paint night," a tattooed girl with violet hair greeted the room. "My name's Maddy and this is the picture we are going to paint tonight," she explained, holding up the painting of two dandelions blowing in the wind against a blue sky. It looked easy enough, but Kensie was only there for the wine.

"First, we are going to start with the background, so taking your second to largest brush, you'll want to dip it in the blue and with a light hand, gently brush it across your canvas."

Everyone did as they were told and the instructor went on, telling them which colors to place where on the board and which brush to use. Before she knew it, the first hour passed. They had a fifteen-minute break for snacks and wine refills while they waited for their canvases to dry.

"See, this wasn't so bad, right?" Quinn asked, grabbing a cupcake from the snack table set up in the back of the room.

"I'd still rather be home drinking on the couch, but it's actually kind of fun," Kensie admitted. She lurched forward as someone brushed past her, causing her to spill wine on her shirt.

"I can't wait for tonight," Tiff squealed in a sugar voice that was anything but sweet. "The guys were awesome on *Big Mike*. They are going to rock the stage tonight, then I'm going to rock CT's world." She was talking to her friend, but her eyes were trained on Kensie.

Fuck you.

Fuck you.

Fuck you!

Kensie chanted in her head. More karma. She was a bitch to Tiff before, and now the bartender was getting her payback. *Way to kick me when I'm down.* Kensie swallowed past the lump in her throat. Yes, they broke up, and yes, he could do whatever the fuck he wanted, but she could barely pull it together for work and he was sleeping with other people?

"He's like totally obsessed with you," Tiff's friend said.

Jamie turned to the two cackling bitches. "What the fuck is your problem?"

"This isn't about you, Kitty Cat," Tiff said.

"You made it my problem when you pushed my friend. I like you—*you know that*—but Ken is my family."

Kensie downed another glass of wine. "It's fine. I'm fine." She wasn't. It wasn't, but her new motto was fake it until it doesn't hurt anymore. She grabbed Quinn and Jam by the arm and led them back to their seats, hoping to avoid further embarrassment. "Are you guys going to the party tonight?" she asked, partly to change the subject, and partly because she wanted them to go and cockblock Fuckface.

Jam and Quinn looked at each other in confusion. "How do you know about the party?" Jam asked cautiously. There was going to be a farewell party for the guys at the Rabbit Hole. Tonight, was their last performance until after the tour.

"Him," Kensie said nonchalantly. She could feel her face heat. She put a moratorium on all things Lithium Springs and Fuckface-related for weeks, and now she was bringing it up so that her friends could spy for her. She knew it was illogical. She knew she didn't have a right to be jealous, but she still loved him. She hated his fucking guts, but she loved him all the same.

"I thought you weren't talking to him."

"I'm not!" Kensie defended as her friends narrowed their eyes. "I'm not talking to him, but he calls and I listen to the messages."

"How often does he call?" Jam pressed. Her inquisitiveness made her a great reporter, but an annoying friend.

"Like…I don't," Kensie ran her fingers through her hair, "every night, I guess."

"Babe," Jam admonished.

"What?" *I'm pathetic? I'm weak? I'm an idiot? I know.*

"I thought you wanted to move on."

"I do. I *am* moving on." It was a lie. She knew it and her friends knew it too.

"You're never going to get over him if you're listening to his voicemails every night and stalking his Instagram all day."

"I. Do. Not." Another lie. She made the account specifically to stalk him. Old habits.

"You do. You've never had Instagram and now, suddenly, you're on it ten times a day."

"I just…I miss him." Finally, the truth. "What would you do?"

"You know what I'd do," Jam said matter-of-factly. Jam didn't tolerate lying, at all, ever. Lucky for her, Ryder was honest, at times brutally so, but it worked for them.

"What about you?" she asked, tipping her chin toward Quinn. She and Quinn bonded in Napa and despite being directly related to Fuckface, Kensie really cherished her friendship.

"I don't know, Ken. I'm biased. He loves you. He fucked up, but I don't think it's something you can't get past."

"He used me."

"You used him, too," she countered. "You used him as an escape. You weren't happy in your relationship and instead of ending it…" She stopped talking, she didn't need to finish. The reality was harsh enough without voicing it.

"But I was upfront about that." Kensie's voice cracked. *Don't Cry. Don't Cry.*

"He confessed. He didn't have to," Quinn countered, softly. She ran her hand down Kensie's shoulder. It was comforting, but it only made Kensie's eyes burn more.

"She has a point there," Jam agreed.

"I don't think I can trust him," she whispered. Another truth, and that one did it. That one broke the dam and the tears flowed freely.

"You're trapped in purgatory. Either tell him to back off or give him a chance, but you can't survive like this," Jam said, wiping the tears away from Kensie's big doe eyes.

She nodded, pulling out her cell phone.

Kensie: You need to stop calling me.

His reply was immediate.

Fuckface: Baby, please talk to me. Tell me what can I do? I'll do anything.

Kensie: Let me move on.

Fuckface: I can't do that.

Kensie: You've moved on, why can't I?

Fuckface: Baby, I'm a fucking mess. I will never move on from you. You're it for me, you know that.

Kensie: I'm staring at your girlfriend right now.

Fuckface: Are you looking in the mirror?

Kensie: Don't play dumb.

Kensie looked up from her phone to see a carefree Tiff laughing with her friends. She used to be that girl, the girl who found humor in the most mundane things. The girl who enjoyed being around people, around friends. Instead, she was this mopey shell of a woman, watching from the sidelines.

Tiff threw her head back in laughter, and her long black hair fell from her shoulders, exposing her neck, exposing the large purple bruise on her throat. The sight of that hickey gutted Kensie.

Fuckface: Baby, I'm glad you're talking to me but I have no idea what you're talking about.

Kensie: Tiff, and it seems as if I'm not the only one you like to mark.

She dropped her phone back onto the table and picked up her paint brush, determined to salvage what was left of her night. *Asshole. I hate him. He probably calls you every night after he fucks her. Fucking douchebag.*

"Now that the background has had a chance to dry, we are going to work on the dandelions," the instructor said, beginning again. Kensie tried to focus on what the woman was saying. She poured her emotions onto the canvas. Her brushstrokes were harsh, giving what was supposed to be an ethereal painting a hard edge. Her eyes wandered back to her phone, the *new message* notification taunted her.

Fuckface: Tiff has never been and will never be my girlfriend.

Kensie: Got it. You're just fucking her. I'm home every night crying my eyes out while you're balls deep in someone else.

Fuckface: I am not fucking her or anyone else.

Kensie: It's fine. We broke up.

Fuckface: You're pissed. You need time, but you never stopped being mine and I never stopped being yours.

Kensie: YOU HAVE TO STOP THIS! We broke up because you lied to me. I don't trust you.

Kensie put her phone down and grabbed Quinn's glass of wine.

"How'd you do that?" she asked, pointing to her friend's canvas. Somewhere along the way, she must have missed a step.

"You two are hopeless," Quinn huffed, dipping her brush in the white acrylic, fixing Kensie's painting.

"I'm trying to get him to leave me alone."

"Sure you are." The redhead rolled her eyes.

Fuckface: I'm not Prince Charming. I'm not the hero. You knew that from the beginning, but got past it then, why can't you at least try now?

Kensie: That was different. This isn't healthy.

Fuckface: Fuck that. I love you. You love me. Why can't we be together?

Kensie: Please stop this. Don't make me have to block you.

Fuckface: Kensington, I need you. Even if it's just talking to your voicemail. I need to feel connected to you.

Kensie: I guess I have no choice.

Fuckface: Don't do this. Please

Fuckface: Please

Fuckface: I'm sorry.

Fuckface: I love you. You're my best friend. Please.

Kensie swiped angrily at the tears leaking out of her eyes. This had to stop. She needed time to herself and as much as she hated to admit it, he needed to move on.

Kensie: I love you. I probably always will, but love isn't enough. I need to know I can trust you.

Fuckface: Don't do this.

Kensie: Enjoy your life. Have fun on tour. You won't even miss me once you're gone.

Before she could talk herself out of it, she blocked his number and then deleted his contact information. She deleted the text chain and every picture of him, except the one they took that day at Gas Works. Was it all a lie? She didn't know. She'd like to think he was sincere then, in the van, and under the stars, but it didn't matter now. They were over. He was leaving and she needed to start living again, this time for herself.

TWENTY-SEVEN

I Fall Apart

"Is this what you want, Kensington?" he asked, walking her backwards. Her legs hit the edge of the bed as she took in the sight of him. Broad shoulders covered in ink, hard chest rubbing against hers, and a face so handsome that it physically hurt to look at him too long. The perfect mix of blue collar and blue blood.

"Yes," she moaned, pulling his mouth down on to hers. He tasted like cinnamon and spice, but there was nothing nice about the way he licked into her mouth. Nothing sweet about the long, lazy strokes he used to claim her.

"You want me to fuck you?" he asked, wrapping his long, calloused fingers around her neck.

"Mmm," was the only response she could muster. It was a heady combination, his tongue dancing with hers, his hands wrapped around her throat like ivy, his scent, clean, with a hint of fireball whiskey. All of it too much, but somehow, not enough. She would never get enough of him. She'd spend the rest of her life with him buried deep inside of her because the opposite, the emptiness, was unfathomable.

"Does he fuck you like I fuck you?" he grunted. His voice hard, almost angry. Like the thought of someone else fucking her drove him mad, but the thought of Trey fucking her pushed him past his *limit*—took him to a dark place.

Kensie shook her head, ignoring the devil hiding behind his blue eyes. She wasn't blind to the devil, not if she was being honest with herself, she'd always known about it. It was there, even in the beginning, but his pull was just too strong. "No one has ever fucked me like you fuck me," she answered. Not because he needed to hear it, but because it was true.

Smirking, he pulled her Lithium shirt over her head, exposing her breasts. Her nipples were so tight, they were almost painful. He eyed her body like she was his plaything, a toy he'd stolen from his friend. A toy he had every intention on breaking.

"Is this mine?" he asked, dipping his hand into her panties. It was rhetorical, of course it was his. It was his since the moment he made up his mind to take her. "I want to hear you say it," he growled. His fingers slid through her folds as he rubbed her, spreading her wetness up to her clit, not too fast, not too slow. His mouth ducked down to her chest. He tugged on her right nipple with his teeth, biting and licking her. Her legs began to tremble as he moved over to her left nipple, giving it the same treatment.

"Of course, it's yours," she whined, "but now that he knows, do you still want it? Do you still want me?"

"Fuck," Kensie hissed, shooting up out of bed. She was wet, from sweat, from tears, and from need. "God, this is so fucked up," she gasped, running her fingers through her hair. It wasn't the first time that she'd had a sex dream about *Him* since they split, but it affected her all the same.

She eyed the clock on her bedside table. Ten o'clock on a Sunday morning, a new day, and she made a promise to herself and to Jam that today would be better. Today, she would try to get back to some semblance of normalcy.

Throwing the covers back, Kensie threw her arms up over her head. Step one in rejoining the real world was a shower, a very long and very cold shower. She needed to wash away the desire, and the regret, and the anger.

Once she was all cleaned up, she got dressed in real clothes, not work clothes, not sweatpants or pajamas, but a pair of shorts and a t-shirt that hung off her shoulder. She put on makeup for the first time in a month, mascara, lip gloss, and blush, then she tied her hair into a high ponytail.

It wasn't fancy, she didn't look like the perfectly polished princess she portrayed when she was with Trey, or like a girl who belonged backstage at rock and roll concerts. It wasn't much, but it was Kensie. She slipped on her sandals, grabbed her bag and headed out of her room. The apartment was quiet. She assumed Jam was still in bed, or at the guys' house, but as Kensie rounded the corner toward the kitchen, she spotted Ryder pouring himself a cup of coffee.

"Hey," she said, choosing an apple from the bowl of fruit on the breakfast bar, "will you let Jam know I'll be back later tonight?"

"Hot date?" he asked eyeing her suspiciously.

"I am going to visit my parents," she bit angrily. *Just walk away, Kensie. Just leave. Just walk away.* She tried to leave, she willed her legs to move, but she was tired of ignoring the tension between them. *Step two: confront your issues head on.* "Do you have something you want to say to me, Ry?" So much for diplomacy.

"I think this whole thing is fucking stupid. You're miserable. He's miserable. All he does is sit in his room writing sad love songs." His voice was severe, his hazel eyes narrowed in on hers.

"I'm sure he keeps plenty busy." Sarcasm dripped from her words as the image of Tiff's bruised and bitten throat plowed through her mind.

"You really think that little of him?"

"Are you really asking me that? *Me?* Of all people? He lied to me. He manipulated me. I turned my entire life upside down for him. I got into a fucking fight with my father. I quit my job."

"But you love your new job."

"That's not the fucking point!" She threw her hands up in exasperation. "The point is I trusted him. I would have done anything for him and all he wanted was revenge. I gave myself to him, mind, body, and soul. He owned me, and then he broke me. Now, because he tripped and fell in love, I'm supposed to forgive and forget because he left me a few voicemails? Fuck that. I need more than that. I need actions. He's already proven that I can't trust his words."

"You want a big romantic gesture?"

"I want it all. I want the small stuff and big stuff and all the stuff in between. I want to be able to trust him. I want him to work for it."

"For him to do that, you've got to cut him some slack."

"But that's just it—I don't. I know I wasn't perfect. I know none of this would have happened if I just stayed away from him. I know no one could make me cheat, I get it, but my mistakes didn't break us, his did. I'm working on fixing my shit. He needs to figure out how to fix his, and don't tell me that's not fair because I've fought for this from the beginning. It's his turn."

"So, you're saying there's a chance?"

"I'm saying that if he really loves me, he'll show me, and if not, then tell him to move the fuck on because this isn't fair to me. It isn't fair that you and Javi make me out to be the bad guy because, oh lookie, Fuckface actually does have a heart."

"I'm not trying to discount your feelings. I care about both of you." She snorted. Like hell he did. He was unequivocally Team FuckFace. "I do," he said setting his mug on the counter. "Look, you're Jam's best friend. I think she loves you more than she loves me," he chuckled, "and you're my best friend's girl—"

"I am not his girl."

Ry looked like he wanted to protest but decided against it. "Whatever, all I'm saying is, you and I might not be as close as you and Javi are, but we are family, and if I thought you'd be happier without him, then I'd say that. But you're not. I know he fucked up, but he loves you."

Kensie shook her head. "It's a lot to forgive."

"I know, but—"

"There is no but," she sighed, sadly. "I should go."

Emotions were immortal spirits hiding in mortal beings. You could free yourself by releasing them out into the world, or you could let them eat you alive—but you couldn't change what you wouldn't confront.

Sunday dinners resumed after the wedding, but they weren't the same. The emotions ran high in Madison Park, yet despite the issues she had with her father, it was still home.

"This is great, Mom," Kensie said, complimenting Jacquelyn's halibut. They spent the afternoon at the farmer's market, picking up fresh ingredients for the meal they now shared.

"Thank you," her mother beamed, "I'm just glad you're eating again."

Kensie half-shrugged, half-grimaced. Of course, her mother didn't have an issue giving voice to her emotions. She not only noticed her daughter's lack of appetite, she never missed the chance to express her concern. Kensie couldn't blame her. She had been thin before, but since the breakup, she'd lost five to ten more pounds, transforming her from fit to frail.

"It's bullshit, if you ask me," Victor grumbled stabbing at his plate. "Sundays are for God, family, and steak. In that order."

"The doctor said your father's cholesterol was a little high and suggested we cut out some of the red meat," Jacquelyn explained to Kensie before turning to her husband. "Having a healthy meal every once in a while, won't kill you, but I might."

Kensie smiled to herself, listening to her parents bicker about steak versus fish; that was the biggest issue in Jacquelyn and Victor's marriage. It was nice, but it made her wonder what was wrong with her. She'd grown up in a house filled with love, yet she constantly chose assholes.

"How's the new job treating you, baby girl?" her dad asked

tentatively. It was strange being disconnected from him. They'd always been so close. She couldn't do anything about her love life, but she could fix this.

"It's great. I'm still learning, but I love my boss and I love the kids. I think I've finally found the right fit." She smiled weakly, cringing at the formality of it all. This was her father she was talking to, not a colleague or distant acquaintance, but her daddy.

"That's wonderful, honey," her mother added, piling another scoop of steamed broccoli onto her plate.

"Subtle, Mom, real subtle."

"I have no idea what you're talking about, sweetie, more fish?"

"Sure," Kensie agreed passing her plate. There was no use arguing with Jacquelyn Roth.

"What made you take the leap?" Victor interjected, passing Jacquelyn his plate as well. For as much complaining as he'd done, he had eaten every bite.

"He did," she muttered, and just like that, her appetite was gone. *He'd* pushed her toward her dream; it was one of the reasons she'd fallen in love with him, but now that was tainted. Was that a lie too?

As if on cue, her mother sensed the shift. "Wanna talk about it?"

"Not if you're going to tell me you told me so," she grumbled looking at her father. There they were, the words that had gone unspoken for a month. In her quest to find happiness, Kensie knew she needed to confront her father for the stunt he'd pulled at El Gaucho's, but she'd been putting it off. The rest of her life was in shambles and, for a time, she needed to pretend that things were fine at home, but she was done sulking and pretending. It was time to put on her big girl panties.

"That hurts, baby girl." Victor's pain was evident in his voice.

"What hurt was you inviting Trey to dinner behind my back, when you knew we were broken up. It wasn't your place to meddle."

"My intention wasn't to hurt you. I just didn't want to see you throw a good relationship away for a fun one. You've kissed a lot of frogs and I just want you to find your prince."

"I love you, Daddy, I do, but you don't get to decided who's worthy of me and who isn't. Trey and I are done. It's over. We will never, ever be together. And if I choose to be with the drummer of a band or an investment banker or a cashier at the Gap, that's up to me. I get that you want what's best, but you also have to trust that I know what that is."

"I was just trying to help, sweetheart. You don't have the best track record when it comes to picking these boys. First Stephan and now this...drummer," Victor countered with a wave of his hand.

Kensie sighed at the mention of her first love's name. Stephan Jones had been her high school boyfriend and the sole reason she chose to go to school in Southern California. He was her whole world. Smart and funny and athletic—perfect.

He'd graduated a year before Kensie and they had agreed not to let the distance come between them. He'd been offered a spot on the USC men's basketball team and he jumped at the chance to extend his career beyond high school.

The plan had been that she'd follow him the next year. It hadn't been her first choice, but she had yet to declare a major, and so she'd followed her heart. He had understood her. He had inspired her and he had pushed her to follow her dreams. He had been like a breath of fresh air, never succumbing to the pressures of growing up privileged. He was his own person and Kensie had been intoxicated by his sense of adventure. He did what he wanted and on his own terms. He had been her whole world, but everything changed.

Stephan became the big man on campus, the sophomore point guard who had led the once losing team to their first finals in ten years. Kensie was proud to be his girl, but she had been so caught up in their bubble that she didn't notice the looks he got from "fans." She didn't notice the looks he gave the girls who wanted to be in the presence of Stephan Jones, girls who didn't give a damn about his high school girlfriend.

It wasn't until one of his groupies messaged her on Facebook, telling her that she was pregnant and Stephan was the father, that everything became stunningly obvious. The late practices, the away games, the long gym sessions, all a front for his infidelity.

She had been hurt and angry and she'd wanted revenge. With Jam's help, she set up a fake Facebook profile and flirted with him. She knew him, what he liked, what he didn't like, what turned him on, and what drove him. It was easy making him fall in love with the fake Kensie, but it backfired.

She only wanted to catch him in his lies, but the more Stephan opened up to the fake girl she created, the more obsessed Kensie became with it. She couldn't stop, inching closer and closer to the edge with every message and I love you that her boyfriend sent to the fake profile. Then one day, he had told her that it was over. He told her that he'd found his soul mate. That was the day she fell.

After the breakup, Kensie had kept the bogus relationship going for another couple of months, pretending to be the girl of his dreams, while also nursing her broken heart.

Jam confronted her, telling her that she needed to stop, that what she was doing was unhealthy, that she had spiraled out of control. But she hadn't listened. She was obsessed with revenge. It had consumed her. Her grades slipped. She sacrificed going out and meeting new people, all because she became obsessed with getting even with a man who never really loved her. It wasn't until her advisor pulled her into his office and told her that if her grades didn't improve, she'd be in jeopardy of failing.

It was the wake-up call she'd needed. She deleted the fake page, got rid of the phone she used to text him, and for added measure, she deleted her real page and swore off social media all together. From then on, she'd done her best to avoid him, to pretend like he never existed. She threw herself into her school work and books and, eventually, she moved on. She made friends and went on the occasional date, but she kept her heart guarded, until Trey, until *Him*.

CT reminded her so much of Stephan. She didn't see it then, that night at the Rabbit Hole, or maybe she didn't want to admit it, but swap out blue eyes for brown, and rockstar for basketball star and they were the same. The realization hit her like a Mack truck. That's why she resisted him, and yet, that's why she was drawn to him. Stephan was her first love, he took her virginity, but deep down it was never meant to last. CT, he was her true love, her other half, her forever. Where Stephan was fun, and Trey was safe, CT, like lithium, recharged her soul.

"I understand that, sweetie, I do," her father said, pulling her back from her dark trip down memory lane, "but you can't keep giving these boys the power to destroy you."

"I love hard, Dad. It's just who I am, it's who you are. It's in my blood."

"Why can't you love yourself as hard as you loved them?" her dad challenged.

Her lip quivered as she fought back the tears. "I don't know how," she confessed.

"Oh, baby, come here." Her mother got up and wrapped her baby girl in her arms. "You owe yourself the same love that you give so freely."

Kensie nodded, burying herself into her mother's chest, shaking violently as she released her emotions into the world. For the first time in a month, she felt like she might be able to endure this hurt.

TWENTY-EIGHT

CRAZY

After leaving her parents' house that evening, Kensie decided to take her own advice. She told Ryder that she wanted to see actions from CT before she would even consider moving on, but where were her actions? So far, all she'd done was get dressed, put on a little makeup, and ugly cry in her mother's arms. It was a start, but she still had work to do.

Why can't you love yourself as hard as you love them? Why couldn't she love herself? Why couldn't she put as much effort into making herself happy as she did in making those around her happy? Outside of work, she didn't even know where to look for happiness.

Three hours and half a bottle of wine later, Kensie was sprawled out on the floor, staring down at a blank page. "What do you want?" she said into the quiet abyss of her bedroom. A loaded question. She wanted to live life on her own terms. She wanted to step outside of her privileged bubble and push herself to be a better person. A philanthropic sentiment, perhaps a little cliché, but at its core, it was honest. The problem was, *how?*

It took another hour and the rest of the wine, but eventually she found an answer to that question, *The List*. It started as a way to organize her thoughts, to narrow her focus, but it ended up being her blueprint.

At the top of the page, she wrote, *What do YOU want?* From there, she let her heart do the talking, no matter how monumental or mundane, if she wanted it, she wrote it.

> *Make a difference*
> *Climb Mt. Kilimanjaro*
> *Dance in the rain*
> *Visit a sex club*
> *Get a tattoo*
> *Run a 5k*
> *Touch the sky*
> *Do something that makes you uncomfortable*
> *Be brave*
> *Write a novel*

The next morning, Kensie awoke with a newfound sense of determination. It wasn't peace, but it wasn't the war that raged inside her body for the past month either.

On her way to work, she stopped at the donut shop she'd heard Tanner raving about last week. Now that she had a plan, she needed a place to start and in order to do that, she needed Tanner. If she learned nothing else growing up around politicians, it was that a little bribery could get you a long way.

"Tanner, this month has been amazing and I'm really grateful for the opportunity, but... No, Jesus, Roth, do you want him to think you're quitting?" She sighed, shuffling the boxes of donuts and coffee traveler so she could push her car door closed with her hip. "Tanner, Safe Haven is great, but the boys aren't being stimulated enough…" *No, too aggressive,* she thought as she made her way to the house. Thankfully the boys were still asleep. The quiet gave her time to quell the anxiety that boiled in her belly. She was the new girl, barely out of training, and in no position to make demands, but her gut, the same gut that threatened to expel the donut she'd eaten on the drive in, told her she was doing the right thing.

"Good morning, Kensie," Tanner greeted from the other side of the breakfast bar. "You're here early." Kind blue eyes assessed her. "Looks like you had a good weekend."

"Oh, hi," she blurted out in surprise. She grabbed the maple bacon bar she set aside and offered it to him with shaky hands. "Good morning, I got breakfast, and yes, it was…cathartic."

"Cryptic." He grinned, biting into the fried dough. "I'm going to throw my stuff in the office and check in with James and Zoe. Can you start waking everybody up?"

"Sure, but…um, do you have a minute?"

He glanced at his watch. "I can give you two."

Kensie smiled, then exhaled, steeling her nerves. "I really love working here."

"We love having you."

"Thank you, but—"

"But?" Tanner arched his brow.

"No but, I mean, there is a small but, like more of a *b* than a full but."

"Okay?" He nodded, taking another bite of her sugary bribe.

"I want to start an art program," she blurted out, throwing the carefully crafted speech she prepared out the proverbial window.

Tanner walked around the breakfast bar and into the kitchen, his eyes giving away nothing. After snagging a disposable cup from the stack, he poured himself some coffee. "Sounds expensive," he said from behind his coffee cup. His face was stoic. She knew it was a long shot, but she wasn't going to back down without a fight.

Make a difference.

Make a fucking difference.

"Probably." *Smooth, Kensington, real smooth.* "I mean, I've thought of that. I know we don't have the resources, but we can do fundraisers—my mother's friends live for fundraisers. I can take care of securing funding. I just think the kids would benefit from having a creative outlet to channel their anger." The words tumbled from her mouth in a rush.

Seconds ticked by and Kensie became less and less sure of herself. The rational side of her brain knew she'd gone above and beyond. She'd done everything that was asked of her and then some, but the irrational side of her brain poked at her insecurities. It told her she'd never be more than a spoiled rich kid living off her trust fund.

"I agree," he said finally. A mischievous grin overtook his features. "You've done a great job so far, as long as you can secure the funding, I think it's a brilliant idea."

"I promise, I won't let you down." Kensie grinned, and threw her arms around his neck, nearly knocking him over.

"Go," he dismissed with a wave of his hand, "wake up the boys, stuff them full of sugar, and send them off to school."

After work, Kensie went home with the intention of ordering Chinese takeout, sitting down with her laptop, and working on phase two of *Operation: Do What Makes You Happy*, but the smell of bacon wafting through the foyer, derailed that plan.

Fuck.

They weren't supposed to be here. The guys were leaving for their tour tomorrow, and Jamie and Ryder were supposed to be at the house, screwing each other's brains out.

Kensie counted to ten, mentally preparing for another

face-to-face with Ryder. She used to love that she and Jam were dating best friends, but she never factored in a breakup.

"What are you—" she started, but quickly snapped her mouth shut. Her heart sank, or, maybe it floated. She didn't know. She couldn't express her feelings. She was just trying not to cry, or yell, or cuss, or kiss. God, she missed his lips.

CT stood in her kitchen like he had many times before, but this time was different. This time, with her pink ruffled apron covering his white tank top, black skinny jeans, and a backwards Lithium hat sitting on his head. She wanted him gone, him and his stupid, handsome face, and his annoyingly perfect body. Fuck him. Fucking, Fuckface.

"I'm making dinner, well breakfast, but it's dinnertime, so." He shrugged. He shrugged! Like it wasn't the first time they'd seen each other in five weeks. Like it was no biggie.

His eyes met hers before briefly scanning her body. It wasn't sexual—though the air crackled between them like it always had—but the look on his face was one of concern. It made her want to scream, *YES, I LOST WEIGHT! You broke my fucking heart. What did you expect?* But she didn't, instead, she calmly asked, "How did you get in?"

The concern transformed to mischief as he reached into his pocket and plucked out a familiar pair of keys and dangled them in the air. "I unlocked the door," he deadpanned.

"Does Jam know you have those?" she asked, crossing her arms over her chest. The gesture, only partly due to anger, but mostly to help muffle the frantic thudding sounds her heart was making.

"I would have asked, but she was kind of busy, if you know what I mean." He smirked, pocketing the keys before turning his attention back to the pineapple he was cutting.

"You need to leave, now. Like right now, like five minutes ago, *now*." She'd finally clawed her way back from the depression he'd left her in and now he was here, making breakfast for dinner.

"No."

"Now, CT, seriously."

"I'm CT again?" he asked over his shoulder. He kept chopping, slowly, methodically, and seemingly without a care in the world.

"Or Fuckface," she seethed. Under normal circumstances she would have commented on his improved knife skills, but this wasn't normal or nice or romantic. "You can take your pick."

"CT it is," he chuckled.

"Get. Out," she gritted.

"I gave you five weeks. I didn't come and break down your fucking door when you blocked me. I'm not going to drag you kicking and screaming on tour with me, although the thought has crossed my mind," he said, pointing the knife in her direction, "more than once."

"I'm really flattered, but I can't do this with you right now. Please, just leave."

"Baby, I'm leaving tomorrow—for three months—I'm not going anywhere. Now, go change out of your work clothes."

"I'll call the police," she said switching tactics. Why? Why? Why was he doing this? She was finally starting to see the light at the end of the tunnel and BAM, just like that, he bulldozed his way back into her life.

"Go right ahead," he challenged, taking a step towards her.

"FINE!" she yelled, throwing her hands up in defeat. She could barely breathe with him in her apartment, she'd surely suffocate if he touched her. "I should call your fucking parole officer," she mumbled as she stomped away.

"I heard that, and I'm not on parole, asshole."

Kensie slammed the door to her bedroom, locking it behind her for good measure. Nervous energy coursed through her bloodstream. Her palms were sweating and her heart beat erratically. She felt like she was going to throw up. Her anxiety was back and the cause and cure was standing in her kitchen, making her dinner—or breakfast. Whatever.

TWENTY-NINE

BloodSport 15

Kensie flopped on her bed with a huff. Her mind was racing, trying to think of something, anything, to get him to leave. Of course, she missed him, she was still in love with him, but that was the problem. She loved him with everything she had and it wasn't enough. Their entire relationship was based on a deceitful game. All her happy memories were tainted.

Her head was at war with her heart. Her brain shouted that this was too little, too late, but her heart—the traitor—prepared for a fight. It warned her that it wouldn't be pretty or easy, but it would be worth it. *Do something that makes you uncomfortable*, her heart chided. They were her words, her wishes, and now she fucking hated herself for being so damn philosophical.

Kensie groaned, knowing that she couldn't run away. Not now. Not when he was leaving tomorrow. Not when she had questions that only he could answer. Questions that ate away at her. Questions that she may never get another chance to ask. Who knew what tomorrow would bring? Who knew what would happen after the tour? The only thing that was certain was that he was here now.

She peeled herself off the bed and stripped out of her business casual attire, slipping into an old, extra-large t-shirt that she'd stolen from her dad. She usually reserved this shirt for sleeping in when she was sick. Then she riffled through her drawer in search of the baggiest pair of sweats she owned. Once she was dressed, she pulled her hair into a messy ponytail on the side of her head and washed off all her makeup.

His eyes followed her with amusement as she made her way back to the kitchen. She looked ridiculous, but they were only going to share a meal and talk. She wasn't trying to impress him. Hell, she was hoping to turn him off.

"Nice try, baby," he chuckled, taking in her appearance, "but I know what you look like underneath all that fabric. You could wear a trash bag and I'd still want to fuck you."

"There will be absolutely none of that," she growled, narrowing her eyes at him. Sex was the last thing they needed. Sex with him clouded her judgment. It turned her legs to Jell-O and her brain to mush. "Why are you doing this?" she asked, her voice pleading. The underlying message clear, *if this isn't sincere, then don't bother.*

"Because," he sighed, cracking eggs into a bowl. Though his back was to her, she could tell his bravado was slipping. His shoulders slumped and his voice lost its confident edge. "I miss you. I love you. I tried to do it your way, but it wasn't working for me."

"Do you think making me crunchy eggs is going to make me forget what you did?"

"No, but I've got to start somewhere," he replied, still focused on his task.

"Or you could just move on."

"You not being in my life is not an option," he stated flatly, like it was a universal truth. Like a *"money can't buy happiness"* and *"all men are created equal"* type of declaration. As if it had been written by God and ordained by their souls.

"I don't get a say?" she croaked, choking on unshed tears. The rawness of his tone unnerved her. She needed to say these things, to ask these questions, but it was easier keeping her emotions in check when he was being a cocky jerk.

"Do you still love me?" he asked, opening the drawer on his left. He pulled out the whisk and began mixing the eggs. It was crazy, the two of them in the same room, saying the words that probably should have been said a month ago, while he made her breakfast for dinner.

Kensie looked everywhere but at CT. She couldn't lie, but she couldn't bring herself to say it in front of him, because despite the way she felt, they weren't lovers, they weren't even friends. They were just two people whose spirits happened to be connected.

"Yeah, that's what I thought." He smirked, the cocky bastard resurfacing once more.

"I need more time," she admitted weakly, shuffling from foot to foot. She still wouldn't look at him. It hurt too much. He was too beautiful, and she was too broken.

"Give me one night, then you don't have to see me again for three months."

"One night," she dismissed with a huff. She made that same promise to herself the night they met and look where it had gotten her.

"Kensington, please," he begged, dropping the whisk and turning to face her.

"Fine. One night. No sex and if I feel like you're lying to me, I'm done."

"No sex. No lies," he agreed. "Should we toast to it?" he asked, offering her a beer.

"No, I need to be sober around you."

"Suit yourself," he said, lifting a shoulder up and popping the top off the bottle. She couldn't help but stare at the way his bicep curled as he brought the beer to his lips, and at the way his Adam's apple bobbed as he swallowed. His throat was so sexy and so, covered in gauze?

"What the fuck is that?" she seethed, marching over to him.

"What?" he asked in surprise, looking from left to right.

"Is that a fucking hickey?" Livid wasn't the word. He came here to beg her for forgiveness with a hickey on his neck? She saw red. She saw black. She was going to kill him.

"Oh, this?" He grinned, rubbing his throat.

"Yes, that." Her hands flew to her hips, but only to keep from wrapping them around his neck. "Did Tiff give that to you?"

"Jealous?"

"No." She shook her head violently. *Calm down, Roth. Calm down.* She did her best to control her temper. She tried, but screw it, no lies, right? "Actually, yes. I am jealous, very fucking jealous, happy?"

"So, let me get this straight," he mused, taking two steps forward, "I can't fuck you and I can't fuck anyone else either?"

She nodded. Was it fair? No, but those where her terms.

"Do the same rules apply to you?" He moved closer still, until they stood toe-to-toe. It was the closest they'd been in months. She could feel his warmth. She could hear his heart, low, steady, sure.

"That depends."

"On what?"

"On if that's a hickey."

The seconds ticked by and the corner of his mouth pulled up into a slow, lazy grin. "No, it's not a hickey and I told you already, I'm not fucking anyone. I got a new tattoo."

"Oh." She breathed in surprised embarrassment. A tattoo. She was so blinded by rage that the thought never even crossed her mind.

"Oh," he mocked, his face inching closer to hers, "wanna see it?"

"Sure, I guess." A tattoo, not a hickey. Not a deal breaker.

"You can't get mad," he warned.

"Why would I get mad?"

His blue eyes held her brown as he slowly peeled back the gauze. He was being dramatic. It was just a tattoo; his body was covered in them. What was the big deal?

"Don't freak out," he reminded her once the bandage was off, revealing the *Kensington* written in purple script across his neck.

"You got my name tattooed on your neck?" she squealed, walking backwards until her ass hit the counter.

He nodded, balling the gauze in his fist, bracing for her reaction.

"You got my name tattooed on your neck," she stated again as she inspected the swollen skin.

"Yup," he confirmed.

"You tattooed my name on your neck!" This time it was an accusation. It was official, he was certifiable.

"Why would you do that?"

"Baby." His voice was soft as he erased the distance between them. He tugged on the end of her ponytail, tilting her head so that their eyes met. "You are all I want, forever, remember?" he whispered, his eyes trailing down to her mouth. Those two blue storms set in the middle of his face held more determination, more love, than she was ready to accept.

"No," she said pushing him back and slipping around him. "No. I've got some work to do. Just let me know when dinner is ready, okay?" She couldn't deal with the tattoo right now. They weren't even together, and he had gotten her name permanently etched on his skin. *His name is permanently etched on me,* her heart reminded her.

CT nodded, pulling at the hair on the nape of his neck. "Okay," he mumbled before getting back to work on the food.

"Why purple?" she called from the other side of the breakfast bar. It was stupid. Did it matter? she asked herself, hoping for clarity. *Yes, everything mattered.*

His eyes pinned hers again. "You said it was your favorite color."

"Right," she whimpered, biting down on her lip in an attempt to keep the tears at bay. He remembered her favorite color, something they only ever talked about once, but was it for ammunition against Trey or was it because he cared?

Grabbing both her iPad and MacBook, she went to the couch with the intention of revisiting the first chapter of *Smoke and Mirrors,* the book she started writing long ago, yet another one of the many things she'd given up on. She tried to concentrate, she really did, but her eyes kept wandering to him. He was handsome, his body, his face, his ink, his everything. On the outside, he was a work of art, a beautiful masterpiece that hypnotized and enticed all who dared stare too long. But inside, he was lost, angry and insecure.

She watched from behind her iPad as he moved around her kitchen like he owned it. Honestly, he probably spent more time in there than he did in the kitchen in the tiny house he shared with his two best friends.

"Baby," he called to her. *Baby, still.* If he noticed her staring he didn't mention it. Instead, he informed her dinner was ready. She made her way to the breakfast bar, eyeing the displayed assortment of food. He prepared French toast, bacon, eggs, and home fries, alongside with an assortment of fresh fruit. It smelled divine and, more surprisingly, it actually looked edible.

"I'm impressed," she said, taking her seat.

"I've been practicing." He grinned proudly.

"Reagan?" she asked, stabbing into her eggs. They were fluffy, but most importantly, not crunchy.

"My mom," he answered around a mouth full of French toast, still her immature lost boy.

"Things are good in Bellevue?" she asked because despite everything, she cared. He needed his family, they were far from perfect, but they were his and they loved him, and he loved them.

"Getting better. It's kind of weird, honestly. It's like I went from black sheep to wounded bird."

"Maybe they're just trying to make up for lost time?"

"Maybe."

It was quiet, then, and not in a good way. Not in the way it was when they could just sit and be. With so much left unspoken, the silence was almost as bad as the distance. It was a physical measure of how far they'd fallen.

"How's Liam doing with all of it?" she asked, unable to take another minute of awkwardness.

"Not great," he confessed, wiping syrup from the corners of his mouth. "It's hard for him because, you know, his new wife wants to strangle his mother."

"I know the feeling," Kensie mumbled, and silence befell them once again. *God, this was awkward.* All she could hear was chewing, the thumping of her heart, and the low hum of the refrigerator.

More silence.

More.

More.

"How's the new job?"

"It's good."

"Did you catch the Mariners game?"

"Really?" she groaned, throwing her fork onto her plate. "Small talk?"

"I'm trying, baby,"

"Stop calling me baby."

"No, fuck that, *baby*," he emphasized. "I'm completely out of my depth here. I know I need to do this right, and take it at your pace, but all I want to do is drag you to the room and make love to you until you remember how good we are together."

Kensie swallowed, picking up her glass of orange juice with shaky hands. She'd be lying if she said the thought hadn't crossed her mind, but sex right now would be like throwing a live grenade into a sinking ship. They didn't need to worsen the wreckage. "Thank you for dinner. It was really good, but I have a ton of writing to do."

"Then write." He stood shaking his head. He was hurt by her dismissal, but he did everything to hide it while he cleared the dishes. "I'll be quiet. I promise."

Kensie sat there and watched him clean for a moment. He wasn't leaving. He was fighting, and that was something, right?

"Okay, well, I'll leave you to it."

I'll leave you to it? Just kill me now, she thought as she made her way back to the living room. Of all the things she wanted to say, that was the best she could come up with? Why was this so hard? A part of her knew the answer even before she asked the question. It was hard because the truth was ugly. It was hard because words mean things and once spoken, they can't be taken back. She needed to know if it was real but asking might undo all the work she'd done.

Smoke and Mirrors
The sky was gray. It was a sign, an omen. I should run far away. I should turn back now before everything changes. I should. I should. I should, but I don't. I need to know. I need to see his betrayal. I need to feel it in my bones, not just know it in my heart. Proof. Unalienable, physical.

"What'cha doing?" CT asked, bouncing down on the couch beside Kensie.

She rolled her eyes and scooted down to make room. "Writing," she grunted, ignoring him. She hadn't opened the *Smoke and Mirrors* file on her laptop since she'd originally written it in college. It was better than she thought, but it needed a lot of work.

Smoke and Mirrors
I stood before the door marked 36B, my hand shaking as I reached for the knob. I turned it with a click—

Thump.
Thump.
Thump.

"Can you not?" she huffed as CT patted out the drum solo to *Sex God* on the tops of his thighs.

"Sorry," he apologized, inching towards her.

Smoke and Mirrors
I stood before the door marked 36B, my hand shaking as I reached for the knob. I turned it with a click. It was unlocked. I was either the luckiest bastard alive or—

Ping!

"What is that?" She turned so that her entire body was facing the source of the noise.

"Pokémon GO." He shrugged. At least he had the decency to look contrite.

"Maybe *you* should go."

"Chill out, Friend. I'll turn it down."

Smoke and Mirrors
I stood before the door marked 36B, my hand shaking as I reached for the knob. I turned it with a click. It was unlocked. I was either the luckiest bastard alive or I was cursed.
The room was dark and—there's an arm draped around my shoulder. Why is there a fucking arm draped around my shoulder?

"CT," she seethed, pushing him off her. "I am trying to write."

"What'cha, writing?"

"My manuscript," she gritted.

"What's it about?" he asked, resting his head on her shoulder, peering down at the screen.

She pulled back, breaking his connection. His breath on her neck sent a chill down her spine, but she ignored it and instead, answered his question. "Love, friendship, and betrayal."

"Sounds interesting."

"Yup," she said, trying to ignore him and his close proximity.

A long, tattooed arm snaked its way around her waist and he pulled her into his side. "I'm bored."

"Then go away."

He plucked the laptop from her hands and set it on the coffee table, then pulled her all the way onto his lap. "Talk to me. Yell at me. Kiss me. Call me Fuckface, anything. I just can't take this…" he paused, searching for the word, "indifference."

"You think this is indifference? CT, I'm experiencing about a million different emotions all at once. This is so overwhelming. I want you to go. I want you to stay. I want you to fuck me into the middle of next week. I want you to beg for forgiveness. I want you to move on. I want you to love me, forever. I just haven't decided what I need."

"I know what I need," he growled into her neck.

Kensie, be strong.

Be brave.

Do something that makes you uncomfortable.

"Let's play a game," she suggested.

"Okay?" His voice was laced with confusion.

"It's called real or revenge. I just made it up. I'll ask you a question and you tell me if you were being genuine or if you were just fucking with me to get back at Trey."

"Kensie," he warned, turning her body so that she was straddling him, "I don't think that's such a good idea."

"I've been obsessing over this for weeks. What was a lie? What was real? I need this if we have any hope of trying again. I can't always wonder." She rested her forehead on his, pushing his hat off so she could run her fingers through his curly hair. She wasn't fighting fair, but she needed to know the truth.

CT sighed. He relished her touch, but his eyes were worried. "Okay," he agreed after almost a full minute, "but you can't shut down if I say something you don't like. You can get mad, you probably will be mad," he clarified, "but you can't shut down."

She nodded, biting her lip. She was prepared for the brutal truth. "I'll start with an easy one, that first night at your party."

"Revenge," he answered without hesitation.

"The no condom thing?" she continued.

His body tensed and he pulled her in, closer still. "Revenge. I'm sorry. I'm a dick."

She figured as much. He told her that he always wore condoms. He wasn't that drunk and as much as it hurt her to think, that first night, she wasn't special. She was just a hate fuck. "You pushing me to apply at Safe Haven?"

"Revenge, but I wasn't trying to be cruel. I just figured Trey was the reason you were so hell bent on staying at a place that you hated because you said, *'sometimes you have to do what's best for your future.'* Trey's dad used to drill that into us. I pushed you towards Safe Haven because I knew he was trying to keep you at CMC, but I swear it was more about sticking it to him than hurting you. I wouldn't have pushed you to quit if I didn't think you'd be happier there."

She was happier, and he is the reason she took the leap, but damn if it didn't suck hearing the why. "Okay. That same night, we talked until two a.m. Were you trying to get to know me or were you digging for clues?"

"Baby," his mouth found her ear, "I sound like a fucking asshole."

"Real or revenge?" she pressed, pushing her palm flat into his chest until his back hit the cushion. His mouth on her ear was sending all the blood from her brain down between her legs, and she needed to focus.

"Revenge," he groaned. "I'm so sorry."

"Liam's party?"

"That's enough, now, Kensington. I don't want to do this anymore. I don't want you to hate me more than you already do."

"Real or revenge?"

"I don't know," he huffed.

"Real or revenge?"

"Stop."

"You asked me not to shut down, you can't either."

Silence consumed them once again, but she wasn't giving up. If he didn't want to play, then there was no point in him staying. She moved to stand.

"Wait," he begged, his hands dug into her waist, forcing her hips back down onto his. "Both, I think. I didn't know about the party. I was honestly surprised to see you there. I was just dropping off some stuff to my dad, and there you were talking to my sister. You looked so fucking sexy and I thought, this is it, I want her and I'm just going to take her. But then you chose him."

"I didn't choose him. I just didn't see the point in humiliating him."

"That's not how it felt watching the two of you. I knew you were with him, but seeing it—seeing him touch you, I was pissed and I was wasted and I wanted to hurt you because you hurt me. So, revenge, but not against Trey, against you."

He exhaled, bracing himself for her response, but she wasn't mad. He already told her that, the day on the couch. She had already forgiven that. She was just happy there wasn't anything else to forgive.

"Real or revenge?" she asked.

"Last one," he creaked, his voice unsure, sad. She could feel his body trembling underneath her. "I don't want to spend our only night rehashing this shit. You can always ask me more later, but this is it for tonight."

"Fine," she agreed. There were a million moments, a million more questions, but only one that mattered. "The van, Gas Works, the Fourth of July. Real or revenge?"

He was quiet, thoughtful. His brow furrowed as he worked through the answer to that one himself. A full minute went by and then another and another before he spoke. "I hated him for texting you," he began. "I hated that he could still contact you. When I dragged you to the van, my plan was to fuck you into submission. I wanted to make you come so hard that you'd block his ass forever. I wanted you for myself. I'd win. I'd get my revenge and the girl, but you were so fucking stubborn. You wouldn't let me touch you." He smirked recalling the memory.

"You were being a dick," she reminded him.

"Anyway. You pushed me. Kicking down all my walls and forcing me to tell you things I'd only ever told Ry and Javi. At first, I was just going to give you the same bullshit answer I gave everyone else, but when I looked at you, when I really looked into your eyes, I can't explain it. It was like drowning, but not dying, if that makes sense?

Like I was being born again and I knew I could tell you anything. I knew I could trust you. I knew that I loved you," he admitted as silent tears rolled down his cheeks. "Real."

"Great answer," she whispered, wiping at the wetness leaking from her own eyes.

His hands wrapped around her throat as he gently pulled her face to his, their lips grazing. "I can't," she breathed against his lips. "I'm not ready for that yet."

"I get it, I can wait." He nodded, kissing the corners of her mouth before pulling back. "What do we do now?"

"Can I have a follow-up question?"

"Sure."

"Why didn't you tell me this at Gas Works? We decided to leave the past in the past?"

"I don't know. Maybe because although I loved you, a part of me still wanted to hurt him. I wanted both. I just didn't realize doing one would jeopardize the other."

She nodded her understanding. She got it. Sometimes it was hard to let go of betrayal. She was still learning that lesson. "I'm exhausted," she sighed. *Mentally, emotional, physically.*

"I'm not leaving."

"I've given up on that," she laughed. She didn't want him to.

"Read me your book," he suggested and she agreed. They spend the rest of the night cuddling on the couch, taking turns reading her words. It was strangely intimate, sharing this part of herself, a part she hadn't shared with anyone before, not even Jam.

Once the sun came up, CT reluctantly untangled his limbs from Kensie's. "I better get back before Jam realizes her car is missing."

"You stole her car, too?" She grinned, sleepily.

"I had the keys so I figured why not."

"She's going to kill you."

"I told Ry."

"She's going to kill him, too," she mumbled.

"Come on, sleepyhead, walk me out." They stood, awkwardly,

realization sinking in. He was leaving. Time was up. "Where's your phone?"

"Umm...in my room on the charger, why?"

He ignored her question and headed in the direction of her bedroom. He reemerged moments later with her phone in hand. "Unlock it."

"Put a please on that," she demanded with a raised brow.

"Please," he said dryly, handing her the device.

"See, that wasn't so hard," she teased, unlocking the phone and handing it back to him.

He smiled, reaching into his pocket and pulled out his phone, holding the screen to her face so she could see the background, which was the same as hers, the picture of them at Gas Works.

She smiled, rolling her eyes. "What are you doing?"

"Unblocking my fucking number," he grunted. "I know we talked about a lot of shit last night, and I don't expect us to fall back into being CT and Kensie. You don't even have to answer my calls if you don't want, but you aren't allowed to block me ever the fuck again, are we clear? And I changed it back to Peter Pan from Fuckface, FYI."

"Whatever." She grinned, pushing both shoulders up innocently.

He slipped her phone into the pocket of her sweatpants, before declaring, "I love you." Placing his hands on either side of her head, he whispered, "And I'm going to miss you."

"We were apart for five weeks, what's three more months?"

"I was never apart from you. Do you know how many times I've slept in my car outside of this building? How many times I've sat outside of Safe Haven and watched you play with those kids? I even followed you to your parents one Sunday, but the guard stopped me at the gate."

"You stalked me?" Her eyes shot up, her early fatigue forgotten.

"Felon, remember," he joked, lifting his hand in the air. "I want to kiss you."

"I'm still not ready."

"I'll still wait," he promised, brushing his lips against her forehead, and then her nose, and across both cheeks, before peppering small pecks on her eyelids, and down her jawline and into the tiny cleft on her chin, then down the base of her neck.

"Carter," she protested weakly.

"Sorry...hey," he smiled a smile that made her want to rethink everything, "you called me Carter."

"That's your name, isn't it?" she retorted, feigning annoyance.

His lips parted as he angled his mouth towards hers again. She wanted to let him kiss her, but she knew it was too soon so she turned, offering him her cheek instead. "Go," she whispered, "before Jam reports her car stolen."

"I love you," he murmured in her ear.

"Break a leg."

THIRTY

Start Over

Two weeks, fourteen unanswered phone calls, and a thousand miles separated Kensie and Carter. True to his word, he called her every night, but every night she ignored it. Her little game was brutal, and while the truth made her happy, it hurt like a bitch.

She'd thought about it a lot in the last two weeks. Could they get past this or was she the biggest idiot in the world for even considering it? She loved him, and he loved her. He confided in her and he confessed his transgressions. He'd given her space to grieve, while stalking her from afar. And then there was the tattoo…

Tattoos weren't always permanent, not with laser and cover-ups, but Carter put thought into his ink. He didn't do things on a whim or a dare. For him, each piece told his story, held his secrets and expressed his greatest fears and wildest dreams. They helped him escape his gilded cage and distance himself from the elitist world he came from, the same world that chewed him up and spit him out, all because his heart was too pure. His tattoos were an extension of his soul, and now so was she.

Real or revenge? she asked herself. *Do you really need more time or are you trying to hurt him like he hurt you?* Kensie tugged on the metal chain dangling from the lamp on her night table, immersing the room in darkness. It was late, and she was too exhausted to answer that question, or maybe it was that she wasn't ready to admit the truth. Either way, she had a big day ahead of her. They were taking the boys to the zoo. It was her first off-site outing, and she wanted to make sure everything was perfect. Those kids deserved a little bit of normalcy.

She lay in her quiet room, praying for sleep to come, but the visions hidden beneath her eyelids were too loud, too frantic.

Buzz. Her phone danced on the bedside table, springing to life and illuminating the dark room. It was him, right on time. *Buzz.* It rang again, and again she ignored it. *Buzz.* Turning on her side, she stared at her phone. She longed to hear his voice but dreaded the feelings it would evoke. *Buzz. Buzz.* She sighed, scrambling to reach the phone. She couldn't avoid him forever, right?

"Hello," she breathed into the receiver, her heart pounding, prepping for the onslaught of emotions.

"You picked up?"

There was enough gratitude in that phrase to melt the ice around Kensie's heart. Everything hit her all at once. His voice, the longing, the nerves, the resentment. Everything that had bubbled inside of her during the last two weeks boiled over as tears flooded her eyes. She didn't know why she was crying, but it felt good. It wasn't pain leaking out of her body, instead, it was relief. "I picked up."

Kensie heard voices in the background, distant, garbled, but distinctly feminine. It stung to know there were other women, but what did she expect? "J, man, can you take that shit outside," Carter growled away from the phone, "I'm talking to my girl."

"My bad, dude," Javi yelled over the giggling bimbos. "Kensie, can you please send CT his balls back? He acts like a real bitch without them."

"Get the fuck out!" Carter screamed, dropping the phone. She heard a loud smacking sound, followed by a door slamming shut and the giggling silenced. "Baby, are you there?"

"Do you need to go?" she asked, wiping at the tears.

"No, Kensie, I want to talk to you." The words tumbled from his lips in a rush. "I've been trying to talk to you for two weeks."

"I don't want you to miss out on the party," she said bitterly, instantly regretting it. She didn't want him to go, she needed him, but why was it so hard for her to admit that?

"There's always a party."

"Are there always girls?" she pressed, swallowing past the lump in her throat. She hated that she sounded like a jealous girlfriend, but she was insecure and the thought of him with another woman made her sick.

"Yes," he whispered softly. It felt like a slap in the face, but she did ask for honesty, she couldn't take it back now.

"I bet that's fun," she bit, fighting the bile that rose up in her throat. They weren't together. She never promised they would be, but he did promise to wait.

"No, it's not fucking fun," he snapped. "I know I fucked up and I deserve every ounce of your doubt, but I'm fucking in love with you. I don't even see other girls anymore, just you. Do you realize how annoying it is to have these bitches throwing themselves at me when the only girl I want hates my guts?"

"I'm sure you manage it just fine," she hissed.

"If by manage you mean I've masturbated more times in the last two months than I did when I was thirteen, then yeah, I guess I'm managing."

"No groupies?"

"No, Kensington, my dick and heart belong to you. I. Love. You." He emphasized every syllable, drilling it into her mind.

"I don't hate your guts," she breathed. Maybe she was naïve, but she believed him.

"I wouldn't blame you if you did."

"I tried hating you. This would be so much easier if I could hate you."

"Then why haven't you picked up until now? Why didn't you let me kiss you goodbye?"

"That wasn't hate. My body is incapable of denying you. A kiss would have led to a touch, and a touch would have led to me on my back and you between my legs."

"Why is that a bad thing?"

"Because we've done this twice already and I'm not sure I can survive breaking up with you a third time."

"I get that. I do. I'll do whatever it takes, and I'll wait as long as I have to because when you finally agree to be mine again, it will be forever. I'm done fucking things up. I'm done making you cry."

She wanted to tell him that he still owned her, that she was still his, but she didn't. She couldn't bring herself to say the words to him aloud. Yes, he got a tattoo and yes, he was being honest and faithful, but she still had to figure out how she was going to get over what he did. He fell for her eventually, by mistake, but for her, it was real from the start. So, instead of saying the thing he wanted to hear, she sighed and asked about his day.

"My day?"

"Yes, no more heavy. Just talk to me." It was a normal request, staying up late, talking on the phone about their days and their dreams, like a regular couple, like it should have been from the beginning.

"Well, we played in Iowa tonight, some college town. Nobody knew who the fuck we were, but we brought the house down," he chuckled. "Creed said they crashed the website."

Kensie smiled into the darkness. It was all happening for them. "That's awesome, Carter, you guys deserve it. Well, Ryder and Javi do. The jury's still out on what you deserve, Fuckface." Light was good. Light was easy.

"Tell me about your day, asshole." She practically heard that panty-dropping grin all the way from Iowa as he spoke.

"I made progress on *Smoke and Mirrors*, and I registered for a 5k."

"I didn't know you were a runner."

"I'm not really," she admitted, "but there's this app that helps you train. I've always wanted to do one of those color run things, but I never really got around to it."

"What gave you the push?" he asked as she shuffled, getting comfortable.

"I made this bucket list kind of thing and it's one of the things on it."

"What else is on your list?"

"I can't tell you. It's personal."

"Kensington, I've eaten your ass on more than one occasion. I think you can share your bucket list with me."

She felt her cheeks redden at his words, words that also sent a flutter to her stomach as visions of riding his face seared her brain. "I'm going to hang up on you," she breathed. It was an empty threat. She was a mess of want and need.

"I'm not sorry," he chuckled playfully, no doubt recognizing the edge in her tone. "Please tell me?" he asked in a low, sexy timbre. He knew what he was doing.

"It's nothing revolutionary," she murmured, fighting the urge to touch herself.

"It's *your* dreams, baby. You are the revolution."

Kensie sucked in a sharp breath of air, as what felt like hope bloomed in her chest. This man, this lost boy, this poet, was trying to understand her better, not for revenge, but for real.

"I mean, there's big philosophical stuff, like make a difference and touch the sky. Then there's normal stuff, like the 5k and get a tattoo…"

"A tattoo?"

"Yes."

"I want to take you to get your first tattoo." The way he said it, with so much conviction, she couldn't help but agree. "What else?"

"Then there's crazy stuff that I'll probably never do, like climb Mt. Kilimanjaro or visit a sex club."

"A sex club?" he snorted.

"Yes." She blushed. "Blame it on reading too many trashy

romance novels."

"No," he said dryly. "What's next?"

"What do you mean, no?" she huffed. If she wanted to go to a sex club, she was going to go to a damn sex club. She wasn't asking for permission.

"I mean, if you want to be tied up and spanked, then all you have to do is ask," he said, dropping his voice again, speaking directly to her core.

"CT," she warned.

"What?"

"You can't say stuff like that to me anymore."

"Why the fuck not? I better be the only one saying shit like that to you."

"I already told you, this is hard enough as it is."

"It doesn't have to be, just give me another chance."

"I should go," she said, knowing she needed to end this call. They'd made a lot of progress and she didn't want to go backwards, not anymore.

"No, baby, don't hang up yet," he begged, desperation piercing his tone.

"It's late and I've got an early day tomorrow. I'll be lucky to get four hours of sleep."

"Kensie," he begged.

"Really, you should go have fun." This time she meant it.

"Will you answer tomorrow?"

"Yes," she replied without hesitation, "I'll answer tomorrow."

"Goodnight, *Friend*."

"Don't. That isn't fair."

"Fuck fair, I want my girl back. I'm putting your little ass on notice, I'm going to romance the shit out of you from now until forever. I'm done going at your pace. I'm about to fuck your world up, and you're going to let me because you need me as much as I need you."

"Goodnight, Carter," she said with a roll of her eyes and flutter of her heart. She believed him, and what's worse, she craved his chaos.

THIRTY-ONE

Gonna Get Better

"When did it become fall?" Kensie asked Jam as they walked around the corner leading back to their apartment. The evidence of the changing seasons was everywhere. Autumn air invaded her nostrils, and trees that were once green were now varying shades of yellows and oranges, signifying the progression of time. Life moved forward.

"Are you kidding me, Roth?" Jam huffed, her hand splayed across her barely noticeable baby bump. "Pumpkin lattes have been back for like a month." Kensie scrunched her nose, looking at her friend like she'd been possessed by aliens. Fall was a season conceived by football and nurtured by her father and his idea that exclusivity sold more coffee than any marketing campaign ever could. "Fuck you, I do realize how basic that sounds, but I blame Victor. There's probably crack in the recipe. I bet there's a story there. You think he would give me a comment?"

Kensie shook her head. "I doubt it."

"You're probably right," Jam sighed. "Anyway, how in the hell did I let you talk me into running with you today? I didn't sign up for a marathon."

"It's not a marathon, it's a 5k," Kensie corrected as she opened the door to their building. She'd been training for her race the past few weeks and although a little over three miles isn't significant for the average runner, she was nervous about finishing.

At Jam's insistence, they took the elevator up to the fourth floor. "Are you expecting something?" Kensie asked, eyeing the package sitting in front of their door.

"You know it's for you. It's always for you."

Kensie smiled to herself, scooping up the package while Jam unlocked the door. Sure enough, her name was on the label. She hurried to the kitchen to grab a knife, curious to see what he sent. Carter kept his word and had been romancing the shit out of her for the past month, sending her random things, things that reminded him of her or things he thought she'd like.

First, came the bouquet of bacon roses he sent to Safe Haven, to which her boys went bananas over. A week later, a box filled with books on hiking and mountain climbing showed up at her door. Then, he sent the dildo, but not just any dildo, one that he cast especially for her, one that was an exact replica of his penis. The note attached read:

> For your pleasure and my peace of mind. Only me and my devil dick allowed between your legs. Friend.
> —C

That same night, he popped her phone sex cherry.

"What is it this time?" Jam asked, twisting the cap off a bottle of water. "And if it's another dick, I'm going to vomit," she added in utter disgust.

Kensie shook her head, contemplating if she should open the package in front of her friend. Carter was unpredictable and his gifts ranged from sweet to completely inappropriate, but that was half the appeal. He was not like anyone she'd ever dated. He was rude and crass, but his heart was pure.

Kensie tore into the box, curiosity winning out in the end. It was only Jam, after all. Her best friend had seen her through the worst times. What was another dildo between friends? Inside was a pair of running shoes and a handwritten card.

> Do your feet hurt? 'Cause you've been running through my mind all day. Good Luck tomorrow. I love you.
> —C

Kensie grinned like an idiot, pressing the note to her lips. He'd written it. This package came from him, not some fulfillment center in the middle of nowhere, but he'd gone out and chosen these shoes for her. He packaged them and took it to the post office, for her. It was small, inconsequential, but it meant everything to her. "He got me running shoes." She beamed.

"What's the deal with you two?" Jam, ever the investigator. "I haven't seen you this smiley since…well, since before."

"He's romancing me." Kensie shrugged.

"Is it working?" Jam asked with a knowing smirk.

"I think so," she sighed. The drummer was chipping away at the calcified remains of her broken heart and stitching them back together, piece by piece, and she was letting him.

𝄞

The next few weeks were more of the same, more small gestures, thoughtful gifts, and late phone calls. She didn't think it was possible after everything, but she was falling in love with him all over again. He was away, traveling from state to state, living his dream, but aside from those first two weeks, she never once felt the distance.

His gifts were thoughtful. He didn't send her pretty things to make up for his ugly actions. Instead, he sent her the tools she needed to chase her dreams. He was persistent in his atonement, replacing every lie, every false memory, with a new, happy one. They could never re-write their history, but Carter was working double time to shape their present and cultivate a future.

To the rest of the world, he was chaos, but to her, he was peace. Then, one Sunday, he did something completely unpredictable, something that shook her to her core. He romanced the shit out of her father too.

"Hey, baby," Carter answered in a sleepy voice.

"Sorry, did I wake you?" Kensie asked, plugging her finger into her ear to drown out the noise from the 40,000 screaming football fans.

Victor yelled over her shoulder, "Tell him I said thanks for the tickets." Kensie nodded at her father, trying not to laugh at his navy-and action-green-painted face. Victor Roth, CEO of a Fortune 500 company, and die-hard Seattle sports fan.

"It's fine," Carter yawned into the receiver, "I'd rather talk to you anyway."

"I just called to say thanks again for the tickets. I think you may have converted my dad to Team Fuckface." She smiled, checking to make sure her dad didn't hear her colorful language.

"I'm shocked he doesn't have season tickets."

"He had them a long time ago, but my mom isn't big on football," Kensie explained. "He sold them when I was like, fifteen. He goes to games occasionally, but he works a lot, so when he's home, he'd rather be with her."

"I understand completely." The way he said it, like she was his reason to stay home, made her knees weak. Kensie spent years looking for someone like her dad, someone to love her so completely that he'd put her needs, her wants, above his own. She had thought she'd found it in Trey, but he had only loved the idea of her, the daughter of the coffee king and member of Seattle's oldest political dynasty, more than he loved the insecure and possessive girl struggling to find her own identity.

"Well, I'll let you get to sleep," she said because she couldn't think of anything else to say and because her heart was full.

"Anything for you, Friend," he murmured, his voice thick with exhaustion. "I love you."

"Me too," she whispered, and suddenly it was just them, Kensie and CT, alone in a bubble, the noise from the stadium distant. All she could hear was his breath on the other line, and the hope that seeped out of his mouth.

"You do?" he asked, and it killed her a little that he had to.

"You know I do."

"But you still can't say it?"

"It doesn't mean I don't feel it."

"Then, I'll wait," he breathed, and she knew he meant it. She could feel his sincerity, even from behind the walls she had erected to keep him out.

The game was the turning point in Kensie and Carter's relationship. Things were light after that. She was still guarded, but for the first time, she felt like they might have a chance.

Life was funny. When they had first found out about the tour, she thought it would be the nail in the coffin of their budding relationship. She had no clue that it would be the thing that saved them.

She needed time to work on herself, and if Carter was in Seattle, he would have pushed his way back into her life before she was ready to accept him. They would have fallen back into their old patterns of lust and obsession. They would have destroyed each other.

But he wasn't in Seattle, and she wasn't the same needy and insecure girl that she once was. Over the last two months, she'd transformed into the person she always imagined she'd be. She wasn't perfect. She drank too much, she didn't recycle, and she ate more carbs than she probably should, but she was happy.

She was doing what she loved, and finally, working on her book. She was spending time with her friends and she was learning to love and trust the man who promised he was done making her cry.

"Miss Kenny! Miss Kenny," Josh, one of the younger boys at Save Haven, screamed as he skidded into the newly assigned art room. The floor was covered by a big blue tarp, and cans of pale yellow paint were scattered throughout.

"Watch it, toad," Chris, one of the older boys, said, trying in vain to rub the yellow stains from his elbow.

"Sorry," Josh huffed. "Miss Kenny, there's someone here for you."

Kensington grinned at Josh, with his bright pink cheeks and wide eyes. "Is it a delivery?"

"Better!" Josh squealed, bouncing up and down. "You're going to love this too, Chris. You know that CD you always listen to? The one with those element things on the front?"

"Lithium Springs?"

Josh nodded eagerly and Kensie's heart did this silly pitter-patter thing. *It couldn't be him, could it?* They had a show in Oklahoma. She saw it on the website. It didn't make any sense. He couldn't be waiting in reception. It was just wishful thinking, right? "What does he look like?" she breathed, preparing for little Josh to send her crashing back down to reality. She didn't realize how badly she wanted to see him until the possibility presented itself. Now it was all she could think of. *They have a show. It isn't him*, she reminded herself.

"He's really tall—taller than he looks on the computer—and his tattoos are awesome."

"Downstairs?" Kensie said, dropping her paint brush.

"Yeah, he's talking to Mr. Tanner, but don't get too excited, he's alone. I asked about the two guys." Josh frowned and mumbled something about wanting to meet the guy with the blond hair, but Kensie barely registered it. Her feet moved forward and she stumbled down the steps, fluffing her hair and straightening her paint-splattered t-shirt as she went, mentally kicking herself for leaving the house without makeup.

She slid to a stop just outside Tanner's office door, giving herself a moment to catch her breath. The door was cracked, and standing there, broad-shouldered and impossibly handsome, was Carter. His hands were stuffed into the pockets of his gray sweatpants as he stared aimlessly out the window.

He's here.

Pushing the door open, she slowly stepped inside. His body tensed as if he could sense her presence. His entire body shifted, turning to meet her chocolate gaze. His face lit up like she was his whole reason for existing. The sight of him watching her with such admiration nearly brought her to her knees.

There was so much shit between them, so much shit that she still wasn't sure if she was ready to forgive, but none of that mattered at the moment because he was there.

"Hey," he whispered, the corners of his mouth pulling up into a lopsided grin. The air in the office crackled. The sexual tension was so stifling that poor Tanner looked uncomfortable.

"You're here," she said in amazement. "How are you here?"

"It's just for today."

"Why didn't you tell me? I would have asked for the day off."

Carter shrugged. "It was a last-minute thing. Our show in OKC was canceled because of a tornado and we don't play again until tomorrow night. I didn't know if we could get a flight last minute and I didn't want to get your hopes up for nothing."

"That makes sense." She nodded. She still couldn't believe he was there. She wanted to touch him. She wanted to kiss him, but she stayed rooted to her spot, nodding like an idiot.

"Can you leave?" he asked, pulling her from her daze.

Kensie looked to Tanner. "Sure, Rebecca's doing a mid today, and Zoe and I can hold down the fort until she gets here."

"Yeah, okay, thank you. Let me just grab my stuff and say bye to the boys." She turned, nearly running into the door as she went. The low, sexy laugh behind her sent a rush of moisture between her legs. Even his laugh was sexy. Grabbing her bag, Kensie ran upstairs to tell the boys she was leaving and they made her promise to get them an autograph, then she raced back out to find her sorta rockstar boyfriend.

"That was easy," Carter said, wrapping his arm around her neck.

"You're here." She grinned, pulling his mouth down to hers. He tasted as good as she remembered.

THIRTY-TWO

Garden

Kensie watched the trees whizzing by as Carter pulled his Mustang into the late afternoon traffic. His left hand draped casually over the steering wheel, while his right rested heavy on her thigh. Heat and want and lust scorched her skin. Sadness did too. He was there, for now, but soon, he'd be off to another city, off to play another show, and she'd be left alone to navigate the conflicting emotions waging war in her heart.

Settling back into the worn leather, Kensie's gaze drifted to Carter as she re-familiarized herself with the nuances of his face. He looked different. The wedding, the breakup, and the tour had aged him, yet, *her* Peter Pan was still there, lingering just below the surface. He was in the stubble growing from his face and in the mischievous twinkle of his eyes, and the purple Kensington etching onto his neck. "I can't believe you tattooed my name on your body."

"Why is it so hard to believe?" he asked, glancing in her direction. *God, he was handsome.* Strong, bearded jaw, eyes that sparkled even on a gray October day, and lips so soft, so pouty, that it took everything she had not to climb into his lap and lick him from one corner of his mouth to the other.

"It's so extreme," she said, pressing her legs together.

"Not really. I love you. I want to spend the rest of my life with you, and you are the most important thing in the world to me. Of course, I'd get your name tattooed on my body."

"But we've only known each other for a short time and half of it was a lie."

Carter winced, tightening his grip on the steering wheel. "Liam knew he wanted to spend the rest of his life with Reagan when they were fourteen years old," he reasoned. "My parents met, got married, and had Grant all within a year. When you know, you know."

They sat in a comfortable silence, letting his words wash over them. *When you know, you know.* But when did she know? When did she fall? Glancing out the window, she watched the city limits fade into a distant memory. "Where are we going?" she asked. They'd passed the exit for both her apartment and his house.

"Hiking," he said casually, like he didn't have to leave tomorrow.

"I don't want to hike." They hadn't had sex since before he left and while she enjoyed their naughty FaceTime sessions, she was desperate for the real thing.

"You think we're going to start with Kilimanjaro?" Sarcasm dripped from his tone. For as much as he'd changed over the last few months, the cocky asshole was never too far from the surface. While Kensie liked the sweet, romantic side of Carter, she couldn't deny her soft spot for the jerk.

"Well, no...wait, we?"

"I'm not letting my girl scale a fucking volcano alone," he snorted.

"Okay, fine, but can't we do this another time?"

"No, I've never taken you on a real date."

A date. It was sweet, and under normal circumstances, she would have welcomed it, but these weren't normal circumstances. The clock was ticking and her clit had been throbbing for the past fifteen minutes. He was here and she was tired of waiting. "Dates are overrated," she grunted, flexing her hand in his.

"I thought you wanted romance?"

"I do, I totally do, but we only have," Kensie looked at her watch, "fifteen hours and forty-five minutes before you have to leave."

"Plenty of time for all the kinky shit I have planned." He grinned, turning up the radio.

One song faded into the next, and a familiar piano riff blared through the speakers. Her entire body tensed as the opening chorus of *Neverland* echoed through the car. Ryder's voice was on the official version, but every time she heard it, all she could picture was CT sitting center stage at Reagan's wedding, singing directly to her. Kensie shuddered and stabbed the power button, clocking them in silence.

"What'd you do that for?" Carter asked, slowing the car to a stop.

"It's a habit," she explained, staring at the glowing red light in front of them. She could feel his eyes burning a hole through the side of her face, but stayed focused on the traffic light.

"You don't like it?" His voice cracked, the sound nearly broke her.

"I do, it's just hard to listen to."

Carter was silent for a beat. "I'm sorry I did this to us."

"You don't have to keep apologizing."

"Yes, I do, because that song was supposed to make you happy, but because I'm a fuck-up, you can't even listen to it." The light turned green and they continued on their journey.

"I love the song, okay, it's just tied up with memories that aren't real and it's hard, but I'm here and I'm trying and I'm fighting." He nodded, munching on his bottom lip. He looked like he wanted to say more, but he refrained. "I don't want you to think that I don't appreciate everything you're doing because I do. It's just hard to forget the bad stuff sometimes. It won't be like this forever," she insisted. "I mean, look at us. Did you think we'd be here this time last month?"

"No, I get it, I just wanted today to be perf—" he began, but the loud roar of thunder cut him off. The sky darkened, lightning cracked overhead, and rain began to spill from the sky. "FUCK," he yelled, banging on the steering wheel, "fucking motherfucker."

"Carter, it's okay. We can go hiking some other time."

"We only have one day. I wanted our one fucking day to be

perfect. I'm sorry I keep fucking this up." Signaling, he veered into the other lane. "Let's just go home."

"Baby," she said putting her hand on his knee, "we aren't perfect. I don't want perfect. I had perfect with Trey and I was bored out of my mind. I want *you*."

"Why? After everything, why?"

"Hell if I know," she snorted, "but, I wouldn't be here if I didn't want to try again."

He was quiet, looking up at the sky. The rain wasn't letting up. He tapped his thumb on the wheel. Kensie could see the gears spinning in his mind. A full minute passed and then out of nowhere, he swerved, pulling the car over to the side of the road. "Get out," he ordered, unbuckling his seat belt. "What?"

"Get out," he repeated, swinging open the driver's side door.

"Carter, it's pouring down raining," she called, but it was too late, he was already jogging around the front of the car, heading for her door.

Opening it, he bent down, resting his forearm on the top of the doorframe, "Kensington," he pinned her with his stormy blue eyes, "get out of the car and dance with me."

She bit her lip. "You're crazy."

"Says the girl who put *dance in the rain* on her bucket list."

"Like a nice warm spring rain, not a cold October one."

Carter offered her his hand. "I'm improvising here, *Friend*, work with me."

"Fine," she huffed with an exaggerated roll of her eyes. Taking his hand, she let him pull her out of the car. The water pelted them from above, soaking through her thin t-shirt instantly.

The rain was cold and relentless, but that didn't deter Carter. He wrapped his strong arms around her body and pulled her close. Raindrops collected on her lashes, blurring her vision, but she didn't care, not while she was in his arms. They turned slowly, their foreheads touching, as he hummed a tune she didn't recognize. "This is amazing."

"You're amazing, Kensington."

"Kiss me," she said as a chill ran down her spine. He gently pressed his mouth to hers, running his tongue across her full bottom lip. She caught it, sucking it into her mouth, and he explored her, tasting her, worshiping her.

"You're shivering," he whispered against her lips.

"Warm me up," she pleaded.

His gaze darkened as he took her in, her clothes clinging to her body, she regained the weight she'd lost during their breakup and her once too thin frame had filled out. She was soft, but toned, thanks to her newfound love of running. His hands gripped her waist tightly as his growing erection poked into her belly. He was losing control and she thanked God for the rain. "What about your bucket list?" he growled, nipping at her ear.

"I think this counts," she said, looking towards the sky, letting the rain splatter across her face. It absolutely counted. Moments like this were why she made the list in the first place. She wanted to be happy, and here, on the side of the road, in the middle of a Seattle downpour, she was.

"Your place or mine?"

"Whichever is closest."

Carter drove them back to his house in record time. Stumbling over the threshold, they peeled off layer after layer of wet clothes as they climbed the stairs to his room. Her tee, his hoodie, her flats, his Chucks, her bra. Their damp bodies collided as they clawed at each other, fueled by months of separation and pent-up sexual frustration.

"Javi? Ryder?" she asked, unbuttoning her jeans.

"Ry is with Jam at your place and J went straight to Houston with the rest of the crew," he explained, jumping out of his wet sweats.

"Good," she moaned, pushing him back onto his bed and launching at him, "because I don't think I can be quiet."

Carter groaned, flipping her on her back and then straddled her. She yelped in surprise, laughing uncontrollably as he pinned her wrists above her head. To think, he wanted to go hiking.

He buried his head in the crook of her neck, biting and licking and sucking on her flesh, reclaiming her body. Kensie arched into his mouth, writhing underneath him, desperate to feel him at her entrance. "Are you ready for me, baby?" he asked grinding his length into her.

Releasing his grip on her wrists, his hands traveling down the length of her body, not stopping until he reached the thin string of her bikini briefs. He pulled at the string until it snapped, dragging the scrap of fabric halfway down her thigh. "I hope you weren't attached to these," he growled, sucking her nipple into his mouth.

"I'm only attached to this," she whimpered, reaching between his legs. His dick was rock hard and the feel of it in her hand sent a rush of moisture to her core that had nothing to do with the rain.

"God, I fucking love you," he murmured around her nipple.

"Mmm," she moaned arching into his body.

"I love you," he repeated, locking his gaze onto her.

"Me too," she whispered, fisting her hands into his scalp. She tried to pull his head back down over her breast, but he wasn't budging.

"Tell me you love me," he insisted.

"Carter," she sighed, "you know how I feel about you."

"I want to hear you say it," he murmured against her lips. He was pushing her, but she wasn't ready for that level of intimacy. Her mind was his and she was willing to give him her body, but she still felt the need to protect her heart.

"Why do you need me to say it when you already know how I feel?"

"Because I need to know that you know it's real this time. I'm not fucking you until this is mine, officially," he said palming her clit.

"I...I...I can't say it," she stuttered. "I'm not ready for that yet."

"Then we aren't ready for this." He sat back on his haunches, watching in amusement as she thrashed backwards on the bed. She grabbed a pillow, pulling it over her face and screamed into it, kicking her legs in frustration.

Carter chuckled, cuddling up beside her, pulling her back into his chest. "You're funny." He grinned into her shoulder. He slipped his hand back between her thighs, sinking his ring and middle fingers inside her swollen lips.

"You are infuriating," she groaned.

"Pot, meet kettle," he said, pumping his digits in and out, in and out.

"No sex?" she asked, grinding down on his hands.

"Not until you say it, Friend." He pulled his fingers out of her center, spreading her juices up to her clit. He then swirled his fingers and applied slight pressure to the tiny bundle of nerves.

"This is manipulation. You can't give me an ultimatum like that after you get me all worked up."

"I'll take care of you," he promised, wrapping his other hand around her body. One hand worked on her clit while the other pumped in and out of her pussy.

"What about you?" she moaned, feeling his cock stabbing her in the back.

"Today is about you. I'll be fine, after all, I spent a year in jail, remember?"

His fingers worked her over, pushing her closer and closer to her release. She turned her head, granting him access to her lips and he obliged, fucking her mouth with his tongue using the same lazy strokes his fingers used to fuck her pussy.

The pressure in her belly built as she moaned into Carter's mouth. His fingers worked faster as he felt her body tense, giving it to her exactly how she needed it, first slow and teasing, then hard and fast. He was in tune with her needs and he played her body like she was his instrument.

"Yes," she whined, as wave after wave of pleasure overtook her. Her breathing was labored as she came down from the orgasm he'd torn from her body. She wanted more, she wanted him, but at least he'd taken the edge off. "Tell me about the night we met," she panted, snuggling into his arms.

He kept his hand between her legs, absently rubbing her. "Baby, we've been over this."

"You won't fuck me until I tell you how I feel and I can't say it without knowing how you felt then. Help me understand."

He sighed and kissed her neck. "I'm an idiot for dragging you into my shit with Trey. You didn't deserve any of this."

"I wasn't that innocent."

"But you were. I mean, cheating is wrong, obviously," he snorted, "but you had nothing to do with what happened between me and him. I should have left you alone, but I'm glad I didn't."

She stilled, turning to face him. "I regret lying and I hate myself for hurting you," he explained, bringing his fingers to his lips, "but if the end result is you and me, then it was worth it, right?" He slipped his ring and index fingers into his mouth. His head rolled back as he savored the taste.

She nodded, reaching for his hand, pulling them from his mouth and inserting them into her own. She was still horny and although they needed to have this talk, she wanted his penis more.

"You aren't going to make this easy, are you?"

"Nope," she murmured, pulling his hand from her mouth with a pop. "Why didn't you send the picture?"

"I told you, I wanted more."

"Why? I wasn't special. If I wasn't Trey's, would you have even looked my way?"

"You were standing next to Kitty Cat in that fucking dress, and at first, I thought, I'm going to fuck Jam's hot friend, but I realized who you were, and I thought, even better, I'm going to fuck Trey's little princess. Then, in the van that first night, I realized that wasn't who you were. You weren't the stuck-up bitch I thought you would be."

"Thanks," Kensie scoffed.

He pressed his lips to hers, shutting her up. "That night, I saw a girl who was lost, like I was. You and I are the same. We were born into a world where we don't belong, and we were killing ourselves trying to fit into a mold, not knowing how to break free. I was going to fuck you because I thought you were his, but ten minutes with you and I knew the truth. You, Kensington Grace Roth, belong to yourself. You were meant to soar, and guys like Trey, like me, we are just lucky to be in your presence. You're special, and I didn't send the picture because I didn't want to lose you for the same reasons I don't want to lose you now. You inspire me. You make me better. You make me whole. I didn't even realize I was broken until I met you. I think," he paused, "I think I loved you even then, I just didn't believe myself worthy of you. I still don't, but I'm selfish and I can't let you go."

They spent hours lying in bed, talking and kissing. She still couldn't say I love you, and he wouldn't budge on the no-sex thing, not for lack of her trying.

They ordered food. Jam and Ryder appeared later in the evening and the four of them stayed up late into the night talking and laughing. The guys told stories from the road and the girls listened intently.

When morning came, long before the sun even rose, Kensie felt Carter's warm breath on her cheek. "Our car's here."

"Okay," she mumbled, swinging her leg off the bed.

"No, sleep."

"I want to walk you out," she protested.

"Babe, sleep. You have to work in a few hours. I'll call you when we land."

"Thank you for yesterday," she said, pulling him into her arms.

"Even though I wouldn't have sex with you?" he asked, kissing the tip of her nose.

"In spite of it."

"Saying goodbye to you never gets any easier. I love you."

"Me too."

THIRTY-THREE

Scared of Happy

Peter Pan: How's brunch?

Kensie: Bacon, best friends, and bottomless mimosas, you know, the important stuff.

Peter Pan: I love how you listed bacon first.

Kensie: You know me. :)

"Oh no, Roth, no phones at brunch," Jam said, sliding Kensie's phone away. "Tell CT you'll talk to him later."

"How am I supposed to tell him if I can't use my phone?" Kensie quipped, sticking her tongue out at her friend.

"She has a point." Quinn grinned from across the table.

"Do you really want to argue with the pregnant girl who hasn't been able to enjoy a bottomless mimosa in four months?"

"No." Quinn's eyes shifted over to Jamie's friend, Lo. "I'm Quinn, by the way."

"Hey, Lorena, but everyone calls me Lo."

"Oh! Oh! You two are Eskimo sisters!" Jam said bouncing in her seat. "Well, not really, but Lo made out with Javi once."

Quinn rolled her eyes. "Who hasn't?"

"Wait, you made out with Javi, too?" Lo grinned.

"They did more than make out."

Quinn turned a bright shade of red. "Can we not talk about this?"

"Why? This is exactly what brunch conversation consists of. How big is it?" Jam asked, just as the waiter came to the table with the food. If he heard the topic of conversation, he didn't let it show.

This was exactly what Kensie needed after a stressful few weeks. She'd been working around the clock to plan a fundraiser for her art program, and to make matters worse, Jam had started house hunting. The tour was nearly done, and she and Ryder wanted to be settled in before she was too pregnant to do it. While Kensie was happy for her friend, she wondered where that would leave her.

After Carter's visit, things got better. They talked and talked, and talked some more, but she still couldn't say I love you. What if she'd never be able to say it? He promised to wait, but how long could she expect him to live in limbo? Sighing, she shoved those thoughts away and resolved to focus on her friends.

"Spill, Cousin Quinn, tell us if Javi is packing?"

"I'll tell you about Javi, if you tell me about Ry. Is it true what they say?"

"Hmm?" Jam hummed around a fork full of Belgian waffle.

"Does he really have a Prince Albert?"

"Oh, that? Yeah." Kensie nodded absently as her friend choked on her waffle. Her phone lit up and Kensie wondered if Jam was too stunned to notice if she slid it back into her pocket?

"What kind of freaky shit are you guys into?" Lo squealed. "And here I thought I was the wild one."

"It's not like I went seeking out that information, it found me," Kensie clarified, signaling the server for another round of drinks.

"How the hell did it find you?" Quinn asked, half-amused, half-horrified.

"I saw it." She shrugged, taking note of the pulsating vein on the side of Jam's neck. She was having fun watching the blonde squirm.

"When?"

"Carter's birthday. I went to get my phone out of your bag and the two of you were passed out on top of the covers."

"And you looked? You perv," Jamie shrieked, throwing her napkin at Kensie.

"I didn't mean to look, but I couldn't not look." Kensie winked, earning her another napkin to the side of her face.

"Oh, you bitch," Jamie chuckled. "I get to peek at CT's dick when they get back."

"Well, technically you already saw it." Kensie felt her face reddening at the mention of the toy Carter had made for her. It was nowhere near as good as the real thing, but FaceTime combined with an active imagination, and it got the job done.

"The dildo?" Jam wondered aloud.

"Yup." Kensie nodded, pressing her legs together.

"I'm impressed," Jam whistled, before adding, "But I still want to see the real thing. Fair is fair."

"Whoa. Whoa, wait a goddamn minute. What am I missing here? Since when are we allowed to even say that name, let alone whatever the hell this is?" Quinn motioned wildly around the table.

"It's a work in progress," Kensie confessed. "They surprised us a couple weeks ago."

"When the OKC show got canceled?"

Jamie narrowed her eyes at Quinn. "How did you know?"

"Carter's my cousin."

"Mmm-hmm."

"It's on the internet."

"Are you sure Javi didn't tell you?"

Quinn blushed again, then turned to Kensie. "Are you guys back together?" Her eyes lit up. She had been rooting for the two of them since she found out they were sneaking around. Quinn and Carter were family, and she was one of the few people who had taken his side in his feud with Trey.

"No, not technically, but he's trying and I'm open to the idea that maybe, someday, we could be something again."

"Maybe and someday?" Jam snorted. Being sober made her kind of a bitch. "You're so full of shit. I could absolutely hear you two having phone sex last night. *Oh, Carter, that feels so good, don't stop.*"

Lo cackled, and Kensie's face turned beet red as she spoke, "Okay, back to Quinn and Javi."

"There is no Quinn and Javi. We hooked up a few times, but that's it," she said. There was something in her voice as she spoke, something sad, but also resigned, as if she'd made up her mind and there was no going back. "And anyway, let's move on to why we're really here, your birthday."

Kensie groaned, "I kind of want to do something low-key."

"Portland?" Quinn offered.

"Not that low-key," Lo chimed in.

"What about Miami?" Jam suggested.

"I don't think so," Kensie sighed. Normally, she'd be into the idea of a weekend away with her friends, but there was only one place she wanted to be. She snatched her phone before Jamie could protest.

"You're lucky the food is here," Jamie grumbled.

Kensie: I wish things were different.

Peter Pan: What do you mean?

Kensie: I mean, I wish we met under normal circumstances. I wish we had a normal relationship. I wish we could just be normal.

Peter Pan: I don't.

Kensie: Why? Think of how much better life would be if we didn't have all this shit between us?

Peter Pan: Different doesn't always mean better. What we have is messy and maybe right now it's a little broken, but it's real and it's ours.

Kensie: How can it work?

Peter Pan: Because it's us.

Kensie sighed, dropping the phone back on the table. "I think I know what I want to do for my birthday."

"What?"

"Vegas."

"But that isn't low-key—" Jam began but stopped as realization washed across the blonde's face.

"Anyone care to fill us in?' Lo asked.

"Kensie's birthday—December eleventh—is also the last date of the tour, which happens to be in—"

"Vegas!" Quinn squealed, jumping up and down in her seat.

"Maybe, someday my ass," Jam mumbled.

The flight from SeaTac to McCarran International Airport was a quiet one. Even with her friends surrounding her and the excitement of the weekend ahead, Kensie couldn't shake her nerves. She'd planned this weekend down to the second, poured her heart into every detail, and now that it was here, she was losing her shit.

Doubt flooded her mind around the same time the 757 landed on the tarmac. Men like Carter were unpredictable. She once saw that impulsiveness as a flaw, and in Stephan, it was, but with Carter, it was magnetic. She was drawn to him, the lost boy searching for his happy place, but never in a million years did she think she'd end up being that for him. What's more, he was that for her.

They were in love and she couldn't fight it anymore. They had the type of love that inspired art and spanned lifetimes. Their bond, no matter how many times she tried to deny it, was unbreakable. But the problem with a love like that was that it could only end in one of two ways, happily ever after or in tragedy.

She was afraid, because love didn't always conquer all, and speaking the words out loud would make it real. Once it was real, there would be no turning back. This was it, her final stand. If they couldn't work this time, there wouldn't be another time. Could she trust him? She had her doubts. Sometimes her insecurities crept back in like a thief in the night, stealing her hope for their future, but she was willing to take the leap. She was willing to let him back into her heart because life was long, too long to spend alone when you'd found your person, and too long to spend with someone who didn't make you feel alive.

Kensie wore her heart on her sleeve. It was who she was, and frankly, she loved that about herself. She wanted to be with Carter, and yes, he'd hurt her, but the thought of life without him hurt more.

That fact is what brought her to Nevada in the first place. As she and her friends exited the plane, collected their luggage, and made their way to the same hotel the guys from Lithium Springs would be checking into tomorrow, it comforted her. She was doing the right thing.

Kensie recruited Ryder and Javi to help with her plan. They agreed to run interference with Carter, making sure he was where she needed him to be when she needed him to be there. Timing was everything. The guys had a show and Kensie only had four hours with the drummer before he had to be back to the arena.

Once they were checked in, she finalized the last-minute details of her plan. All that was left to do now was wait. "You want to get some food?" Jam asked, picking up the menu from the desk.

"No, I don't think I can eat. I'm too nervous," Kensie said, pacing the length of their room. It wasn't anything lavish, two twin beds, a desk, a mini bar, and a long window that overlooked the strip.

"I don't know why you're so nervous. He's obsessed with *you*," Jam emphasized, the *not with revenge* was implied. "He's going to shit himself when he finds out you're here."

"I know but what if it's different? I mean, it's nice that he's trying so hard to get me back, but what happens next?" Kensie asked, voicing the worry that had been nagging at the back of her mind. What if the thing that made them so good in the beginning was gone?

"You get to be happy, babe. Isn't that the goal?"

"Yeah." Kensie nodded, and her eyes glistened with unshed tears as she took a seat next to her suitcase on the bed. Happy, finally, and not just in one area of her life, but utter bliss across the board.

"Did you know that Ryder had to talk him out of flying to Cabo directly after the show tomorrow?" Jam continued. They came up with the idea of telling Carter they were going to Mexico for the weekend so she wouldn't have to explain why she wasn't home when they FaceTimed later. "He's sick over missing your birthday. He would do anything for you, Kensie. It's not an act. I think your Peter Pan is ready to grow up."

Kensie smiled at her friend, knowing deep down she was right. Carter wasn't the same man he'd been when they met, and more importantly, she wasn't the same woman. They'd grown, both together and independent of each other. They respected each other, and yes, they were still obsessed with each other.

Kensie: Hey, we just landed. Cabo is as beautiful as I remember it.

Peter Pan: FaceTime?

Kensie: No, we're about to find some food. I'll call you later, though.

Peter Pan: I'm sorry I'm not there.

Kensie: Stop apologizing. I knew what I was getting into when I started dating a rockstar.

Peter Pan: Dating?
Kensie: Well, we aren't fucking.

Peter Pan: Whose fault is that?

Kensie: Mine, I know…I gotta go.

Peter Pan: I love you.

"Okay, I need to do something," Kensie squeaked, throwing her phone on the bed. "I'm freaking out."

Since that day at brunch, she had to bite her tongue every time Carter told her he loved her, and he never missed the chance to tell her. In texts, phone calls, and in video chats, there had been a million times when she wanted to put him out of his misery, but she needed to do it in person. She needed to show him her love. She needed him to feel it, the same way she felt his.

"Now you're making me nervous," Jam said, digging through her luggage. "We need to get out of this room. Let's go explore the strip. It is your birthday weekend and we should be celebrating."

After a quick shower and change of clothes, they set out to see what Vegas had to offer. They spent most of the night wandering up and down the strip, drinking frozen margaritas sold by street vendors and taking touristy photos in front of the fountains at the Bellagio. Vegas pulsated with an energy that was unlike any other place in the world. It was a city built on luck, spontaneity, and excess. It was the perfect setting.

"I know! Let's go see a show!" Jam suggested, sucking down the dregs of her virgin margarita.

Kensie shook her head. "I think we'd need tickets in advance."

"What about a strip club?"

"No, I'm not going to a strip club with a pregnant girl."

"Party pooper," Jam pouted, rubbing her tiny baby bump.

"Honestly, I'm beat. I think I want to just head back."

"No, the night is still young, Roth, let's do something fun!"

"We can have fun tomorrow. I think I'm going to go call Carter."

"Kensie," Jam scolded, "stop worrying. Everything is going to be perfect."

"I know and I'm sorry for being a Debbie Downer. I just want to hear his voice."

"I forgive you this time, also, my feet hurt." Jam grinned. They linked arms, making their way through the hordes of tourists. On their way back to the hotel they stopped at a taco truck. The sight of it comforted her, the smells evoked memories of that day at the Rabbit Hole. She didn't realize it then, but that's when she fell for him, and now, hundreds of miles from home, the universe was giving her a sign. They would be okay because a love like theirs was already written in the stars.

"Kensie?" a familiar voice called out from across the hotel lobby.

"Reagan? Grant?"

"I gotta pee, I'll meet you upstairs," Jam said, smiling to CT's siblings before snagging the tacos and sprinting for the elevator.

Grant chuckled, "Pregnancy suits her."

"Yeah, she's going to be a great mom." Kensie nodded. "So, what are you guys doing here?"

"We wanted to surprise Cart." Reagan grinned, pulling her in for a hug. "Mom and Dad are here too, somewhere, probably in the casino."

"Ah," Kensie said. She didn't think to account for his family. Of course, they'd come to see him perform, especially after everything came out about Trey and Annabelle. Carter said they'd gone above and beyond to make up for lost time.

"So, you two are back together now, officially?" Grant asked, hopefully.

She grinned, shaking her head. "Not officially, but I think it's time to end this standoff."

"Finally," Reagan said rolling her eyes. Just then, Liam came up behind his wife, wrapping his arms around her waist.

"Finally, what?" he asked, nodding a hello at Kensie.

"Kensie here has come all the way to the desert to claim her man," Reagan explained. Liam's body tensed and to his credit, he tried to hide the tightness in his jaw, but everyone within a ten-mile radius could feel the animosity rolling off him. "No, you don't get to be upset," Reagan chided. "Trey is not a good person. He doesn't get to nearly ruin my brother's life and still get the girl."

"I get what he did was wrong, and I'm glad CT's happy, but Trey's my brother and he was in love with her," Liam argued, pointing to Kensie.

"Look, Liam, I get it, but Carter or not, Trey and I were never going to work. We were two different people and we wanted different things."

"Hey," Grant interrupted, glancing around the crowded lobby, "this isn't the time or place to rehash all this shit. It's done and we all need to just move on."

"Whatever," Liam said, storming off in the direction of the casino.

Kensie got the feeling that this was a fight they had often. Guilt washed over her for the part she played, but she knew this would be a part of the package if she signed up for a life with Carter. She only hoped time would heal the hurt, and their love would outweigh any residual awkwardness. "I should go," she said, "but please, Carter doesn't know I'm here and I have this whole surprise planned."

"Our lips are sealed," Grant said, closing an imaginary zipper over his mouth.

"Thanks, have a good night."

"Wait," Reagan said reaching for her arm, "don't let Liam get to you."

"It's not that. I know what Carter and I are facing and I'm just sorry our shit spilled over onto you and your marriage."

"It's not your fault and Liam knows that. He's just having a hard time accepting he comes from a family of assholes." She grinned.

"But are you two okay?"

"Yeah, I mean, we have our moments, but he is the love of my life. Nothing can change that." Kensie nodded. For the first time in her life, she understood what a love like that meant.

Kensington stared at her reflection in disbelief. She bit down on her plump bottom lip as she took in the sight of a woman she barely recognized. Her hair was piled high on her head in a messy bun, her face was bronzed and dewy, her eyes smoky, and her lips were fuck-me red. A black leather jacket was draped over the gray Lithium t-shirt that she had to beg Javi's brother for. The shirt was tucked into the waistband of a black leather mini and her legs were covered with sheer black thigh highs. She felt like Sandy at the end of Grease.

"They're on their way," Jam said, popping into the bathroom. "Holy shit, Roth." The blonde's eyes widened as she took in her friend.

"You don't think it's too much?" Kensie asked, spinning around. They'd arrived at the T-Mobile Arena earlier to set up the drum kit and speakers she'd rented for the occasion. Once that was done, she ran to the bathroom to change and do her makeup while her friends went in search of food.

"Hell no, he's going to want to rip your clothes off." Jam whistled, appraising her once more. "Are those thigh highs?" she asked, pointing to the lace peeking out from under her micro mini skirt.

"Yes, it's too slutty, right? I should take them off."

"Absolutely not! Just imagine how hot it's going to look when your legs are wrapped around his head. God, can I watch?"

Kensie rolled her eyes. "I'm being serious, James."

"Kensie, he loves you. It doesn't matter what you wear, all that matters is you're here." The blonde grinned, pulling her from her spot in front of the sink. "Now move your ass, they'll be here any minute."

Kensie followed Jam back out to the main floor. The atmosphere in the arena was calm, but not in an eerie, calm before the storm kind of way. It was peaceful. The large space would soon be filled with people preparing for the big show, but for now, it was just Kensie, her drums, and her heart.

She took her seat behind the drum kit sitting at half-court. Exhaling, she grabbed the sticks with shaky hands and waited. Her friends were there, sitting courtside, silently cheering her on.

Her breath hitched as she heard the door to the right fling open. He was here. This was it. *Be Brave, Kensie,* she reminded herself. She heard him before she saw him, his voice echoing through the tunnel as he advanced. Ryder came into view first, winking at her before making a beeline for Jam. Javi was next. He gave her a thumbs-up before pushing Carter towards center court.

The drummer turned to his friend, poised to attack, but froze as Kensie brought the drumsticks down onto the snare. He turned, cocking his head to the side, his blue eyes meeting her browns in surprise. His grin slipped and love washed over his features as Kensie butchered the drum solo to *Sex God.*

Carter stalked towards her, his long, lean legs walking purposefully. His black joggers and gray Lithium t-shirt, the same one she wore, clung to his body.

She continued banging aimlessly at the drums as he advanced. His steps were sure. He crossed the floor in no time, taking the sticks out of her hands, one by one, and throwing them aside. "Is this why you haven't been answering my calls today?" he asked, pulling her up from the stool, his face inches from hers. She nodded, focusing on his lips. "You're supposed to be in Mexico."

"I know, but I wanted to spend my birthday with you."

"Why?" he asked, running his hands down the length of her body. He stopped low on her thighs, playing with the lace there.

She closed her eyes. After months of fear and uncertainty, the time had finally come. "Because I wanted to spend it with my best friend, and because I love you," she breathed, exhaling any remaining uncertainty. She was all in. She was his.

"What did you say?" he asked, grabbing her ass, pulling her into him.

"You heard me," she lifted her chin in invitation, silently begging for him to kiss her, to claim her.

"Say it again."

"I love you," she whispered, as he kissed the corner of her mouth.

"Again."

"I love you." This time he kissed the other corner.

"Again," he growled, yanking the bun on top of her head back, exposing her neck.

"I love you. I love you. I love you," she chanted as he walked her backwards, his mouth warm and wet on her throat.

"Thank God. I don't think I'd be able to hold out much longer," he murmured against her skin. "I'm going to fuck you now."

"Wait. Wait. Wait," she said, pushing against his chest.

"Baby, I've been waiting," he said as his hand flexed on her rear.

"But there's more. I planned a whole first date."

He groaned, burrowing his face in her neck. "You're killing me."

She smirked. "Payback's a bitch."

He looked at her, and she could see the mischief in his eyes. "Hey, douchebags," he called over her shoulder to where their friends were waiting, "find another way to the hotel."

Her eyes narrowed as he laced his fingers with hers. "Come on." He moved so fast that she stumbled to keep up.

"Where are we going?"

"Tour bus," he grunted. "I need to be inside of you and I don't want to miss our first date. I get to have my cake and eat it too."

"How romantic." Kensie grinned, pushing him forward.

He led her around the back of the arena as crews were starting to unload trucks of equipment on the dock doors. Carter navigated them through the madness around to an all-black bus. Kensie gave the driver the address as Carter pulled her up the steps and into the main cabin.

The interior of the bus was wood paneled with a small kitchen and black leather sofas stretched across both walls. A flat screen was mounted in the corner, and if there was more, she didn't notice. Carter somehow sat down on one of the sofas and had her straddling him before the bus engine even roared to life.

"This is where you lived for the past three months?" Kensie asked, looking around the confined space.

"Yup," he said, pushing the jacket off her shoulders.

"Where do you sleep?"

"Back there," he answered with a tilt of his head. His hands traveled up her thighs as he pulled at her G-string.

"It's nice," she said, biting down on her bottom lip.

He yanked the ponytail holder off and her hair spilled out around her shoulders and down her back. She groaned as he massaged her scalp. "I want you."

"I'm yours, but I think I was promised cake." She pushed herself up, kicking off her heels, before sinking to her knees. "It is my birthday after all." Her voice dripped like honey as she tugged on the elastic waist of his joggers.

"Who am I to deny the birthday girl?" he muttered, lifting his hips for her. He looked down at her with hooded eyes as she wrapped her hand around the base of his shaft. Slowly, she began pumping up and down, leaning forward to kiss the little "v" where his hip connected.

"Can I have a taste?" she asked, teasing his cock. A low, throaty growl escaped his lips and she took that as a yes. Her mouth fell open and she licked the underside of his cock from the root to the tip, swirling her tongue around the tiny opening.

Carter's head fell back against the seat as spit dripped from her mouth over his dick. "Fuck," he hissed as she moved her hand up and down spreading the wetness before finally sucking him into her mouth. Her bright red lipstick staining his dick as she sucked him to the back of her throat. "Shit." His hips bucked up, causing her to gag.

She pulled back, hollowing out her cheeks, bobbing her head up and down, up and down, making a show of choking and gagging, pushing him closer and closer toward the edge.

She was relentless, bearing down on him until her forehead pressed against his abs. She could feel his body tensing beneath her, his moans of pleasure increased in frequency and in volume as she squeezed his balls, milking him. "I'm going to come," he moaned, trying unsuccessfully to pull her up, "babe."

"Cake, remember?" she mumbled around him and that was all he needed to hear as he bucked his hips up once more, hot cum shooting into her mouth. She swallowed as much of it as she could, but it was too much. Spit and cum seeped out of her mouth, streaking her already ruined makeup. Lipstick was smeared across her face, her eye makeup running down her cheeks, but she could only think of one thing, him filling her so deeply that she'd feel it in her womb.

"Come here," he said, pulling her on to his lap. "I love you so fucking much."

"I love you, I want this, and I am willing to do whatever it takes. I am here and I'm not going anywhere, okay?"

He nodded, pushing her hair back, doing his best to wipe away the red staining her lips, before pulling her mouth over his. Their tongues danced for what felt like hours, as they explored each other. The feelings came flooding back. There was no awkwardness, no uncertainty. It was just CT and Kensie, how it should have been from the beginning.

She could feel him growing under her. She wiggled her hips. "Is that for me?"

"Happy birthday." He grinned, lifting her hips up over his semi-erect cock.

She pushed her panties aside and sunk down on his length. "I missed this," she moaned, letting her head fall forward. "I love you."

"I love you more."

Twenty minutes later the bus pulled to a stop in front of a small night club.

"So, what are we doing?" Carter asked, stuffing himself back into his joggers.

"You'll see," Kensie teased, doing her best to fix her makeup in the tiny bathroom. Once she was satisfied with her appearance, she led him off the bus and up to the building. The word, Voodoo, was scrawled across a purple awning.

"Hi, may I help you?" the man at the desk greeted them as they walked in.

"Yeah, we have a three-thirty reservation."

"Thayer?" the man asked.

"Yup, that's us?" Kensie nodded, as Carter wrapped his arm around her neck. "Soon," he whispered in her ear, and she had to take a moment to catch her breath.

"Have either of you ever been on a zip line before?" the man continued.

"A zip line?" He looked at her with equal parts confusion and excitement.

"Well, while I don't know what's on your bucket list, I did finally get the courage to listen to your new album," she explained. "I figured this would be perfect."

"I still don't get it."

"I want to soar with you."

𝄞

"Alright, Las Vegas, you guys have been amazing tonight," Ryder drawled into the mic, sending the crowd into an eruption of cheers. "Our time is just about up." This elicited a low grumble of boos. "I know, I know, but The Unburned are going to fucking blow your minds." Kensie giggled as the cheers boomed through the audience once more. "But, before we go, we've got one more song for you. This one, you may have heard. It's doing pretty well right now. It's the title track off our new album, *Neverland*."

Kensie had to plug her ears at that. The sound in the arena was deafening. She looked over at her friends, the four of them stood off the side of the stage, watching the guys, their hearts into the performance. The night was amazing, from the bus to zip-lining to racing back to the arena to make it in time.

"We're going to do things a little different tonight," Ryder announced. "CT, man, get up here." There was more screaming as CT rose from behind his drum kit. Javi handed Ryder his bass and went back to sit behind Carter's drums. Ryder slapped CT on the back before releasing the mic stand.

"How y'all doing tonight, Vegas?" CT asked, adjusting the stand. The crowd went wild. "Okay, okay. So, what a lot of people don't know is that I wrote *Neverland* for my girl." *AWW,* the crowd cooed. "I put her through hell and she stuck by me when most people would have bailed. She is my Wendy, my best fucking friend, and she happens to be here tonight." *Wendy! Wendy! Wendy!* "So, if you guys don't mind seeing my ugly face on the big screen, I'd like to sing it for her. Is that okay?" *YESSSSS!* "Alright, enough of the sappy shit, Kensington Grace Roth," he said, pointing to where she stood off to the side of the stage, "this one's for you, *Friend*."

THIRTY-FOUR

All Night

Smoke and Mirrors
As I sit at the end of the old oak bar, swirling the ice around my empty glass of whiskey, I can't help but wonder if this is the life I chose or if this life chose me. The last year was hell, finding my best friend in bed with the love of my life sent me into a downward spiral. I never understood what pain was until that moment. I never knew what loss felt like before then. The pain and betrayal was suffocating; I died a gruesome death at the hands of the ones I loved. I didn't know that it was darkest before dawn. I didn't know that joy cometh in the morning. I didn't know that I would soon be reborn.
The hurt lingers on, but now I endure it; I wear it like a talisman. It protects me and it reminds me not to fear love or companionship, but to welcome it, to nurture it, and watch it flourish. Because pain is fleeting, and because love is everlasting, and because this heart of mine, fractured though it may be, is still beating.

The backyard erupted in applause as Kensie finished reading an excerpt from her book. It had been a long road, many a sleepless night, but she finally finished. *Smoke and Mirrors* would be live soon, and she could officially cross another item of her bucket list.

Tomorrow was still a mystery, but today, at Safe Haven, surrounded by the people she loved, Kensie could truly say, she was happy.

Josh and another little boy ran up to her, throwing their arms around her. "Can we cut the cake now?" They didn't care about the book, just the party.

"We can cut the cake now," Kensie giggled, and the boys went darting across the lawn. Kensie took in her surroundings, canvas posters lined the perimeter of the yard, showcasing the creations that came from her art class. In the center, hanging from a large tapestry, held the cover of *Smoke and Mirrors*. She commissioned Chris, one of the older boys at Safe Haven, to design the original cover art. He took it seriously, even sketching a few ideas before they settled on one.

~~*Make a difference*~~
Climb Mt. Kilimanjaro
~~*Dance in the rain*~~
Visit a sex club
Get a tattoo
~~*Run a 5k*~~
Touch the sky
~~*Do something that makes you uncomfortable*~~
Be brave
~~*Write a novel*~~

"Not bad," she muttered to herself.

"Not bad at all, Friend."

Kensie smiled as she felt the warmth of Carter's body on her back. Settling into his embrace, she asked, "When did you sneak in?" She angled her head slightly to take him in, the purple *Kensington* scrawled across his neck still took her breath away.

"Twenty minutes ago, but you were reading, and then the little ones attacked you, and after last night I figured I should lie low."

"Don't remind me." She cringed, recalling the night before.

After work, she had gone right into decorating the yard for the party. It had been late, the boys were supposed to be in bed, so she'd recruited Carter to help. That was her first mistake.

They'd gotten the chairs set up and were halfway through the tables when his hands had started to roam her body. She had tried to focus on the task, pushing him off every time he'd wandered up her shirt or down her pants, but she could only resist for so long. It was physics, his touch, gravity.

Before she'd known what was happening, she'd been sitting on top of the table, her blouse unbuttoned, with her rockstar boyfriend standing between her legs, palming her breast through her t-shirt. That's when Chris and Josh had walked out, wanting to know if they could help. It was a miracle they didn't tell Tanner. "It's not like we were fucking on the Xerox machine." Carter shrugged.

"That's easy for you to say, you're famous. You don't have to worry about keeping a nine-to-five."

"We're hardly famous," he scoffed.

"Baby, *Neverland* is in the top ten on iTunes and you guys just signed a three-album deal with a major label and—"

"Lots of people sign deals and never make it," he clarified, tightening his grip around her shoulders.

"Last week a group of teenage girls asked me if I was Wendy," she countered, arching her brow.

"My bad," he chuckled, "I posted the picture of us from Gas Works up on my Instagram."

"Oh, so only five million people saw it." Kensie shrugged. "No big deal."

"Okay, so we might be a little famous now, but I'm still the douchebag you fell in love with."

"Well, douchebag, I'm going to say bye to Tanner and the boys, and then you can take me back to your house and show me why I fell in love with you in the first place."

"My little nympho," he said, swatting her on the behind as she went. She rolled her eyes. Only Carter would smack her ass in front of a bunch of children. He was right though; no amount of fame or fortune would change her lost boy.

Before this summer, happiness was always abstract, but now it was tangible. It was the six-two drummer who couldn't keep his hands off her. It was the bucket list she carried in her wallet, reminding her that she could do anything she set her mind to.

Kensie said her goodbyes, hugged her friend, then went in search of her man.

It didn't take long before she found him, standing at the edge of the yard, body rigid, fists clenched into balls at his side, lips pressed into a thin line as he stared down her ex. Rage coursed through her veins. Of all the places for him to show up, why here? Why now?

"What the hell are you doing here?" she hissed, storming over to where the two men stood. The last time the three of them were in the same room, Carter almost broke Trey's nose.

"I didn't come here for you. I came to see him," he said coolly, not bothering to look in her direction.

"We don't have anything to talk about," Carter replied with an equal amount of frost in his tone.

"You should go."

"What, do you speak for him now?" Trey's body tensed as he said the words, still refusing to look at her. The bitterness cut through the air like a machete.

Kensie had to mentally count to five before answering. "Actually, we speak for each other, but you wouldn't understand anything about that, would you?" The nerve of him, barging into her party, making demands on Carter's time as if he hadn't had ten years to talk.

Trey looked down at her for the first time since she'd walked over, his brown eyes filled with regret. "Was I that bad to you?"

Kensie sighed. She didn't want to rehash all this shit, especially not when her co-workers stood within earshot, but he was here, and for whatever reason, she still felt the guilt of what she'd done to him. "Look, Trey," she said, taking a step towards him. Carter snaked his arm around her neck, pulling her back into his front, halting her forward progress. She glanced up at him, watching as he shook his head making it clear that she was to stay put. "I'm sorry it didn't work out between us, okay, but this is my job. Can you just go, please?"

"Not until he talks to me."

He was as stubborn as she remembered. "I can't believe you're doing this here," she snapped, eliciting a few curious glances from people standing nearby.

"I've been trying to do this for weeks and he's been ignoring me. This was my only option."

"Maybe you should have taken it as a sign to fuck off," Carter growled. "I'm not buying whatever it is that you're trying to sell."

"Just give me ten minutes, and then I'll leave. No harm done."

Kensie looked back and forth between the two men. To everyone else, Carter wore a mask of indifference, but she knew better. She saw the resentment that lingered behind his blue irises. Trey, he was desperate, but she couldn't read his motive.

"Fine," Carter gritted.

"Are you sure, baby?" she asked in shock. She never thought she'd see the day that Carter would voluntarily have a conversation with Trey.

"Baby?" Trey snorted.

Carter turned Kensie around, pulling her to him by her ass. He looked up at Trey mumbling, "Baby," against her lips just before covering her mouth with his. He kissed her deeply, the kind of kiss he usually reserved for the bedroom, but she understood his need to do it, so she let him. They kissed like that, indecently, for almost a full minute before Carter pulled back. "Sorry," he whispered in her hair.

"It's fine," she said, placing her hands on either side of his face, forcing him to look at her. "I'm yours. You can claim me wherever and whenever you want."

"Ahem." Trey cleared his throat, pulling them from their bubble. Kensie felt her cheeks heat as she glanced around the yard. Thankfully everyone's attention was on Josh and the cake.

"Five minutes, cornball," Carter grunted, shouldering past Trey through the gate. Trey looked at her for just a moment before following his former friend.

Kensie wasn't sure how much time passed before Carter came back into the yard, but his face was pale. "You ready?" he asked, grabbing her hand and pulling her into his arms.

She planted her feet. Her mind was working overtime trying to figure out what the hell just happened.

"Wait, what did he say?"

His jaw twitched, and she could see the walls she'd fought so hard to tear down, slowly going right back up. "He apologized."

"Apologized?"

"He said he knows it's too little too late, but that he felt like it needed to be said. Now can we please get the fuck out of here?"

"Do you agree?" she pressed. There would be no going backwards. When they agreed to try again, they agreed there would be no more secrets, no more lying. He was going to talk to her, whether he liked it or not.

"I don't know," he said, rubbing the back of his neck. "I thought I needed to hear it, but now that he finally said it, I realized something."

"Realized what?"

His voice softened as he lifted her arms and brought them around his neck. The wall that he'd temporarily erected had vanished and her Carter was back. "I let go of that shit the moment you walked into my life. Trey was the first person to ever break my heart, but if he hadn't, then maybe I would have never met you. Maybe I was meant to lose him so that I could find you."

Tears welled in her eyes. It was in that moment that she knew they would make it. Their love wasn't a fairy tale. It was dirty and damaged and there were times she wanted to give up, but he possessed the other half of her soul. With him, she could fly. "I love you," she whispered, because what else was there to say.

"I love you more. Now, let me take you home so I can show you."

She nodded, following him out to the car. Her words, the words she'd spent months bleeding over lingered in her mind, was *this the life she chose, or did this life choose her?* In the year, Kensie drifted from purgatory and down to hell, before making her final ascent up to heaven. She was living her life on her own terms and it wasn't fate that got her to that point. She'd done the work. She clawed her way out of the pit of complacency on her hands and knees over the shards of her broken heart to find her happiness.

It wasn't easy, but she did it, not for her parents or for her friends or even for Carter. She did it for herself. Because pain was fleeting, and because love was everlasting, and because her heart, fractured though it may be, was still beating.

THE EPILOGUE

Tanzania, 1 year later

"I can't do this," Kensie sobbed, dropping to her knees. *Climb Mount Kilimanjaro.* It was one of the few things left on her bucket list and, with Carter's encouragement, she'd signed them up to for a nine-day trek up Africa's highest peak.

"Come on, baby, you gotta keep moving," Carter said, lifting her up by the arms of her forest-green jacket.

"No. Just leave me here," she whined. Not only had she already fallen behind the rest of their group, but now she was cold, dizzy, and mentally and physically drained. To make matters worse, she was struggling to catch her breath. The tears fell hot and wet down her cheeks as she broke down, realizing for the first time that she might not be able to conquer *Kili*. "I don't know why I thought I could do this. I'm not strong enough for this."

"Kensie," Carter kneeled in front of her, pulling off his glove to wipe away her tears, "baby, you are the strongest person I know. You can do anything."

"I..I...I...I can't...breathe," she stuttered, panicked. She looked up towards the peak. It was right there, taunting her, hiding behind a white wall of clouds and ice. Africa had been as beautiful as she imagined, but that beauty was ruthless.

"Just calm down and take deep breaths. If you freak out, it will only make it worse," he coached, handing her a canteen filled with water. "Drink this, you need to stay hydrated." Kensie tilted the water up to her lips. The liquid, though not cool, was refreshing. "Make sure you keep breathing. When you're ready, stand up, slowly."

She nodded, using the breathing technique their guide taught them on their first day on the mountain. Once she got her breath under control, she stood, using her trekking poles to help support her weight. Her legs shook and her head was spinning, but she couldn't quit. They'd come too far. They spent seven days slowly making their way up the north side of the mountain, traveling through four different climate zones that spanned nearly forty miles. No, she wouldn't quit, not when they'd planned this trip for six months, spending every weekend Carter was home, hiking up and down the mountains of the Pacific Northwest in preparation. Not when they were mere miles from the summit.

"Okay?" one of their porters asked in broken English.

"Ndio Asante," she replied, telling him she was fine in equally broken Swahili. The porters, along with their guide, had been incredible, helping them, pushing them, preparing them. They couldn't have made this journey without them. She couldn't let them down. She couldn't let herself down.

"That's my girl," Carter said, kissing the tip of her nose. Their time in Africa was life changing. They were excited to take on this adventure together, bonding and growing while camping under the stars. She was grateful to have him there with her. Whenever the altitude or exhaustion started to take its toll on her body, he was there, reminding her that she was strong. He never gave up on her and he encouraged her to fight. She realized their first day on the mountain that this would be one of the hardest things they'd ever do, but that it would further solidify their bond. They were more than lovers and soul mates. She was him and he, her. They were one in the same.

"That's it, baby, you've got this," he said from behind, as they continued their climb. Slowly, one foot in front of the other, they went. Up further and further, climbing higher and higher, and finally, their guide announced they were coming upon the summit. This was it.

Just a little further, she just had to keep walking, keep breathing. It wasn't a race, it was a journey and it was coming to an end.

"I hate this so much," she gritted, stabbing her pole into the frozen ground.

"Yeah, but check out the view."

"Fuck the view," she grumbled, but couldn't help sneaking a glance at the clouds and sky. Blue and white swirled all around them, combining to make a color she'd never seen before. It was the color of perseverance and strength. She smiled, after all, she was touching the sky. "Oh my God," Kensie cried. "I did it. I fucking did it." Tears of relief fell. Her whole body shook as she walked past the achievement marker to the edge. Looking down on the world below, she exhaled in amazement, *"As wide as all the world, great, high, and unbelievably white in the sun."*

"Miller?" Carter asked coming up behind her resting his chin on her shoulder.

"No, Hemingway, a line from *The Snows of Kilimanjaro*. It's a short story he wrote about a couple on safari," she explained.

"Like us?"

"Well, the guy dies, so no." Kensie grinned.

Carter chuckled, "That's pretty fucking morbid, Friend."

"It was the only thing I could think of to encapsulate the moment."

"I can think of something better," he said, lifting his chin and taking a step back.

"What?" she asked, turning. She gasped, and this time it had nothing to do with the altitude and everything to do with her boyfriend, down on bended knee. "What are you doing?"

"What does it look like I'm doing?" he teased, pulling a black velvet box from the pocket of his pants.

"I can't breathe."

"Kensington Grace Roth, you are my best friend, the love of my life, my happiest thing. You are the place between sleep and awake. Wherever you go, I will follow, whether it be up the highest mountain or down into the depths of the sea. I will support your dreams and do my best to help you make them come true. You are my home, my family, my everything. Will you soar with me, forever?" Tears fell silently down his face.

"Forever." She nodded, yanking her hiking glove off, offering him her hand, her heart.

Vegas, 1 month later

"I can't believe we did this," Kensie squealed, looking down at the black *Mrs.* scrawled on the inside of her left ring finger.

"It's too late to back out now, we're already married," Carter said, as the tattoo artist finished the *Mr.* on his finger.

"My parents are going to lose it."

The realization of what they'd just done began to sink in. They were in Vegas because Lithium had a show. They crushed it. Reeling from the high of the performance, they decided to continue the party. CT, Kensie, Ryder, Jamie, Javi, and his flavor of the month hopped from club to club, and somewhere along the way, they ended up at one of those cheesy wedding chapels. Before she realized what was happening, Elvis was asking if she did, and what was even crazier was that she said yes.

"I was sick of waiting." Carter shrugged, flexing his finger to admire his new ink.

"My mother is going to kill us," she huffed, pacing the small room as the artist smeared ointment on CT's finger, "and your mother is going to dispose of the bodies." As soon as they'd gotten back from Africa, Jacquelyn and Penelope went into full-on wedding planning mode. Their mothers were fast friends and this wedding was an excuse for the two women to get together for weekly brunches. They'd gotten so much done in under a month, Kensie wondered if they started planning even before Carter asked. Apparently, everyone knew he was going to propose up on that mountain but her.

"We don't have to tell them," he said, as if it were simple. As if her mother couldn't smell bullshit from a mile away. While Carter paid their tab, she silently contemplated how she was going to keep their marriage a secret. She could wear gloves or maybe she could avoid Madison Park and Bellevue all together. The band was constantly traveling and she was deep into the editing stage for her latest project. They didn't need her to plan the wedding. She even considered emailing them her measurements. "Ready, Mrs. Thayer?" CT asked, pulling her from her thoughts

"Of course, we have to tell them," she blurted out, throwing her hands in the air. "We got married, six months before we were supposed to."

"We can still have that wedding," he said, pulling her out the door of the tattoo parlor. "No one has to know."

They walked hand in hand down the street, towards the little diner where their friends were waiting for them. "You've met my mother. I can't lie. She's going to smell it on me as soon as our flight touches down at SeaTac."

"Don't worry, I'm a great liar, remember."

She froze, elbowing him in the ribs. "You're a fucking asshole."

"What? Too soon." He smirked, rubbing his side.

"That's never going to be funny," she grunted, pulling open the door to the restaurant.

"Hey, it's the happy couple," Javi said as they neared the table. He held up his phone towards them. "Let our audience see the ink."

"What audience?" Kensie asked, confused.

"Instagram Live. I streamed the whole wedding."

Kensie's face fell. "I guess we have to tell them," Carter murmured into her ear, before giving his new bride a kiss for their fans.

Seattle, Two Months Later

"We are not doing this," Kensie said, pointing to the large Neil Young poster Carter was hanging over the mantelpiece. They'd closed on their new house the week before they'd gotten everything moved in and were mostly unpacked, but she was kicking herself for inviting their families over for Sunday dinner in their half-furnished and still undecorated house. She spent the morning buying groceries, only to come home to this? "You were supposed to be moving those boxes to the garage," she said, glancing at the mess still waiting in the corner.

"I started, that's where I found the poster," he explained, hopping off the step ladder.

"Please, take it down."

"Why?" he asked, grabbing the bags from her hands.

"Because this is our home, not some bachelor pad. You can't just hang a poster over the mantle. It's for art or family photos, not that," she explained, gesturing wildly.

Carter shook his head, taking the food into the kitchen. "Baby, Neil Young is The Godfather of Grunge. He's family," Carter argued. "Everyone always credits Cobain, but if it wasn't for *'Rust Never Sleeps,'* and *'Ragged Glory,'* there wouldn't be a Cobain."

"Take. It. Down," she gritted, putting her hands on her hips.

"No," he said, unpacking the first bag. He took out each item and placed them on the kitchen island. He'd graduated from breakfast and moved on to pasta. Kensie got everything he needed to make his famous spaghetti with meat sauce.

"Now, Carter," she insisted. She needed dinner to go smoothly. Their parents were still pissed about Vegas. She wasn't backing down, and judging by the determined glint in his blue eyes, he wasn't either.

"Is this our first argument as husband and wife?" He smirked.

"It isn't an argument," she said, shaking her head, "it's coming down."

"But why?" he whined.

"You know that room above the garage, the one filled with all your instruments? The one you said would make the perfect studio? The entire reason we bought this house?"

"Yeah." He nodded.

"You can put your godfather there, but that is coming down, before our parents get here for dinner."

"Baby," he took a step towards her, the determination replaced with lust, "you're hot when you're all bossy and demanding."

"No, it's not going to work," she said, pushing him away.

"Please," he pouted, walking her backwards into the kitchen island. His hands wrapped around her throat and his mouth was inches from hers.

"N.O."

"Please," he asked again, brushing his lips over hers.

"Carter, it's not going to work." His mouth found her jaw and he trailed small kisses from her chin up to the spot behind her ear. "Please," he whispered in a voice that made her heart race.

"Carter," she moaned, as his hands slid from her neck down to her breasts. Their parents were due to arrive in an hour for Sunday dinner, and so far, all they'd accomplished was unpacking the groceries and hanging up a Neil Young poster.

He dropped to his knees, tugging down her shorts and burying his face in her sex. "Let's make a deal?"

"What?" she asked, hooking her leg over his shoulder.

"If I make you come in less than ten minutes, the poster stays."

"And if you don't?"

"Trust me, I will," he growled, before sucking her clit into his mouth.

"Deal."

The End

A PEEK INSIDE CARTER'S HEAD

The whiskey flowed freely in Dave's office. Excitement crackled in the air. The bar was at capacity and the line of people waiting to see them perform wrapped around the building like ivy. It was a special night, not just for the band, but for him. His birthday.

Twenty-seven years old, and in many ways, CT was still that nineteen-year-old kid whose best friend betrayed him. Impulsive, and at times immature, but who could blame him?

"I feel fucking invincible," he yelled bringing the handle of Fireball to his lips. The small crowd of people in the office erupted into cheers as he chugged.

People were always around them now, friends, groupies, fans. Everyone wanted to get close to the band. Everyone wanted their chance to say they knew them when. Everyone but his family.

People were simple, as quiet as it was always kept, everyone wanted fame. The illusion of stardom, even if they experienced it from the fringe was more alluring than reality. They wanted to be a part of something great and Lithium Springs was their way in.

It should have bothered him. It bothered his bandmates, but he didn't mind. He spent his entire life around vultures. The person he loved most, stabbed him in the back. What did he care about a room full of strangers?

"Okay, birthday boy, slow down," Ryder, the lead singer, guitarist, and one of his best friends in the world, said, slapping him on the back. "We still have a show to do."

CT wrapped his arm around a curvy blonde girl standing near them. She wasn't anything special; pretty, big tits, and the way she looked at him—eyes wide and lips parted—confirmed what he already knew—she'd do anything to have him between her legs. "I'm ready, man. I have a good feeling about tonight."

The blonde giggled, leaning into his embrace. "You guys are going to kill it."

"You think so?" he asked, smirking at her.

"I know so," the girl purred, dragging her nail down his chest. Yeah, she was down to fuck. Women were easy. Even so, he had it. That thing that made heads turn when he walked into a room, charm, charisma whatever name you wanted to give it, he possessed it in spades. They all did. It's what made Lithium Springs kings of Seattle and what would one day make them gods around the world. Their time was coming. The summer was theirs.

"You hear that, Ry?" CT wagged his brows at his friend.

"Yeah, dickhead man."

"Don't listen to him, sweetie," Javi, the bass player, said from across the room, "he's just mad his girl isn't here yet."

"I can keep you company," a leggy brunette said seizing the opportunity.

"No, thanks," Ryder said, discreetly taking a step back. He'd always been the one to crave monogamy but since he started dating Kitty Cat, he'd been unbearable.

"Come on," she said, "I've seen your girl, she isn't that pretty. Plus, I won't tell if you don't."

CT cringed, feeling bad for the girl in desperate need of a clue. "You can have fun with us," he said extending his hand to her, trying to save her from embarrassment.

"I was kind of hoping to get a taste of the *Sex God*."

"Sweetheart," Ryder cooed in a deceptively soft voice. He was usually the nice one. The guy who made sure the girls he and Javi gave the boot got home safely. The one to hold their hair back when they couldn't handle their liquor, but he had his triggers and Kitty Cat was at the top of the list. "I wouldn't fuck you with his dick," he growled nodding towards Javi. "Now get the fuck out of my face."

"Should have just taken the hint," Javi chuckled, as she stormed out of the office. "Where is Kitty Cat anyway?"

"She's coming with her roommate later. They're having a girls' day, shopping, dinner the whole nine," Ryder pouted.

"What's the occasion?"

"Nothing, they just don't get to spend much time together and her boyfriend's out of town or some shit. I don't know."

"Hmm," CT said grabbing the bottle off the table. "You never met him?"

"Nah, Jamie hates his guts."

"What about her, the roommate, is she hot?" Javi asked.

"I don't know."

"You don't know because you've never seen her or you don't know because you don't want Kitty Cat to cut off your balls?"

Ryder rubbed the back of his neck, grinning. "A little of one and a lot of the other. We met once, when Jamie and I broke up, but I was a lunatic then and wasn't really checking her out, you know? I guess she's pretty, in an 'I'm completely in love with her best friend, and I don't need those problems' type of way."

"I bet she's hot. Have you seen Kitty Cat? Hot girls travel in packs."

"Fuck you, Javi," Ryder said, getting defensive.

"Chill, bro. Jamie is hot, but we love you more." CT laughed, blowing kisses at his friend. He really was an unbearable ass when Jamie wasn't around.

"Dibs on the friend," Javi said.

"No, I don't want you bastards fucking her, plus she has a boyfriend."

"Are they married?"

"No."

"Engaged?"

"I don't think so."

"Then fuck it. I can't make her cheat, but if she's willing." Javi winked.

"I don't need you fucking shit up with me and Jamie."

"I won't, trust me." He smirked.

CT shook his head, pulling the blonde across his lap. Tonight, was going to be epic. He could feel it in his bones.

Their set ran long that night. The crowd was intense, and the guys fed off their energy. When they stepped on stage they transformed from a group of immature fuckboys into rockstars. They poured everything they had into each song.

"Alright, Rabbit Hole," Ryder growled into the mic. Despite his annoyance with Jamie's tardiness, he had the crowd eating out of his fucking hand. "You guys have been amazing, but I can't let you leave here without introducing you to the Sex God." He stalked across the stage, pausing at the end, his eyes searching, searching, searching. A slow smile crept across his face, and his body relaxed. Kitty Cat must have been in the building.

CT followed his gaze, the lights from the stage made it difficult to see, but the blonde looking up at his friend with so much love and adoration was impossible to miss. He was happy for his friend, and Jamie was like a sister to him. Since his blood sister couldn't make it, he was happy to have her there to help bring in his twenty-seventh year of life.

His eyes shifted, next to Jamie was one of the most beautiful women he'd ever seen. He couldn't take his eyes of the striking woman with the espresso-colored locks and warm-brown eyes that were eerily familiar. His grip on his drumsticks tightened, his body went rigid as a strange sense of dread flowed through his body. He knew this girl, but how?

As their set went on he continued watching her, mesmerized but the way her tight red dress hugged every curve of her body. He was so lost in her movements, he nearly fucked up his drum solo. Javi was right, hot girls traveled in packs. Fuck his dibs. CT wanted her and judging by the way she was eye fucking him, she wanted him too.

God, where did he know this girl from? Did he fuck her before? Then again, something told him he'd remember if those lips had ever been wrapped around his cock.

Think, Carter.

Think.

Was she a fan of the band?

No.

Did Jamie ever show him a picture?

No.

One of Reagan's friends?

Reagan.

She knew Reagan.

How?

How?

How?

Fuck.

Fucking, shit fuck.

She knew Reagan, because they were dating brothers. Her boyfriend was out of town. Half his family was too. The bachelor party. Her boyfriend was in Vegas. Her boyfriend was the one person he hated most in this world.

Trey Knight.

She belonged to Trey fucking Knight and she was here, looking like a snack, waiting to be devoured. She was better than birthday cake. He was going to fuck Trey's little princess and he was going to enjoy it.

After their set the guys hopped off the stage and headed straight for the van. Every other night they stuck around to sign autographs, take pictures, and have drinks with their fans, but it was CT's birthday and they were having a party.

"Where are the girls?" Javi asked as they made their way down the long, dark hallway that led to the side door where the van waited to take them back to the house.

"Tee took them to the car," Ryder said pulling his shirt back on. "He couldn't find your blonde though."

"It's cool, I think I want Kitty Cat's friend." He contemplated telling them whose she was, but he knew Ryder would put a stop to that shit. He knew what he was doing was fucked up, but what Trey did was fucked up too. He deserved this, and if the girl in the red dress was willing to cheat on that fucking cornball then she was no angel either.

"Hold up, ass wipe, I called dibs."

"It's my birthday, and my dick is bigger."

Javi laughed, grabbing his junk. "You wish."

Ryder pushed through the door making a beeline for the van. It was certified, he was pussy-whipped.

Javi pushed CT aside and jogged over, climbing into the van behind Ryder. He extended his hand to Trey's girl. "I'm Javi," he said, his voice dripping with sex.

She blushed and bit down on her bottom lip, and in that moment, CT made up his mind. Fuck Trey, and as much as he loved him, fuck Javi too. Grabbing his collar, he yanked him back from the van. "Back off, homie, she's mine."

Javi looked at his friend and then back to the girl in the red dress, before groaning, "You're lucky it's your birthday, motherfucker."

CT smirked, pushing his friend towards the passenger side door before climbing in next to Trey's girl. He pushed his body against hers and dropped his arm around her neck. A jolt of adrenaline rushed through his blood. She fit perfectly underneath him, and he was willing to bet that he'd fit perfectly inside of her.

"I'm Kensie," she whispered, all breathy and seductive. She wanted him just as badly as he wanted her.

"CT." He grinned, as the van pulled out into the night. The house was about a twenty-minute drive from the Rabbit Hole, and that gave him plenty of time with them trapped in such close proximity to come up with a plan.

He could tell by the way she was squirming that she was attracted to him, but what he didn't know was if she would actually take the bait. Trey was a douchebag, but did she love him?

As if she could read his mind, she winced, shifting her body away from his. "Everything okay?" he asked, pulling her back into his side.

"I have a boyfriend," she murmured, biting down on her lip. Her eyes shone with regret, but was that regret for cuddling with him in the back of the van or was it for what he was going to do to her later?

"I'm not trying to be your boyfriend." He smirked, bringing his thumb up to her mouth, gently wiggling her lip free. Even as he said the words, something deep in his gut flipped. He wasn't Ryder, he didn't do the girlfriend thing, but he couldn't deny his attraction to Kensie. He had never wanted anyone as badly as he did her. Part of it was because she belonged to the cornball, but he'd be damned if there wasn't something addicting about this girl.

"Good." Kensie shifted, trying to put as much distance between them as the cramped space would allow.

"Not so fast." He pulled her back under his arm and his hand traveled from her knee up to her thigh. This was happening, revenge probably never tasted as good as sweet little miss Kensie's cunt. Fuck, even just the thought of tasting her made him hard as granite. He wondered if she was as turned on as he was. "This is short," he mused, ghosting his hand up her thigh. Higher and higher it went as he buried his face in the side of her neck. He inhaled, and she smelled of flowers and tequila, a combination he didn't know could be so intoxicating.

She gasped when he nipped at her earlobe. "I have a boyfriend."

"But tonight, I'll be the one fucking you." *And maybe again in the morning,* he added mentally.

"Listen, I know you're probably used to girls throwing themselves at you, but you're barking up the wrong tree. I have a boyfriend and he's the only one who gets to fuck me."

A smile played at his lips, and amusement danced behind his blue eyes. He was trying not to laugh, but he failed miserably. He could feel the dampness between her legs. He could see the desire in her gaze. Him fucking her was no longer in question, it was a matter of how many times he could make her come.

Kensie didn't get the joke. She wiggled out from under his long arm and gave him a hard shove, causing him to fall over on the seat. Her little temper tantrum just caused him to laugh harder. It was cute watching her fight her attraction—pointless, but cute.

"Care to tell us what's so funny?" Javi asked from the front seat.

"Nothing," he croaked, slowly regaining composure. He pulled himself upright and returned his arm to its home around Kensie's neck. "You're funny," he whispered, his mouth on her ear. If her ear tasted this good, how would her pussy taste? He couldn't wait to find out.

"And you're a pig," she huffed, crossing her arms over her chest.

Slipping his hand back up her thigh, he went in for the kill. "So, where is this boyfriend of yours tonight, and why was he stupid enough to let you out of the house in this?"

He knew exactly where the bastard was, but he wanted to see if she'd lie. Would she tell him he was home waiting for her, in one last-ditch effort to get him to back off, or would she tell the truth, which was hundreds of miles away, and that she was his for the night.

She let out a shaky breath before answering, "His brother is getting married. They're in Vegas for his bachelor party."

"I should send his brother a thank you gift then." He gently massaged her leg, creeping his hand up centimeter by centimeter until it reached the edge of her thong. "These are drenched," he groaned into her ear.

She trembled, he could tell her brain was starting to accept what her body knew the minute he sat next to her. She may hate herself in the morning, but before the night was over, he'd be balls deep in Trey Knight's pussy. It was the best birthday present he'd ever received.

And then it happened, she let go, parting her legs for him. He didn't hesitate, his fingers dove into her panties, pulling them, and letting them go with a soft thud against her wet flesh, playing with her body as if she was his instrument, one he'd long since mastered.

"I have a boyfriend," she begged. She fucking begged him, but unfortunately for her he wasn't in a merciful mood. He was impulsive and his hatred for the man she chose to align herself with overrode any sense of morality he felt about dragging her down into the mud with him.

"Do you get this wet for him?" he mouthed, as the car lurched to a stop.

"No," she breathed, and he couldn't help the wolfish grin that spread across his face. He was going to enjoy fucking her. He was going to enjoy making her scream out his name, and then he was going to send Trey a picture of his cum dripping out of her slit.

The party was in full swing by the time they arrived. As soon as they entered, CT was swallowed by a sea of people; neighbors, fans, and friends he'd made in the last few years, but no one from his family. Not one of his childhood friends. Not his brother, because he too was in Vegas with the enemy, not his sister, no one. They were gone, absent from his life and his birthday party, because of Trey.

That fact motivated him. He couldn't let his attraction to the smoking-hot girl in the red dress cloud his judgment. She was the bait, and Trey was big game—he couldn't lose sight of that. "Hey, Kitty Cat," he said, grabbing the blonde by the hand. Ryder growled at him, as if he'd ever cross that line. "Calm the fuck down, dude, I'm trying to fuck her friend."

Jamie rolled her eyes, giving Ryder a light peck on the lips before grinning at him. "She likes you, and I'm committing at least fifteen girl code violations by telling you that, but she does. She's just having a hard time admitting that to herself. She's stuck in a situation she thinks she wants, but I know her. She isn't happy, but she can't admit it to herself."

"Is that why you brought her here tonight?" he asked.

"I brought her here, so she could meet Ry, officially. She's like my sister and I have this whole life that she isn't a part of, and I hate that," Jamie confessed, and he couldn't fault her for that. He too led a double life. "But I see the way she looks at you, the way you look at her, it's like nuclear fucking fusion."

"You're giving me too much credit."

"I'm not saying you guys have to get married, but I am saying, maybe a night away from him will give her some perspective."

"Just call me Mr. Perspective." He grinned.

"Okay, Mr. Perspective, just know, if you hurt my friend, I will cut off your balls and shove them down your throat."

"Noted," he said shifting under her gaze. He felt a pang of remorse for what he was planning to do. He was hurt and his aim was to hurt. Ryder was going to fucking kill him.

"Here's your chance." Jamie nodded, her head in the direction of the keg.

Kensie was there, her long chocolate hair twisted up into a bun as she pumped the keg up and down. "She's too good for him," he muttered under his breath.

"Huh?" Jamie asked.

"Nothing," he muttered absently, making his way over to her. God, Trey was a lucky bastard. Everything about this girl was perfect, but the way her ass looked as she bent over the keg, drove him insane. He wanted to bite it. "You're good at that," he said coming up behind her. His groin grazed her butt as he leaned over her, to grab the faucet from her hands, and refill his cup.

"Thanks," she said with a shrug. "Happy birthday, by the way." He watched, amused as she dipped down and picked up her discarded stilettos, and turned to leave without another word. She was going for nonchalant. It was cute, the way she tried to pretend that she didn't want him. It was going to make fucking her that much sweeter.

"Can you not stare at my ass, please?"

A slow grin crept across his face. "I can't help it. You have a very nice ass." His voice dripped with sex. "I've been fantasizing about bending you over and licking you from here," his knuckles drew a path down the small of her back, all the way down the hem of her too short dress, and he palmed her ass, "to here." His hand continued lower still, down to her soaking-wet panties, and he hooked his fingers around the back edge of her thong, gently pulling it and releasing. He plucked at her panties as if they were strings on a guitar.

"Also, can you also stop putting your hand up my skirt?" she bit. Her mouth was saying one thing, but her body said another. He could feel her lust, hell, his fingers were coated in it, but for whatever reason, be it loyalty to Trey, her moral compass, or her subconscious screaming at her to run as far away from the wolf in sheep's clothing standing in front of her—she fought it.

Unfortunately for her, it only made him want her more. He couldn't remember the last time he had to chase a girl. Even before the band, he'd always been blessed with a handsome face, lean body, and a healthy trust fund. If his looks failed to get him laid, his money certainly never did.

"For now," he grumbled as they reached their friends, "but make no mistake, tonight you are mine. This," his hand was on her ass pulling her into his erection, his mouth on top of hers, "is mine." His kiss was slow and deliberate and possessive, all tongue. The long, measured strokes claimed her mouth, as the hand on her ass claimed her body.

"Damn, C, you're turning me on, my guy," Javi joked, pulling them back to reality. "Kensie, when you're done with him, I want a turn."

"You couldn't handle me, bro," CT chuckled and the game resumed as if his hand hadn't been up her skirt just moments before.

"I hope you know what you're doing," Ryder said as they loaded the DJ equipment into the van. It was three in the morning.

"Will you relax, man. Kitty Cat's cool with it, why aren't you?" CT said to his friend.

"She has a boyfriend."

"It's just sex, Ry, not everyone falls in love as easily as you."

"You sure about that, bro?"

"When have you ever seen me following a girl around like a love-sick puppy?"

"Tonight. You're different with her. You've barely let her out of your sight to take a piss. The kissing and touching? It's worse than me and Kitty Cat."

"Look, it's my birthday, and I'm about to have very pornographic sex with a super-hot chick while her douchebag boyfriend is out of town. So what, I'm a little eager, sue me."

"How do you know he's a douchebag?"

"If he wasn't, she wouldn't be with me," he said with a raised brow. Ryder let the subject drop as they headed back inside.

Jamie and Kensie sat on the couch. "What do you want to do?" Jamie asked her friend.

CT raked his fingers through his slightly overgrown hair; his tongue swept across his lips as he took her in. Her hair was a disaster, her makeup was all smudged and her feet were dirty from walking around all night barefoot. He knew in that moment that he had to have her. Wild and carefree, easily the most beautiful woman he'd ever laid eyes on. Trey didn't deserve her. Hell, neither did he, but that didn't stop him from walking over to her. Bracing his hands on the couch, he bent over, trapping her between his arms, with his face inches from hers. "What do you want?"

AUTHOR'S NOTE

Dear Reader,

This book inspired a dream. This book, these characters, possessed me in a way no other characters' have before, or since. I ate, slept and breathed Carter and Kensie, and I'm so proud of their journey. They inspired this entire Lithium universe, as well as my entire writing career. I owe more to them than you could ever possibly know. Thank you for reading. Thank you for loving them as much as I do.

As always,
Unedited and Slightly Inebriated.
Carmel.

Please review and share this story with your friends!
Sign-up for my newsletter to stay in touch.

Playlist: open.spotify.com/user/author.carmelrhodes

Pinterest: www.pinterest.com/authorcarmelrhodes/lithium-tides

ALSO BY
CARMEL RHODES

Novellas:

Shipwrecked
Anarchy

Lithium Springs Novels:

Book One: *Lithium Waves*
Book Two: *Lithium Tides*
Book Three (Coming Soon): *Lithium Oasis*

For the most up-to-date list check out my website!
www.carmelrhodes.com

ACKNOWLEDGEMENTS

To my Husband: Thank you for the endless love and support.

Gerannda: Once again this wouldn't have been possible without you.

Erica, Brittany, Lexi, Meli. You guys keep me sane. You keep me laughing. You keep me writing. I love you.

Diana and Kelly: CT's number one fans and my biggest cheerleaders. I'm lucky to know you guys .

Betas: Helen, Suzan, Lori. Thank you for always keeping it real. For telling me your thoughts and encouraging me to keep going.

Stacey: You never stop blowing me away. Thanks for making my book babies beautiful.

Kristen: Thank you for helping make my words sparkle.

Jen: Thank you for accommodating my last-minute requests with a smile. You rock.

The Army: Everything I do, I do to make you guys proud.

Readers: Thank you for loving my boys as much as I do!

ABOUT THE AUTHOR

Writer of words. Mother of Joy. Wife of Compassion. I like to write stories about real people who go through real struggles and come out the other side stronger. I also like to write smut. Welcome to my brain. It's a little screwed up, but always well intended.

Sign-up for my newsletter for exclusive content, and to stay up to date with all things Carmel Rhodes.

Website: www.carmelrhodes.com

Facebook: facebook.com/authorcarmelrhodes

Reader Group: facebook.com/groups/299310880471688

Goodreads: www.goodreads.com/author/show/17070667.Carmel_Rhodes

Instagram: www.instagram.com/author.carmelrhodes

Twitter: twitter.com/AuthorCarmel

Made in the USA
San Bernardino, CA
26 April 2018